AF191988

THOMAS W.J.
SIMPSON

FOOTBALL THANK GOD FOR *MOHAMED* FROM A *MARRIAGE LICENCE* TO A *SEASON TICKET*

novum ▲ pro

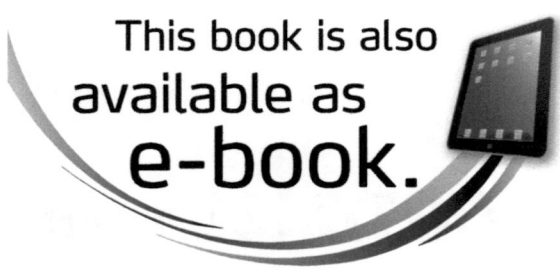

This book is also available as e-book.

www.novum-publishing.co.uk

© 2024 novum publishing

ISBN 978-3-99146-741-0
Editing: Gillian Fisher
Cover photos: Cornelius20,
Eugene Onischenko I Dreamstime.com
Cover design, layout & typesetting:
novum publishing
Author's photo: Thomas W. J. Simpson

www.novum-publishing.co.uk

Print product with financial
climate contribution
ClimatePartner.com/16547-2311-1001

THIS BOOK IS DEDICATED TO THE MEMORY OF
DOUGLAS JOHN MCMANUS
31 MARCH 1949–22 JUNE 2005
NEVER HAS THERE BEEN A BETTER
OR MORE LOYAL FRIEND
GOD BLESS ALWAYS
NEVER TO BE FORGOTTEN

ALSO, IN LOVING MEMORY OF
MY SISTER PATRICIA ANNE LEWIS (SIMPSON)
14 MARCH 1947–28 MARCH 2021
FOREVER FULHAM

AND

MY NEPHEW SIMON JAMES POWELL
1 JANUARY 1966–2 JANUARY 2022
SPURS TILL THE END

BOTH SADLY MISSED

Contents

There's an old saying in football:

'You can change your wife, or partner but
you can't change your team.'

Football, Thank God for Mohamed: From a Marriage Licence to a Season Ticket is a light-hearted look at the life of a boy developing from a young child to an adult. It covers his everyday highs and lows over the years; his family life and the trials and tribulations which that brings; and his meeting and falling in love with members of the opposite sex and how they treated him. It also explores how his everyday personal life has changed over the last sixty years: from school days through to marriage, and eventually retirement.

At the same time, *From a Marriage Licence to a Season Ticket* shows the development of that same small child growing up and becoming a full-time football supporter. Being a child in a football family brought similar trials and tribulations: how he picked his team and fell in love with it; how the team treated him; and how being a football supporter has changed over the last 60 years in almost the same way that his personal life has changed.

It tells the details of all the years of supporting his team, Fulham, the cost, the long away trips, freezing cold evening matches, soaking wet Saturdays, scorching hot Sundays, the verbal abuse from the opposition's supporters, and the long hours sitting in cars, trains and coaches, the pain and suffering, especially when losing at those long, long away matches (which always made the trip back home feel even longer).

BUT NOT ONCE IN ALL THAT TIME DID HE ASK HIMSELF:
'WHY AM I DOING THIS WEEK IN AND WEEK OUT?'

9

Hopefully this book will explain why fully fledged supporters do it. This book is based on the author's own personal experiences, therefore, the book is written from a male point of view.

I first started writing this book about eighteen years ago, but due to work commitments (being a Class 1 HGV night driver) I never seemed to get the time to sit and write it. But over the last couple of years, I've since managed to put more hours into getting it finished, so hopefully you will forgive me if there are pieces in the book that on the football side might be a little, or a lot, out of date, or totally wrong. (What do you expect? I'm a lorry driver not William bleeding Shakespeare!!) Over the years I have had to rewrite parts of the book due to the way certain things have changed in the football world. Also, because Watford didn't stop sacking their managers, and West Brom, Norwich and Fulham didn't stop fucking yo-yoing in the league, I thought I'd never finish the fucking book.

My name is Tom. Pleased to meet you. I hope you enjoy the read.

The wedding bells ring to start our future
THE REFEREE'S WHISTLE BLOWS TO START OUR GAME
Wedding bells
FOOTBALL CLAPPERS

The registry office

'Do you (groom), take (bride) to be your lawfully wedded wife,
   To have and to hold from this day forward,
   For better, for worse, for richer, for poorer,
   In sickness and in health, until death do you part?'
   'I do.'
   'I now pronounce you man and wife. You may now kiss the
   bride.'

THE REFEREE'S WHISTLE BLOWS TO START OUR GAME
The wedding bells ring to start our future
FOOTBALL CLAPPERS
Wedding bells

The ticket office

'Do you (supporter), take (team) to be your only football team,
   To follow and to support from this season on,
   For better, for worse, for richer, for poorer,
   In winning, drawing or losing, until death do you part?'
   'I do.'
   'I now pronounce you a season ticket holder. You may now
   kiss the badge.'

'Women and football are two of the
most beautiful things on earth.'
(Apart from my wife's banoffee pie.)
MOST FOOTBALL SUPPORTERS LOVE THEIR TEAMS
AS MUCH AS THEY LOVE THEIR PARTNERS.

What shape do you like your women to be ...
32–22–32 or maybe 38–26–36 or even 42–36–46?
WHICH FORMATION DO YOU LIKE
YOUR TEAM TO PLAY ...
4–4–2 or maybe 3–5–2 or even 4–3–3?

Do you like your women to be direct
or
do you like your women to tease?

DO YOU LIKE YOUR TEAM TO PLAY DIRECT
OR
DO YOU LIKE YOUR TEAM TO PLAY KEEP BALL?

Whatever your preference, it's all about
'THE LOVE'

Life can be hard no matter which street you live in,
from the poorest streets of England to the richest streets.

THIS IS A BOOK OF TWO HALVES.

GAMES CAN BE HARD NO MATTER
WHICH LEAGUE YOU PLAY IN,
FROM THE LOWEST AND POOREST LEAGUES
IN ENGLAND TO THE RICHEST LEAGUES

**FOOTBALL, THANK GOD FOR MOHAMED:
FROM A MARRIAGE LICENCE
TO A SEASON TICKET**

Chapter One

The Perfect Match

Good days, bad days:
GOOD MATCHES, BAD MATCHES

It wasn't until I was about seventeen or eighteen that I personally knew of anybody by the name of Mohamed (apart from a
couple of blokes that worked in the local newsagent's and the
takeaway), but none really to say I knew up close and personal.
Back in the 50s and 60s there weren't many foreigners on the
estate where I lived, and only a couple at my school. So I didn't
really get to mix with many people from a different culture. But
then, in the late 1990s, as if by chance, two Mohameds came
into my personal life, and also my footballing world. Two men,
whose worlds could not be further apart if they were living on
different planets.

One was a very, very famous rich Egyptian shop owner, known
as Mohamed Al-Fayed. The other was a not very, very famous rich
Tunisian hotel entertainments manager, known as Mohamed
Ali Amroussi. But these two men between them showed me two
different footballing worlds that I could never have envisaged.

The second of these two men, the poor old entertainment
manager, Mohamed Ali Amroussi, took my son Lee and me on
an absolutely mind-blowing and amazing adventure into the
football experience of the Africa Cup of Nations in 2004, which
was held in Tunisia. This story you will be able to read (if you're
bored and with nothing better to do) at a later date under the
heading of *Extra Time* when it has been published.

The first of these two men, Mr Mohamed Al-Fayed, changed
the whole meaning of football for me and many, many, other
Fulham supporters who watched my beloved team Fulham playing mainly in the lower leagues for over 30 years sadly without

much success, apart from an amazing 11-match cup run in the 1974–1975 FA Cup (which is still a record today. And due to rule changes regarding the cancelling of replays, it will stay a record). Sadly, this ended with a Wembley 2–0 defeat to West Ham (Wet Spam) in the final. If you can call losing a success, I suppose getting to our first ever major final was our success, after having been beaten in a few more minor semi-finals in previous years.

Fulham, as I said, hadn't had a great deal of success over the years. In 1996 they were languishing, or should I say slowly dying, in the Third Division, under the guidance of Ian Branfoot. Branfoot was soon then replaced by Micky Adams who had been at the club as a player for a couple of seasons. Adams took over the role as player–manager and helped us slowly up the table. Fulham, at this time, looked as if they were about to go out of the league altogether due to a financial meltdown. And the rumours were that the ground had been sold to a company called Cabra Estates for about £14 million, and the club would possibly go out of business altogether, or have to find another place to play.

Then, on the 5th of April 1997, Fulham's future was about to change dramatically. Fulham were drawing with Carlisle United at Brunton Park, United's home ground. Then with about 35 minutes to go, a goal by the legend that is now Rodney McAree changed the whole destiny of Fulham FC. That goal won us the game 2–1 and guaranteed us promotion to Division Two. The song 'Rodney McAree, Rodney McAree. Who put the ball in the Carlisle net, Rodney McAree' is still being sung at just about every Fulham game.

Cabra Estates thankfully went out of business for some reason or another that I'm not too sure about (or really care about to be honest). The bank resold the ground back to Fulham, thanks to the hard work and dogged determination of the then chairman Jimmy Hill, and they were back on track. Things were starting to look up for Fulham FC, and the Fulham faithful. But what was to come next was even more of a shock, not only to us Fulham fans, but to the whole of the English football leagues.

The announcement on the 29th of May 1997 was that Fulham football club had been taken over by a billionaire shopkeeper. This breaking news left us all totally shocked and stunned. Was this some kind of a sick joke perhaps, or a rumour started by Ken Bates, the then chairman of Chelsea FC, to wind up the Fulham fans?

A little Second Division family club like Fulham being taken over by a billionaire? It couldn't be true, could it? It would have been less of a shock if it had turned out to be old Arkwright (Ronnie Barker of *Open All Hours*).

BUT IT WAS TRUE!!

Mr Al-Fayed, the then owner of one of the world's most prodigious stores, Harrods, purchased Fulham Football Club in 1997. There was no prior speculation and no rumours going around. Not a word to be heard on *Sky Sports*. (Where was Jim White when you needed him?) After the initial shock of the announcement had worn off, and our hearts started to get back to somewhere near the normal rate, there was quite a lot of speculation among the supporters as to what his reasons were for buying such a small now Second Division club that only had a fan base of about between four and five thousand. Why, when you have the financial clout to purchase almost any other more salubrious and successful club in the world, then why pick little ol' Fulham?

Most of the opinions among the Fulham fans suggested that he wanted the ground, which is superbly sited alongside the River Thames, for the purpose of moving Fulham out to pastures new. He would then demolish the stadium and build luxury top-of-the-range apartments, each having a value of around the £1 million mark.

Many of our earlier fears were laid to rest when out went the very popular Micky Adams (who is still revered today by all the Fulham supporters) after one season. The board then brought in two football heroes: Ray Wilkins (sadly no longer with us) as manager, and Kevin Keegan as chief operating officer. When

Ray Wilkins left in 1998, King Kev then took over the reins as manager.

Fears raised their ugly heads again when the proposed extension of Craven Cottage to a 40,000 all-seated stadium was blocked by a few local residents complaining about parking, the extra noise, and basically anything else they could moan at. Why buy a house near a football ground? Or an airport, as in the case of Heathrow (especially with all the ongoing issues of the third runway)? The cost of the court case and the lawyers escalated until it became too costly for Fulham to carry on the fight.

Regarding those who opposed the rebuilding of the Cottage, I hope that their drains get blocked and their houses flood and fall down, then when they apply to rebuild, we'll oppose it, and they can then sod off, just like they wanted us to do. (There, rant over!!)

There were also more concerns regarding the stadium when there was talk of Mr Al-Fayed buying an old milk depot in Shepherd's Bush about three or four miles away from the Fulham ground but only a five-minute walk from Loftus Road, the home of our dreaded enemy, QPR ha ha ha. There was talk that Fulham was looking to build a stadium there, and share the ground with the old enemy, which didn't go down well at all with both sets of fans. That would be the equivalent of asking the Rooneys and the Vardys if they'd like to go on holiday together ... or have a nice night in and share a KFC family bucket ... It ain't going to happen. FULL STOP.

So, after all that fell through, and having weighed up all options, it was decided by Mr Al-Fayed and the board that they would refurbish and extend the Cottage. We did also eventually groundshare with QPR ha ha ha for two seasons while the building work was carried out before returning to our spiritual home by the river after the revamp.

The Fulham rollercoaster was now on the move, taking me, along with the rest of the Fulham faithful, on a 14-year unbelievable adventure. When Kevin Keegan left to become the

England manager, Mr Al-Fayed then appointed a French football legend called Jean Tigana.

Jean Tigana was a true football maestro. He had represented France in the 1980s, alongside two other French legends, and they were Michel Platini and Alain Giresse, who won the 1984 EUFA European Championship. At that time, they were seen as being one of the greatest mid-fielders of that generation. Tigana totally changed our style of play, and took us back to the top flight for the first time since 1968 with an incredible 101 points out of 138, and with an unbelievable style of football that I'd never, ever seen before at the Cottage. Jean Tigana then led us to a massive 5–3 but forgettable win in the 2002 Intertoto Cup final against Bologna. It was a terrible competition, in which three teams: Fulham, Malaga and Stuttgart, were all declared winners. All three winners were presented with a cup that made the Ashes cricket trophy look like the Champions League trophy. The competition was a complete and utter farce and, quite rightly, was abolished in 2008. However, after a few twists and turns, it has now ended up as the Europa League. Then in 2002–2003, Fulham lost in the later rounds of the UEFA Cup to Hertha Berlin. After a good start for the first two or three years in the Premier League, Fulham started to do what Fulham do best (struggle). Tigana then left.

Chris Coleman, who had had to retire due to a serious car crash in 2001, took over the reins until April 2007. Then in December 2007, with Fulham now facing relegation again under yet another manager, Lawrie Sanchez who again they soon replaced, and appointed Roy Hodgson as manager. Roy Hodgson did an absolutely incredible job of not only keeping us up by the skin of our teeth, but he also took us to a memorable 2009–2010 Europa League Cup Final. This sadly ended in defeat (another final defeat) against Atlético Madrid, in Hamburg. This was a team full of stars, and stars in the making: players such as David de Gea, Cabrera, Raul Garcia, Maxi Rodriguez, José Reyes, Diego Forlán and a certain Sergio Agüero-o-o-o (WHO?).

The 35-hour coach trip that my son and I endured for both the semi-final (the first leg in Hamburg against Hamburg where we drew 0–0, who we then went on to beat 2–1 at home in the second leg) and the same 35-hour coach trip back to Hamburg for the final, was worth every second of the trip.

Even though some of the years since have been a struggle, I will always be grateful to Mr Al-Fayed for taking us from the football poorhouse up to the dizzy heights of the Football League and eating off the Premiership table, and finally rubbing shin pads with some of football's elite.

With Mr Mohamed Al-Fayed in mind (and his wonderful cheque book), *Football, Thank God for Mohamed: From a Marriage Licence to a Season Ticket* is by way of a thank you to him. It's a light-hearted look into the similarities that I (and no doubt you too will have) had growing up from a child to what I am now: a senior citizen. From our first encounter with the opposite sex up until the time we commit ourselves to them by marriage. And that same young child (me) growing up to become a staunch football supporter. From our first encounter with our football team up until the time we commit ourselves to them by way of a season ticket. The strange and uncanny parallel life in which I, and most other supporters, have lived. That same parallel life is one that so many other supporters out there are also living now. Until we come to realise we have found 'THE PERFECT MATCH.'

Chapter Two

Pre-match Warm-up

Lay your love on me
LAY ME OFF IN THE BOX

This book is dedicated to Douglas (Dougie) John McManus, a good friend (or should I say more like a brother), who sadly passed away in June 2005. This was a friendship that lasted almost 35 years. During all those years, he could never understand how anyone could get so worked up and excited over any kind of sport, especially football.

Dougie was the typical couch potato. He was a big guy, not only in heart, but also in size so to indulge in any kind of sport was a problem for him. No, sport was not Dougie's forte. But in all fairness to him, he did try playing squash once. However, for health and safety reasons (my health and safety), I thought it better he gave it up. At the time I was about 5 ft 8 inches and 6 stone, fully clothed and soaking wet (I made Mr. Muscles look like Arnie Schwarzenegger), the original size O, whereas Doug was about 6 ft 2 inches and about 25 stone. If you can imagine it, it was a bit like Julian Clarey versus The Incredible Hulk. So, with him running around the court like a headless chicken, and bouncing off the walls more times than the squash ball, I felt it was in my best interest to keep him to the type of games he could play at home. I think he thoroughly enjoyed this type of activity and was willing to partake in at any time of the day or night (not with me, I hasten to add).

He might watch the odd Scottish international rugby or football match on the box, being a very proud Scot as he was (and only because he thought it was unpatriotic not to do so). But he wasn't really that bothered. Therefore, he was somewhat bemused and baffled by my passion for the greatest game in the world. He could not see why I, or thousands (no millions) like me worldwide would want to travel the length and breadth of their country in all weathers, come rain or shine, spending a fortune, just to watch twenty-two blokes kicking a ball around a park (as he saw it).

It didn't matter how much I tried to explain, he couldn't, or wouldn't, understand what the game of football means to millions of people all round the world. It also made me realise that there must be thousands of other people just like him, who don't understand the mentality (if we have one!) of the true football supporter.

There must be wives and husbands, as well as girlfriends, boyfriends and family relatives, who watch their partners and family members going off to a match each week, wearing their team's shirts, scarves, hats etc. in all types of weather, wondering what it is about the game of football that can turn grown men, women and kids, no matter what their age or mentality, into a mass of mindless cretins (as they would see it).

Why do even the hardest of men, men who would stand up to anybody, fight to the death against anyone, then cry like a baby who's just had their ice cream taken away when their team has just been beaten?

Why does it make well-to-do young girls and respectable married housewives scream and shout obscenities that you would normally expect to hear when passing a building site, a pub, a betting shop, or a Weight Watchers weighing in session?

Why does it make much older men and women, who possibly already have a heart condition, start putting it under even more pressure by standing up screaming and shouting at the top of their voices, questioning the parenthood of the players, the ref and the other supporters? These are the same men and women you wouldn't look at twice, who next week will attend a Cliff Richard concert. (I know who I'd rather shout obscene remarks at out of the two. Sorry, Cliff mate.) Sadly of late, we've seen more and more people in the crowd collapsing. Sadly, some lose their lives. This is mostly brought on by the emotions and excitement that the game of football brings.

I remember not so long ago I was at a game at the Cottage and I felt really poorly. I was about to tell my son I was going to leave and sit in the car because I felt that bad, but a minute or so later it went off. About two or three weeks later, I was taken into hospital and had two stents put into my heart after suffering a silent heart attack. (No, it wasn't due to how bad Fulham play!! Yes, I know what you other team supporters think). I was a very lucky man that day.

Why does the game of football also make successful businessmen all of a sudden start spending money like a poor man who's just won the lottery? Throwing caution to the wind, and doing things with the club's finances that previously they would never have risked, just to keep up with their football neighbours? Or chasing a dream: that pot of gold at the end of the footballing rainbow.

Well, if you're like my mate Dougie, then hopefully this book might just try to help you to understand why I think we do what we do, and maybe it might just answer any queries or questions that might have been driving you all mad.

There must also be thousands of football supporters who do what they do but never realise why they're doing it. They just go with the flow. Week in and week out. Just like lemmings, they turn up to watch their team, come hell or high water, win, lose or draw, and never stop to ask themselves why? Why am I here? Why am I soaking wet? Why am I trying to eat a lukewarm dried-out excuse of a thing they have the cheek to call a burger? (Have you noticed they have even stopped calling them beefburgers?)

Do supporters ever ask themselves why they have paid a fortune for a match or season ticket just to sit (or stand in some cases) in the freezing cold or pissing rain, trying to cheer their team on from losing its tenth straight defeat. Meanwhile their new, overpaid, and overrated Tibetan Division One striker, whom their team has only just managed to sign on at the bargain knockdown price of £8 million (having fought off some Tibetan Division Three side), is being paid an astronomical wage.

At the press conference, the translator (because the player doesn't speak any English) has had the nerve to say on the player's behalf how it's been a lifelong ambition and a dream come true for the player to play for the club, and that the player has been a supporter of the club ever since his dad or granddad took him home the club's football shirt.

That shirt was most probably an old shirt some backpacker had discarded some years back while travelling through that part of the Tibetan outback. 'NO,' Mr Translator, it's all lies. The player had never seen or heard of the club until some clown of a scout or agent, who, by the way, is going to get a nice backhander after he's managed to persuade a manager with a big brown paper bag, to sign him. They then dragged this poor sod across the sea, dumped him in front of a load of media at the training ground, and told him to smile and nod now and then.

Now that same player who said he would give his right arm to play for the club (well, pal, he might as well give both his feet as well, because apart from walking on them, they aren't any good for anything else) is now sitting in the comfort of his paid-for house or his paid-for 5-star hotel, suffering with homesickness, or depression, or getting over a drink or drug problem, and is unavailable to play. If he wants to see suffering, he should come and sit where we are.

Depression! Depression! You don't know the meaning of the bloody word. (I'm getting depressed just writing this.) If they didn't pay him so much fucking money, he couldn't afford to take drugs or drink so much so that he's unfit to play, and if they cut his wages to what he is worth, which is basically zilch, sod-all, they could then cut the ticket prices. Then perhaps we, the supporters, could afford to drink and take drugs (no, cancel the bit about taking the drugs, that's not a good thing to do). And if any members of the PC brigade are reading this, PLEASE ONLY DRINK IN MODERATION (which might help us when we're watching our teams playing crap).

There are lots of books about football that cover just about everything in the game. These range from ex-managers spilling the beans about ex-players turning up late for training, if they could be bothered to turn at all, or turning up straight from a night on the tiles still hung over. I remember hearing a story from a manager (can't remember exactly who, but I think it might have been big Ron Atkinson) about a player telling him that he wasn't going to be at training the next day for some reason or another, so the manager told him if he didn't turn up, he would be fined a week's wages. Apparently, the player got out his cheque book and wrote him a cheque for the said amount, and went AWOL the next day.

They give us stories of fights in the changing rooms, flying cups and saucers. They tell us all about the awkward bastards who upset the rest of the squad, which is why he (the manager) lost the changing room, got the sack, and is now slumming it working for Sky Sports, BT or the BBC as a so-called top analyst after getting the sack from his fourth relegated club (aye, some analyst he is!). Because instead of getting rid of the bad influence, this soppy bollock of a manager gave them a longer contract and a massive pay rise, then moaned like crazy when he was then sacked, of course with a massive golden handshake. ('Unbelievable, Jeff.')

We then get tears from the poor sod of a manager who apparently didn't choose the particular player his chairman decided he wanted, so he agrees to pay an absolute fortune in transfer fees and wages for this player who's been recommended by his agent. Unfortunately, it would seem the chairman was blinded by the agent, and they have brought in an unknown quantity who can't head, tackle, dribble or pass, and can only shoot with one foot (and not even straight at that)! Ah, back to the Tibetan striker.

When the team finally gets relegated, the manager (not the player or players, who didn't play for him or the shirt) is the one to get fired, owing to the fact that *he* didn't get the best out of the player.

You also get the manager whose team is relegated, then moans like fuck that the board didn't back him enough financially in the transfer market, even after spending between £50 million and £80 million plus in each of the last two or three transfer windows. The fact that the club has now down a division means they are now on the verge of extinction.

The shitty manager has been paid well to have his contract cancelled, and all the crap players he brought to the club have been sold at a massive reduction, just to get the wage bill down. So now the chairman has stood down, the club is up for sale, the roof of the half-built brand-new stand is unfinished (and leaking), and the building contractor won't come back and repair it because they haven't been paid for the work done so far. Not that it matters too much about the roof, because since going down a division, a lot of so-called supporters have now pissed off to the enemy down the road, so there is no one sitting in the new stand anyway.

The grass on the pitch is too long because now having no money, the club have had to swap their lawnmower for a player from a team in a much lower league, a team which five years ago was in the Champions League and was well established in the Premiership until the chairman and board decided to sack their LONG-serving, LOYAL manager, or release him by mutual consent (whatever that means). Just to chase the impossible dream. Look at what's happened to Charlton since the sacking of Alan Curbishley. And Stoke with Tony Pulis.

Whenever a team sacks a manager, it's always the same old names that come to the top of the betting list when they're looking for a replacement. Managers like Steve McClaren, Alan Pardew, Avram Grant, Ian Dowie and Mark Hughes, to name a few, all had very little success previously, or had not long been sacked by their last club, and should, in my opinion, never be let near another football club again as a manager. Some of these have had some minor successes but are now out of their sell-by dates. When will football clubs ever learn?

All in all, it creates a bleak outlook for the club you love: so much doom and gloom all round, a bit like the Alamo or Custer's last stand. If Custer had to fight today, it would have to be known as Custer's last seat (no standing allowed). So, it's backs to the wall stuff, and let's face it there have been a few cowboys at our club, who unfortunately were not as loyal or prepared to die for the cause as were Davy Crockett's or General Custer's troops. So, apart from the old tea lady, a one-armed programme seller, and us the faithful, there is nobody left to fight the fight for our beloved football club. But fight we will (without the violence).

We then get books written by ex-footballers, telling all about how they wasted every hard-earnt penny that you worked your bollocks off for in order to buy an overpriced season ticket, which then goes towards paying their exuberant wages so they can go and piss it all up the wall. Or so they can pay £1,000 a night to shag some old tart in a top London hotel, who then tries to accuse them and three or four of his mates of rape. (WHY go to his room with him and his mates, love? What did you think you were going there for: to play Monopoly or Happy Families?)

I remember someone asking the late great George Best once what he had spent all his money on, and his reply was: 'I spent a lot of money on booze, birds and fast cars. The rest I just squandered.' George was one of the greatest players to ever grace a football pitch, so it was funny at the time. But looking back, it didn't do George's career any good at all. Sadly it cut short his playing career far too early, as it possibly did his life.

We were lucky enough to see George and his great friend Rodney Marsh, who himself was a fabulous player and one of my all-time favourites, down at the Cottage. This was a memory never to be forgotten, especially if you're a Hereford supporter, as George and Rodney in a match back in 1976 ripped them apart. Fulham was so superior on that day that the two maestros, at one moment in the game, even had fun tackling each other for the ball, with Fulham running out as 4–1 winner.

We've also had books written by football thugs who try to justify their right to kick the shit out of the opposing supporters all in the name of their club. Mindless morons, who over the years have caused more problems for the football clubs they claim to follow and love so much. Total arseholes. These pricks are so brave that they have to go about in groups, completely bevvied up so that when they're caught, they can blame the drink. When they go to court (if they ever get caught), they turn up in a nice suit. They've had a shower, shit, shave and a haircut, and they've got a nice clean shirt on, looking like butter wouldn't melt in their mouths. So there they stand, all apologetic, saying they don't know what came over them, and they've never done anything like this before (what this toe rag means is, he has never been caught before), pleading that 'it must have been the drink, Your Honour.' Or they blame their childhood upbringing, coming from a poor family (this poor little sod was deprived of all the good things in life), saying his mother was a junky, his father left home two years before he was born (honest). And the soppy judge swallows all this crap, slaps his wrist and sends him on a two-week community order, and that's if he chooses to turn up for it.

The club will put him on a banning order (big deal). I don't care what anyone says; a banning order means nothing: a determined thug will still get into a match one way or another. Not everyone on the turnstile will recognise him. He doesn't care about the match. It's only the fight he's interested in.

What should happen is, when these thick scumbag bastards (I'm not a bitter person, you understand) are caught, their clothes and boots should be taken away, and when they go to court, they should be made to wear the blood-stained clothes they were arrested in. And the boots, with the blood, skin and hair of some poor sod's skull still around the metal toe caps. The judges would then see these bastards in their true light.

If they blame the drink, then they could not only nick them for assault but also for being drunk and disorderly. And if the judges wanted to send them somewhere for their punishment, then they could put a gun in their hands and send them to fight (which they obviously like to do) in one of the many wars this country seems to get involved in. Or if that is not agreeable to the human rights lobby (you know the group, those who like to defend the offenders and not the victims), then how about on football match days these thugs are made to report to a room at a police station where an off-duty policeman who wants to earn some extra cash, could check these people in, and sit with them for three hours before the game starts until three hours after the game finishes.

These cretins have set clubs back years, and they have also cost football clubs millions of pounds over the years in lost revenue and European experiences due to overseas violence. Teams such as Everton, Norwich, West Ham, Southampton, Oxford, Luton and Wimbledon, to name just a few, were all denied European football during a five-year ban (1985–1990) on all English teams playing in Europe. The sad thing was that for lots of these teams and their supporters, they had nothing to do with any of the trouble relating to the ban. For some, it would have been their first chance to venture into a European competition, and sadly, for a few, their last chance. But worst of all, the thugs have tarnished the names and reputations of some great clubs and countries worldwide.

It's quite strange that the England team hooligans only seem to travel and cause a riot overseas, but we don't seem to get much trouble with them when we play at home. Can it be that the overseas police can go a bit over the top with their security measures?

Now, I know we're not angels when we've all had a bit of a skin full, and I do know that we have made a bit of a reputation for ourselves, but hopefully we won't see the same scenes in the future as those we have in the past.

I was also under the impression that we were made to have all-seating stadia for safety reasons as well as to cut down on hooliganism. But after watching the Liverpool versus Manchester United game where both sets of fans behind both goals stood upright through the entire match, it would seem that nobody in authority was able to do anything about it. It makes it seem a bit bloody pointless ever bringing in the law to have seated grounds when the majority of fans don't want it.

Although nowadays, most away fans stand, I see lots of clubs are now testing the idea of bringing in safe standing, as they have in Germany, which hopefully will make for better and safer standing over here.

There have been many other books covering other different footballing matters and footballing experiences: books written by famous authors such as Nick Hornby, my favourite being *Fever Pitch*. Another great read is Simon Jordan's *Be Careful What You Wish For*, which is about his time as chairman of Crystal Palace and the problems he had to go through when he was running the football club: dealing with the players, their agents, and some of the managers with whom he didn't quite see eye to eye over the team and the transfer market.

But I haven't found a light-hearted one that covers the relationship that a full-blown totally dedicated football supporter has with his club. A club they dedicate their lives to, and a club they will follow to the ends of the earth no matter how badly they treat them. They will even go where Captain Kirk wouldn't (to the Ryman League).

SO WHY DO WE DO IT?

The answer is,
We do what we do for the love of our club.
The name of our club. And our football family.

The people of the club, such as the players, managers, chairmen and backroom staff will all come and go. Some will become heroes, as Johnny Haynes, George Cohen and Gordon (Ivor) Davies are at Fulham, and now 'Mitro … Mitro' (well, he was!). Jack Walker is one such at Blackburn Rovers; King Kenny, Stevie G and Emlyn Hughes at Liverpool; Bobby Robson the Toons. others in the football family will see him as their favourite grandfather. Bobby Moore and Mark Noble of West Ham; Alan Shearer and Robert Lee of Newcastle; Matt Le Tissier of Southampton;

and Jimmy Greaves, Glenn Hoddle and now Harry Kane at Spurs. That's just to name a few. I'm sure all supporters have their own heroes.

Also, for some supporters, there are some people who will be better forgotten: Mario Balotelli wherever he played, I would think; Winston Bogarde at Chelsea; Karel Poborský at Manchester United; Ken Bates at Chelsea and of late, at Leeds; Alan Sugar at Spurs; and the late Doug Ellis at Aston Villa.

One of the worst cases of hero to zero was Sam Hammam. Under his reign, Wimbledon and The Crazy Gang (due to the antics they got up to) got promoted to the then First Division in 1986. They then won the FA Cup in 1988, beating the then League Champions Liverpool, but sadly, Hammam, then tried back in the 90s to take Wimbledon FC (aka The Dons, or The Wombles) to Dublin, Ireland, due to the poor fan base Wimbledon had at their home games. Having seen that move fail, Wimbledon was then sold to two Norwegian guys who eventually went bust. But thanks to Pete Winkelman and some of the loyal supporters of the original Wimbledon, they eventually moved the team to Milton Keynes, and it was renamed as Milton Keyne Dons. As for the rest of the loyal supporters of the original Wimbledon who refused to go to MK, they all fought together to get their team back to Plough Lane, and eventually won. A new team was born, and it is now back in business as AFC Wimbledon, with a nice new stadium. And most importantly, the club is back at its spiritual home in Plough Lane.

Now ... possibly regarded as the last football villain of them all is ... (roll on the drums) Mr Mike (Sports Direct for Thailand) Ashley. This is all due to him having more meetings in about two or three years with potential buyers of Newcastle United than Parliament had had since Guy Fawkes tried to blow up its very Houses. These meetings with a billionaire or two, who were trying and failing time and time again, to take over Newcastle FC, took what seemed like a lifetime to the sad supporters who desperately wanted him out. Now finally after years of saying it was for sale, it has at last been sold to a Saudi Arabian-backed consortium (and that news went down as well as a bacon roll at a bar mitzvah).

But I will try and stand up for some of these owners, chairman and managers because I do believe that 99 per cent of them try to do the right thing by the clubs they run, refusing to bow to supporters' demands, such as spending a fortune, and they try to run a tight ship to survive and compete the best they can. Alan Sugar and Doug Ellis kept a tight rein on their clubs' spending, as does Daniel Levy at Spurs, but we supporters are so fickle, and if we're not at least winning the odd match or two, or for the bigger teams, winning the odd trophy or two, then heads must roll, and normally it's the manager's.

But after all this, the name of the football club in most cases carries on in one form or another, even when going out of business. For example, Accrington Stanley, Aldershot Town, AFC Wimbledon and many, many more, old, well-established clubs have all fallen on hard times, but thanks to those loyal supporters who have stood by the club they love and cherish, those same supporters that were treated so badly by the rulers of the club in the so-called good old days when things were going well in the pockets of the bosses; those supporters who were taken for granted; those same supporters that now are the saviours of the club, and, in many cases, go on to become the guardians of their clubs.

Sad as it was with Covid-19 causing not only health problems but also many financial problems, I hope clubs will now appreciate the importance of their supporters. Unfortunately, I doubt it.

Trying to explain to someone like my friend Dougie, who as I say wasn't into football, about my love of the game was very difficult, until one day, my wife, for whatever reason, pointed out that she thought that I thought more of Fulham than of her. Well, I think we've all heard that line from our spouses before about one thing or another, and we tend to shrug it off with a 'yeah, yeah, alright, here we go again' attitude. But this time it started the little old grey cells working (as Poirot would say). Even though I thought that she was wrong, I wondered if perhaps she had a point to some extent, and I started to realise that I did tend to give up lots of time, consideration and money to the club.

She also pointed out that she felt she was fighting a battle with Fulham for my affections, and that I would rather go to a match than go out with her. She then said the one thing that really hit home and made me realise what the relationship between a football supporter and their football club is. My wife said it was as if 'I was having an affair with another woman.' I laughed at first when she said it (as you do), but those words kept going around and around in my mind, and I started to see similarities between my life as a boy, and then as a young single man, growing up into what I am now: an old married family man, and my life as a young football fan, moving through my teens, and becoming what I am now: an old grown-up season ticket holder.

There are many more women involved in all sorts of different roles in the world of football. Just look at the USA: women's football is massive and growing day by day, as it is now in England. Another footballing great, Arsenal's Tony Adams, stated he still keeps a check on Arsenal's results because it was 'like keeping an eye on an old girlfriend.'

Rudd Gullit talked about playing 'sexy football', saying we call it the 'beautiful game'. All these statements or comments regarding football seem to be in some way female-related.

OK, so imagine your football team as a woman. Now, I'm talking about the style of football in which the team portrays itself on the pitch, not just anybody at the club. And if you do, who would your club remind you of? Is your team the equivalent of Rachel Hunter (mature and beautiful), or sexy like the gorgeous Kylie Minogue? Or is yours more like Nora Batty (*Last of the Summer Wine*) stockings rolled down and getting stuck in?

Unfortunately, at times, I see my club Fulham as a bit like Hyacinth Bucket (*Keeping Up Appearances*). Sometimes we want to be something we perhaps aren't (well, not yet anyway). No disrespect to the Khans our owners, the manager, or anybody at the club, who no doubt are all working their butts off to get us the success we supporters yearn for, but to be seen as a sexy gorgeous club is going to take us even more years than we'd hoped for. After going up and down between the Premier League and the Championship, it's going to take quite a few years and a massive makeover, which perhaps even old Trinny and Susannah might find a bit daunting.

Rachel Hunter I see as perhaps Manchester United or Liverpool, because they, like her, seem to have been around for years, but have kept their top-class standing, and still turn people's heads wherever they go. Manchester City and Arsenal, to some extent, have got to be sexy Kylie, because their movement and style of football is so sleek and precise, and they make everyone drool with envy when they start to move. When Chelsea had those two big ones up front, Drogba and Anelka, they were like Jordan (Katie Price), sometimes looking very tasty, and sometimes a bit average, but when they decided to thrust those two big ones up front forward (nudge, nudge, wink, wink, say no more) then, like Jordan, they'd frighten the life out of anyone.

Unfortunately for Chelsea towards the end of their reign, Drogba was still like the real thing, but Anelka was moving more like an implant. Derby and West Brom at the moment remind me of Miss Marple and Hetty Wainthropp respectively, running around try to work out where it's all gone wrong, and who did what to kill their season while trying to find solutions to resolve the problem. However, it was pointed out to me they can't be like those two ladies, as both of these ladies tended to have a bit of a clue, and these clubs don't at this moment in time. Still, I'll leave you to decide who your team reminds you of, and I have no doubt that whoever you decide it is, you'll still love them to bits.

So, it's as simple as that: the reason we do what we do.
It's for the love of our football team, and our football family.
Everyone who supports my football team is a member
of my football family.

Chapter Three

How I Think It All Started

As life is inbred into most of us:
FOOTBALL IS INBRED INTO MOST OF OUR LIVES

Hopefully this book is going take you back in time to when your mother or father first held your hand and took you through those great big intimidating gates of your first school, and right up to where you are now in your life. If you're of a more mature age like me, and married with a family, then I hope this book will remind you of some of the silly and stupid things that you might have done, and events that maybe went on around you in your younger years. Things that you might have encountered while growing up from boy to man, girl to woman, or man to woman, or … (you get my drift).

Maybe it will bring back some great, and perhaps not so great memories of yesteryear's encounters with everyday life. If, on the other hand, you're young and just cutting your teeth in the big wide world, just starting on your circle of life, then this might well give you an insight into some of the obstacles that I, and thousands like me have had to overcome to get through in life, to get to where we are today, and finding that right partner with whom you want to spend the rest of your life.

The years of hard work ahead, the highs and lows, the pain and suffering, spending your hard-earned money, both of you chasing a dream of success and prosperity in life (like doing the lottery): that only comes true for the chosen few.

Everyone is hoping to go from rags to riches, struggling one day, hoping to be overnight lottery millionaires the next, like the so-called stars of reality shows, with their fifteen minutes of fame: people who had never been heard of before (and possibly will never be heard of again) but for one reason or another, became very successful in a short space of time. But sadly in life it can also be the other way around, as it has been in many cases. In a short space of time, failure can also be so easy to come by.

Some of the top entrepreneurs, movie stars, and sportsmen have gone from riches to rags, mostly of their own doing, not concentrating on what their life is about. Or maybe it was too much 'sex and drugs and rock and roll', as the brilliant Ian Dury and The Blockheads sang about in the late 70s. (Fifty years on and The Blockheads, sadly without Ian, are still rocking today. If you've never seen them, then you're missing out.)

During our lives we will meet up with some wonderful and very interesting people. People to whom we will listen intensely. People who will broaden our minds, and educate us. People who know far more about life than we ever will. We thought we knew it all.

Unfortunately, we'll also meet some right arses, the 'I've been there, I've done it, I've got the T-shirt' people, the dreaded 'know-alls', or should I say, 'know fuck-alls'. We've all met them; it doesn't matter what you've done, they've done bigger and better. You tend to find them at the local pub every night on their own. They boast and try to make out that they're fairly well off. And you can't get rid of them. It's like having piles: a proverbial pain in the arse.

They all make out their lives are so perfect. They're most probably not married, have never been involved in any type of long-term loving relationship, but they imply that their girlfriends are 'drop-dead gorgeous', apparently the best in the world, so beautiful that nothing can compete with them, and they are so deeply in love with them. But a lot of the time it's bullshit. Their so-called girlfriends are never about when you're there, and no one's ever seen them. If they do have someone sitting at home or waiting in the wings for them, then they're most probably not enjoying the same sort of relationship that you're having with your partner. That's why they're sitting on their own each night in the bar. They take the piss out of what you're wearing because it comes from a charity shop, or Primark, or some other cheaper store, and also because it's not got a top designer label attached, and even if it has, then it's most probably a cheap copy. Whereas they have the lot; they're wearing Gucci this, Armani that: all the top brands.

You mention that you're just popping out to Lidl to get your shopping and they look at you with disdain and say, 'Oh no, we shop at Marks & Spencer.' (Arrogant turd.) Sadly for some of them, they live in their own sad little world. Your other half may be not as attractive as theirs, not exactly 'drop-dead gorgeous', but at least your relationship is for real. They can criticise and turn their noses up at you and your other half. Compare what you have to what they say they have. But it doesn't matter what you say, they have better.

Unfortunately, they paint a picture of their lifestyle that makes it difficult for you to argue with, as much as you try to do so. And doesn't it piss you off big time? Even though you know you have a better life and relationship, it still gets right up your nose to listen to them bragging on. It gets to a stage where you actually laugh about them, treat them as a joke, and in some very rare cases feel a bit sorry for them. So then it's better that you just nod your head and agree with them as you get to realise after a while that you're wasting your breath trying to argue.

But there are lots of folks out there that do have 'drop-dead gorgeous wives' and a big house and a big bank account, they do wear top-of-the-range sports gear and have a great lifestyle, but they never, ever rub it in your face. They don't brag about it. They appreciate what they have. Lots of them have been where you are now and have total understanding of what struggles you have to face week in and week out in life. But no matter how many struggles you and your partner face, you'll face them together, and fight them all the way to the end.

Hopefully, this book is also going to take you back to the time when your father or mother first held your hand and took you through those great big intimidating gates to your first ever football match, and up to where you are right now in your footballing life. It might make you reflect on things that you might have seen or encountered during your footballing life. Maybe you're like me, a mature season ticket holder, or perhaps on the other hand you're a long-standing football supporter who has signed up to a club membership because you're still not sure if you want to fully commit yourself to a permanent relationship with your club, preferring to play it safe and keep it casual.

You will meet some really interesting supporters who will teach you all about the game. You'll learn about the good grounds to go to, and also the best ones to avoid. How to get to watch some of these teams away from home. They'll give you all the knowledge you'll need to make your footballing life that much better. But you'll also meet some really painful footballing dickheads.

Now the worst pain of all that you will almost certainly encounter in your football life, and the biggest problem that all true supporters have to overcome, is the dreaded armchair or bar stool fan. You know the sort (they're like the 'know fuck-alls'). There's at least one of these in every pub, and you can bet a pound to a pitch of shit that they are, if you're living in London, a Southerner who supposedly supports one of those big northern clubs like ManUre (no, it's not a spelling mistake, it's the way they have been since Sir Alex left, and may it carry on that way forever), Liverpool and, of late, Manchester City. Teams who have been so successful over the years.

It's funny how money not only gives power, but also that power can make people oh-so arrogant, and therefore hated, as many of the so-called big clubs are nowadays. These guys brag about how brilliantly their teams are doing, and most of the time they are doing well (unfortunately). They boast that they're the best, no one can get near them, they're going to win this, that and the other (and sadly they most probably will). But these so-called supporters(?) are never there in body to see or feel the emotion of the game on the actual match day.

They sit in the comfort of their homes or the local pub and wallow in the glory. When you ask why they profess to support a club they've most probably never seen in the flesh, and why they supposedly support a club 200 plus miles away, their answer is nearly always the same (and I think it must be rule number one in the *I'm Not Really a Proper Supporter, I Just Don't Have Anything Else Going For Me* manual), and that answer is, that their dad or grandad took them once to see the team play about 25 years ago, and they've supported them ever since. Well, my mum and dad took me to see Vera Lynn once (and I never did forgive them), but I never rushed out to buy her records afterwards, or had 'VERA' tattooed up one leg, across my forehead or across my arsenal. It's like buying *The Sun* newspaper and looking at the girl on page three, and then telling the world she's your girlfriend. (Just like the bloke in the pub who made out his relationship was better than yours). They slag you and your team off, giving it large because you haven't won anything for years (if you've ever won anything at all), and they take the piss out of your team who isn't doing very well (yet again).

I remember a couple of years ago when Fulham were in the Championship. I was having a beer in my local, chatting with a Chelsea supporter when this dickhead of a southern Manchester United supporter came in. We were just chatting away about football in general when the subject turned to the transfer market. As the conversation went on, I happened to mentioned that Fulham were in the market for some player or another when this United prick looked at me and said, 'We're talking about shopping at Marks & Spencer, not Help the Aged' (arrogant turd).

These people end up boring you to death, going on and on about their so-called team, but the one thing they don't realise is that for the true supporter, it's not only about success (although it's something we all crave for); it's also about being involved with the club, being part of the club, being part of the football family. Something these guys, and in many cases girls, will never experience.

No, I'm sorry, lads and lassies, you're not supporters of your so-called clubs in the true meaning of the word; you don't spend any time, or money, following these clubs. You are just mere fans who sit on your arses and admire from a distance, and you have no allegiance to these clubs whatsoever.

I remember a few years back, arguing with a young lady about this very subject. She said she had supported Manchester United for about ten years or so. I asked her if she had ever been to Old Trafford, which was about 250 miles north of where she lived, at which she confessed to never, ever having been there. I also asked had she ever been to a football match anywhere. Her answer was no. I then asked her why she supported Manchester United. Her answer was that her new boyfriend at the time was a Bournemouth supporter, and they were playing Manchester United on this particular day. When he asked her who she supported, apparently, she looked at the television for inspiration. And this is what she told me: 'Just then David Beckham was walking on to the pitch, and I thought he's got a nice arse.' And that was why she was a Manchester United supporter! (There are some sad bastards about.)

There are however people in life who are successful, and do have beautiful wives, and a lifestyle you'd die for. There are also many southern-based supporters that do travel 200 plus miles or so, week in and week out, to watch these northern clubs, but these people don't get in your face bragging away, driving you potty, and trying to put you or your club down all the time. They appreciate what a lot they have, and appreciate what very little you may have.

We are all part of the football family.

Chapter Four

Fan or Supporter?

A penny for your thoughts:
£100 MILLION FOR YOUR STRIKER

It's been almost 60 years of previously standing, now sitting (well, most of the time), watching and supporting my football team playing in all the four English football leagues.

During this lifetime of watching my team win, lose or draw, I've experienced, like most hardened supporters, the highs and the lows of what a result can bring. And no matter how bad times got: relegation, early cup exits against lower league teams, humiliation when beaten 6–0 or 7–0, I've never, ever thought about packing it all in, or giving up my sacred seat in the Hammersmith stand at Craven Cottage, home of the mighty Fulham Football Club. Nor did I even think of giving up going to away matches, no matter how bad results were. I was always there, hoping the next result would be a better one, or at least the next one, or maybe perhaps the next one, and so the hope goes on, and on, and on. Although unfortunately at my age now (72) I can't seem to get to go to as many away games as I would like. Of course, I, like most supporters would get upset and angry every time results went against us, but I would still be there at the next match no matter what.

I have been asked so many times over the years why do I bother spending lots of time and money, following a team that over the years has won sod-all, and, what do I get out of watching a team that gives me so little back? Surely, I'm told 'there must better things to do on a Saturday afternoon' ... (or, as it is now, whenever the TV companies decide that we should be able to watch our teams). And do you know what? I never knew the answer! I just did it, it's part of my life, it is part of who I am or who we supporters are.

Now at the ripe (actually overripe) old age of seventy-two, I think I've actually come to realise the reason, and that is a four-letter word (no, it's not FIFA or UEFA). It's LOVE. It's as simple as that. We supporters love our teams as much as we love our wives and husbands, girlfriends or boyfriends, and our families. I have a family life, and I have a football family life, and they run along side by side, a parallel life. I help support my family, and I help support my team. I watch both daily, checking that they are both fit and healthy. They have both made me laugh, cry, and cost me a fortune over the years, and I've loved every minute of it (well most of it). Family dedication for most people in life is a natural thing, to make sure your family are OK.

BUT to live, eat, drink, breathe and feel the same way about your team isn't quite so natural; you really have to be a true supporter (or, as some would say, a complete frigging head case), and I mean a true supporter, totally dedicated, ready to give your all for your team, and to understand why you do it.

I have also come to realise that in this wonderful world of football, there are football fans, and football supporters. The differences between these two are, fans may like a certain club, but very, very rarely go to a game. They don't spend any real effort, time, or money on their chosen club, so they can't really be classed as a supporter, they tend to FANtasise. Supporters do just the opposite; they support their clubs no matter what the sacrifice or cost may be.

I've also come to realise that there are three different types of football supporters. Well, actually there are four, but I can't really class the fourth one as a serious contender for this category (or any other type of category) because that's the one that has absolutely no relationship or bond with a team anywhere within a 100- or even 200-mile radius of where they were brought up, or where they live now. But sadly, they pretend to support a team, and normally it's always a successful team that is over 200 miles away from where they have lived at any time in their life. If I were to include them, it would definitely be under the category, THE DREADED GLORY HUNTER.

For example, many years ago back in the 50s, Chelsea weren't all that good. Then came the 60s, and the place to be seen, other than Carnaby Street in the West End of London, was the King's Road, Chelsea. At this time these two places had taken off in the fashion world and everyone who was anyone, from top film stars, famous singers and part-time royalty, could be seen walking these streets on a daily basis. So, Chelsea football ground was to become a plaything for a lot of the rich and famous, as it still is even today. Chelsea started to become successful on the pitch and lots of so-called Fulham fans hoping to see the so-called famous celebrities jumped ship and followed the glory trail (or, as I would see it, the *gory* trail). I must admit Fulham at this period in time weren't playing all that well, which was also another reason to wander off down the road. Alas, the glory hunter came to be, and sadly that trend still carries on today.

Chelsea wasn't the only team to have this sort of follower. Manchester United is possibly the most well-known for this trend because of their success. Liverpool, Arsenal, and now Manchester City are the people's choice brought on by success (which is fair play if you're that way inclined). Lots of these fans change their teams like they change their socks, and they only change their teams from one to another because of the success of that club, and for no other reason.

THE GLORY HUNTER CHASES THE GLORY,
NOT THE ADVENTURE.

I'll try to explain which category I put these other three so-called football fans and supporters in.

In category number three is THE TOURIST. Most of these are supporters of football teams in their own country, but they are also perhaps fans of certain teams abroad. They are the ones who enjoy going to a match that appeals to them for some reason: maybe they are going to watch a certain team who have just signed a superstar player, or perhaps a player from their own country or continent.

I remember when Fulham signed Junichi Inamoto on loan from Arsenal in 2002. All of a sudden, we had loads of Japanese tourists turning up with their cameras flashing all over the place (their cameras that is). There were more films on show there than at the Cannes Film Festival. But as soon as Inamoto got in his moto and left the club, so did his fans. Brian McBride and Clint Dempsey brought lots of American tourists, and Dimitar Berbatov brought just about every living southern so-called Manchester United supporter that had never been to Old Trafford to see him (sad).

Lots of these people don't follow any particular team outside their own country. They have very little knowledge of the teams they're going to watch, but if they're in an area working or maybe on holiday somewhere, they will go and see a match if one's on locally.

I have done this myself while having a short break in Prague some years ago. I took my wife to watch Sparta Prague. (She was over the moon, bless her. You should have seen the tears of joy!!) That was on a Wednesday. The following day, Slavia Prague were playing, but sadly, for some reason my wife said she didn't feel very well. (I think she was overwhelmed by the surprise of me taking her to the game on the Wednesday).

Lots of top teams get these tourists from all around the world. They mainly only go to the Premier League games to see the so-called top stars. Sadly, they're not queuing up outside or fighting to get in to see the lower league teams like Wycombe, Rochdale, or Darlington (and this is no disrespect to them). These tourists I class as football fans in this country, but they are most probably supporters in their own.

You can always spot the tourist fans; they tend to turn up mob-handed, fifteen or twenty minutes late. Firstly, they stand in the aisle, spinning around and around like a lighthouse, taking a shit load of pictures of everything and everybody around them, blocking off all that's happening on the pitch. Then they try and work out what their tickets about. They walk up and down the aisle more times than Liz Taylor has ever done. Bumping into each other as they twist and turn, they look like they're doing the conga, unable to find the right row for their seats. (I suppose if you're from somewhere like Asia, Africa, or the Middle East, then our alphabet isn't as simple as it seems to us.) When they have finally located the right row, they nearly always seem to have seats in the middle of the row. So again they frustrate everyone around them who have to get up as they squeeze their way in, trying to find the right seat numbers, only to realise that their actual seats are in the middle row on the other side of the aisle. So everyone has to get up again to let them back out. And now it's time for them to cause mayhem for all those people across aisle. Now they have all got into the middle section which is great, but instead of just sitting in the ten or twelve seats they have been allocated, each individual wants to sit in the exact seat number which is on their ticket. The people sitting behind that row can't see anything now for all the bodies weaving and bobbing in front of them (I'm all for taking the knee, but at this moment in time l just wish they'd take the bloody seat). All this mayhem is nearly always at a time when your team is on the attack, or they have just scored and you've missed it.

They'll all be carrying a club shop bag containing just their match day programme. They've already got their brand-new shirt on, and a brand-new scarf is also hanging around their neck. They'll most probably also be wearing a brand-new cap with its label still attached and hanging down the back of their neck. They have spent a fortune in the shop which is great for business and long may that carry on, but for fuck's sake, in future buy a ticket in another part of the ground, cos I'm sick to death of having to keep getting up and down like a lift operator, and missing the rare goals we do score. Then at half-time, they come back from getting their refreshments late, only to start the whole rigmarole of finding their seats again!

Lots of clubs at this moment in time are petitioning for safe standing. I want to start a petition for some sort of tourist area. There should be a tourist enclosure: like there is for families with kids. These fans have no feelings for either of the teams; they're just on a day out (like old Dell Trotter, they're just on a *Jolly Boys' Outing*). They have no feelings for whatever the result may be, and you see them walking out after the game, all smiley faces, laughing and joking with their friends, and you've just been stuffed out of sight. Your team has had a shit game, and a shit result, and here they are all happy. They've had a good day out, the result means very little to them, and they will move on to another ground somewhere else in the world, and cause chaos all over again. Sadly, as much as I moan about them, football teams still need these types of fans to help the club flourish. And for lots of teams like Fulham, to get bums on seats, and a few extra pounds in the till.

In category number two is THE PART-TIME SUPPORTER. These are the ones who turn up as often as they can. Sadly some are fair-weather supporters, or maybe they cannot give their all due to family or work commitments. But they are *supporters*, not *fans*. These supporters will often go to a rare away match, mostly to grounds they haven't been to before. But they don't always turn up if your match is on the box, or it's a mid-week game, and especially not if money is a bit tight, preferring to save the few pounds they might have for the next home or away game. But they are always there in spirit if not in person. They still feel the pain or joy of whatever the result is. Many of the more well-to-do season ticket holders just pick and choose which matches they want to see, and mainly they're there when the bigger teams or bigger names are coming to town.

There are so many different reasons for the odd no-shows. It could be that lots of them were regular supporters in the past and used to attend week in and week out. But, due to moving away, getting married and having a family, mortgage, ill health, or in lots of cases being outpriced by clubs (due to the cost clubs put on their season ticket prices), they can just no longer afford it. Others get tickets on the day when they can, and that can be a problem in itself nowadays, as lots of clubs now have a limited number of tickets to sell for each match.

Many pay for club membership in the hope of getting a ticket now and again. But whatever their reasons for not being there, they are still totally committed to the club no matter what. They will see more games than they miss during the course of the season. They spend a limited amount of time and effort when they do make it to a match. They spend a limited amount of any money that they may have spare. They still wear their shirts, scarves and hats that they bought many years ago (when you didn't have to remortgage your house to pay for them and when they were able to attend on a more regular basis). They have been coming and supporting their club over many years.

Most were born local to the ground or in the local borough. They have ties to the club. Possibly their mothers and fathers were supporters and they have followed in their footsteps. Lots of them were born somewhere else but have lived in the area for quite some time, and they have developed a loving relationship with the club. They also feel the pain, anguish, and hurt when the team is going through a bad spell and results are not going their way. The one important thing is that they know the history of the club and what it stands for. They are supporters.

Now in category one is THE TRUE FOOTBALL SUPPORTER. These are the supporters in the true meaning of the word. Supporters who, no matter what or why, will be there: home or away, rain or shine, whatever the country. They will follow their team through thick and thin to the end of the world, or as Meatloaf sang, they would 'run right into hell and back' (OH, and they will do that).

Most of the old-timers are kitted out in discoloured washed-out shirts from yesteryear. Some are so old (the shirt as well as the supporter) that there are no names or numbers on the backs, and no sign of a sponsor, or if there is a sponsor, it has most probably changed its name, or gone bust. There's a tatty old scarf with frayed edges, and a mixture of badges (which weigh about half a ton) from all the different grounds that they've attended, attached to their woolly hats. Some have a great big bobble on the top. If not a hat, then a discoloured sweat-stained cap.

Then there is the must-have for all: the sacred match day programme, held carefully (like a newborn baby) so as not to damage or crease it. It's usually stored in an A4 plastic bag to keep it in mint condition. They turn the pages over as gently as if they were turning the pages of some delicate ancient manuscript. I can just imagine them at home, wearing white cotton gloves, opening the programme in dark surroundings so that the sunlight won't fade the ink or the print.

They stand outside the ground with all the kids waiting for the team bus to arrive. And like the kids, they get just as excited. They're there, waiting with their scrapbooks open, pens at the ready, to get yet another signature across yet another picture that they've stuck in another of their many precious scrapbooks.

They have their social gatherings with other like-minded supporters at the local pub. Wetherspoons is always a popular watering hole, being cheap and cheerful. Or it's a real ale pub for the connoisseurs prior to the home game.

Before the away games, they meet at pubs in far distant lands (depending what league you're in!!), such as Sunderland, Nottingham, Norwich, Exeter, or even Shepherds' Bush: places that they have all been to so many times before over the previous years of encounters with the opposition. Some will meet up with supporters from the opposition at away games (perhaps not in Shepherd's Bush). These will be supporters they have befriended owing to playing against them so many times, and who are now good drinking buddies, and they will return the compliment when the opposing team visits their ground.

Not all true supporters dress and act as I've described above, more so the old-timers, as I say. Lots just wear their colours and go about their usual match day routine. They're quiet and inconspicuous, but totally, totally dedicated to the team, unlike those I pointed out as glory hunters.

There are thousands of dedicated supporters all over the country that still travel 200 plus miles to every game despite the fact that they are now living miles away in different parts of the country. This could be because they've moved away from where they originally lived or were born, or some might be working away from home, and only come home at weekends. Lots travel from Ireland, Scotland, and Wales, whether they're going to Manchester, Liverpool, or London, or from the south coast to the north, east to west or vice versa to see their teams home and away. I know of a few people who travel from the West Country to all the Fulham home matches and back home again afterwards. They will spend every last pound on their club.

The younger up-and-coming dedicated supporters turn their bedrooms into shrines, with pictures plastered all over the walls of their favourite players, scrapbooks and autograph books filled with pictures and autographs signed by all the players.

It's a pity that nowadays a lot of players in the top leagues tend to ignore the kids as they come off the coaches. Wearing headsets bigger than Mickey Mouse's ears, they pretend not to notice little Jimmy or Jane, who absolutely idolises them and has been standing there in the rain and cold for an hour or two with Mum or Dad, just waiting for the coach to arrive to get a close-up, a glimpse and a signature, maybe even a quick picture. The kids are then left teary-eyed, looking at their heroes' backs as they disappear into the distance, leaving their parents to console the children and make up some excuse as to why they were ignored. I know, as I've been that parent on many occasions. There are some real MISERABLE BASTARDS.

These youngsters have club flags or scarves proudly hanging in their bedroom windows. The club duvet and pillow cases are on the bed, and they have matching curtains. They are proud owners of DVDs showing all the seasons gone by. They wear the club shirt with their favourite player's name blazoned across the back, which is fine when you're an adult, but when little Jimmy or Jane (who is only about seven or eight, and whose body is no wider than a lolly stick, or measures about 12 inches across their back) wants Ibrahimovic, Alexander-Arnold or Aubameyang printed on their shirt, it starts getting awkward.

The older ones will have signed shirts framed and hanging on living room walls. Boxes of programmes of home and away matches they've seen in years gone by are in pristine condition and chronologically arranged in nice football folders on shelves, or neatly packed away in their lofts. Cups, slippers, and dressing gowns, all proudly display their team's badge. These are Christmas and birthday gifts from their families and friends.

No matter what their ages are, these supporters dedicate their lives to their teams. Unlike The Tourists, and some part-time supporters who fit football around their personal and private lives, these supporters are (or for the younger ones in the future, will be) living two lives. They'll have their own private day-to-day family lives, and they'll have their everyday football family lives. These two lives run alongside each other day by day and have so much in common. The only time there is a problem for them in this parallel life is when their two lives clash, then they'll be asking themselves: 'Do I go to my brother's wedding ... or go to the cup match at Liverpool?' Or to their wives or partners: 'Is there any chance, darling, that you could give birth without me, as the boys are playing at Old Trafford tonight and it's a really important game?'

It's very difficult to decide which is more important, because it's a bit like having two wives or girlfriends who both want to see you at the same time. Now, if you're a young lad or lassie reading this, beware, because you could be asking yourself the same questions in the not-so-distant future. There are lots of young supporters who even now follow their teams week in and week out. If they stay loyal over the coming years, they will be the fresh blood, they will be the ones to keep the heart of the club beating for many years to come.

And it's so good to see young kids wearing their local team's shirts no matter what division they're in, and not the shirts of teams 200 or 300 miles away, that they most probably will only ever get to see on the box. Many of these young ones will earn their stripes and badges and become the next generation of THE TRUE SUPPORTERS.

The book is based on some of my own experiences; therefore, the book is seen from a male point of view.

Chapter Five

KICKING OFF
How We Met

The world of girls:
THE WORLD OF FOOTBALL

I was born in Notting Hill, West London on 10 October 1951. My family moved to Putney SW15 when I was a just a few months old. We lived on the Lower Ashburton Estate, Chartfield Ave. My father, Tom, was a qualified bricklayer who, during the winter months when it was too cold to lay bricks, was a totter (a rag and bone man, like old *Steptoe and Son*). A few years later, he took over Sheen House riding stables in East Sheen, near Richmond in Surrey, where he taught people to ride. My mother, Kathleen (Kitty), was a housewife-cum-school cleaner-cum-shop assistant, cum just about everything. I have two older sisters, Joan, and Pat (who, since writing this, has sadly passed away).

My first school was Granard Infants School, and like most infant schools back then (and I suppose now), the teachers mostly taught us about playing and getting used to mixing with other small kids: boys and girls, all equal, all playing together in sandpits, and with paint and plasticine and anything else you could get all over your clothes. Your mother would go potty when she came to pick you up. (I think they're called preschools nowadays.)

I was then to go on to Granard Junior School, where it was more about the learning game. I remember my first day, my mum holding my hand as we approached the school gates. They looked so big and frightening, but in truth the reason they looked so big was that I was so small. I remember being so nervous as she took me in. There I stood, frightened but proud, my skinny little legs dangling from my short trousers, shaking in my shoes, frightened to move from her side, not knowing what the hell was going to happen to me, or what I was supposed to do. Then the bell went and it was game on.

Along with about 250 to 300 other kids, I was taken by our new teacher to meet my new classmates. There I was kitted out in my new school uniform: a blue blazer with the school badge of a cedar tree (the tree which stood proudly in the school playground) stitched on the left-hand side of the blazer, a blue jumper, a blue polo shirt, short grey trousers and long grey socks that came up to my knees. Almost everything we wore was blue and had the cedar tree badge on it.

The colour blue and the badge were symbols of the school, showing everyone around who we were, and who we stood for. It was there that kids became different; boys and girls selected mates and went around in little groups or gangs. For the boys, the girls became fair game. Pigtails or ponytails, it didn't matter, if it was hanging, it got pulled by the boys. Boys and girls called each other names, but mostly it was only really hiding the fact that they quite liked each other, nothing sexual, far too young for those types of thoughts. No more sandpits, paints, and plasticine; now it was kiss-chase, and doctors and nurses (no, not that version).

It wasn't until I went to Elliott Secondary Modern, when I was about eleven, that the world started to take some form of shape; and so did gender. Now my blazer had gone from blue to black. The badge had an elephant's head on it (which again was on just about everything). While researching for this book (yes, I know it may not read like I have), I have only just found out that the reason for this is that back sometime in the 50s, the playground was redeveloped and shaped like an elephant's head with the trunk and all (I'm not sure whether it was planned to be that shape, or whether the builder had had a few too many beers the night before), and so it was called the elephant's playground, and they adopted the elephant's head on the badge.

Here I was now in a different kind of environment, a school with about 1,100 kids, most of them trying to be the best in the class; this was the time when the you had to get your head down to some serious hard work. No more playing about at school. The teachers were strict. No more silly kids' games, now it was pure work. (Well, for some it was.)

This was where your life was about to be structured for your pending future, and where girls were also starting to take shape. Up until now I had never really noticed girls as anything other than friends, just like all my other mates, just someone to play with. But that all changed as I got a little older. By the sixth form (I was now about fifteen or sixteen), I was no longer playing doctors and nurses. I was more into practising gynaecology, and meeting girls for a quick fag and a grope behind the infamous bike sheds. There were sometimes a few problems with the girls I was seeing, because they wanted to see me on such and such a day, which coincided with meeting my mates for a kickaround, so sadly I had to let them down. Well, you couldn't let your mates down, could you?

As the years went by, I had a few different girlfriends, and each new one brought a different type of personality. It seemed that with each different personality I found myself trying to fit in with their ways, rather than finding one that matched mine. Eventually though, after a few dates here and there, I finally found the right one for me, and after a short while, I decided to make it official, and commit myself to a long-term relationship. A MARRIAGE LICENCE was taken. So that was how my young personal life started and progressed up till now.

My football life started in the same fashion, and the similarities are amazing.

My dad was a QPR supporter when he was younger, but then due to working seven days a week, alongside the long hours it took running the stables, he only took me to see two QPR games. It was in the early 60s. I was about ten or eleven. I can't remember who they were playing, but I remember it was when they played at the White City Stadium, which was built in the early 1900s for the Olympics. It was also used for matches in the 1966 World Cup. Apparently, QPR were looking to move there on a permanent basis, but for whatever reason, it didn't happen, I vaguely remember it being so vast and empty. Rangers, like Fulham, had their regular supporters, but I don't think there was much hope of them ever filling the stadium that was built to hold about 90,000. I think at that time they were in Division Two or Three so perhaps it was for that reason they didn't move grounds. As I have said, due to his work, my dad couldn't take me often enough for me to get too involved with the Hoops (I'm pleased to say). Now although this was a general coinage for the team, to Fulham supporters they are better known as QP-R ha ha ha.

A schoolmate, Graham Alexander, and his dad, Arthur, had started taking me along to Fulham for each home game prior to my dad taking me to the Hoops, and so, unbeknown to me at the time I was basically already committed to Fulham. Fulham was just a 30-minute walk from where we lived. We'd walk down Putney Hill, through the High Street, over Putney Bridge, and into Bishops Park, and it was then a great stroll along the river to the ground. And that's how I became hooked on football and the Mighty Whites of Fulham. I was introduced to Fulham by my friend, a sort of blind date, and I fell in love. I remember the excitement and yet trepidation when getting to those big doors with those turnstiles, which are still there today.

I remember standing on the terrace with my black and white scarf, bobble hat, a big black and white rosette, which almost covered my scrawny little chest, with Fulham written across it. Everything then, as now, was black and white with the Fulham badge on it. Back then we also had the equivalent of today's clappers, but unlike the cheap advertising cardboard clappers they give out now, we had big wooden rattles. They had a handle that you held and you spun them around and around as fast as you could. The faster you could spin them, the more noise they made. There were two cogs attached to a wooden box, and the box itself had two thin strips of wood. As you spun it around the strips of wood would hit against the cogs making a clattering sound. And if you didn't take care when spinning it you could do permanent damage to anyone close by. I doubt you would be allowed to take one of those to a game today.

So, here I was wearing my team's colours, very proud to show everyone who I supported. And over the coming games, the passion grew and the fear of what might be grew less. I only had a short fling with QPR; we only dated twice (not really long enough to get to know each other). Lots of other teams I had seen occasionally on the TV brought so many different styles none of which I could say tickled my fancy. So, after many years of supporting Fulham, I decided to make it official and commit to a longer-term relationship. A SEASON TICKET was taken.

I can remember in the earlier years coming home from the Fulham games and Mum asking whether we'd won. Normally I'd reply, 'I don't think so' because normally we didn't (ahh, some things never change), but at that age I was more interested in kicking an old Bovril cup or some rolled-up newspaper around the terraces with my mate Graham than watching what was actually going on on the pitch. (That was in the good old days when you could stand at matches.)

Even though Fulham had some great players back then, they had not long been promoted back to Division One(Premier League, as it is now known). They had the Fulham and England captain Johnny Haynes, who could put a 70-yard pass on a sixpence. Everyone raves about David Beckham's passing ability, which was outstanding, but I don't think even he would come near to the ability that the maestro had. It should also be remembered that the ball in those days was more like a medicine ball and made out of leather, so when it rained, it soaked up the water, and it was then more like kicking a cannon ball (not like the beach ball they use nowadays). My uncle broke his foot kicking a ball as, sadly, it was chained to his ankle. (How prisons have changed!) And my cousin was a half-back. He worked at the local cinema, taking the customers' entry tickets, tearing them, and giving them their half back! (Ah, the old jokes are the best!! Well, some are.)

We also had the bowlegged left-back Jim Langley, who put more balls into the River Thames than the Cambridge boat race team did with their boats. Then we had the soon-to-be World Cup winners: George Cohen, Alan Mullery, the flying Scotsman

Graham Leggat, Bobby 'killer' Keech, and later one of my all-time favourites, Steve Earle, who could score fabulous goals from all over the pitch. Even with that glorious team, Fulham always struggled, and were always close to relegation.

Like with football, when I was really unaware of what was going on with the game, it was the same with girls. After school I would normally go out and play with a girl called Shirley. When coming home for tea Mum would ask, 'What have you and Shirley been doing?' My answer was normally the same each time: 'just playing.' And that's all we had been doing.

Shirley was my age and lived two blocks away (she was also the only other kid living near), so after school we would meet up and play kids games that meant nothing. Most of the time I couldn't remember what we had been playing, and even now 60 or more years later, still nothing comes to mind as to what we did actually do. There was most probably a doll, some soldiers, or a ball was involved. Then, when I was about thirteen or fourteen, football was about to change for me.

Up to that point, football for me was a kickaround with about twenty or thirty kids who lived on the estate. One of these was a young future Terry McCann of the brilliant *Minder* series. He was also in *The Sweeney* and latterly *New Tricks*. (He is better known as Dennis Waterman.) There we were, all running around like headless chickens, chasing a ball all around the playground, or the large open green, much to the annoyance of the people who lived in the flats next to it, who were forever lambasting us, frightened we were going to put their windows in. No one knew who was on which side. We just chased the ball and kicked it when we had the chance (which was pretty rare with the number of kids that were playing), and we'd all chase it wherever it went. Jumpers were for goalposts.

As I say, it wasn't until I got to be about thirteen or fourteen that I started to see football in a totally different light. By this time, I was starting to play football on Saturday and Sunday mornings. It was still pretty well disorganised, but we had a manager whom we called 'Prof' (as in professor). I remember he was also into the Scout Movement; a strange sort of person but harmless enough. He was a bit like the Pied Piper: he'd call and we'd all follow.

We now had a proper kit that almost fitted us; a great big leather ball, which I think is now classed as size 5; and massive great goalposts, where, with the best will in the world, the poor little sod who had aspirations of being the next Ron Springett, Gordon Banks, Peter Shilton or Peter Bonetti, was about to have his dreams squashed after the first shot. Sadly, ball after ball flew into what looked like an empty net, if we were lucky enough to get a net. If we didn't, then after every goal (and there were many that were let in), some poor sod of a keeper had to run and retrieve it.

Unlike nowadays where the keeper does very little running about, back then the keeper did as much running to get the ball back as we did running up and down the pitch. After retrieving the said missile for the umpteenth time, this poor little sod then had to take a goal kick, and with the best will in the world, he could hardly kick it out of the 6-yard area, let alone the 18-yard box. Remember, this was a full-size pitch.

Many a tear flowed, and many kids walked off, crying because they were being substituted for letting in too many goals, their parents screaming at them. These boys, who were about 3 ft 6 in tall, and about the same again when they spread their arms out wide, were put in a full-size goal that was 8 ft high and 8 yds wide. These balls were flying in quicker than planes were flying in at nearby Heathrow, with Prof the manager, shouting encouragement from the touchline; urging us to get our little legs running up and down this enormous ploughed-up pitch (which was full of divots, holes and dog shit); pushing for us to chase up and down, and back down and then back up again (we were like the Grand Old Duke of York's men); and to tackle nonstop for ninety minutes. With the best will in the world, this was tantamount to child abuse. And all through this torture, our parents were screaming at us when we did a bad pass or missed an open goal. But we were in a league, so we had to give our all for the team, the manager and, most of all, our mates.

The headless chicken syndrome we had at school had been well and truly stuffed out of sight. We were now being taught how to play the greatest game on earth properly, or, so we thought. And after all the screaming and shouting that went on, on match day, it was a matter of 'I will (would) love it ... love it' (as Kevin Keegan once told Sir Alex Ferguson).

But no matter what the result was: win, lose or draw, we'd be back again for even more parental verbal abuse the following week. Thankfully nowadays, the big wigs at the FA have now come to their senses and changed the size of the ball, the goals, and the pitches to suit the age of the players, and that can only be to the benefit of the up-and-coming youngsters, and the future football generation.

By the time I'd reached puberty, it was a toss-up between my girlfriend and football. If she was not prepared to tag along for the match on a Saturday or Sunday, no matter what the weather, and give us total support, well, there was no true love in her heart and she'd have to go. After all, you can't let the boys or the team down can you? If you were lucky enough to have a couple of girls on the go, as many of us would have liked, it was great if you could find one that liked football and was willing to turn up each weekend, and one that didn't. That way you could use football as an excuse to meet one at the weekend, and the other one in the week (two-timing bastard). If there are any young ladies reading this, don't try to say you didn't do the same to us boys back then.

They do say you never forget your first love, and it's true for most people. It's the same with football. Most people go to their first game and that's it, they're hooked, for whatever reason: maybe the atmosphere, the excitement of the game, or the feeling of being part of it (it certainly isn't the food). But they almost certainly fall in love with one or the other of the two teams, which becomes 'the one' for them. Nine times out of ten they pick their home team rather than the team that won, even though that might mean going to see the team that loses week in and week out (which isn't very appetising), but it's kind of love at first sight.

If you were a very young kid and you went to football with your dad, you could say this is like one of those arranged marriages where you had no choice about your footballing future. Your dad takes you along to each home game to meet your future football spouse. To not follow his choice could end in family disgrace, arguments and match day upset. Luckily my dad didn't have enough time to convert me to his team.

All my family members have been brought up the Fulham way, except for one, my beautiful granddaughter Ella, who tends to wind me up by telling me she likes Chelsea. But I know she really loves 'the Whites'. However, a good friend of mine, Paul (aka Icky) has two teams on the go, one being Chelsea, who he used to go and watch now and again, and Fulham, where he has a season ticket (two-timing bastard).

Unlike today, back then you could go to a match with a mate who supported the opposition, and wear your team colours. (But it was wise if you remembered not to cheer too loudly if your team scored.) I can really only remember that things changed back in the 70s when football hooligans made it virtually impossible to go with your mates and stand or sit together. At that time Liverpool and Everton were seen to be the exception to the rule. Here you could find kids from the same families either being 'a Red' or 'a Blue'. They even sat or stood next to each other at matches, and it didn't matter who the home team was, whether it was being played at Anfield or Goodison, they would sit next to each other in their red or blue shirts without any problems. Sadly, Mrs Thatcher put a stop to that with all-seating, and segregation. So now, although you can still go along with a mate to watch your team play at your mate's ground, you can't wear your colours, *and* you have to sit on your hands.

Years ago, all local lads and lasses tended to marry the kid next door, or somebody from the same town, or at least the next village. It was very, very rare for someone to fall in love with somebody from another part of the country. People rarely knew, or had contact with, anyone from outside their zone. This might happen if you lived near, or visited, a holiday resort, but even then contact was short and sweet. There might be a holiday romance but this usually only lasted a month or two via the telephone as you had no other way to see each other. So, to give yourself to anyone far away was as I say, very, very rare.

Many years ago, people would have pen pals. These were people they met perhaps on holiday (or friends that used to live nearby but had moved and now lived miles away), so they would keep in contact by letter. Very rarely would they meet face to face unless they became long-term pals, then, sometimes love would develop between the two and perhaps it would end in a long-term relationship or even marriage. I think nowadays online dating has taken over the pen pal state of affairs.

Over the past few years this has all changed owing to social media and dating sites. Through Facebook, Skype, X (formerly Twitter) and the like, people from all over the country get together and date. Quite a lot get to meet the partner of their dreams, and it's the same with football.

Years ago, you would hardly ever have seen another team's shirt worn outside of its home town, and if you did, the person wearing it was most probably not quite all there, or had a bit of a death wish. But nowadays the local loyalty has been pushed aside. Parents are more relaxed about who their kids want to support. As I said, my dad didn't really have a choice in the matter with me because he couldn't take me to see 'the Oops' (no, not a spelling mistake, just the way they play), so it was OK for me to go to Fulham.

Now due to TV coverage by Sky, BT and internet streaming, youngsters see teams from all over the country and the world. Pre-1967, if you were lucky enough to have a TV it would have been watched in black and white. This sometimes caused problems working out which team was which, especially if the TV reception was bad. I can remember one time the brilliant TV commentator, the legend that is John Motson, who was well known for some brilliant gaffs, saying, 'For those of you watching in black and white, Spurs are in the all-yellow strip,' which meant absolutely nothing to anyone. We didn't have computers, Xboxes, iPads or laptops, and really the only live football matches were the FA Cup matches.

In the 1950s, the World Cup was shown for the first time on TV showing some of the greatest teams from all over the world. In that same decade *Miss World* was also shown on TV displaying some of the most beautiful women from all over the world. (What a coincidence; the football and women connection pops up again!) In 1955 ITV televised the European Cup, and in 1964 the BBC brought us *Match of the Day*, but that was it: one match a week. So with matches now shown every day, it's given way to the glory hunters. Lots of these people have never even seen their so-called teams in the flesh but still wallow in that team's glory. As I said at the beginning of this book, how these people can confess to liking something or somebody hundreds of miles away that they have had no emotional or physical connection with just amazes me.

Some people find it hard to meet a partner; they may be a bit shy and they don't want to go alone to find someone, so they need a helping hand. They like girls (or maybe they like boys, or someone of their own gender), but for one reason or another they need that little push. That's when they need someone to take them along on a blind date. (Where's Cilla when you need her?)

Trying to find the right partner whether it's male or female is not always that easy. Good looks, wealth, personality, a good sense of humour and kindness are all things we look for when trying to find the Mr or Mrs Right of our dreams. But some of those ingredients aren't always the right things. Sometimes the good-looking ones that have a few quid tend to have lots of admirers, so, perhaps you're not going to be the first in line as you'd want to be. Their diary is possibly too full to allow you the time you want to spend with them. Perhaps you can't afford to keep up with their financial needs to follow them to the places they like to be seen. So, unless you're pretty well-to-do yourself financially, or know the right people in the right places, and able to do the things they want or need, then as they get more popular the less interested they are in you.

Football can be the same: going to your first match on your own when you're young can be a bit daunting. It's better to go with someone who knows the ropes. If you're a football virgin in your late teens or early twenties, you like the game but are finding it difficult to find the right team, then you might have to find someone to take you along and introduce you to a team or two. As I said, it's a bit like going on a blind date. Eventually, or hopefully, you will find the right one for you. Unfortunately, we can't all meet the gorgeous, glamorous successful teams. The one that's going to sweep us off our feet. But when we do finally give up our football virginity, sometimes we have to settle for the steadier, homely sort, the more down-to-earth type, as it maybe with our partners.

As I pointed out, the more glamorous types tend to have men falling at their feet or queuing at their door. Football teams tend to be the same. The bigger, more glamorous, and richer teams tend to have the most supporters queuing at the turnstiles. So you can't always get in to see them as often as you would like. Therefore, you're sometimes better off with a steadier team in the middle or lower half of the league. But once you've made your mind up and decided on the right team for you, then you've made your bed and now you have to lie in it. There's no going back.

It's not always a bad thing supporting a lesser club. At least you don't have to worry so much about the loyalty that they will show you. Yes, they will take advantage of you; they will bleed you dry; have you in tears one day, and over the moon the next. But they tend to need you a little bit more than the more glamorous clubs do. These bigger clubs will have many more like you waiting at their turnstiles to take your place.

With our steady partners we don't expect too much of each other, especially on the spending side. The cost of keeping each other happy is small compared with the so-called posher types. So by the time you've reached the age of false teeth, meals on wheels and Zimmer frames, it's very rare if you haven't been married, or in a long-term relationship, with a partner or a football team at one time or another. Sadly, some people can't deal with relationships, so those that have been practising celibacy will get a lot of their sexual pleasure from having pictures of nude big-busted young ladies (or well-hung men) stuck up around their bedrooms; top-shelf porno books, or kinky videos. You might be a sadist or masochist and get your pleasures though other people's need to be hurt, or personally enjoying the pain, using sex aids to pleasure yourself. You might even park your car somewhere out of the way in a wood, with a strong pair of binoculars, to simply watch others doing their thing.

It seems that dogging became a trendy thing to do or watch. I do believe a certain famous ex-footballer (who shall not be named) was caught in the act, or was seen doing a bit of voyeurism. (There's nothing wrong with that!! Isn't it a bit like twitching: you're just going into the woods with a pair of binoculars to watch the birds do their thing, and seeing if you can recognise any of them.)

If in your football world you've been practising football celibacy, and you haven't got a club, you've most probably become an armchair voyeur: getting your football pleasures at home in front of your television. You're watching matches where there are plenty of sending-offs and bad tackles, or football cock-ups on DVDS, and you can most probably get your football relief reading soccer manuals, or magazines like *FourFourTwo*, *Shoot*, or *Match*, watching games that have pain and suffering, like the time Southampton beat Manchester United 6–3 back in 1997, or when Liverpool thrashed my beloved Fulham 10–0 in the League Cup in 1986–7. Or even the Stevie Gerrard slip-up against Chelsea 2014.

I can picture you now, sitting there in your front room, surrounded by pictures of Graham Poll, Mike Dean and Rob Stiles, in front of the television with a whistle (the equivalent of a sex aid) in your mouth, red and yellow cards in your pockets and with your ref's kit on, rubbing your hands together, laughing out loud, while watching these games and seeing the goals raining in. You're probably wallowing in the pain and suffering of all the loyal supporters on the terraces who are crying and sobbing their hearts out as their teams get relegated or lose important games. And you're loving every minute of it.

So, you could meet the partner in your life by:

1. Going it alone (bars, singles club, or internet).
2. Through the family (arranged marriage).
3. Through a friend (blind date).

And you could meet the team in your life by:

1. Going it alone (different grounds, TV or internet).
2. Through the family (Dad's team).
3. Through a friend (blind date).

These are some possible ways you could have met your girl, or your team, and your relationship has kicked off.

So now let's go and see how our houses and stadia have changed over the years, and how those changes are similarly parallel.

Chapter Six

Our Home Life
OUR FOOTBALL LIFE

Home is where my heart is:
MY HEART IS WHERE THE GROUND IS

This chapter basically speaks for itself. It's about how our daily lives and football lives have changed over the years. The ground, as you would expect, represents the family home where you would go to visit your newfound love, her family and friends, and regarding your football team, your newfound love, your football family and friends.

After the Second World War, when Adolf Hitler and Germany had given up trying to copy Sepp Blatter and FIFA and take over the world (as FIFA has done in all football matters), prefabricated houses were used by local councils to replace the houses and buildings that the Germans had bombed in the Blitz in most major cities. They were single storey, cheap and quick to build. Any houses that did manage to survive those terrible onslaughts, that were still standing and habitable, were perhaps two-up two-down properties. The roofs most probably leaked when it rained, and there would be old tin buckets or bowls lying around the floor to catch all the water. (Mind you, lots of properties were like that even before the bombings!)

The walls were so thin that you could hear just about everything that was going on next door. If the neighbours were having a bit of a disagreement or maybe just having a bit of the other, then you could hear everything that was going off. If they had youngsters then the sound of their gramophones (renamed as record players) would really get on your nerves especially while you were trying to watch your black and white TV, with programmes like *I love Lucy*, or *Bonanza* with Little Joe and the rest of the Cartwright family; *The Roy Rogers Show* with the singing cowboy; or *77 Sunset*

Strip with the cool Ed 'Kookie' Burns continually combing his hair back. I think most of the male population wanted to be as cool as that bloke, driving around Sunset Strip in his 1950s T-Bucket custom car. But all you could hear was Bill Haley 'rocking around the clock'; Elvis's warning to whoever: 'don't you step on my blue suede shoes'; Tommy Steele sorting out his 'little white bull' problem (which at the time I thought was a medical condition); or Lonnie Donegan scrubbing away on his washboard and wailing from next door. And if you complained, they would turn the volume up even louder just to piss you off even more.

The rooms were dimly lit and very small, and consisted of an old settee, a sideboard and a couple of armchairs, one of which was always kept for Dad, because that was his: his throne in his kingdom. I can still remember the feeling of grandeur, sitting in my dad's chair after school watching the TV. It was like I had become the boss of the house. This chair was so comfortable and massive to my little frame, but I felt all grown-up, sitting there like Lord Muck. My mum would then say, 'You'll soon move yer arse out of that chair when yer dad gets in.' And sure enough, when I heard the front door go, and his voice booming out to announce he was home, I was out of that chair faster than a Roberto Carlos free kick.

Because the size of the room was so small, the number of family or friends you could invite around on those special occasions was limited. Most of the visiting adults got an old wooden fold-away kitchen chair to sit on (if they were lucky). The kids just had to stand or sit on the carpet. There was very little heating in many of the rooms, so when you were getting dressed for work or school in the mornings, you didn't hang about as the bedrooms in the winter were freezing cold. If you were lucky, you might have small piece of ground at the back of the house which you would use as a yard or garden. Most had coal bunkers and outside toilets. Some only had a shed at the bottom of the yard with a bucket half filled with water. This was to use as a toilet.

I remember in my later years going out with a woman whose family had just that: a bucket in a shed at the bottom of the garden (I'm now talking about the 1980s, not the 1890s), and there was no light in it, so if you were caught short in the middle of the night, you were knackered. It was OK if you just needed a Jimmy Riddle (piddle) or now aka a Matt Le Tiss (piss), because you had a pot under the bed for that. If not, then you'd open the back door and Matt Le Tiss in the bushes. But if you needed a Tom Tit (I'm sure you know what that is), then you had a problem, because then you had to find a torch and hope that the batteries lasted long enough until you'd made your way to the shed, sat on this makeshift toilet, and done your deed.

Once you were through, you had yesterday's newspaper to wipe your arse (not a Labrador in sight when you needed one); no nice soft Andrex. If you were one of the lucky ones and could afford toilet paper, it was most probably called Izal. This stuff was more like greaseproof paper than the luxury tissue paper we have nowadays. It was tougher and not so tender on your butt, so it was best not to have any late-night snacks before bedtime to save going through all this trouble just for a crap.

There was no running water either to flush any bodily discharges away, so this woman's brother had the wonderful job of emptying this bucket half full of urine and crap daily. It was a great fertilizer. I once asked him if he put it on his rhubarb to which he said "No, I'd rather have custard"! (Boom, boom!) I suppose it was just as well that curries weren't as popular in those days as they are now.

The cottage her mother lived in was on the borders of Welsh Wales, just outside Leominster, in a small village called Kimbolton. So there I was one morning sitting in this shed, on this bucket, out in the middle of the garden, reading yesterday's news, when I heard this rumbling sound which started to get louder and louder. At first I thought it was my stomach rumbling, then all of a sudden there was this almighty whoooooosh! that went over my head. I even ducked, which was a bit pointless as I was already sitting down. This all happened in a spell of about five or six seconds, then all was quiet. The whole time I had my eyes closed as tight as a duck's arse.

When I did finally have the courage to open them again, I expected the shed to be gone, and me to be sitting there on this makeshift toilet with my pants and trousers around my ankles: something you might see in a sketch with Kenneth Williams or Charles Hawtrey in a *Carry On* film. Of course, being near the borders of Wales, it was one of the Red Arrows planes on exercise. I'll tell you it was just as well I was sitting where I was because I nearly shat myself (well, I would have if I hadn't already done so).

Because the poorer family homes didn't have bathrooms, they would most probably have had an old tin bath, which was normally brought in from the back yard and put in front of a small coal fire in the front room one night a week. This would normally be on a Saturday night when everybody would share the same bath water. There would be kettles, saucepans and large pots and pans boiling away to fill the bath.

Father would be first before he went to the pub, then each child in order of age, the oldest being first up. Mum would have hers when all the kids were nicely tucked up in bed. (She most probably changed the water without us knowing.) It was a bit of a bummer if you came from a large family because you could end up dirtier than when you got in, and some dirty little sod was bound to have pissed or pooped in it.

The daily morning wash was taken in the outhouse, lean-to, or the scullery (the outside kitchen). With no hot water or heating, Mum would again have to boil a kettle or saucepan. It certainly didn't take you very long to wash in the middle of winter, and if you stayed outside too long, Mum or Dad would have to come to your aid to defrost your frozen hand, which might be stuck to the tap (and we tell our kids about the good old days).

To build or buy a home fifty or so years ago would cost on average about £2,000, and everything in it was very basic. But these new prefabs did have inside toilets, heating, and hot running water.

With the average wage about £10 a week, most working-class families could only afford to furnish their homes modestly, with possibly an old cottage suite or a settee with the springs coming through (which had more lumps in it than your mother's custard); an old sideboard or a Welsh dresser; a few black and white family pictures; and some cheap mementos, like the flying ducks Hilda Ogden had on her walls in *Coronation Street*. There might also be some glass bottles with different coloured sands in them, or a cheap ornament that had been won while playing Bingo during a two-week camping or caravan holiday to the local seaside resort. If you were really lucky, this might be instead a two-week holiday at a local Butlin's or Pontins holiday camp (*Hi-De-Hi!*). In most of these houses, the carpets were so thin that after a short time they became so worn out and shiny that you could use them as a mirror to comb your hair.

The boys would all meet up after school in the street (or in the park if there was one locally) to play football. It was very rare for girls to join in: they'd be playing with their dolls or indoors helping out Mum. Mum would call us in for our dinner (tea as we used to call it back then) at about five o'clock. This would been eaten so fast you wouldn't even know what it was, then it was back out to meet your mates and join in the game, which had carried on without you while you were eating (whatever it was).

Games would last for two or three hours and could end up with some amazing scores like 20–20, or even more. It got to a point where no one could keep up with results. Games would go on well into the dark night, and that's when Mum would call you in for bedtime. As some of the younger kids were called in to bed so the team got smaller and smaller. There was no subs in those days. But all the time you were playing, there was one thing you had to remember, and that was not to piss off whoever owned the ball, because if they got the hump and took the ball home, then that was the game over. Not many of us had a decent football. It was one ball, one game. There was no such thing as multi-ball like there is today. There was very little else to do back then other than play football, cricket, or rounders (like baseball). Most other types of sport were confined to school time.

Board games were for indoors when the weather was really bad, and even then, most of us would still try and go out to play football no matter what the weather, come rain or shine (although Mum wasn't too happy when you came in with your clothes caked in mud).

There were a few TV programmes that grabbed young minds: programmes like *Alvin and the Chipmunks*; *Bill and Ben the Flower Pot Men* (and even they had a little bit of weed between them. Tut tut!); *Torchy the Battery Boy* (who was actually held up by string); *Fireball XL5*; and *Thunderbirds* with Lady Penelope. Later, there came better programmes such as *Zorro*, *Batman*, *Bewitched*, the amazing dolphin *Flipper*, and the equally amazing dog called *Lassie*, just to name a few.

We had board games such as Twister, Mouse Trap, Hoopla and many more, but these were for those cold and miserable rainy days, or when the owner of the ball wasn't playing ball. X-boxes, Game Boy and the internet were about as far away as the moon (and we never, ever thought we'd get there). So, for most of us it was football, football, football, and the odd game of cricket. Sadly, nowadays it's not as safe playing in the street as it was way back. And regrettably, in lots of roads and streets signs have been put up saying NO BALL GAMES.

Unfortunately, lots of kids now live in places that don't have the playing areas that we had. In the big cities, most of the parks and fields where we all met up and played for hours on end, have been taken up by shopping precincts, council car parks, offices or large private housing estates. Lots of kids now don't have a choice after school whether to stay in or go out, unless the school has an after-school football club. Sadly too, lots of kids now prefer to sit indoors and play football on their Xboxes, Game Stations or the internet and watch programmes on YouTube. Most of the games we had back then came in a cardboard box: Monopoly, Scrabble, Game of Life, and Cluedo. Kids can now download all these games and play them on their phones. Today's state-of-the-art technology now rules over most of our lives in one way shape or another.

Back in the dark old days of football, the sport was mainly seen as a man's game, no place for girls. Although women had been playing since the late 1800s, women's football wasn't taken much notice of, or taken very seriously. Even though women were allowed to vote at that point, sexism was still rife. The majority of women were expected to stay at home and do the household chores, have kids, and make sure the old man's dinner was on the table when he got home from work. Some wives had part-time jobs, cleaning at the local school or cleaning for some well-to-do family who lived close by.

Most men went to work, got paid on a Friday in cash at the end of their shift, and went to the pub for a few pints with their workmates afterwards. For most men Saturday was all about football. Three o'clock on a Saturday was always kick-off time. A pint or two might be taken in the local pub before or after the match, and on the Saturday evening you might take the wife back to the local for a few more bevvies, a good old sing-song, get pissed, and back home to try for more kids (at which, under the influence of alcohol, wasn't always successful).

While Mum and Dad was in the pub, the kids were outside kicking a ball around the car park or up against the pub wall. Every so often Mum or Dad would come out with a glass of lemonade and a bag of Smith's potato crisps. These crisp packets had a small blue bag inside which contained salt. You would open this and pour its contents all over the crisps, and shake the bag like Mick Jagger did with his maracas on the Rolling Stones song 'Not Fade Away'. Failure to do this meant you got only a few crisps totally coated in salt and you were left gasping for your lemonade, which didn't last very long. Why they didn't just add the salt when they were packaging the crisps, God only knows. (Sadly, Gary Lineker hadn't been born yet. Perhaps his parents stayed in the pub too long?)

If you tried to eat the crisps in the dark, you could quite easily forget about the blue bag and pop that in your mouth along with the crisps too. I vaguely remember my mum or dad would bring me out a great big biscuit called an Arrowroot, which back then cost about a penny. It was rock hard and took ages to eat, which I suppose was cheaper that buying two or three packets of crisps. I later found out that people bought these biscuits for their dogs because it was hard and good for their teeth. (I was being fed bloody dog food! And I thought my parents cared!) And my teeth still fell out, as the bloody thing loosened them because it was too hard.

If your team was playing away from home, then you could get the result on the BBC radio with James Alexander Gordon (very posh). Failing that, you would have to wait for the Saturday evening newspapers with all the classified results and write-ups from matches all over the country. There would be a queue a mile long outside newspaper shops of people waiting for the vans to deliver the bundles of *The Evening News* or the *Evening Standard*.

Once the papers arrived, they would be grabbed up and sold before the poor old newsagent had time to count them, or even put them on the shelves. Everyone was eager to get home and check their weekly pools coupon, looking to get (if I remember rightly) the eight best results, and hoping to clinch the jackpot with 24 points or as near as.

I remember doing my Saturday evening paper round, with my bag full of the latest addition, delivering to the local houses that had a weekly order, and walking around the streets shouting out loud, 'Papers, papers. Classified addition. Get your football results here.' And people would come out of their houses and buy them.

Sunday lunchtime for men was back to the pub with your mates to pick the bones out of the previous day's football results, and the world in general.

In the 60s and 70s, lots of people went very plastic and colourful (not the people themselves) with just about everything there was to buy: chairs, tables, and all different types of household goods. This suited the slightly poorer families as you could get now get rid of the old furniture for new, for a fraction of the price, and it tended to last longer than the more traditional wooden furniture. The more affluent families also enjoyed this newfound fashion, and they would buy the more expensive and most outrageous and colourful items of furniture, just so they could show off to all their friends and neighbours.

Household flooring over the years has also changed dramatically. In the 50s, lots of middle-class households had rugs covering their carpets, because the rugs were easy to clean. You just picked them up, took them outside, and beat the shit out of them with a stick or an object that looked like a tennis racket. If you lived in an upstairs flat, you'd hang them over the balcony railings and God help anyone who was walking underneath, because they would get covered in dust and all sorts of crap. Rugs and mats could also help prolong the life of their carpets, because it was cheaper to buy new rugs or mats than recarpet the room when they started to get worn out.

Later, vinyl tiles were the in thing because they were cheap and easy to lay. But in the 1980s, it was found that the vinyl had asbestos in it and it was deemed to be a health hazard. As a result, lots of people changed to different types of floor coverings: lino, cork, laminated hardwood, brick, and some even went back to stone, but most ended up with good old-fashioned carpet. It was much softer to lay or roll about on (although you could get carpet burns if you and your young lady weren't too careful). Gradually over the years, most of those old houses were knocked down and they have been replaced with much better accommodation.

Most people back in the day were unable to afford to buy their properties, but Prime Minister Maggie Thatcher decided in the 80s that people should be given the right to buy their council homes at a vastly reduced market rate, so many did, which even today has had an adverse effect on the property market. Due to the sell-off finding somewhere to live is now a massive problem for many. Lots of people who were unable to buy their council properties still pay rent on their council homes. Due to the sell-off there is currently a massive shortage of social housing, so those that are unable to get on the council's list are having to pay rents to private landlords at a massive price.

The councils started to build more high-rise flats and houses to eventually sell off, and as bigger council estates started to develop, London became Greater London, towns like Luton, Crawley, Slough, Basingstoke, Hemel Hempstead and later Milton Keynes, all

popped up as overspill towns as the council moved people out of London's poorer areas into the new towns. Flats and houses were built to a better standard, and the furniture companies built better furniture (no more of those old wooden arse-numbing chairs and settees to sit on). People bought their furniture from places like Courts, F. W. Woolworths, G Plan and Harveys.

No more going down to the second-hand shop to get your furniture, unless you were really hard up. Houses now had modern kitchens (no more sculleries) and bathrooms with posh baths and hot running water. There were no more outhouse toilets or lean-tos, no more toilet buckets to have to empty each day, the rooms were better designed, more spacious and heated. The gardens were, if you were lucky enough to have one, bigger and they had grass not concrete as before.

The air was cleaner. In fact, everything was cleaner and greener. Trees replaced lamp posts, and the world seemed a brighter place again. People also moved away from using door numbers, choosing to name their houses Maple Leaf Cottage, Acorn Villas, or even good old *Fawlty Towers* ('BASILLLLLLLLLLL!' I can hear Sybil screaming even now). Many people after a short while wanted to expand their properties and so they applied to the local council for permission. For whatever reason, many applications were denied. Only the chosen few were granted.

Unfortunately, lots of people didn't like the idea of moving from where their roots were formed. Sadly though, people *were* moved out so that their houses could be demolished, and highrise flats could be built. The councils realised that if you built upwards rather than building outwards, you could house more people in a smaller area. But, for the elderly as well as the young teenage kids, the last thing they wanted was to move home (even though the houses and flats were now clean and modern).

The trauma it brought them was unreal and they didn't want to move away from where they had been living for so long; a move for them was out of the question. It was fine for some of the kids' parents who didn't see that moving to another area would mean losing contact with your family, friends and neighbours: your whole identity, your local meeting and playing areas.

Lots of the elderly were now living five, ten or even twenty floors above the ground: prisoners in their own homes, especially when the lifts were out of order. Sadly, they now looked out of their windows down at the busy ant-like figures of those who used to be their friends and neighbours. But now they were totally cut off from everything and everybody that had been part of their lives for so many years: through the War, the Depression, and thick and thin. People fought with their councils to stay in their properties. They refused to move until the bailiffs and police physically removed them. But it suited the middle-aged parents to have a nice new home with all the mod cons.

Many people now got decent jobs as companies moved into new offices and new shops. There were lots of better opportunities for everyone, and people could now afford a car to get about. I remember we had a motor bike and a sidecar (well, it wasn't so much a sidecar, it was more like a coffin on wheels without the lid). I remember my dad dropping my sister Joan off one morning at the bus stop that was about two or three minutes' ride away. Then about 25 minutes later, she came storming back home, cursing, to redo her hair. (She had one of those bouffant hairstyles which meant that her hair sat about two-foot high on her head, making her look like a guard at Buckingham Palace. Whatever happened to motorbikes and sidecars?

For lots of young teenagers, moving was a no-no. But it didn't matter how hard they fought with their mums and dads and whoever, they were never going to win. They had no right to a say in the matter.

The small local shops were nearly all privately owned and family-run corner shops (much like Arkwright's in *Open All Hours*, with the late great Ronnie Barker and the ever green David Jason as G-G-G-Granville). I remember seeing the grocer's, butcher's, and greengrocer's boys on their bikes, delivering to the local houses. They were just like G-G-G-Granville and they were 'open all hours. The high streets were booming, and, as I said, most shops were family-owned and family-run. Dad would run the shop all day with the help of Mum, and when the kids got home after school and had had their evening meal, they would then help out as well.

From what I can vaguely remember, it all started to change around the 70s. This is when bigger companies and large conglomerates started to push the smaller stores out of business by offering people a larger range of products, cheaper goods and cut-price deals. And because of the size and financial power these companies had, it meant they were able to negotiate better deals with manufactures from abroad, therefore buying goods cheaper, and buying in bulk, which smaller independent tradesmen were unable to do.

Shop hours also changed. Lots of the bigger stores, like British Home Stores, the Co-op and Woolworths opened at 9 a.m. and closed promptly at about 5 or 6 p.m., five days a week, with half-day closing on one day in the week. But now some of these new stores started to have late night opening when on one night of the week the store would stay open until 9 or 10 p.m.

Due to families' work commitments, this was a success and eventually stores went on to open almost 15 hours a day over six days, and opening for half a day on a Sunday. This pissed off a lot of God-fearing people who went to church and argued that Sunday was, in their eyes, a day of rest. Fortunately, it didn't affect lots of other religious groups who argued their religious day wasn't a Sunday, and so local councils allowed the shops to open. It was then that the local high streets started to suffer. Lots of these big companies were so financially powerful that with the backing of local councils (and maybe a few dodgy dealings), they started to erect purpose-built complexes and malls on the edges of the new towns, with easy access for car parking and everything under one roof. Even some of the bigger and middle-of-the-road stores like Woolworths and BHS cracked under the pressure, being taken over by bigger companies, and they were eventually stripped of their assets and closed down. This trend carried on right through the nineties with old established companies like Cadbury's Jaguar, Asda taken over by foreign investors, and lots of the production lines taken abroad, which entailed lots of job losses.

Sadly, most high streets offer very little nowadays; even the pound shops have competition from the 99p shops; there are more and more charity shops; and even some of the local pubs are struggling to keep their businesses from going under due to the larger stores and supermarkets taking their customers at will, selling cheaper beer and spirits (whatever happened to Watney's Red Barrel?)

It wasn't only the shopkeeper who was affected by this transformation. All local businesses such as builders' merchants, the greasy spoon cafes, and small restaurants were affected by overseas companies trying to buy into all different types of businesses. And it still carries on to this day.

Richer families didn't have so many problems; they could afford the better things in life, and most had, and still have, big houses out in the country away from the grubby, polluted life that the city had to offer. Most new private houses that were starting to be built had all mod cons: en-suite bathrooms, showers, bidets, fitted kitchens, carpets that felt like you were walking on a cloud, and central heating throughout the house. The furniture was also top of the range and probably handmade. If you were blessed with a nice few quid and came from an important or famous family or knew somebody in high places, then adding an extension to your already oversized property was not a problem. The bigger the extension meant that you could invite more family and friends around.

The rich and famous, on the other hand, had enough clout to persuade MPs, councillors and other top officials to get whatever they desired; dodgy handshakes and brown bags would fly in all directions, with a 'you scratch my back, I'll scratch yours philosophy. A driveway was a must, as was a carport or a garage for all the family's matching top-of-the-range cars. They had all the up-to-date electrical mod cons, colour TVs, and top-of-the-range audio equipment (things which most of us could only dream of owning). Their holidays were abroad and they travelled in first-class only of course.

The cost to build or buy a house nowadays can run into the hundreds of thousands of pounds. Unfortunately, those of us with a small income are unable to move on up and into that market. Sadly, some did try and failed very badly. Many lost their homes when the financial market collapsed and the interest rate went through the roof.

Unfortunately, there are still many homes all over the country that remain in a bad state of repair, because some of those who were fortunate enough to buy their properties were unable to afford their upkeep. Some now have built bigger and better houses; some sadly have to continue to live with what they have.

OUR FOOTBALL LIFE:
Our home life

Years ago, football grounds where our football families lived were exactly the same as those old houses we lived in. The small stadia meant limited space for the supporters at the bigger games. Most of the smaller grounds only had a roof covering the main stand, so on rainy days, we not only soaked up the atmosphere, we got soaked as well. Most grounds didn't have any heating, only freezing cold changing rooms. If you were lucky, you might have a few old showers to wash in. If you were not, there would be a large communal bath that the whole team had to share after the match. (It was sometimes thought better to get sent off just so you got your bath before the rest because some dirty sod of a teammate was likely to do something in it that wasn't very pleasant.) I heard a story a long while back regarding a famous footballer who had taken an early bath and left a rather large deposit floating for when his teammates came in to take theirs. I won't say who I think it was, but I believe he was a Geordie.

Teams were forced to find a small piece of land locally to train on as very few teams had their own private training facilities, and I think I'm right in saying I'd seen the old Wimbledon team (the real Dons, or the Wombles as they were also known as) back in the late 60s and 70s training at the Richardson Evans Memorial Playing Field in Putney Vale, London. There they were training on the same pitches that I would be playing on the following weekend.

A long, long time ago, I went to (I think) Chesterfield's ground, Saltergate (my apologies to Chesterfield FC if I've got them mixed up with some other team). Here the away supporters' toilets were just four walls with a gutter to piss in and the stench from the urine was absolutely disgusting. Also, there was no roof, so you got soaking wet when it rained. I'm sure that Saltergate was not the only ground to have had those facilities back then, and I'm sure that they're not like that now.

Most grounds had one main stand with limited seating on old wooden chairs (no leg room), so unless you were very short, or a contortionist, you had to stick your legs up your arse, or if you were really lucky and no one was sitting in front of you, then you could put your legs over the chair in front. The Johnny Haynes stand at Fulham is still a bit limited with its leg room, even to this day.

Most supporters who sat in the stand (*sat* in the *stand* ... that's doesn't sound right, but they did) would sit in the same seat at each game, or stand in the same spot on the terraces. There used to be, or still are, in the lower leagues club grounds, parts of the terrace where the all-seating is not compulsory, but there are metal barriers that you could lean on, or sit your kids on, which helped when there was a full house and a bit of a crush, and again you would see mainly the older men and ladies leaning on these same barriers each match. That was their spot.

Apart from a new up-to-date team photo, a few old black and white pictures of past players hanging on the walls, and a bare trophy cabinet, which was nearly always empty apart from an odd Mickey Mouse cup (our Intertoto Cup comes to mind) in the main hallways, there wasn't too much to write home about.

The grass (what there was of it) also left a lot to be desired. I can remember back in the late 60s and early 70s when there was more grass to smoke, than being played on. Past pitches were like ploughed fields, places like the Baseball Ground (Derby County), Elm Park (Reading), and City Ground (Nottingham Forest) to name just a few. You were then better off wearing welly boots rather than football boots. If you were going to do a sliding tackle in the middle of the park, you might well have been in danger of running out of pitch and end up crashing into the advertising boards around the edges of the ground.

Lots of the games that were played in these muddy conditions looked very similar to what the contestants had to endure on *It's a Knockout* or *Jeux Sans Frontières*, with the very funny pair of Eddie 'up and under' Waring and Stuart Hall with his totally infectious laugh.

Our own ground at the Cottage wasn't always at its best. But just like our flooring at home had changed, so did the pitches in the following years.

Underground heating was first introduced in the late 50s but wasn't used by many clubs at that time due to the cost. In the early 80s, QPR was the first professional British club to install an artificial pitch of Omniturf, a sort of plastic pitch, which they kept until 1988. Luton Town and Preston North End also installed these types of pitches.

It was great for the clubs in the winter, because if it snowed, they could just sweep the pitch and go on to play, whereas other teams were calling off matches left right and centre. But there was some controversy regarding the safety of the players when going into such things as a slide tackle, which could give you a nasty burn (a bit like at home with your girlfriend on the carpet). Unlike turf, it didn't give way, so it was easy to twist an ankle or knee if you had a heavy fall.

It was also great as the pitch remained nice and flat for the players. On the previously poor grass pitches, it was difficult to judge the bounce of the ball. Now I might be wrong, but I think there was some uproar by other clubs who didn't agree with the use of the surface, stating it gave an advantage to the home team as they played on it on a regular basis, and the opposition only on the odd occasion. Eventually, it was either banned or the clubs agreed to stop using it.

Stadia nowadays are being knocked down where the clubs can afford to do so, and they are being replaced with state-of-the-art facilities costing millions of pounds. Just like the high-rise blocks of flats the council built, the new stadia are two and three tiers high in order to accommodate more supporters.

Back in the day lots of clubs rented their grounds off the local council, but as the years went by lots of clubs managed to purchase their grounds although some still pay rent: teams like West Ham and Manchester City. Chelsea has a sort of part-ownership thing going on, owning almost every inch of Stamford Bridge except the Chelsea pitch, which is owned by the Chelsea pitch owners.

Lots of the clubs' old communal baths have gone and been replaced with hot showers, ice baths and spas. The cold changing rooms and training pitches have been replaced by multi-pitch training complexes with all-purpose gyms and equipment to keep the players as fit as a butcher's dog.

The bigger and richer the team, the bigger and more upmarket the stadium is required to be, and, it seems, the more influence they have with the Government or local council to be able to get permission to expand, or at least get the decision pushed through quicker. It's amazing what the contents of a brown paper bag can do to help someone sort out their itchy back.

The poorer teams have had to put up with what they've got. Or if they do wish to move to another spot in the area, like Brighton or Barnet FC had been trying to do for what seems like a lifetime, then they have to wait for someone in local council or parliament, who has absolutely no interest in the survival of these small clubs to decide their fate. After all, who in government is interested in free VIP tickets to the smaller teams like Barnet versus Leyton Orient or Hartlepool versus Exeter (no disrespect to these clubs).

The powers that be (if at the football club, that is the club owner or the chairman) or the local council then decide the fate of our clubs. It's fine for them to decide that they are going to uproot the club and move it miles away (look at the old Wimbledon). The owners said they would consult with the supporters before making a decision. What a load of old bollocks! They had already worked out the whys and wherefores. They possibly did indeed consult with the supporters, but I'm pretty sure that they'd already made their minds up.

West Ham have moved to the Olympic Stadium against the wishes of most of the supporters. But the club played on the sympathy of the supporters by saying, 'We have to move to survive.' And the supporters, like us kids years ago when told we were moving home, have to accept it or simply not go. Everton are also moving, but only a mile or two from their old ground, so they will not be as affected as they will still be in the area that has been their home for many years.

The Goldstone ground was the home of Brighton & Hove Albion FC for over 90 years, and then the major shareholder, Bill Archer, decided to sell up his shares to a large supermarket chain, who then got permission to knock down the ground and put up another supermarket (as if we don't have enough). This was despite a protest march, which my son and I joined, along with a couple of thousands of supporters from other teams on a match day. Marching from the town centre to the ground was fine, but it all fell on deaf ears. The authorities gave the OK and Brighton & Hove Albion became homeless (nomads) for twelve years, sharing for two years with Gillingham FC, until they then moved to the Withdean stadium. They were then given permission to build a stadium in the Falmer area just outside of Brighton. I bet it didn't take twelve years for the supermarket chain to get permission to build the supermarket.

My own club, Fulham, tried to get an extension to its ground, but because of four or five families opposing the plans, and with of all the delays and all the farting and arsing about by all the bureaucrats trying to decide whether we could or couldn't, the cost just kept rising, until it was no longer viable to carry on. Can you imagine Manchester United being told all those years ago that they couldn't extend their capacity past fifty thousand? I don't think so.

I'm sometimes sure that the powers to be who have to make a judgement on these smaller club's proposals, just keep making excuses so things get delayed so this sort of outcome happens, where clubs financially can't afford to fight anymore, so it takes the decision-making out of the council or government's hands, and clubs just concede (we obviously didn't have enough big brown paper bags).

Some of the bigger more successful clubs weren't always lucky enough to be able to extend their grounds due to lack of room, so they looked to move to somewhere else in the local area, and guess what ... the council and the government seemed to fall over themselves to help Arsenal. Apparently compulsory purchase orders were made by the local council on local properties, and companies were forced to move out to allow a new 60,000 all-seated stadium. I think that also happened for Spurs and Liverpool.

Lots of new grounds are now built out of the towns, nearer the motorways which is great for a lot of local and travelling away supporters. Better parking facilities and access out the ground, after the match straight into your car or coach and straight onto the M whatever. Lots of clubs (like the new houses) have also changed the names of their new grounds. Southampton's (The Dell) is now St Mary's stadium, Leicester stadium (Filbert Street) went from the Walkers stadium to the King power stadium, Arsenals (Highbury) is now the Emirates stadium and Manchester City (main road) is now the Etihad stadium. But sadly, the local businesses that were near to the old grounds have suffered badly. Shops, takeaways, bars, restaurants, and the sacred meeting place for most supporters THE PUB.

The local pub is the inner sanctum for most supporters; it's a bit like our church, after games and especially on Sunday mornings. This is where we dissect the last game, drink our holy water, and thank God we won or didn't get to much of a pounding if we lost. We then all give a sermon on the outcome of the next match, deciding who should or shouldn't play, debate the manager's decision, and normally slag the board off. This is where we drown our sorrows when we lose, and carry on celebrating if we've won. Sadly, due to cost, the pubs are going down as quickly as Uncle Albert's ships (only fools and horses), also our brethren in the churches, are slowly getting smaller due to the cost of going to the matches.

I suppose the one good thing that comes out of all this is that the weekend shopper can go about their business in comparative safety with fewer football thugs about. And like the large stores that changed their opening and closing hours, thanks to Sky and BT lots of games now aren't played on any set day or at any set hour.

Years ago, we knew what times the shops opened and closed, we knew what time kick-off was: three o'clock on a Saturday afternoon. As soon as the fixture list was announced we knew who, where and when we were playing. We didn't have to keep checking each day or each week to see, we knew and could plan our away days. The time we needed to leave home to get to the away ground, what time the train or buses run, and the time we would, if possible, get back to our own drinking hole to meet up with our mates for a few bevvies.

But now thanks to the TV companies we don't know if we're on our Arsenals or our Everton's as they change the days and the times. You try to save money on the rail or coach fares by booking four or six weeks, ahead only to find that the Saturday three o'clock match is now a Tuesday match at eight o'clock in the evening! And if you're a supporter of a team that's playing at the other end of the country, you'll find yourself having to take two days off work, no refund on your previously booked road or rail fare of £40 or £50, which you have to pay again plus an extra £30 for the match ticket and the cost of a beer and a pie. The same goes for the supporters who have to travel the other way, especially for the supporters of some of the Northern clubs. With the job situation as it is in the North, it makes it a darn site harder for them poor sods. It's OK if you support Liverpool or Manchester United as most of their supporters seem to live down south anyway. (It doesn't come cheap being a football supporter.)

Again, we come back to it's not *what* you know, but *who* you know that gives you that extra lift. Look at all the big football finals: FA Cup, the World Cup, the Champions League where we see all the famous faces in the posh seats; family and friends of the rich and famous, people who only ever go to the prestigious games. You don't see many super stars at the Bluefin Sports Challenge Cup Final (the WHAT Cup you're asking yourself; look it up!!), but somehow they get hold of the complimentary tickets, they get to go to the after-match jaunt, all free, thank you very much, and it's only because of who they know or what their name is. (Their backs must be red raw with all the scratching that's going on.) Such is life.

Now getting back on track regarding our houses and grounds, the most important thing about keeping a good and prosperous home is good housekeeping. There is a fixed income, so keeping your spending within that budget is of the uppermost importance. But sometimes, due to overspending, just trying to keep up with their rivals or next-door neighbours (keeping up with the Jones's), you fall behind with loans or mortgage repayments, the bills mount up, reminders are followed by red letters, and this almost certainly leads to possible financial ruin. The banks refuse to extend their overdrafts, your credit ratings plummet (you've got more chance of borrowing a pound off Daniel Levy) and you end up living in financial Shit Street.

Some households do manage to clear their debts by remortgaging their property or cutting back on their expenses, such as less housekeeping money to buy all those extravagant items that they were so used to having, or by selling the car and using cheaper forms of transport (biking it), less pocket money for the kids, and if that's not enough, they then have to sell most of their prized possessions, such as their family heirlooms or jewellery. Most of the upper-class families have enough assets that the banks and financial sector are falling over themselves to help them out when they get down to their last few hundreds of thousands of pounds.

Clubs are in the same boat, overspending in the transfer market or paying overly high wages to too many mediocre players, which leads to the path of ruin. Look at the state Barcelona and Real Madrid have got themselves in, paying Messi almost €1 million a week and most of the other players €3–400,000 a week. The collapse had to come sooner or later. This then means the clubs end up over the years having to get rid of *their* prize possessions to keep their clubs afloat, selling their star players and best youngsters, those who have come through the ranks ('He's one of our own, he's one of our own', as the song goes) at clubs like West Ham, Manchester City, Leeds, Sheffield Wednesday, Coventry, Leicester, and the list goes on. Over the years they've all had to sell, sell, sell the little gems they have so carefully nurtured over many years. Some are sold so cheaply due to the club's financial situation it then becomes a buyer's market. Some clubs sadly didn't have assets to sell, and have, or, almost have, gone to the wall: teams like Aldershot, Wimbledon, Accrington Stanley and, of late, Bury, just to mention a few.

Sensible spending is most important for a good stable future, not only for your club but your family life as well. Leeds is a prime example of making sure you keep to your budget. Champions League one day, down the pan the next, trying to buy that elusive dream.

I think lots of the smaller clubs have now decided to let the bigger clubs fight it out at the top, and they are just hoping to pick the bones off what is left available. They have come to realise that chasing the dream is now like doing the lottery; you spend a certain amount and hope like fuck that it's your turn to be the lucky one. But it doesn't matter how much money you invest; you don't always get what you deserve because luck plays a big role. Covid-19 was a warning to many clubs, big and small, not to overspend or take things for granted now or in the future.

Unfortunately, there are still many grounds just like some of the houses all over the country, that are still in a bad state of repair. Some owners who were fortunate enough to buy their grounds and houses were fortunately able to afford their upkeep. When you think about our family lives, and our football family lives, do we control them? Do we get a say in the way things are or what we desire? The answer to both is NO.

The Government at this moment is run (for a better word) by the Conservatives, and the other shower (Labour). They make the rules that run our lives, they decide what we do, and when we can do it.

We have no say.

The football side of our life is run (for a better word) by FIFA (Gianni Infantino), and the other shower, UEFA (Aleksander Čeferin), who between them make the rules that run our football lives. They decide what we do, and when we can do it.

We have no say.

(AND THE BACK-SCRATCHING STILL CARRIES ON TODAY, BUT ONLY FOR THE MIGHTY FEW.)

My love lives in a quaint little cottage (Craven) that sits right next to the River Thames. Number 44 Stevenage Rd, Fulham London SW6. The number 44 is the turnstile number, which is the equivalent to the front door number of the house.

As I stated earlier, some families and teams were more popular than others, so sometimes it wasn't always best to go and watch the one you wanted to. Fulham, like some of the girls I dated all those years ago, were for one reason or another not all that popular (ugly football? ugly birds?), which is a bit of a cheek on my part, I suppose, because I wasn't exactly stepping over girls that had fallen at my feet. Anyway, it wasn't much of a problem getting to see my beloved team or the girl of the moment unlike with some teams and some of the girls who went to my school who were so popular that you couldn't get near them.

Teams of the day back in the late 50s and early s60s were Preston, Blackpool, Aston Villa, Newcastle, and Manchester United, who were just coming to the fore. Spurs, doing the double in 1960–61, put themselves on the map and then in the 70s and 80s the might of Merseyside, Liverpool, not only took English football by storm but also Europe, winning just about everything Europe had to offer.

The tragedy of Hillsborough led to the call for all-seated stadia, which we have today. Most of the tragic events (Bradford being the exception) are due to fans being crushed. Teams playing to packed grounds week in and week out and too many fans being allowed in (or trying to force themselves in) to matches led to the need for extra safety so we don't get another repeat of these disasters. It has taken Liverpool over 30 years to get back to where they were in the title race. And they're back now with a vengeance.

The 90s saw the trophies move from Merseyside to Manchester, with the United lads and the class of '92: Beckham, Giggs, the Nevilles, Scholes etc., taking over the mantle from Liverpool. United's reign was to last up until 2013 when Sir Alex Ferguson left. And so did all the trophies.

Over the last 20 years, Arsenal, Manchester City and Liverpool have all come to challenge each other for the top spot. All these clubs are now performing to packed houses.

There were also two or three girls who went to my school that performed to packed houses day in and day out, especially when their mums and dads were out (nudge, nudge, wink, wink, say no more). The trouble I had trying to get into their homes uninvited was unbelievable. The difference between getting into a popular team's ground and getting into a popular girl's house: you needed a bunk-up to get into the ground, and you needed to get into the house for a bunk-up.

Like most young lads of the day, it was fun climbing over the wall or blagging your way into the match without paying. I was lucky my uncle worked on the turnstile at Fulham, so he used to let me slide under the turnstile and in. HAPPY DAYS! It made life much easier for me than it did for my mates who tried climbing over the wall at the Putney End, most got caught and slung out, and some were unlucky enough to get their clothes caught and either ripped the arse out of their trousers or had to shout for help to get untangled from the barb wire.

One mate of mine ended up in Putney Hospital having ripped his hand open, but within a few weeks he was back there again, climbing the wall trying to save a few coppers. Back then you had the difficult choice at each home game, it was either pay to get in, or get a bag of chips and a pickled onion on the way home, in those days for a young kid that was a major decision and nine times out of ten the chips and onion won.

Now if you go along with me on this, I will now show you how your team, players, managers and backroom staff, compare with your family members, what part the ref and their assistants have to play in your parallel life and how winning a cup or trophy is like having a baby, and how your season ticket is your marriage licence.

That's the house and ground of our 2 daily lives covered, so now let's go and meet our family and our team.

Chapter Seven

The Family
THE TEAM

You can't choose your family.
You can choose your friends:
YOU CAN'T CHOOSE YOUR MANAGEMENT.
YOU CAN CHOOSE YOUR TEAM

If you look below, both sets of families have the same sort of roles in their daily football or working lives. The parallel carries on within the families as we see them:

The owner and chairperson are the father of the football club.
The manager and coach are the mother.
The players are the children.
The referee and linesman (lino) are the brothers and sisters.
The assistant managers are the aunts and uncles.
The Academy trainers are the school teachers.
The physio is the doctor.
The club sponsor is the bank manager.
The stewards are the police.
The food outlets and bars are our restaurants and pubs.
The rest of the matchday staff are our everyday work force.
And finally, our legal eagles ... PGMOL (the Professional Game Match Officials Board) is the Law Society.
The FA tribunal acts like our criminal courts.

The parents: father and mother
(Our in-laws to be)
With each new parent, we get a new girlfriend.
(A new personality)
(With each new chairman or manager,
we get a new style of play)

If you're going to be successful in life then both the parents must work together and be as one. If we start at the top of the list of our home life, the father is probably the most important one in the family for financial reasons, and that's not taking away anything that the mother does, but the father's job is to work hard and bring in the right number of finances into the home, otherwise the mother's job becomes that much more difficult (no money, no food).

The more the mother has to spend, if done properly, then better and hopefully the happier and more successful the family should be, although there are lots of rich families like the Kennedy's or the Hiltons, where endless amounts of money have just led to a lot of pain and misery. Well, they do say money is the root of all evil.

Nowadays the roles are reversed in many homes. Years ago it would have been unthinkable that a fit and healthy man would stay at home all week and look after the kids, and do the house work, while the wife would go out to work and be the main bread winner.

Years ago, even in the poorest of families, most of the male egos would push a man to go out to work. Men were seen as men after all. The other women living in the street would all gossip about the wife, and their kids would have had the piss taken out of them at school or in the street, and the neighbours would have had a few choice words to say about him behind his back: 'lazy bastard, scrounger, layabout, ponce' (and they were some of the nicer ones).

Although there were some men who were so lazy and just didn't give a damn about what the neighbours thought or said. They were content to let their wives struggle on, choosing the pub and betting shop to lose their money, rather than going to a place of work to earn it. But to most, the man was meant to be the boss, the king of the castle, and that was the way life was. Sexual equality had not quite yet been invented. Probably 99 per cent of what the man said went, 'no arguing'. He ruled the roost. (Well, at least the wife let him think that.)

The women were there to have children, cook, clean, wash, and more importantly make sure the old man's dinner was on the table when he got in from work. I don't think back then we realised how much work our mothers did. They did literally run everything in the house, and with money being so tight, wages poor, and very little financial help from anywhere (unless you borrowed from the loan man and paid exorbitant amounts of interest back each week), people really did struggle to keep their heads above water.

As well as bringing up the kids properly: making sure they got a decent meal (although any kind of meal for most would have sufficed back then) while also teaching them the rights and wrongs of the world and keeping them safe. Lots of the mothers also had part-time jobs, such as being cleaners for the rich families, or in offices. My mother did cleaning in my school, just to get extra cash to help with the household expenses. I can always remember when my sisters or I got home from school, Mum would already have left to go to her cleaning job, so the front door key would be hanging on a hook on a very long piece of string behind the letterbox. You'd slide your hand in and pull the string through in order put the key in the lock and open the door. We were all known as the latchkey kids.

It was quite strange when you think about it as nearly everyone did it, and everyone knew that everyone did it, so, why bother doing it at all. You might as well have got a load of keys cut and handed them out to everyone in the street. Or why not just leave the key in the lock? Some people also left keys under front door mats or under flower pots, others just left keys with the next-door neighbours for emergency reasons. Can you imagine leaving a key under the mat today? You'd come home to an empty house, and I mean literally empty. Everything gone, nicked, stolen.

Slowly over the years things got slightly better; the 1960s and 70s were seen as our better years; wages went up, and the unions held the Government to ransom to get better pay, working conditions and better hours. Everybody seemed to have that little extra for the nicer things in life. Work started to pick up as well, and basically life seemed a lot easier financially.

Lots of parents were still struggling, but banks were becoming more obliging and helpful, throwing money to whomever wanted it. Credit cards became easier to get as people had a lot more control over their finances. The running of the house got a lot better for most too. Unfortunately, lots of families still went silly and borrowed much more than they could afford to, so their overspending eventually caught up with them and they were unable to pay it all back.

A lot of so-called posher families thought they had very little to worry about. They had the money and the clout to buy all the things they wanted. The dads were high flyers, bringing in wads of money each week to the extent that their wives could afford to hire a maid or housekeeper to do the all their chores. No scrubbing floors for them. No part-time cleaning at the local school. They had nowhere near the financial problems that most had to suffer. They had money dripping out of their backsides. Lots of them were on different types of boards, dealing with charities and a school's PTA and such like. They were out rubbing shoulders daily with all the top councillors and people that had a lot of local influence.

Nowadays life's a bit different. Lots of fathers choose to stay at home and look after kids, and it's now accepted that women are the breadwinners in so many households and are doing a great job. Unfortunately, there are still some blinkered people today who continue to think that women should still be chained to the kitchen sink.

It's always been the parents' job to make any family more stable mentally, physically, and financially, and as I've already stated, safe and sensible spending is the key to a long-term safe environment in which the family can grow big and strong. Setting out certain criteria according to which all the family must work and adhere is important to make sure everybody works and pulls together towards reaching that all-important goal in life.

Without a strong leader at the head of the family then all hell can be let loose. How many famous families do you know that were once outstanding pillars of the community (the sort that if they fell into shit, they would still come out smelling of roses)? Everyone envied them, and they seem to have everything going for them. Then all of a sudden, for whatever reason, they lose everything. They end up having to sell their prized possessions, their jewellery, the cars, their businesses and eventually their houses. Their lives are in ruins because they took their eye off the ball. They got into a situation of thinking they were financially indestructible and didn't have to live by the financial rules.

The end result is that the father blames the mother, while the mother blames the father. The kids start to get unruly and end up not taking any notice of anything the parents say or do. The parents split up or get divorced. In some cases, one of them won't agree to a divorce straight away and it might take a while for them to agree to it.

The father sods off leaving the mother with the kids, and then the father has to struggle to pay maintenance to the mother. She is happy to take the kids but can't afford to keep them with her small income. One parent families are as common as a cold in winter. In some cases, one or both of the parents piss off and the kids end up in some council-run home. Lots of the unwanted kids will end up in places like Dr Barnardo's, or they are sent out into temporary foster homes until someone comes along to adopt them (hopefully to give them a good home where they can settle down).

Over the years more and more children have become homeless and lost in the system. We see them sleeping in doorways, begging on the street. More and more have health issues and are just unable to settle into everyday family life. Many turn to alcohol or drugs to try and help ease the pain of seeing their family lives coming to an unhappy end.

Sadly, with the problem we have had with the Covid-19 virus, it has shown how financially unstable lots of families have found themselves to be in. Lots of workers have been unable to work due to contracting the virus. Lots were laid off work. Companies have been forced to close down or furloughed their workers. Smaller companies lost thousands, and some of the larger conglomerates even millions of pounds. Many are looking for government aid to help them with their financial outgoings and to get them through these dark financially testing days.

Unfortunately, at this moment there is no end in sight with the cost of oil, gas and electricity rising through the roof. The old saying of 'take care of the pennies and the pounds will take care of themselves' is still very prevalent today.

THE MANAGEMENT
chairman and owner, manager and coach
(our in-laws to be)

As the years move on, the two leaders of our beloved club will be seen as our football family in-laws to be. And as in real life we don't always see eye-to-eye with our loved one's parents. It's the same with our beloved clubs.

Now, as supporters we don't always see them in a good light. Some that have run my club such as Tommy Trinder, who used to take the piss out of Fulham while doing his so-called comedy act, and Ernie Clay, who allegedly tried to sell the club on many occasions, were both in my eyes terrible as fathers-in-law. But we have had some great fathers-in-law like Jimmy (the chin) Hill, Mohammed Al-Fayed and now Shad Khan.

As far as mothers-in-law go, Felix Magrath, Lawrie Sanchez and Mark Hughes were lousy. On the other hand, we've had several great ones such as (and I'm not going to go back too far) Micky Adams, Kevin Keegan, Chris Coleman, Jean Tigana and Slaviša Jokanovic, who was probably the one that gave us our greatest day out at Wembley. Now we have Marco Silva. And of course, we cannot forget the wonderful Roy Hodgson who, because of his age (sorry to bring that up, Roy), is our great-fairy-grandmother. I'm sure you all have your own good and bad ones.

The running of a football club is exactly the same as running a house. The owner and manager, as the parents of the club, have to work hand in hand to keep the club in good order.

The football clubs back in the 50s and 60s was predominately male-run organisations. Things were tough for most clubs. Money was scarce. Lots of clubs were owned by local businessmen who did their best to keep the club going financially. The owner (father) was the most important person at the club for financial reasons. He had to try and supply as much money as he could to help the manager (mother) with the running of the club and help keep the club afloat. Money was hard to come by. Although there were a lot of owners who were quite happy to run their clubs on a shoe string and let the manager struggle along without any input. There were very few investors in those days so the manager not only looked after the team but they also had all the other chores to do as well, such as cutting the grass and painting the lines on the pitch, cleaning the changing rooms and the toilets.

Women had very little to do with football. Over the years though this has changed; woman now have a much bigger say in football and are now leaders in all different areas of the game. Years ago, women as I've said, had only a small, if any, voice in the world of professional football. Mostly they would have an office position: secretary or PA to the chairman, working in the ticket office, cleaner or possibly a tea lady. Could you imagine back then what football would have been like if a club had put a woman in as manager. I'm sure there would have been uproar, and I'm sure the FA would have tried to find some rule somewhere in their ancient book of rules to ban it. It was still widely believed that a woman's place was in the home.

I don't know how long it will be before we see a female manager or coach in the men's professional league. Now that really would upset the footballing suits and old farts at the FA. Although apparently Crawley Town did try to persuade the Chelsea Ladies manager, Emma Hayes, to become their new manager or coach. And, with the equal rights of today surely the FA would have had to have sanction it.

Things started to get better financially over the years with the introduction of televised games. Sponsorship and shirt advertising brought in lots more pennies. Banks were willing to lend more money on the promise of things to come. Lots of companies were fighting to link their brand names with the top clubs, throwing bundles of cash the club's way. Companies like Carlsberg, JVC, Sharp, Peugeot, NEC, and Holsten were just a few. Financially, clubs could now loosen their spending belts to attract better players and add better infrastructure.

Some of the smaller clubs could now complete with some of the bigger clubs, but only through sensible spending. Unfortunately, though, lots of top clubs had it all: plenty of income through all kinds of deals. They didn't have a thing to worry about!! Or so they thought.

The purchase of bad players led to bad football on the pitch, which led to bad results, which led to relegation, which led to sponsors not renewing their deals, which led to loss of income. Players on big wages and long contracts led clubs into massive financial problems that led to the loss of almost everything. This was all due to a club's bad housekeeping and spending far more than their income should have allowed.

The list of big supported football clubs that have fallen into that same trap is almost as long as the Beckham's wedding guest list: Sheffield Wednesday, Leeds United, Portsmouth, Nottingham Forest, Sunderland, Derby, and Sheffield United. Although Sheffield United did reach the Premier League after many, many years of struggling, even though it was only for a short time. And what a great job their manager (mother) Chris Wilder did! Alas, on relegation, Chris Wilder and the Sheffield United board decided to part company. And now after 23 years and a lot of soul-searching, Nottingham Forest are finally back in the big time. But for how long depends, like for most teams, on their financial prowess.

I suppose Derby is one of the biggest and most famous clubs of recent times to go into financial meltdown due to the leader of the day losing control of the purse strings for one reason or another. Whether it's through their own misjudgement or their manager pushing too hard for more housekeeping, only they will know the truth.

In most cases the chairman blames the manager, and the manager blames the chairman, but who suffers the most is us, the supporters, because after the collapse the chairman and manager have parted company. In some cases the split might not be as amicable as it could be, and the manager is often put on garden leave until a solution can be found. Sometimes some of the players are sent out on loan to (fostered by) another club, who unfortunately are unable to meet the full wages, so the parent club has to pay part of the cost (child maintenance). If lucky, they may be transferred (adopted) for a smaller fee.

Dele Alli and Donny van de Beek are prime examples of not fitting in with their parental clubs for one reason or another and being sent out on loan (sent to foster homes). Sadly, Dele Alli doesn't seem to be fitting in very well where he is now either.

Many players in the big clubs are sent out on loan. Chelsea at one stage were like Dr Barnardo's; they had somewhere in the region of thirty plus players on their books who were surplus to requirements, or were learning their trade, and who have been sent out all over the world on loan.

Other players like Sheyi Ojo, Ben Woodman of Liverpool, and Fulham's own Jean Michaël Seri and André-Frank Zambo Anguissa (the cost to have his name printed on the back of your shirt would be about £50, and you would need a body like Tyson Fury) have all been out on loan many times with the chance of trying to settle down at different clubs. Unfortunately, not all of them are able to settle down in a permanent place they can call home. You could say they are all just looking for someone to adopt them, and show them love.

There are lots of clubs that appear to be run mostly by the managers only (one-parent family): Pep Guardiola, Jürgen Klopp, Brendan Rogers. It seems that these managers have the most control over the running of their clubs. They are all left to it, and most of them have the final say.

When you think back, Leeds were in the Champions League and the UEFA Cup and that was only back in the late 90s. But under the guidance of chairman Peter Ridsdale and manager David O'Leary, they took out large loans on what they thought was to come (but didn't) i.e., more Champions League revenue. The club found itself unable to pay back the repayments, leading them to financial disaster, relegation and years of struggling to get back onto a sound footing. I don't think that now they've finally reached a position to get back to the promised land of the Premier League again, they will make that same mistake again … Or will they? Or it might turn out to be that some people just never learn.

The parents of teams like Manchester United, Manchester City, Liverpool, and Chelsea, to mention a few, should also beware. It's OK spending someone else's money, providing they don't want it all back in one go. Or you stop paying the weekly and monthly instalments to the creditors. I'm not saying it will happen with these or many other clubs, but at the moment there are many clubs who are sailing close to the wind. And as I've already pointed out, who would have ever thought it would have happened to the once mighty Leeds.

And don't forget rumour has it that Chelsea was on the verge of joining the dodo just before the Roman Empire took over. Also, I think I am right in saying the Romans ending up going on to rule most of the world. They also built a wonderful and regularly packed arena in Rome once, and look at the state that's in now. Also, a lot of Chelsea managers should have been aware of the Ides of March, April, or May, because if a trophy or two isn't within their grasp by then, I think the knives might well be out again (*Et tu, Brutus*).

And now that Mr Abramov-ery-rich has departed, with the possible loss of his money, we might well see Chelsea go down a division or two, then we might hear the almighty roar of the Lions of Millwall, who may well return to haunt another once almighty Roman Empire, in their almighty arena?

Teams like Burnley, Sheffield United and Bournemouth have all come a long way over the last few seasons. Well done to Sean Dyce, Chris Wilder and Eddie Howe and all the rest of those at those clubs that have done very little spending but got promoted the right way. OK, it will always be difficult for them each season as they've already found out, but heigh-ho, enjoy it while it lasts. Some of them have tested the water with a small amount of overspending, nearly drowned, and now realise what they are, where they have come from, and the depth of water they are swimming in. So, unless a sugar daddy comes along, they will always have to live within their means.

Although Eddie Howe has now joined Newcastle and with the backing of the Saudis, if he needs to strengthen his team, he can just say 'Oil well, I'll buy another player.' (Get it? Oil well ... Saudis ...)

Now, once the financial rules have been put in place by the chair (father), he hands over the reins to the manager and coach (mother) to run the family home, and it's their job to bring the kids up and help them develop into fine outstanding well-educated young men (and women for the ladies' teams) in the social and football community. The right food, a good solid education and a limited liquid intake of the alcoholic type is all important. Plenty of sleep too. Just basically a good clean lifestyle.

Why is it that these things seem to be important to mostly only the foreign managers and players, and not a lot of the British ones? Although things have changed a lot over the last few years with the British players taking better care of their bodies, it seems that whenever there's trouble or there's a punch-up in a nightclub, it nearly always involves a British player.

While most of the French, the German or the Italian players that have won World Cup, Euros or Champions League medals are at home resting with frogs' legs (that's not an injury), Schnitzel (bless you!), or a nice glass of vino before a big game, some of the Brits are out hitting the town in a nightclub, or hitting some poor sod who dares to question why one of the players of the team he loves (and helps to finance by paying to watch week in and week out) should be out at four in the morning pissing it up, with a couple of players whom he's supposed to be playing against in eleven hours' time (or six hours if Sky had their way). The fan then gets a slap from the player for his cheek.

Sometimes the Brits don't always wait until they get to a nightclub for a good old punch-up. Back in 2005 while both were playing for Newcastle United against Aston Villa, a certain Mr Lee Bowyer (the ex-Birmingham City manager) and a Mr Kieron Dyer decided to have a punch-up on the pitch, which resulted in them both being sent off, leaving the Geordies with only eight players as defender Steven Taylor had seen a red card earlier for a blatant goal line hand ball.

It seems to be that if a woman gets attacked in some hotel room, it's normally eight times out of ten a British player whose names in the hat for doing it. And we can't understand why we don't do very well in World Cups and the Euros. ('Duh!' as Homer would say.)

I'm not saying that all Brits are bad and all foreigners are angels, but we do tend to give ourselves a bad press at times.

It's not always bad parents either who tend to bring up bad kids; sometimes even good parents' kids can turn bad and go off the rails. But good caring parents soon get them back on track. We've all got those little shits in our towns, some as young as fourteen or fifteen, just roaming the streets in the early hours of the morning. Where are their parents?

These little sods don't care about other people, or other people's property. You see them rat-arsed almost every night in town centres making everyone's life a misery, and it doesn't matter what you do to them, or how much you fine them, they couldn't give a toss.

Some players, too, over the years have been caught up in trouble of one kind or another, but mostly they have done more damage to themselves than to anybody else. Some great players over the years have blighted their reputations. Sadly, and in many cases, it's helped to shorten their playing careers. I could be wrong, but we seem to have had fewer bad boys back in time, probably because they were just seen as players and not held up as so-called superstars (which is who they are perceived today). Did this also mean their egos were not so big?

Those that did have the reputation of being a bad boy did themselves more damage than anyone else. I'm not going to mention the managers who I think should have perhaps done a bit more in the way of disciplining their players on and off the field, nor am I going to name all the players at this moment (but I will in a while) who did themselves no favours by the lifestyle they kept. I think we can all name our own players who we wished had acted in a more professional manner.

I will though mention those who have been outstanding in their different footballing fields. George Cohen is one such (and one of my favourite players), a Fulham legend and one of the 1966 World Cup winning team. Gordon Banks is also a 1966 World Cup winner. In addition, Kevin Keegan, Gary Lineker, and latterly, Stevie G, the Neville Brothers, James Milner, and Mark Nobel, have all served, their clubs professionally over the years (and some are still serving).

There are many other players also in the lower leagues who don't get the accolades they deserve because they're not big names in football. There are too many to go through, but all these players are a credit to the sport.

The managers who I think deserve a pat on the back are Sir Alex Ferguson, Arsène, Wenger, Jock Stein, Harry Redknapp, Bob Paisley, Sir Bobby Robson, and Ron Greenwood. Again there are far too many others to mention. These great managers of the past have all been the mothers to some of our greatest players, some of whom have been awkward to manage, some easy to manage, but these managers have got the best out of their kids.

Nowadays, it's different apparently. Managers have to be careful what they say or how they treat their players or they'll run crying to their agent for a transfer. It's also been said that some players have phoned the owners direct and had a moan (player power).

I don't know if you've noticed over the years of supporting your club, that each time you get a new chairman or manager, it's like getting a new girlfriend. The new parents will bring in a new way of thinking and playing, which brings a whole new personality to the love of your life.

When we (Fulham) lost Kevin Keegan to England, we lost the fast attacking up-and-at-them carefree attitude, the good-time girl, the out-for-fun type. When he was replaced by Jean Tigana, we got this beautiful sleek flowing sexy erotic-style football. With his replacement Chris Coleman, we got a more of a shelf-filler type (Pot noodles no doubt). No disrespect to Chris, but it was no airs or graces, do the job the best you can, and go home. Chris went on to be the Wales manager and had great success, and I thank him for the great times he gave us, not only as a great player, but his time as our manager.

He was then replaced with Lawrie Sanchez coming in as caretaker manager in 2007. With his Irish connections (still manager of Northern Ireland at that time) and with his Irish purchases, it seems our back four were now all Irish jigging together in a straight line, instead of doing the twist as they seemed to have been doing under Chris. (It was now *Riverdance* at the river side).

After a disastrous spell, Fulham soon parted company with Sanchez. Sanchez had left us in total limbo (see what I did there? The Twist? *Riverdance*? The limbo? Not impressed? Please yourself). Then in came the wonderful Roy Hodgson, who took over at a time when we were not only dancing the limbo under that relegation line, in the bottom three, but under Roy, we started to slowly waltz through the games, until we ended up doing the Fosbury flop over the relegation line, and just about managing to stay up.

By now Mr Fayed had had more partners than Peter Stringfellow. Roy steadied the club and took us to new heights and proved to be as steady and solid as any manager we've ever had. All different types of managing (mothering) brought us different results, Roy Hodgson's experience bringing the best out of the team. Roy turned out to be one of the best mothers-in-law we've had.

The parents in our private and football family lives have at times made decisions that all loving family members and supporters are affected by. Those decisions, whether right or wrong, have moulded our lives forever. Sadly, the problem that we had with the Covid-19 virus has shown how financially unstable lots of football clubs were.

OK, so you've met the heads of the family. Now let's see how the rest of our relatives will affect our day-to-day lives, and our football lives.

The children:
THE PLAYERS

Youngsters back in the 50s and even the early 60s didn't move around the country as much as they do now. Life was difficult. Some kids stayed on at school to get better qualifications with the hope of getting a better chance of securing a better job. Some stayed on at school just because they didn't know what they wanted to do for a living. Some stayed on so they didn't have to find a job; they had no ambitions, they weren't concerned about the future, or what it might bring. Lots were clever but were basically just too lazy. School taught them nothing. Lots of them didn't even bother to turn up for lessons. Most of them left school with very little education and took whatever job they could find. This could be working in factories, down mines and even joining the forces. Lots were only interested in earning a wage to survive, others so they could go out on the piss at night.

Once you left school and managed to find work somewhere locally, there you stayed long-term if you were lucky. And after 50 years (yes, you youngsters out there, 50 years) you'd normally receive an engraved gold watch or a crystal-cut glass decanter, a golden handshake and a company pension on retirement. I don't think that people can do 50 years' service now that they have changed the school leaving age. Although if the Government keeps raising the age of retirement, you'll have to work until you're seventy-five before you can pack it all in. Even then, they would most probably have invented some way, some type of machine, which they will plug into your cadaver to bring you back to life for however long is required so that you can keep working even longer, and with no wages to pay out.

From 1966 on, things started to change with easier access to travelling abroad, thanks to Freddie Laker and his cheap budget airlines. But even then, the world was still a giant ball into which only a few had ventured.

The old saying is 'you can pick your friends, but you can't pick your family.' Well I suppose that's true in our everyday lives, but it's only slightly different in football life. We are born into this world whether we like it or not. We don't get to choose to whom, where or when; that's left to our parents and the rhythm method to decide.

Once we get to a certain age, as I've already said, we are now in the hands of our parents to show us wrong from right, respect and everything else that goes along with growing up. Some kids have great family lives and prosper; some think that they know better and can't wait to reach the legal age when they can spread their wings and leave the nest ASAP. And some do go on to better things whereas unfortunately others make the biggest mistakes of their young lives. Oh, they won't admit it, but the old sayings 'it's better the devil you know' or 'the grass isn't always greener on the other side of the fence' (at one stage it was Astro turf) spring to mind.

I've had many good friends, who secured good jobs, decent wages, and a happy environment after leaving uni or college, but the most important thing was they had a secure future. Then in no time, their heads were turned by a larger company who would offer this and that: the world on a plate. But for most of them, like the grass being greener, the plate turned out to be made of paper, and soon they lost their jobs and their income, along with the security they had had. Was it chasing a dream, or was it maybe just greed? They each tried to get to the top long before their time. They should have stayed where they were, learned their trade for a little longer and slowly worked their way up the ladder, one rung at a time before even thinking about moving on. Now they have had to get their heads down and start all over again (wasted years). It can work for some, but for many it doesn't.

We pick our friends and sometimes we can be led astray by them, doing things that are not normally in our personality. We soon realised that we're on the wrong path and move away from them, and then find the right people to fit in with our thoughts and plans.

It's so difficult knowing who to trust when you're young. You've not long left school, college or university and you're doing well at a job, when along comes someone and throws a complete spanner in the works by offering you a job somewhere else, which is great, BUT, who do you go to for advice? Family members are fine if they're in the same type of business as you are, but they are not really much help if they're not.

A friend might be useful if they know your industry or perhaps someone who works for the company which is offering you a position. Most will say it's too good an opportunity to turn down (follow the money). But is it too good to turn down? Your whole future depends on your decision. It's one of the biggest decisions you'll have to make.

Many people have gone on to greater things, but sadly others have had their lives totally ruined by false promises. Lots of those that leave school or college still need guidance along the way, an arm around their shoulder when making the big decisions, or a shoulder to cry on when things are not looking too good.

There have also been a lot of kids over the years who have had talent academically but unfortunately due to laziness never got anywhere. They never pushed themselves to get any further in their line of work. They were just happy to sit back and take it easy, happy with what they were getting paid. They did just enough to keep their bosses happy. They stayed where they were until it was time to retire never caring about what might have been.

Years ago, certain jobs, such as being a dustman, and many factory vacancies were handed down to relatives of the workers already employed, a helping hand you might say. As the saying goes: 'It's not *what* you know, it's *who* you know.' With the invention of the internet and more media sites up and running, it's now easier for people no matter what age they are to show more of their talents by placing their CVs online for the world to see, to hopefully become more successful. And with airlines, trains and buses travelling the globe, those who can't find the right job in their own country can now find work overseas without any problem. The world has shrunk as far as work opportunities go.

Learn your trade before moving on.

THE PLAYERS:
The children

Like the kids back in the 50s and 60s, movement of footballers was minimal. Squads were a lot smaller, just like the classrooms were. Most players stayed where they were until they had got enough playing time and experience to be able to entice any top team to even consider trying to poach them from their existing clubs. Lots of players in the early years also had daytime jobs. Football was a secondary job for many of them.

Unlike today, the players in the 60s through to the end of the 70s were only paid between £25 and £125 per week and they played near to where they were born. Players like Sir Thomas Finney CBE played 14 years for his home town of Preston; Billy Wright was born just outside Wolverhampton and played 20 years at Wolves; Jimmy Armfield, born in Greater Manchester played 17 years for Blackpool; Stevie G and Jamie Carragher were both born and grew up in the Mersey area and spent all their playing careers at Liverpool; and latterly the wonderful Mark Noble, born in Canning Town, who, apart from a couple of short-term loans, has played for West Ham since 2004 and only this year (2022) decided this will be his last season after 17 years.

Although not all players played for the team that they supported, some played for a local team close to that area. Fulham's own Sean Davis (the love of my daughter's life, even now after all these years) was born just a few miles from Fulham and spent 8 years at the club, coming through the youth team and rising to the first team. He played for England at Under-21 level even though he was a Spurs supporter (and we forgive him for that … well, just about).

The Fulham legend that is Johnny Haynes was born in Kensal Rise, North London, but signed for Fulham at the age of fifteen and spent 18 years man and boy with the club, and I can say I was proud to stand on the terraces and watch the maestro at work. Then there's Matt Le Tissier who was born in Guernsey but played his entire 16-year career across the English Channel at Southampton. Some players like Alan Shearer OBE and Paul Gascoigne finally found there's no place like home after leaving their own parental city.

Lots of players nowadays have done just like my old friends from school. Instead of staying put with their clubs in the lower leagues and learning their trade thoroughly before moving on, they've suddenly got noticed by a lot of scouts from all sorts of the so-called bigger clubs and made location-changing decisions. These scouts are just like vultures. They come circling around these youngsters, and I mean *youngsters*. If a kid drops his dummy out of his mouth and catches it, you can be sure there's a scout waiting to sign him up as a potential goalkeeper; it's got that bad.

Clubs are now signing kids straight out of the playpen. If any kids show any kind of promise, then the scouts or agents are there, letting it be known to the kids and their parents that they are interested. This then straight away unsettles the kids. It's also been known for certain clubs to bypass the club that the kids are already playing for, by knocking on the family door offering a five-year deal, doubling or sometimes tripling what they're earning, and then going straight in to offer the families of their potential superstars incentives, such as cash, or houses, and paying to relocate them to the new area. Plus, they offer the chance for these kids to play Champions League football playing in front of 50–70,000 fans. Then these young kids and their parents with a star in one eye and pound notes in their other eye just get blown away with the limelight, and they are taken in by it all: all the bullshit the clubs are offering, and especially by what their agents are telling them and selling them (who, by the way, stand to earn a fortune if the kid signs for the club). After selling the dream to the kid and their parents, they then go to the existing club and offer a pittance of what that kid is really worth, and the existing club has very little chance of persuading the kid to stay. The vultures have done their job picking the best meat off the other team's carcass.

Sadly, there have been lots players, for example, John Bostock, who was at Crystal Palace as a young kid of 15 when Spurs came calling. Instead of staying with a good solid club like Palace, who are renowned for bringing on the youth, he (I would like to believe he was badly advised) upped and left for the bright lights of White Hart Lane, and although he was at Spurs for 5 years, he only played a few senior games for them. Now I don't know whether he never made the grade or that they didn't give him the time he needed to bring on the obvious talent he was showing when they brought him. Even now he is still only at the tender age of twenty-six, but he went on to play in America, Belgium and then in France with Toulouse. I believe he's now playing for Doncaster Rovers. Let's hope this time it works out for him there.

Another promising young player was Jack Rodwell, who, at the tender age of sixteen, made the first team for the Toffees (Everton) where he stayed for 5 years. But he only played just over 80 games, which may seem a fair number until you understand that teams play 38 league games plus cup matches, so it isn't very many for a team that used to run with such a small squad. Then along comes Mansour City, offering a great big juicy carrot, and young Jack took a great big bite, far more than he could chew, and off he went to the land of hope and sadly not so much glory. He lasted, or should I say he wasted, 2 years playing (or not) before he moved to Sunderland where he played about 67 games in about 4 years. He then went on to play in the Premiership with Sheffield United but was released last year on the first of June 2021. The last I heard of him he was playing in Australia with Western Sydney Wanderers FC.

Scott Sinclair is another prime case to me of stupidity of the greatest order. He was just under sixteen when he played his first game for Bristol Rovers and after amassing an incredible number of games for The Pirates (just two in total), was signed by Chelsea and then went from sitting out on the wing, to sitting out on the bench (that was if he was lucky enough to even make the squad. In four years, he played just five games out of a possible 200, and I think you'll find most of them were cup games. Still, unperturbed, he went out on loan to six other clubs before finally moving to Swansea City where he had a great two years playing 82 games, and scoring over 20 goals.

Now you would think after all that went on at his time with Chelsea, that when Manchester City came for him, it might have been 'once bitten twice shy', but oh no, off went silly old Scottie to City where between 2012 and 2014 he played less than a dozen games. He then went on loan to The Baggies (West Brom), then on loan to Aston Villa and then four years later, in 2016, he signed a four-year deal with Celtic in Scotland. In the four years before signing for Celtic, he played about 57 senior games, and some of those were as a sub. He stayed at Celtic for four years, playing just over 100 games and scoring 40 plus goals. He is now plying his trade, as far as I can see, at Preston North End.

Another one to fall foul of the big clubs was Patrick Roberts who played for Fulham for about four or five seasons. Then at the ripe old age of seventeen or eighteen, and having played about twenty times for Fulham's senior team, he went off to join Manchester City.

As I write this on the first day of July 2022 he has, I believe, just signed a new two-year deal with Sunderland, after actually having been released by them at the end of last season due to his contract coming to an end, having been on a short-term loan. He is now playing for Bristol Rovers in League One. Having spent about eight years with City he had amassed, from what I can find, one senior game, having been sent out on loan to about seven or eight different clubs. All these players no doubt have earned a good few quid but unfortunately very few footballing memories or trophies considering their potential.

There are many, many more players who have done the same, who were too young to listen, and too immature to understand. In all fairness, all the said players have earned a great amount of money, but I think a lot of them might well have done things differently if they could turn the clock back. Sadly, some of the players I've mentioned have had their careers dogged by injuries that have also held them back to this day.

Like most clubs, Fulham have had and still have lots of good youngsters coming through their Academy. I just hope that some of these lads and lassies stay and don't get the money bug before they fully learn their trade.

Lots of players that did make the mistake and moved too early in their careers for whatever reason ended up going out on loan rather than sitting on the bench at their parent club. Lots of the clubs that take these players on loan are like the foster parents for these poor lost souls of football. They are like the ones that parents can no longer handle or afford. Quite often, the clubs they go to on loan can't afford to pay their full wages, so the parent club ends up paying a percentage of their wages (a form of child maintenance if you like?).

There are lots of players who even though they had talent, were late in their development and so struggled to get a chance in the game. Take the Arsenal legend Ian Wright who didn't get a look-in until the age of almost twenty-three before being spotted by Crystal Palace. It was then that he was given the opportunity to play and show what he was good at, and well … the rest is history. Players like Kevin Phillips, D J Campbell, Jamie Vardy and an all-time great, Mr Drogba, were all late in their years before going professional.

There are lots of players with ability, but who have fallen by the wayside. This might be because maybe they needed an arm around their shoulder, or because they were just yet another player alongside more important names were coming through (or should I say, that were being *pushed* through because of who they are). Again, as the saying goes 'it's not what you know, it's who you know' that helps you get on in life.

Everyday life is the same. Look how many so-called stars' kids or relatives have got that leg-up in life because of who they are, or who they are related to: Stella McCartney, Michael Douglas, the Fox family (Laurence, Emilia, and a lot more). No doubt the Beckham kids will go on to be stars in some shape or another, and good luck to them all. Football is the same: the Allen family with Les, Martin, Clive, and Bradley; Ian Wright's son Bradley and his adopted son Shaun; Kenny Dalglish and his son Paul; the Cruyffs, Johan and Jordi; and lately, Gus Poyet's son Diego, who was at West Ham. Now I'm not saying that any of the aforementioned don't deserve to be where they are, or that they are not talented in their own right, but I'm sure that if it wasn't for a little help from people they know, or who they are related to, it might have been a little harder attaining their success so quickly. Whereas Tom, Dick, and Harry's son (perhaps not Harry's son Jamie) might have to work a lot harder to get noticed. (OH well, that's life. OH well, that's football.)

Players like the long-serving ones I've mentioned used to get a testimonial after playing 10 years for the same club. The gates receipt was kept by the player as wages weren't all that good back in that period between 1950 and 1970s. Nowadays, top players earn so much money that they (and good for them) give the money to a worthy charity of their choice.

Loyalty between company employers and employees, just like in football between clubs and players, has gone down the proverbial tube. People stay in jobs whether they like it there or not, and players stay with clubs in the same manner. Most people used to take pride in their work, and players played for the badge, but over the last 20 or 30 years, society has changed, workers' and players' mentality has changed. Now for most it's all about how much they are being paid.

Lots of people stay in their jobs because they wouldn't get the same money if they went somewhere else. Lots of players stay at clubs for the same reason, and they wind down their contracts and go on a free holiday at the end of it. Take Winston Bogarde (I can hear the Chelsea supporters shouting out, 'Please please') for instance. Here was a player who had signed on a massive four-year deal by Chelsea, and he only played about ten or eleven times. When it appeared he was not going to make the breakthrough at Chelsea, they tried to sell him, but they were unable to owing to the large salary he was on. Now that's not the player's fault, it's the club's fault. The player isn't going to turn down a massive contract. So when they wanted to sell him, knowing he wasn't going to get the same money anywhere else, he decided to sit out his contract and collect his salary each month. He hardly played a handful of games in the four years he was there. They tried to get him out by making him train with the youngsters, but he just sat it out until the end. He later retired at the age of thirty-five in 2005, earning a reported £15 million in the short time he was with the club. It's rumoured, and I say rumoured, that he used to fly in from Holland each day, go to training, then afterwards fly back home to Holland. But as I say, it's a rumour.

With scouts now travelling the globe, plus the social media network, those who can't find the right club in their own country can now find clubs overseas without any problem. The world has shrunk as far as footballing opportunities go.

Learn your trade before moving on.

Brothers and sisters:
REFEREES AND ASSISTANTS

Next in line in the family is the one all kids love to hate: their brothers or their sisters. Now it doesn't matter whether it's the older ones or it's the younger ones, but they will for some unknown reason despise each other. While everybody is having fun, they will find a way to bring everything to a halt, sometimes, it seems, just for the fun of it. Everyone is playing nicely then for no reason they have to get involved.

Now, most of us boys as teenagers would invite a girl home (as I have no doubt girls did the same), with the excuse that we wanted them to help us out with something, with

Whatever feasible reason we could invent and one that they would believe (homework was a good one). And, funnily enough it was always a coincidence that your mum and dad happened to be out.

So, after totally pushing aside all thoughts of any homework, there you would be sitting on your sofa, all soppy like, then very gingerly you'd put your left arm around the back of her neck. Slowly you'd lower it down on to her shoulder, giving a minute or two between each manoeuvre while waiting to see if there was any negative reaction from her. She'd look at you and giggle, you'd blush. Then you'd pull her head towards you, lean forward and bingo, you'd give her a gentle kiss. Slowly you'd start to move in closer.

Your right hand is now nestling on her knee. Still there's no reaction. You try your luck by sliding your right hand up her skirt, not going too far in case she realises what's happening. Your tongues are going like knitting needles in her mouth. Your left arm slowly comes down over her left shoulder and you let your hand settle on her left breast. You move it gently so you can just feel the shape of it.

Everything is now in position and you're just about to strike for goal when all of a sudden, the door bursts open and in walks your older brother or sister. 'What you doing?' they ask. Well that's it; that's killed that attack. Or maybe you're just about to strike when your little brother or sister comes in, and they just stand there watching you. You scream at them to get out. They run out and call for your older brother or sister to 'come and see what so-and-so's doing.' They tell on you, just to stop your fun. So you have to settle for a bit of foreplay but don't get to actually get the chance to score.

Now, when you want your siblings to be there, they're nowhere to be seen. For example, you get bamboozled by a girl who fancies you like mad, but you're not too sure how you feel about her, but finally she persuades you to take her back to your house (to help her with her homework?). But as soon as you get through the door, she's all-out attack. She's all over you within minutes. You now realise she's not the one for you. All you want to do is get her out of your house and keep your defence intact. But it's like trying to fight off an octopus. Her hands are all over the place, and so is your defence. You keep pushing her back, but to no avail, she keeps coming back for more, and no matter what you do, you're struggling to defend yourself. Where are your brothers and sisters now when you need them to help slow her down and take the pressure off you? They are nowhere in sight. And in the end, you collapse under the pressure and concede. You give in. She scores. And she wins.

You keep thinking that if you didn't have brothers or sisters to tell on you, you could get away with almost anything. Still, love them or hate them, there are times when they're needed. If there's any unrest in the household it's normally the mother or father having a moan at the eldest one for one reason or another.

It seems being the oldest you think you know more about life than your parents, and you feel you're also old enough to make your own decisions because you know best. But unfortunately, Mum and Dad think *they* know best, and you all end up at logger-heads. And in the end if it gets too bad, they all end up blaming each other for whatever's happened. Eventually they all end up storming out of the room in a huff. As far as you're concerned, you were right, and they were wrong. Unfortunately, they feel the same way. But whatever the final outcome of the row is, neither will concede that they were wrong

REFEREES and ASSISTANTS:
Brothers and sisters

Now it doesn't matter what team you support you will have to agree that the most hated man on the pitch is the referee, and after him are the linos, unless you include Robbie Savage. How I hated that man whenever he played against Fulham. But since his career has come to an end and he no longer plays against us, I have come to appreciate what he did do for his team, and how I wish he had played *for* us, and not *against* us.

A total pain in the arse, he was like a wasp that keeps flying around your head when you're having a nice barbeque in the garden, one that no matter what you do, you can't swat. Or he was like that itch that no matter how much you scratch it, it won't go away. He had amazing energy; he'd run all day and night for his club, country, and teammates, giving a hundred per cent in every game. To you Mr S, I salute you, and apologise for everything I called you (although at the time I meant it).

Now it doesn't matter which team you support you have got to agree that referees and their assistants do exactly the same as your brothers and sisters did (get involved when you're having fun). There you are, your team, the love of your life, playing all nicely. They're all over the other team. You've got one winger feeling his way down the left, another fiddling down the right, everything is in place for your striker to score when all of a sudden, the ref blows and stops the action for some unknown reason. If it's not that, then it's the ref who's missed something, and you think great, We've got away with that, but then his assistant starts waving his bloody yellow or orange flag as if to say 'quick, quick, look at what so-and-so's just done.' And that's it, the action stops there and then. The foreplay was great, but you didn't get to score.

Then on the other hand, sometimes you do need the ref and his assistant to help. For example, when teams such as Liverpool, Chelsea, Manchester City, and the like come to play at your ground, and you're taking a right pasting. No matter how much you try to defend yourself, it's like they've got 22 players, and they're all over you. All you want to do is get them out of the stadium with your defence still intact. They've got four or five of their players all coming at you at one time. You try to play high up the field, but there's nothing you can do to stop attack after attack. You're praying for the ref to intervene, to give a foul and help relieve the pressure, or the linesman to give an off-side, or to see something the ref's missed. Ahh, but no, now they are nowhere to be seen. So in the end, your defence collapses and you concede and you give in. They score, they win.

This is like in life when the parents disagree with the kids. In football it's the same: match after match, the managers are in disagreement with the referees over decisions made during the game. The manager knows best. The manager says that the referee or his assistant got a decision wrong and that's why that team lost. The ref said he was right and the manager was wrong.

Nowadays, referees seem to prefer their assistant not to get involved too much with what is taking place on the pitch and decide for themselves regarding what they see happening. So, sometimes now the players can get away with almost anything. As far as your manager is concerned, he was right and they were wrong. Unfortunately, they feel the same way, and eventually they all end up storming off the pitch in a huff.

But whatever the outcome of the row is, neither will concede that they were wrong.

Aunts and uncles:
ASSISTANT MANAGERS AND COACHES

The next on the family list is our aunts or uncles.

Years ago, lots of families had a neighbour who were called 'auntie' or 'uncle', even though they weren't related in any way: just good neighbours. They lived close by and were a great help to you and your family in times of need. Some families had a real aunt or uncle who lived local, which was even better. They'd come around every day to give a hand with all the daily household chores: helping mother with the kids; helping with their upbringing, advising them about the rights and wrongs of life; helping to keep them fit and well, clean and tidy. If Dad was out at work, and mother was not well, or had to go somewhere for an urgent appointment, then they were there to step in and take over the reins for a short spell. Some mothers are unable to cope without their relatives, who are there as a back-up, and sometimes as a go-between, between Mum and kids. When the arguments start up, they're there to keep things from getting out of hand.

Some aunts or uncles tended to live on their own, being perhaps a spinster or bachelor. They may have been married, but are now divorced or separated for some reason or another. They may have tried married life, but soon realised it wasn't for them. Perhaps they've never had kids themselves but love looking after someone else's, happy to be part of the family and looking after their young nieces and nephews.

It has also been known that lots of times when the mother ups and sods off with someone else, having being courted with the promise of a better life (or they've just had enough of the pressure that daily life can bring), well, that's the time when the aunt or uncle will move in and take over the running of the household. Sometimes for only for a short time, to help out until the father can get the house back in order. Lots of times they stay for a longer period than they intended, just trying to keep the family stable. They take over sometimes, to the disagreement of some of the kids (especially the older ones). They don't like what's going on, being told what to do by someone else. They get the attitude of 'who are you to tell me what to do? You're not my mother.'

Eventually the older ones, not happy where they are in life, will start to look around for a new home somewhere else. The younger ones tended to carry on regardless: too young or inexperienced to move. So, they wait to see how they're treated, to see if they're in favour. But sooner or later the aunt or uncle will almost certainly end up moving out of that home, especially if the mother calls for help with her new family. They end up going to give a hand there. Eventually the father gets himself sorted out, and meets up with someone else who's willing to move in and take over the family. Nowadays, there are lots more people in the background to help out with the home life and care than there was years ago.

And so the circle of life goes on (as Elton sang).
And I bet you'll be singing that now all day.

ASSISTANT MANAGERS and COACHES:
Aunts and uncles

In football we see the same thing with the assistant manager as we do with the aunts and uncles. They're there on a daily basis helping out the manager. Some have flirted with management, but somehow it didn't work out for them. Others for some reason just don't feel it's for them and would rather assist the manager than take full control themselves. Some managers find their jobs that much more difficult without their assistant. The great Brian Clough was more successful with Peter Taylor by his side; Big Sam always has Little Sammy Lee; and Roy Hodgson has Ray Lewington. All three, Peter, little Sammy, and Ray have been managers previously but for some reason or another seem to be better suited as assistants. And all three of the managers have seen more success with these guys by their sides.

Often when a manager moves on, the assistant will take over as caretaker. This was the case with big Duncan Ferguson at Everton, Roberto Di Matteo at Chelsea, and John Carver at Newcastle, to name a few. This can upset some of the so-called big names at the club as some unfortunately have bigger egos than names. I think they feel the assistant isn't a big enough name, or lacks the experience or personality to tell them what to do. So, as soon as the old manager has departed, so do some of the so-called stars. Most of the younger, less experienced players wait to see what will become of them.

Lots of ex-pros say it's hard to go from being assistant manager to manager as the transition from being close to the players to becoming their boss can be very testing and difficult to make. It can be that some do so well that they get the job on a full-time basis, like Chris Haughton at Newcastle. After Alan Shearer in 2008–09 failed to keep Newcastle in the Premiership, the then owner, Mike Ashley, who was about to sell up and get out (again for the umpteenth time), then gave the job of caretaker manager to the first team coach Chris Haughton. This man changed the club around, and in the following season 2009–10 got them promoted back into the big time. (Well done, that man!) Sadly, his reign didn't last very long because he was sacked in December of the following year. There's nothing better than doing a great job for a great boss. (Well done, Mike! And you should be.)

Normally when a manager leaves a club, whether by choice or so-called mutual agreement, they don't tend to be out of work for long. Soon another club is vying for their signature. And not long after that, they call in their assistant and all the backroom staff of their previous club to go with them, to take on a new football family.

Now it depends on your age as to how you see your team's players. If you are young, then the players look like old men, or older relatives (like brothers-in-law) and there's a tendency to look up to them with respect. If you are in your late teens or early twenties, then they might look like more cousins or mates of the same age as yourself, so then you might tend to judge them on what you would do, or how you would act. You might start moaning, be short-tempered and curse each time your players put a foot or a pass wrong, thinking they should know better with all their experience. As you get older, you might start to see the players as your kids or young nephew' or nieces. You might start moaning, be short-tempered and curse each time they put a foot or a pass wrong, but you do your best to try and forgive, and hope that they will learn as they grow. You want them to make you proud. All the other backroom staff act as other family members (more distant relatives perhaps). However, all are there to help the family in maybe a less substantial but still important way.

And so the circle of football life goes on (as Elton sang).
And I bet you'll be singing that now all day.

School teachers: ACADEMY STAFF TRAINERS AND OTHER COACHES

What we don't learn from our parents at home we have to learn from our teachers at school. This is where we go to be taught the meaning of life, the everyday knowledge we will need to survive, to help build us up ready for our futures in the big bad world. But like all places of learning, it has to be fun as well as interesting, otherwise kids lose interest and, like many a promising youngster, they can lose their way and get left behind. With the Government giving grants to the better schools, it can cost a school financially if they don't meet their expected targets set by OFSTED.

Lots of kids are slow learners so when they leave school, they go and do apprenticeships with very different types of large companies, but, sadly halfway through they're told that they're no longer required for one reason or another, and off they plod into the ether only to reappear on the scene four or five years later after working their socks off at a small little back street company. They've passed all their exams and are now a director or owner of a company that is now taking the business away from their previous large company that thought that they weren't going to make it because they weren't good enough.

It happens so many times in all types of industries. Companies want instant results. They don't want to waste time on those that don't show their potential straight away. This then is when these large companies realise their mistake, and they try and headhunt them back into their fold. This costs them a shit load of money and benefits to get them signed back up again.

I'm sure there are lots of famous entrepreneurs, such as Lord Sugar or Sir Richard Branson, who had some great ideas when they were young and up-and-coming only to be shown the door by the people they went to for backing. They will then have lived to regret it after someone else showed faith, backed them, and made a shit load of money themselves off them.

Lots of slow learners often come back to bite your arse.

ACADEMY STAFF
TRAINERS AND OTHER COACHES: School teachers

What the players don't learn from the manager, they learn at the Academy. The Academy is the same as our everyday school; this is where the players in your football family start to grow and take shape. This is where the players go to get their football knowledge and train for their futures in the big bad wide world. The director of football and the Academy staff are equivalent to the headmaster and the teachers.

These wise men and women mostly have been there, seen it, or done it. They know the game inside and out. They are there to give you all the knowledge they have amassed over the years and it's up to you to listen and learn. Obviously, like schools with their OFSTED targets, academies have their targets too, and bad results could cost them their EFL or Premier League funding. Some of these young players (some as young as five or six) would have been scouted by a big club and spent years of hard training and learning, missing out on their childhood, just hoping to make the big time. Wanting to fulfil a dream.

Sadly, some don't always show their potential and after spending many years with the club, will, for whatever reason, be told that they no longer have a future at the club and they will be released. Teams like Chelsea, had Lukaku on their books in 2011 at the age of eighteen only to let him go in 2014 to Everton for £28 million after playing just ten games. Lukaku then went on to prosper at Everton, Manchester United and Inter Milan, only for Chelsea to buy him back from Inter for the princely sum of £97 million. And after just one year, Chelsea has decided he has no future with them. At this moment in time he has gone back to Inter on a year's loan.

Manchester United had Paul Pogba from 2009 until 2012, again 18 years of age. They then released him in 2012 after just three appearances. After that he went to Juventus for the grand sum of zilch, sod-all, only for United to buy him back four years later for what was then a world record fee of £89 million. Now after six years, he has left the club on a free (unbelievable, Jeff).

These are just a couple of the many that have been let go because clubs didn't show faith and patience in them. And because they couldn't wait, it cost them a shit load of money when they did decide to bring them back.

Lots of even younger players, when released, will go to a smaller lower league club and be signed up as apprentices. Then after five or six years, they will come back as a star player for a team that has just knocked their previous team out of the cup by scoring a hat trick. It's happened at my beloved club, as I'm sure it has at yours. The big club, realising the total cock-up they have made by not nurturing the player when they were younger, will, as Chelsea and United have done, have to pay a fortune to re-sign the player they already had.

Lots of slow learners often come back to bite your arse.

School dinners:
ACADEMY MEALS

There's an old saying that goes: 'Eat shit. A million flies can't all be wrong.' Well, I did that for about ten years in the 50s and I can honestly say that the shit our school dished up even flies wouldn't touch. Most of the other kids that I went to school with had nothing good to say about the food either. We were fed things like spam fritters with mash (which was so watered down it was more like tapioca), mince and potato pie, cheese and tomato pie, some sort of meat stew with undercooked carrots, swede and peas, and overcooked greens and cabbage that stank the whole school out. Friday was always fish and chips and a few green peas (that were more like bullets).

For afters (puddings) we were given spotted dick (that's a pudding by the way, not a disease) with warm lumpy custard; or treacle sponge or jam roly-poly with custard; tapioca (that looked more like frogspawn); or semolina with a spoonful of jam.

Now I know you can't please everyone, but there are limits to what they should dish up to young kids. But on saying that, at least a lot of kids who were from a poorer family didn't have to pay for it. The rest had to pay about 1 shilling (5p) a day, and if I remember correctly, you paid in full at the start of the week. I vaguely remember being given five tickets on a Monday and then we had to hand one a day to the dinner monitor or prefect who was on dinner duty so they knew you had paid. No ticket, no food. Some who lived locally to the school were allowed to go home at lunchtime, and some who didn't like the school dinners could take a packed lunch with them.

Luckily, for some reason, from the 60s onwards, school dinners started to get slightly better. The quality of the meat and vegetables seemed better and tasted as they were supposed to taste. This was just as well, because if we'd carried on eating the 50s menu, we would have all ended up looking like Billy Bunter did at Greyfriars School.

At home, lots of families were only too pleased to get anything that resembled a decent meal on the table. Rationing had not long been stopped after the War, so people ate whatever they could get to fill the bellies. There really wasn't any thought about health and fitness. Our parents fed us with what they could afford and not what we would have wanted. And if we didn't like it, well, it was too bad.

I remember making a stance on this when I was about eleven or twelve. I was adamant that I wasn't going to eat something that was given to me at tea time (six o'clock). To this day I can't remember what it was, but considering the pain it put me through, I should really remember.

l sat at the table in the kitchen and watched my parents and sisters eat their meals, but I was determined I was not going to touch mine. I was told that there was nothing else: 'Eat that or you go can go to bed hungry.' No way was I going to give in. I was sure that later my mum would dish up something else for me, but how wrong I was! I asked if I could leave the table and go and watch the TV, and I was told, 'You can stay there until you eat your dinner.' My dad was not a happy chappie. I sat there from six until about nine when I was told to go to bed. Off I went, leaving my meal still intact, thinking how bloody hungry

I was, and what horrible parents they were. But I was all proud thinking I had won.

I woke up the next morning with terrible hunger pains, and was happy to hear my mother shout out that breakfast was ready. I think you might know what I'm about to say ... yes, I got the meal from the previous night, warmed up and put in front of me. Defiantly I picked at it and never ever moaned again. Lesson learnt.

Everything to eat was about cost back then, and our food was very basic. Pie, mash, and liquor; sausage and mash; bread and dripping. Plenty of vegetables. Princes tinned Spam or corned beef; Fray Bentos tinned steak and kidney pies, or steamed pudding; and plenty of spuds. A company called Shippam's, who do all kinds of different types of sandwich spreads (paste), such as salmon, crab, beef, and fish, was ideal for making the school lunches or Dad's packed lunch, or even for a nice picnic at the park or seaside. We ate food that was reasonably priced, if not exactly healthy. On Sundays, if we were lucky enough, we would get a roast dinner with whatever meat we could afford, with all the trimmings.

For lots of us, our diets started to change in the 60s when Britain was invaded by the American fast-food culture. In the mid-60s we got Colonel Sanders, and the wonderful KFC, then in the 70s the golden arches of Ronald McDonald started to light up all over Britain. Up until this time we had only really had the Wimpy bars selling burgers and chips. With the American influence, our chips were now called fries. Burger King also started up in the same year as McDonald's but never took off. However, it did reappear as a household name in the 80s.

All different types of restaurants, bars and bistros started to open up, selling food from all over the world: Chinese, Indian, Thai, and Italian, all serving their own special dishes. More pubs moved into the food market. We used to just put salt and pepper on our food way back then. Now there are no end of spices to enhance our food: garlic, cinnamon etc., or if you take advice from Simon and Garfunkel, you would use 'parsley, sage, rosemary and thyme.'

Nowadays, it's all about healthy eating at school. Over the years we have been educated and informed more and more about what is in the food we're eating, which has made us more aware of what was good, and what was bad in what we ate. We have begun to take more interest in things like our health and well-being. Gyms and fitness centres are more and more popular. Running, walking, and swimming have been taken up by the old and young alike. Diets today are so important to many people.

I'm still not sure though if school dinners have changed much for the better. According to my grandkids, they haven't. But I'm sure they can't be as bad as they were way back then.

ACADEMY MEALS:
School dinners

The football players in the 50s right through to the mid-90s were seen as footballers, not as athletes. Athletes were people like the first sub-4-minute milers: Dr Roger Bannister, Chris Brasher, Lillian Board, Seb Coe, Steve Ovett, and Mary Peters. More recently, we have had Mo Farah, Chris Hoy, and Steve Redgrave, to name just a few of many great athletes of the track and field, and winter sports, swimmers, ice skaters were all seen as athletes. Cricketers, tennis players, rugby players and footballers were never put in that class.

If you asked anyone to name their favourite athlete, the chances are they wouldn't name a footballer. Football players ate almost the same as we did through these years. It's been well documented that some players would have a main meal before playing a match. Most of them drank too much. They smoked too much. And they ate all the wrong things.

Some players struggled even to do warm-ups, as it made them tired. For most of them, their diets were terrible. They would eat steak and chips, a full English breakfast, a steak-and-kidney pie, or fish and chips, followed by a good few beers, all before running around for a full 90 minutes. It wasn't until the mid-60s that substitutes were first allowed by the football league. So if you were feeling a bit bloated, it was too bad, you stayed on the pitch no matter what.

It wasn't until we had an influx of overseas players that, all of a sudden, our British players seemed to take note of what these continental players' diets were. It was one man who changed the way that footballers' diets changed and that was France's answer to Jamie Oliver: Arsène Wenger. When he took over at Arsenal, he changed the whole culture at the club with regard to eating, drinking, and thinking. He banned lots of different types of food too. Out went the pints of beer or lager, and dinner was now taken with a glass of wine. Less of the snooker, betting shop and pub culture after training. Players were now weighed on a more regular basis. He changed the way they trained and the players' mentality regarding health and fitness. Lots of overseas managers and coaches came over to England and brought this new way of thinking to the benefit of all the clubs.

Many players moaned about the new health and fitness regime. But the style of football was now changing. Instead of playing the so-called long ball, the type that Tony Pulis and Sam Allardyce were always accused of playing, it was now all about keeping ball, speed, and a matter of breakaway football. To do this you had to be as fit as a butcher's dog and have less fat on you than on a butcher has on his pencil. (That's not Terry Butcher's dog; I don't even know if he has a dog.) Almost every player (and his dog) is now as fit as they will ever be.

My grandson Oscar is eleven and when we went to see Fulham play Bristol City last season (2021–2022), Harry Wilson gave him his shirt after the game. Now Oscar is quite stocky for his age, but the shirt fitted him perfectly. That's how slim today's footballers have to be. Sadly, for a player's shirt to fit me, it would have to be the brilliant Adebayo Akinfenwa's. What a great servant he has been to the game. Retiring at the ripe old age of thirty-nine going on forty. What a fine figure of a man! Unfortunately like me, the figure is a big sort of 0. Most Academies way back were like the schools we attended, with the dinner ladies cooking the meals. But nowadays they are only serving good healthy food and drink, and most often this is by Cordon Bleu chefs.

Bank managers:
SPONSORS

Whether it's a bank loan, a credit card, or an overdraft, we all need some kind of financial aid at some stage during our family life. The bank is where we used to go with a cap in one hand and a begging bowl in the other, pleading for financial aid, whether to help us build on what we already have, or to get us out of a mess we're already in. This has gone on since the year dot.

Most families live on some kind of credit or HP. With the cost of living spiralling out of all proportion as the weeks go by, it's important to watch every penny. Food, petrol, household utility bills have all gone through the roof. Whether you're buying a house, a car or having a holiday we all need some sort of financial backing.

Nowadays, it's so much easier to get some sort of financial aid. Just go online and fill out a simple form and nine times out of ten, it's yours. Lots of finance companies can't wait to get you signed up, some at extortionate rates. But making sure you get the right deal is so important because, as I've ready said, borrowing too much can lead to total disaster. But most families must adjust for everyday needs.

Sadly, since Covid-19, at this moment in time, lots of poorer families are struggling to keep up with bills and feed their families. Hopefully, all families that suffered will eventually come out of this situation and get their lives back on track, safe and sound.

SPONSORS:
Bank managers

Almost every day, football clubs, especially those in the lower leagues, are looking for new financial investment. This could be a new shirt sponsorship deal or a TV broadcasting deal, i.e. Sky, BT. Or it could be thinking about selling the naming rights to the stadium to help keep the club's head above the water line. This is in the hope that the fans, who themselves are also struggling to buy a season or match day ticket, will also buy the club's shirts, scarfs, hats etc. All clubs need some kind of financial aid during the course of the season.

Lots of the football families are no different to lots of everyday domestic families in that they may have to borrow to survive. They themselves have to go with the begging bowl to the banks for assistance just to help pay the staff wages. But making sure you get the right deal is so important. As I've ready said, borrowing too much can lead to total disaster.

Since Covid-19, at this moment in time, clubs in the lower divisions are looking for some kind of assistance from wherever they can find it in order to survive. Hopefully, all those clubs that suffered will eventually come out of this situation and get their supporters back in the grounds, safe and sound.

Police, fire and ambulance staff:
SECURITY AND FIRST-AIDERS

Their duties have been more or less the same since we started to send all our villains and criminals to Australia (who, sadly, through the years, have had offspring after offspring, and now after all these years, have come back to beat us at fucking rugby and cricket).

Today we still have crime on our streets, and even with the excellent police force we have, things are never going to change. It's a social issue. Idiots get pissed and start trouble no matter what time of the day it is. Stabbings seem to be on the up. The police fight an endless battle week after week, trying to clean up the streets, but it's like trying to turn back the tide. The police in high-speed car chases are going into situations blind, not knowing what dangers they will be facing. They attempt to break up pub and bar brawls and act as go-betweens to settle domestic differences, which can sometimes turn quite violent. Over the years, to aid our police force, more and more CCTV cameras have been installed all over the bigger towns and cities. Due to the amount of CCTV's, we now have, there are slightly less police patrolling the streets

The fire service also does a fabulous job, but accidents unfortunately happen every day. Their not only there to attend fires but also for numerous other events and happenings while putting their own lives at risk daily. All these services are so vitally important in our lives for our safety. The brave members of the fire services go running into burning houses with intense heat to rescue people trapped in the flames and they're often blinded by the smoke. And there is the biggest and bravest task of course ... that's getting some one's cat out of a tree.

Those working in the ambulance service are there saving lives on a daily basis while putting their own lives at risk, most of the time from the people they're there to assist. There are a wide range of traumatic experiences for all the people in these three services: accidents with horrendous scenes, Grenfell Towers, London terrorists' attacks, the Manchester Arena bombing, and all kinds of motorway accidents. They're there in the front line during and after these events to help clean up all the devastation that's left behind.

SECURITY AND FIRST-AIDERS:
Police, fire and ambulance staff

The football stadium safety officers and security companies are our footballing police force. Along with the first-aiders, they do their best to keep everyone in our football families safe and sound on match days. They are backed up by the orange jackets of the safety stewards. They, like the PCSOs who help the police, have no legal authority, but are there when, unfortunately there are any outbreaks of violence instigated by a few brainless idiots. They are paid little for big risks, keeping the fans in the best of order, and specially making sure they keep the fans apart (a thankless job), doing spot checks, carrying out safety procedures and directing supporters when their lost or can't find their seat. They put themselves at risk, like our police officers, for a few paltry quid each home game. We do have to have a small contingent of recognised law enforcement officers, as they're now known (policemen and women in old money), at the lesser high-profile matches. But whenever and wherever the so-called bigger supported clubs play, then they're out in force trying to make sure the games go ahead without incident.

Unfortunately, it doesn't always go to plan, as happened in the Heysel Stadium in Belgium in 1985 when 39 football fans lost their lives when a wall collapsed, crushing them to death. Four days later, UEFA banned fans from British clubs from attending all European matches for five years. Liverpool fans were banned for six. Then in 1989 tragedy struck again at the Anfield Club. Ninety-six Liverpool supporters were again crushed to death at Hillsborough, the home of Sheffield Wednesday, as they were preparing to play Nottingham Forest in the semi-final of the FA Cup.

In 1985, we also had the Bradford Stadium fire which sadly killed 56 fans when an old wooden stand caught fire during a Third Division match between Bradford City and Lincoln City.

In 1971, Scotland had their own disaster: 66 fans were crushed to death at an old firm match between Rangers and Celtic. It's so sad to think these people lost their lives doing the one thing in life that they loved most: watching their great clubs and their heroes.

There has been violence in football since the game was invented, but it really took off in England back in the 1960s and early 70s when the infamous skinheads appeared with their shaved heads, Dr. Martens boots and Crombie overcoats. They were more interested in kicking heads than in who was kicking a football. Total scum professing to stand up for their club. Luckily, they seem to have grown up and although we still have some mindless morons intent on bringing the beautiful game into disrepute, they are few and far between, and they are to be pitied. The stadium security officer's job is now slightly easier than it was 40 or 50 years ago, although, sadly, we still have the problem with thugs raising their ugly heads when following the National team in Europe.

Football stadia have done exactly the same as our local councils; they have installed more and more CCTV and television cameras everywhere so football grounds now have better safety measures inside the grounds. Unfortunately, violence still goes on outside many of them.

You cannot compare what the security men, women and stewards do at football matches to what the brave men and women of our three emergency services do on a daily basis, but I have tried to show there are some parallels in terms of their role, which is to keep people safe. Hopefully I haven't caused anybody any upset in doing so.

Doctors and physios:
CLUB DOCTOR AND CLUB PHYSIO

Years ago, going to the doctors was pretty straightforward. You phoned up, got an appointment, you arrived, booked in with the receptionist, and waited in a room with the rest of the attendant patients. I can remember as a young boy there were two lights above the doctor's door: one red, one green. I remember sitting there willing this red light that was on (indicating to the rest of us that the doctor was busy with a patient) to go green for the next in line to go in after the last one had just left. It was important that you got in to see the doctor as quickly as possible in those days due to the fact that while you might only have come in with a snotty nose, by the time everyone around you had coughed and sneezed their germs around the room, you now had just about every other ailment man had discovered (and possibly some that they hadn't).

Now I don't know about your doctor, but it seems that no matter whether you go to see them about a headache or an in-growing toe nail, they always ask the same questions: 'Do you smoke? ... Do you drink ...?' If your answer is no, then the response might be to 'take two of these, twice a day after food, and come back in a couple of months if it's no better'. You get the same questions and the same reply even if you answer to say that yes, you do smoke, 80 a day, and drink 10 pints a day.

Nowadays you have more chance of seeing Ronaldo playing for Manchester United than getting to see a doctor. I don't mean to paint a bad picture of the medical profession, because our NHS staff are doing the best they can with what they have, but it is frustrating when you're ill and struggle to book an appointment. It often involves having to go through all the rigmarole of sitting forty-sixth in line on the telephone, then after two hours of holding, being informed that 'you are now second in the queue.' Sometimes even you get a PING, and a voice says, 'Sorry, but the surgery is now closed for staff training.' Perhaps having a degree in IT would help so you can book online.

One day they will find one pill that will cure everything so the country will only need one doctor to prescribe it. Then you will hear: 'We're sorry but all lines are busy at the moment. Our operator will get to you as soon as possible ... you are now 6,587,328th in the queue.'

Now, if you were suffering with aches, pains, and stiffness in parts of the body you didn't want to get stiff, then you would almost certainly be sent to see a physiotherapist (a bone cruncher). I'm sure some of these people think that we are made of rubber. I have seen some of the old 60s and 70s wrestlers, like Jackie Pallo, Big Daddy, Giant Haystacks, Mick McManus, Les Kellett and Johnny Kwango (or for you younger readers, wrestlers like 'Oooh Yeah' Randy Savage, Jon Cena, Dwayne 'The Rock' Johnson, and 'Stone Cold' Steve Austin) scream and submit to some of the positions that these physios twist and pull your body parts into. They dig their knuckles into your back and spine as if they're kneading dough.

I went to one once and I'm pretty sure that this bloke had another job down at the local bus depot changing the tyres on the buses. Unfortunately, lots of us will need such medical attention, whether it's a doctor or a physiotherapist. Long may these people be there to aid us when we do need them.

CLUB DOCTORS and CLUB PHYSIO:
Doctors and physios

Nowadays, when a player goes down screaming his head off and rolling around in agony as if he's just been run over by an articulated lorry, holding his ankle or shin, waving his arms in the air, the ref waves to the dug-out for urgent medical aid. Then you see the physio or whatever he is, and his assistant run onto the pitch with a great big bag full of enough medical supplies to fit out a local pharmacy. Then after about ten minutes of checking out the player's medical history, the player and the two medics (?) decide he's not going to need a blood transfusion or an operation to get his boot back on. So what do these medics do then? They dig deep into the bag of medicinal delights and bring out a can of some sort of medical cure, spray the point of the concern (if they actually know where the point is) and lo and behold, the player is now fitter than ever and soon running around like a rabbit.

It's quite strange that all the falling about and medical aid requirements and time-outs usually occur when a team is either under pressure by the opposition or leading 1-0 and time-wasting.

Years ago, if a player went down after a bad tackle and stayed down, you knew he was hurt. Players then didn't scream blue murder, roll about and wave their arms in the air. If a player was not back up more or less straight away, then you knew there was a problem. Most of the players were as hard as nails: goalkeepers weren't protected, they were battered; tackles were tackles; and players went in full-blooded, and came out with their shirts full of blood. If a player walked off the pitch rather than hobbled off the pitch, he hadn't put in a full shift.

When the ref called for medical assistance, you would see a little tubby bloke (usually the assistant coach) come waddling across the pitch with a sponge and a tin bucket of cold water that splashing everywhere as he made his way to the player. For some reason, this magical bucket of water and accompanying sponge strangely seem to work better in the winter months than in the summer. Those cold winter days back then were bitter, so if you got hurt, the last thing you wanted to see was that sponge and bucket coming to your aid. Old tubby would dump the sponge into the water and wallop it onto the spot that was giving you grief. Now that was bad enough, but should you have got hit in the knackers, then your eyes would drip out water as much as the sponge. And when he put that freezing wet sponge down your shorts and squeezed the water over your nuts, my God, did the world stop still (and so did your breath)! You screamed at him just like your partner screamed at you when she was giving birth, calling him all the names under the sun.

Over the years, things have changed so much in terms of health and safety, not only in the workplace but also in sport. And for athletes, the pitches and fields are their workplaces. Most clubs now have a full medical team who work in the same manner as our family doctor does, treating the team for all kind or injuries and ailments, prescribing what types of medicine they should and shouldn't take, and generally looking after all health and body matters, from exercise to diets. They also advise the mother (or manager) about the condition of everyone, and decide who will be fit enough to carry on working, or who might need some time off to recover for the next game.

There's not much to write about the family and the club doctors other than you hope you don't see too much of them too often while you're alive and the players are still kicking.

Postman:
PROGRAMME SELLER

Since the year dot, we've always relied on the postman, or should I say post person, to bring us our mail. Whether it is good news or bad, from our loved ones, or companies trying to sell us something we don't really need, bills or just general information, no matter the weather, come rain or shine, they'd be there.

Nowadays, with the invention of the internet, letters are getting fewer and fewer (a bit like the milk person). Emails and social media have taken preference over letters to give us the information we require even though some people would still rather put pen to paper to tell their friends and love ones how they are, and how they feel about them. Receiving a letter feels more personal than getting a ping on your phone, that ping which could have come from anyone. But when a letter arrives, and you see the handwriting, you know straight away who it is from. A letter is something to hold and keep, something you can look back on at a later date.

I don't remember the last time I got a love letter from a friend or family member, do you?

PROGRAMME SELLER:
Postman

Programme sellers are equivalent to our post person. They convey messages and information regarding the team in the shape of the match day programme. There they are inside and outside the ground no matter what the weather, come rain or shine, with all the up-to-date information about our football family in one book. Good news and bad news on our favourite loved ones, a message from the manager (mother).

Again, because of the internet, fewer and fewer programmes are being sold. With social media, emails and the like, we can keep up to date with all that's going on with our football family. But some supporters still prefer to pay and collect their programmes because, to them, it feels more personal. A programme is something they can keep, something to hold which they can look at again at a later date. Let's hope that the post person and the programme sellers don't go the way that the milk person has gone.

Our mum:
THE KIT MAN

My mum was our Kit Lady (well, her name was Kitty). Anyway, she used to do the washing and the ironing. There was never a doubt in the early years about who did the washing in the house. It was always considered as the mother's job to keep the kids' clothes nice and clean. Washing machines were around in the 50s but very few people had them or could afford them. So mothers used to wash the clothes in the sink or a big bowl, and use a scrubbing board to rub the washing up and down (a bit like Lonnie Donegan playing his old washboard, and asking, 'Does your chewing gum lose its flavour on the bed-post overnight?' They don't make classics like that nowadays).

If it wasn't Mum doing the washing, then it was left for the oldest daughter, if there was one. Very rarely did the man of the house do it. An aunt or neighbour might be asked to come to your aid if there was no one else to do it. No, the poorer families had to do their own. It was the same with polishing your best shoes. The kids helped out by doing Dad's while he was at work.

If you were well endowed financially, then you possibly had some sort of housekeeper, or a daily cleaner whom you could pay to do the washing for you, but that was really only for the richer families. Some of the elite families had a valet whose job it was to make sure that the washing, ironing, and dry cleaning was done to perfection: clothes all laid out ready to wear when the family members were venturing out on that special occasion.

THE KIT MAN:
Our mum

Lots of football clubs back in the 50s, and still many do today, relied on the manager, his assistant, and players to wash and iron their kits. Some managers managed to get their wives to give a hand, and some had supporters who'd volunteer to help out, free of charge. Nowadays, it's really just the lower league teams where the players still have to wash their own kits and clean their boots. It doesn't matter whether they're male or female, they do their own laundry, ironing, and dry cleaning.

Years ago, the young trainees used to help out the kit man. Their job was to clean the pros' boots after each match before going to the Academy, just like kids helped to clean their dad's shoes.

Some of the slightly better off clubs have washing machines and pay someone a few extra pounds to make sure that the players' kits are spotless and hanging on their pegs, or folded on their bench in the changing rooms, all ready for when they're going to play.

Now, the big clubs have it all sorted out just right; they have a full-time kit man. He's like the valet of the rich and famous. His job is to make sure on match day that everything is ready for the players, the managers, and Uncle Tom Cobley and all.

Our mum:
THE TEA PERSON

We all like a nice cup of tea or coffee at any time of the day, so whoever makes it in our house is an absolute diamond. Nine times out of ten it's your mother. Not only was she our kit lady but also our tea lady. When times were rough, she was there, putting the kettle on, helping to keep the morale of the house up.

I remember we used to sing to my mum: 'Kitty, put the kettle on, Kitty, put the kettle on, Kitty, put the kettle on, we'll all have tea.'

And she would shout back lovingly, 'You make it yourselves, you lazy sods! I've been on my sodding feet all day.'

Bless her, but she would do it. She was totally the family's most valuable assist.

THE TEA PERSON:

(Or, to be politically correct, the supplier of liquids and refreshments person. Na, balls to that, it's the good old tea lady–man–person):

Our mom

The person who makes the tea and pushes the trolly (there, is that OK, PC people?), whether male or female, are one of the most valuable assets to any football team. They are nearly always happy and smiling, going around with their mobile tea bar, giving out tea, coffee and biscuits. They help to keep the morale of all the football family up, especially if results are not going too well. They rub shoulders with everyone connected with the club from the top brass to the juniors. These are like the neighbours that always seem to be there when things are going wrong, offering to make the tea and coffee, and helping everyone to keep their chins up. A total asset to everyone around.

(God, how I hate all this politically correct nonsense! Postman ...? No ... post*person*. Milkman ...? No ... milk*person*. If that's the case, then you can't now have a landlady or a landlord. So, what do you have ... a land*person*?)

Family pets:
TEAM MASCOTS

After the War, when money was so tight, only the few had any type of family pet. The only animals that were really needed was a cat, most probably called Tiddles, to keep the mice, rats and any other vermin away; a dog called Rover, for reasons of security; a blue or green budgie called Joey to keep you company; and a couple of goldfish named after your favourite celebs: Stan and Ollie, or Andy Capp and Flo. Later would come Starsky and Hutch, or Ronnie and Reggie (perhaps the last two are better names for a couple of piranhas). Or, if you were more into pop music, then you might choose such names as Simon and Garfunkel, Aretha and Otis, or Ike and Tina. Today if you're really sad, it might be Ant and Dec, or Itchy and Scratchy. If you were into food, how about sausage and mash; mac and cheese; or lastly, just chips (well, you've already got the fish: two of them ... gold).

I know if my two grandsons had a cat and a dog each, they would call them Palhinha (Joao) and Wilson (Harry).

Some families had so-called pets, such as chickens, geese, or rabbits, that were sadly sacrificed for the dinner table when times were bad. As the years moved on, families started to get more involved with their pets, seeing them more as a family member rather than just as an animal. Guinea pigs, mice, hamsters, tortoises, rabbits, and parrots, were now all popular with kids and parents alike (no more eating the cute little bunny).

Pet shops started to sell a bigger range of animals as pets were imported from all over the world. There were all different types of reptiles and exotic birds. Snakes, lizards, parrots, chinchillas, and different kinds of small primates also became a thing to have.

Some of the rich in society even had lions, tigers, bears, and crocodiles in their back gardens. All types of wonderful species are now part of family life. All these pets have brought happiness to family life, especially to the kids. (Really? Lions? Tigers and the likes? I don't see that.)

TEAM MASCOTS:
Family pets

In earlier years, only a very few football families had pets. A few used real animals, such as dogs, the odd bull, or goat maybe? But it wasn't until the 80s when clubs started to think that it would be nice for the younger supporters to have a football pet (mascot).

So teams like Blackburn Rovers decided to get a dog and they called it Rover (that was original). Leeds had a cat called Kop Kat, and Norwich City had a couple of canaries. Preston had a duck, whereas other teams went for more of an exotic or different type of pet. Aston Villa had a lion and so did Middlesbrough and Millwall. Hull had a tiger. Crystal Palace had a couple of eagles. Sheffield Wednesday have an owl called Barney. Swansea has a couple of swans called Cyril and Cybil. Watford have Harry the hornet. Brighton has a seagull called Gully. Everton went really big time and got in an elephant.

Lots of football families have all sorts of weird and wonderful pets. Wolves have wolves, and my own family have a badger called Billy, although in 2008 we nearly had to have Billy put down after a vicious unprovoked attack by him on the then Chelsea manager Avram Grant. But the RSPCM (the royal society for the prevention of cruelty to managers), aka the FA, just gave Billy's owners a stern warning.

West Brom has a baggie bird and a … combi boiler? (Don't ask.) Mind you, I shouldn't take the Matt Le Tiss really, as Fulham once had Sir Craven of Cottage, a bloke dressed up like a knight. (Oh, how embarrassing that was!) He was enough to scare the shit out of most kids, wandering around the ground with two big bloodshot eyes peering down at them through his steel-clad helmet, waving a great big sword and a shield about.

I wonder what Cockfosters and Pratts Bottom FCs' mascots are??

All these pets brought happiness to the football family life, especially to the kids. And presumably the boiler kept the West Brom family nice and warm, especially those on the bench.

To end this section about pets, in our family and football family lives we have our legal eagles.

The Law Society: PGMOL
(PROFESSIONAL GAME MATCH OFFICIALS LIMITED)

The Law Society according to Google is the voice of solicitors, which I think means that basically they are the advisers for all types of solicitors to be, and advisers to any solicitors that may need help or information. Also they're there to make sure the rules of the law are upheld and understood.

Whenever we have a problem or dispute in life there is always a solicitor or lawyer to turn to for help. These people are there to see that justice and fairness are seen to be done in the courtroom. But should they be accused of doing something that is unlawful, unethical, or against their 'code of conduct' (whether it's in the courtroom or outside of it) then they are brought before the SRA (Solicitors Regulation Authority) to explain their actions. After stating their case, if they are then found to be guilty, depending on how serious the offence is, they could be suspended, sent down (prison), or even struck off.

PGMOL:
The Law Society

Professional Game Match Officials Limited, or PGMOL as they're also known, are the rulers of the referees and all match day officials for all the leagues. They're there to make sure the match officials are fit and prepared for the matches they have been chosen to preside over. Whenever we have a problem or dispute on the football pitch there is always the referee or the assistant referee to turn to for help. These people are there to see that justice and fairness are seen to be done on the field of play or even after the match ends, i.e., in the tunnel. But should they be accused of doing something wrong, for example, making a wrong decision regarding a bad foul, or failing to send someone off that they should have, or going against the rules of the game, they are then brought before a FA disciplinary committee to explain their actions. After stating their case, if they are then found to be guilty, depending on how serious the offence is, they could be suspended, sent down (referee a game in a lower division) or even struck off.

The law courts:
THE FA TRIBUNAL

This is where the bad boys and girls go when they've been accused of doing some sort of misdemeanour. Here you're up before a judge and jury, the bigwigs who will judge after hearing the evidence from all parties concerned, whether you're guilty or innocent of all charges. And they will hand out the appropriate sentence if there is to be one.

'DO THE CRIME, DO THE TIME.'

THE FA TRIBUNAL:
The law courts

This is where the bad boys and girls go when they've been accused of doing some sort of misdemeanour. Here you're up before the FA committee, the bigwigs, who will judge after hearing the evidence from all parties concerned, whether you're guilty or innocent of all charges. And they will hand out the appropriate sentence if there is to be one.

'DO THE CRIME, DO THE TIME.'

Chapter Eight

Family Feuds
FOOTBALL RIVALS

Protecting your family:
DEFENDING YOUR TEAM

Ever since I was old enough to understand what my elders were shouting and screaming about (which most of the time was about nothing and everything), I realised that family life wasn't a bed of roses. And just like a bed of roses, there's always a prick, or two, that will start a family bust-up.

There have always been family feuds and family arguments since the days of the cavemen and women (although I don't think that there was much arguing going on after the old man clumped his missus on the head with a large piece of wood and dragged her back into the cave by her hair). Famously, Henry VIII (who had six wives) got his old chopper out (steady now) and chopped off the heads of two of them: Catherine Howard and the one whose name West Ham chose for their old ground: Anne of Upton Park (hands up those who thought I was going to write Anne Boleyn), when they pissed him right off.

The present royal family (the real one, not the one on TV) always seem to have some sort of in-house family dispute going on, what with Sarah Ferguson and Prince Andrew, then Charles and Lady Di (sadly, that in-house feud didn't turn out at all well), and now we've got the Harry and Meghan fiasco. It's all going on at Buck House. There's Britney and her dad, Johnny Depp and his ex-missus, and the Gallagher brothers, Noel and Liam, who once proudly sang, 'Don't look back in anger'. But unfortunately for all Oasis fans, they are doing just that. And I've just heard that even the Lighthouse family have called it a day.

The in-house fighting goes on just about everywhere, in every street and behind every closed door. Some of these families couldn't survive without a good old argument. Lots of the parents' arguments tend to be over money, kids, or one of them feeling that they're not being appreciated by the rest of the family (taken for granted). If one partner is drinking, gambling, or maybe buying expensive shoes or clothes too often, then sadly that problem tends to carry on indefinitely and usually ends up with a total family split. Most, of the kids' arguments are over whose clothes are whose, and rows over who gets to use the bathroom first. I remember my son Lee used to say to me about my daughter Gemma: 'You love her more than me; she's your favourite, blah, blah, blah.' Twenty-five years later, he's still saying it.

The list of reasons goes on and on. Sadly, some do go on to end in violence. Years ago, if you were rude or out of line with your parents, then you got a clip around the ear or a smacked arse, and were sent to bed. Now I'm not saying that it's right to hit your kids, but I don't think a smack on the bum does too much damage, physically or mentally, if it's only on a very, very rare occasion, and I think there's a big difference between smacking and hitting. No one should hit a child, but a smack on a flabby bum ...? (C'mon.) No doubt I'll get castigated by the civil rights movement for that view; they'll be outside my house with their banners soon, shouting obscenities.

Anyway, where were we? Ah yes, sadly, as I stated, lots do end in violence, as in the case of the White House Farm murders when in 1985, Jeremy Bamber was found guilty of murdering five of his adopted family for a large inheritance. The soul singer Marvin Gaye was killed by his own father in 1984. In 2002, Martin Baker was sent to jail for killing his wife and feeding her to the pigs. There are many cases of husband and wives killing not only each other but also, sadly, their children.

Over the years we've even had similar arguments on the telly. TV families like the Ewings in Dallas, with the old nasty backstabbing bastard J.R. (Larry Hagman), his pissed-up wife, Sue Ellen (Linda Gray), whom he romantically referred to as a drunk, a tramp and an unfit mother, and his poor little brother Bobby Ewing (Patrick Duffy) strange that...? I didn't realise that he came from Dallas. I thought Patrick Duffy was the *Man from Atlantis*. It's no wonder that J.R. got the best of poor old Bobby. Well, he was wet behind the ears (*Atlantis*? Wet?) The Ewings were all going at it ten to the dozen back in the 70s. So were Basil and Sybil Fawlty, played by the wonderful John Cleese and Prunella Scales: Connie Booth as Polly; and Andrew Sachs as Manuel, who apparently comes from 'Barthelona' and he knows nu-u-think. There were arguments among members of *The Royale Family* (not the real ones), *The Simpsons* (the TV version) and my own Simpson family.

Families arguing and fighting with another family, was, and is, a part of everyday life. I've seen many a neighbourhood argument over the years: mums rowing with mums, dads threatening dads, and kids telling other kids, 'My dad's bigger than your dad, and he'll come and beat your dad up.'

This could often be followed by: 'Yeah, well, my dad's stronger than your dad, cos my dad's a weightlifter.'

And in reply, 'Yeah, well, my dad's a shoplifter, see, so there.'

It's family life

Now, if the trouble involves two or three different families, then that's when you find the bigger problems start. Even today we've had the Rooney's versus the Vardy's, both families showing themselves up with a 'she said, she said' load of old nonsense.

Many arguments are of a trivial nature, rows starting when the neighbours spread unfounded rumours and gossip. Now no matter how friendly you are with your neighbours, or how calm you are in life and easy-going, sooner or later a neighbour or two are going to get under your skin. Usually, it's for such reasons as they have parked their car outside your house, or their kid's ball keeps coming over your fence, or the worst one of all: their dog keeps shitting in your prize garden. There's going to be a row, and once there's one argument, you can bet your life it won't end there.

It's been going on through the years and it isn't ever going to stop. And we've all had our share of noisy neighbours, husbands and wives screaming and shouting at each other, kids playing loud music, dogs continually barking, driving us mad. Most family versus family feuds tend to be with the bigger families in the area.

Lots of the more ongoing family feuds tend to start in the local pub, bar, or nightclub, or basically anywhere there is alcohol. The kids of one family would be all out together having too much to drink, then the odd fracas might start. One member of family A might try and chat up a member of family B, who is already going out with someone from family C, and that would start an almighty argument between the lot of them, no doubt leading to some sort of confrontation. Or, it might be that someone from another local family would say something nasty about someone's girlfriend or boyfriend: call her an old slapper or an ugly old cow, or say he was a dickhead or arsehole, or say something even worse like ... insult your football team ...!! And then it would all really kick off big time.

Tables, chairs, and glasses would fly across the room, and quite a few punches thrown. It would usually end up with one or two people being decked, then both lots would walk away declaring themselves to be the victors. Lots of times though, the families would not let it end there, and whenever they got the chance to get revenge, they would take it with both hands (or bike chains, lumps of wood, a very large metal bar or the good old trusty knuckle-duster). Eventually the police would have to step in and try to resolve the problem. But if that didn't work, then it might well end up in court, with some sort of injunction or banning order given.

My dad always told me when I first started to go out drinking never to discuss politics, religion, or football in the pub. It was a sure sign to start an argument or a fight.

In the 50s, families like the Krays and the Richardsons ran the streets of London. These families had taken family feuds to another level for years, fighting over who had a bigger share of the ill-gotten gains that London had to offer. But, from what I've read about these two firms, they never hurt the general public who weren't involved in anything underhand. Films were made and glorified these gangsters: in 1990 *The Krays*, and in 2015 *Legend*, both about the Krays, and in 2004, *Charlie*, a film about Charlie Richardson.

Books have also been written, such as *Gangland UK: The Inside Story of Britain's Most Evil Gangsters* and *British Gangsters: Faces of the Underworld*. Problems evolved from just a couple of rival family gangs over the years, and things seemed to escalate out of control. In the 70s, 80s and 90s, it moved on from family gangs like the Richardsons and Krays to just local lads starting up gangs. Rival gangs from different boroughs of London and all of the big cities, such as Liverpool, Manchester, and Birmingham (the *Peaky Blinders*), would cross areas and fight, again trying to take control over their rivals' patch. More films were made regarding gang rivalry: *Lock Stock and Two Smoking Barrels* and *Snatch*, both with the ex-footballer Vinnie 'HA-HA, HA-HA, STAYING ALIVE, STAYING ALIVE' Jones. *Layer Cake* with Daniel Craig (sorry, 'the name's Bond.' Or *was* James Bond).

I read an article once which stated that after going to watch a *James Bond* film, many people get into their cars and drive up to fifty per cent faster than they would normally. How the fuck they know that I can't imagine. Do they follow these people before they go to watch the film, and check their speed ... and follow them again when they come out? How did they know they were going to go to watch the film in the first place??

Back in the 50s and 60s, we had Teddy boys and girls (known as Teds). They were the boys and girls with the drainpipe trousers. The boys, with their DA (duck's arse) haircut and winkle-picker shoes, the girls with their beehive hairstyles, would fight with the leather-clad, metal-chained bikers known as rockers or greasers (most probably due to the fact that their hair looked as if it hadn't seen water since they were baptised) on the beaches at

Brighton, or in some car park behind a greasy spoon cafe, or on an A road leading to some seaside resort.

This would put the fear of God into some poor family who just wanted to go and have a good day out, sitting on a beach with their kids, watching Punch knocking the crap out of Judy, killing the baby, and then attacking policeman Jack, with Punch telling the kids, 'That's the way to do it.' Sadly, even though the Punch and Judy shows were supposed to be funny, real-life tragedies like these show's seemed to be happening in families daily. And it's still going on today. So, instead of fun on the beach with the Punch and Judy show, here's this family watching a drunk and looney show. Yes, the Teds and rockers were a pain in the arse, but mainly only in the summer months. During the winter, they would have a set-to in a car park behind the back of a large pub after a local dance.

We then got the Mods, who started to evolve as the Teddy boy era was slowly coming to an end.

Now some of you younger readers might think I've been drinking too much or have something wrong with me writing about Teddy boys with ducks' arses and drainpipe trousers and winkle-pickers; and metal-chained rockers riding a Triumph; and Punch kicking the shit out of Judy ... and now the mods ... Well, for those of you that don't know what the fuck all these words mean, ask your mum or dad because they were probably one of them in their younger days. I'm sure they'll have a fine tale to tell.

The mods came along just as the Teddy boys were going out of fashion, and they were so called because they wore the more modern and up-to-date clothes. These were loafer shoes, Ben Sherman shirts or Fred Perry polo shirts, and two-tone tonic strides (trousers). The girls had almost the same attire and haircuts as the blokes, all looking very much like the all-American college boy. They rode on scooters, such as the Vespa and the Lambretta. And for some strange reason they always had to have a fox's tail hanging from a metal rod or aerial on the back.

What the fuck a fox had done to deserve that I don't know. And what happened to the rest of the fox? God only knows!

Should these three groups meet, they would have a set-to. But when they fought, they fought among themselves and very rarely involved the public.

The 50s Teds were into rock 'n' roll: Lonnie Donegan, a young Cliff Richard, Bill Hayley, and of course Elvis Presley. The bikers were into the heavy metal music of bands such as AC/DC, Led Zeppelin, Judas Priest and Black Sabbath. The mods were into The Jam, The Kinks, the Small Faces, and The Who. A great song out in 1971 was 'Johnny Reggae' by The Piglets, which was about a girl and her love for her mod boyfriend. The video is well worth watching on YouTube.

At this time, you may be thinking why have I gone from family feuds to gang feuds? And what have all these gangs got to do with the family feuds? Well, that's what these guys and girls became when they joined these gangs: they became part of a family. Members of these gangs like the Hell's Angels, who I think were possibly the most famous or infamous bikers (rockers or greasers) of the day, had different members and gangs (or chapters, as they were known) all over the country, and when called on, they would join forces to fight other gangs. Thankfully, over the years these tribes have slowly died out or are not so prominent.

Unfortunately, though, we do still have gangs of little shits running the streets, calling each other bruv, bro or cuz, and there will always be gangs, drugs, violence and organised crime, ruining many family lives. (And perhaps it's hardly surprising, seeing as we took these kids when they were about five or six to watch Punch beat up Judy, kill the baby and attack old Jack the policeman and tell them, 'That's the way to do it.')

The police managed to quell a lot of the fighting and made lots of arrest. Some of these thugs were taken to court and were handed out silly little fines, and community services, and in some cases a short term in the nick, which did nothing to deter them.

We even had families arguing on the TV. In 1975, we had *The Good Life*, with Richard Briers and the beautiful Felicity Kendal as Tom and Barbara Good, driving their next-door
neighbours Margo and Jerry Leadbetter crazy with their attempts to be self-sufficient.

In the 80s we then had *Dynasty*, which was similar to *Dallas*, with the Carringtons versus the Colbys. This had Linda Gray, JR's now ex-wife Sue Ellen, who apparently had sobered up by now, so no longer a drunk (but apparently still a slut and an unfit mother) as Krystle Carrington, and Joan Collins as the evil Alexis Carrington Colby, both fighting over money and oil.

Albert Square had its family rows, what with Dirty Den and Angie Watts, the Beale family, and nasty Nick Cotton, all at loggerheads. Then there's *Corrie* with Ken Barlow (who's had more girlfriends than Peter Stringfellow), Sally and Kevin Webster, Gail Platt, and Rita Sullivan, all fighting in the Rovers Return over Betty's hotpot. Then there was dodgy Mike Baldwin, Vera Duckworth, and Elsie Tanner, my God … the list goes on and on all the way back to 1960, with Ena Sharples, Martha Longhurst and Mini Caldwell and her pussy called Bobby, all sitting in the snug, all drinking their bottles of milk stout.

Nowadays, it's the Trotter family (in answer to the Krays), that is Tony and Danny, the Driscoll brothers, and also Del trying to get one over on Boycie, and trying a leg-over on Marlene, having their arguments in *Only Fools and Horses*.

Unfortunately, there are families that love to be the centre of attention and no matter where you look, they're there: the Kardashians, the Beckhams (when they first arrived on the scene), Peter Andre and Katie Price (aka Jordan)

YouTube has loads of families now that are all looking out to become the next …

FAMILY IN YOUR FACE.

Now that would make a great TV game show. Each family would get points for who has the best fake tan, or lips that look like a trout's, the biggest boob job, the biggest six-pack, the best facelift, and who's the best worst actor. Then they would have to talk about how completely uninteresting they are. Finally, they would get bonus points for being up themselves so much that they totally piss you off, and bore you the most. Sadly, it can't be hosted by anyone who has previously been on any of the reality shows, such as *Love Island*, *The Only Way Is Essex*, *Made in Chelsea* and *Ex on the Beach* as no doubt they will all be applying to participate as contestants. It could be hosted by Ant and Dec, because those two seem to be in most things nowadays (what they bring to a show I just don't know). It could be about as much fun as watching that exhilarating programme *Gogglebox* (zzz...).

The majority of families just kept themselves to themselves, helping friends and other neighbours when needed, but preferring to live in the shadows of these more robust and overpowering families. I criticised the Beckhams for being an in-your-face family when they first arrived on the scene, which I felt they were, but I must say that they now seem to be a prime example of how to be famous and stay out of the spotlight.

Lots of famous people like singer Elton John, designer Stella McCartney, actors Harrison Ford and George Clooney have all kept their family lives in the background, going about their business quietly without too much fuss and attention.

We've had TV families like that. We had *The Waltons*, and what a family they were! There were about a dozen of them living in that house (talk about overcrowding), and all that shouting at bedtime: 'Good night, Mary Ellen' ... 'Good night, John-boy,' then it's 'Good night, Ben' ... That stuff would do your head in every night: by the time they had all said good night to each other, it was time to get up again. Why the fuck John-boy couldn't just shout 'good night, everyone' beats me.

Then there was the Ingalls family in *Little House on the Prairie*, with Michael Landon, who was better known at the time as Little Joe from the 60s TV series *Bonanza*, now playing Charles Ingalls, with his wife and kids. Both these families lived a reasonably quiet life (well, except at night in the Walton household), all struggling through day to day. They didn't want any hassle with their neighbouring families so it was better for them to keep their heads down and stay out of the way.

Sadly, some arguments never, ever heal for some people, and can cause a lifetime of hurt and misery. The feeling of being let down or wronged in some way will never be repaired.

Everyday life has always been a struggle for most families over the years. It doesn't matter whether you're posh and eating off the top table, or poor and eating off a park bench, there's always someone or something to have a row with or about. But nine times out of ten, most disagreements or arguments are normally sorted out with one big bust-up, then it's kiss and make up, and it's back to normal (even if only for a short while until the next one). Families stick together no matter how they feel about each other when a problem arises.

No matter what happens to you during the rest of your life, your family and loved ones will always be there for you, and you for them.

FOOTBALL RIVALS:
Family feuds

Over the years my Fulham team, like my family, has had its ups and downs (mainly downs). This has caused me grief and upset, especially when they've made a decision that I didn't agree with, but it's soon forgotten and life goes on. I, like most supporters would have to sit back and watch our owners, managers, and players fall out just like our mother, father and siblings did (and even me sometimes, well, quite a lot of times to be truthful), having a barney with each other.

Lots of owners and managers (like our parents) argue over money or feeling unappreciated or in some way let down. The players' (kids') arguments with their parents (owners and managers) are mostly about one player getting more game time than another ('he's your favourite, you prefer him more over me … boo hoo'), or one getting paid more than another (pocket money), even getting to wear someone else's shirt (clothes). This was the case with Edinson Cavani, who didn't take it too well, when after signing Ronaldo, Manchester United gave Cavani's number 7 shirt to old Ronnie boy. You can just imagine it: Eddie's gone to his locker to get ready to go out and play footie with his mates. He's looked for his favourite shirt, the one with the number 7 on, and it's missing. Well, you can almost hear him screaming and crying all over Trafford Park, 'Olieee? Olieeee? Ronnie's wearing my shirt again …! It's not fair. He keeps doing it. Tell him off, or I'm leaving home.'

Well, he didn't get his shirt back, and he did eventually pack his bags (minus the number 7 shirt), and he left home. In-club feuds and rows are nothing new.

Over the years, like most supporters, I have seen and heard of many in-house problems, arguments, and feuds. In the earlier years there were managers like Jock Stein, Bill Shankly and of course Brian Clough, who would all stand their ground against any owner or chairman, and certainly wouldn't take any crap from anyone.

Not long ago we had managers like Arsène Wenger, Sir Alex Ferguson, José Mourinho and of course, the one manager that has possibly had more rows with his bosses than Maggie Thatcher had with Arthur Scargill during the miners' strike in the 80s: that's Neil Warnock. Love him or hate him, he said it as it was, and he took no shit.

All these managers would row and argue with the owners of their clubs, especially if the money for new players wasn't available, or their results were being questioned.

There were players like Billy Bremner, Norman 'bites yer legs' Hunter, and big Jack Charlton at Leeds United; Tommy Smith, Emlyn 'crazy horse' Hughes, and Graeme Souness at Liverpool. And at Manchester United there was Gordon McQueen, big Joe Jordan, and Roy Keane. Spurs had players like Dave Mackay,

Alan Mullery, and Graham Roberts. All these, and many more players over the years, would have arguments on and off the field with their managers and teammates, time and time again. All these men were as hard as nails. Bill Shankly once said of Tommy Smith, 'Smith wasn't born, but quarried.'

They would fight each other, and they would fight *for* each other. But no matter what, at the end of the day, they were a family. Not so long ago we had Sir Alex Ferguson allegedly throwing cups and saucers about the changing room. Now, as I stated earlier, a smack on the bum is fine by me, but hitting your child with a boot is not on, which again allegedly is what Sir Alex did to poor old Becks. (Bet the civil rights weren't at his front door. Did he get done for assault? No, he didn't even get done by the courts for illegally driving up the hard shoulder of the motorway, stating he was dying for a crap, and looking for a shithouse.)

I wonder, as the old joke goes, when he told the policeman he was looking for a shithouse, did the policeman reply, 'You've found one'? If that had been me or you, it would be a £500 fine, a loss of licence for a year or two, and ten lashes in the stocks. (I think I did mention earlier my not having much time for Manchester United, or some of their southern supporters)

Back in around 1999–2000, Fulham's Chris Coleman allegedly had a set-to with our striker 'su-u-per, super Geoff (repeat twice more), super Geoffrey Horsfield' behind closed doors. And in 2008 on the pitch, Aleksandar Mitrović was not on fire but absolutely fuming when he and Aboubakar Kamara had a set-to after a disagreement over who should take a penalty. Against the wishes of just about everyone in the ground, Kamara won, and the silly bollocks went and missed it. Luckily Mitro was on fire a little later in the match and scored the winner.

We've seen the Newcastle pair, Lee Bowyer and Kieran Dyer, both getting sent off for fighting in 2005, and Emmanuel Adebayor and Nicholas ('I didn't say "I am the best in the world") Bendtner, having a confrontation while playing for Arsenal in 2008. In 1993, Steve McManaman and Liverpool goalkeeper Bruce Grobbelaar had a handbag ruck after a bad pass by McManaman led to a goal for the bitter enemy ... Everton. Just about every club and every supporter throughout the divisions go at it at one stage with other.

It's family life

Then there's the other type of family arguments, those between two clubs (family versus family) and we have all seen them over the years. We've seen the parents of these clubs arguing on the touchline, the same as our mothers used to when I was a kid, and I've done it myself several times over the years, protecting my family. There they are on the sidelines, screaming and shouting, pointing fingers, accusations flying in all directions, blaming the opposing players when there's a bad tackle or a fight on the pitch.

There always seem to be one or two parents that are bigger and louder than most. José Mourinho, Sir Alex Ferguson, Arsène Wenger, Antonio Conte, Pep Guardiola, Jürgen Klopp. All parents of bigger families, all fighting and arguing, defending their kids. We've watched Fergie and Kevin ('I will love it ... love it!') Keegan, Fergie and Arsène ('I er ... er coudder not see dat') Wenger, and José Mourinho having handbags at dawn (or it could be at half past twelve, four o'clock, quarter to eight or eight o'clock, depending on the TV networks) with just about everyone in the league (the street).

Every parent of every club, no matter what size they are, or what league they are in, will defend their family. Lots of opposing players on the pitch will end up having a set-to during a match. In the 2011–12 season, Joey Barton tried to take on the whole Manchester City team. In 2001, there was heat between Roy Keane and Alan Shearer, and in the same year, Keane's over-the-top tackle on Alf-Inge Haaland. Then in 1998, there was a

Paolo Di Canio and Patrick Vieira fight that not only involved them both getting red cards but in the melee, the poor ref, Paul Alcock, fell to the ground quite dramatically when pushed by Di Canio.

Then there was Eden Hazard, who in 2013 got a red card after trying to retrieve a ball back from a ball boy who decided not to do what his job was. This was because his team Swansea were 2–0 up against Chelsea so he laid on top of the ball to waste time. (In my mind, the ball boy, whom I will not name as I don't want to make him out as some sort of hero, should be banned from ever working for the club again, if he isn't already.)

During all these, and many other on and off the pitch fights, the stadium security (police) have many times been involved, trying to calm things down, but no matter what the outcome is it will almost certainly end up in the court of the FA. They will give out fines and bans to the culprits, and fines, bans and threats of ground closures to the clubs.

Then there's the argument over tapping up (chatting up) or poaching, trying to break up a relationship between a team and a player, which is deemed illegal by the FA if written consent isn't first agreed upon by the player's club. But it goes on, on a regular basis.

Then there's gazumping, coming in with a late bid and nicking a player who was just about to sign for another club. That goes on a lot. Apparently in 2004, Arjen Robben was about to sign for Manchester United then Chelsea came in at the last knocking, presumably with a better offer, and he signed for them. In 2001, Ben Davies was about to sign for Celtic only as Neil Lennon states 'to be gazumped by Liverpool'. In 2013, Liverpool's hopes of signing the Brazilian player Willian was knocked back when Chelsea came in and pinched him from under their noses. They tell the player that they will shower them with all the riches in the world, that they are top of their wish list, they have admired them from afar for years, and they beg them, their agents and family with pound signs. They want them for the next four to five years, unless you get too old before then (like a lot of boyfriend–girlfriend relationships when one gets too old or is not performing, it's time to look for a younger model).

Like the gang problems that we've had in our private lives, there have (and unfortunately will always be) gang problems at football matches, such is the passion that the game brings. It's normally matches between two clubs in the same city, such as United and City in Manchester; Celtic and Rangers in Glasgow; Hibs and Hearts in Edinburgh; Arsenal and Spurs; West Ham and Millwall; Aston Villa and Birmingham. Sometimes the rivalry is between clubs that are just a good few miles apart, such as Newcastle and Sunderland, or Portsmouth and Southampton; the list goes on. Lots of these derbies have always brought out bad rivalry and hatred between the supporters of their football families.

Sadly, some of the hatred goes back so far that most of the fans and supporters don't even know why, or what's it about, such as the problem between Portsmouth and Southampton that started in 1930. Crystal Palace and Brighton, although 50 miles apart, have been bitter rivals since before most of their supporters were born.

The Tottenham–Arsenal supporters' hatred is just because they live near each other, and I suppose it didn't help matters too much when Sol Campbell signed for the arch-enemy, Arsenal, especially after Tottenham made a statement to say that there was no way he would ever be seen in an Arsenal shirt. Well, he was. And he doesn't regret it one ounce. The youngsters hear about the stories of old, and they feel it's OK to carry on with the nastiness.

If we go back again to the 50s and early 60s, going to a match was something special. There was no segregation at the grounds, and all supporters were standing together, YES, standing. They were all singing their own songs of praise to their own team, shouting out encouragement. Now we have to sit. Have you ever tried to sit and sing out loud? I've only ever known one person who could actually sit in a chair (and occasionally on a stool) and sing, and that was Val Doonican. (I can hear you youngsters now singing ('Who are yer?' 'Who are yer?') and to be fair, did you ever hear him? Sorry, Val but it was crap.)

Unlike nowadays, the players used to get the bus or walk to the games with the supporters from both sides and they'd have a great banter with everyone. Could you imagine Robbie Savage walking to a game in Nottingham or Derby now? I don't think the banter would be quite the same. Or Gary Neville walking through Stanley Park on his way to Anfield, having a jolly with the scousers. Or how about Big Sol Campbell walking down White Hart Lane. Or Stanley Victor Collymore walking along the road to St Andrew's, Birmingham. It just isn't going to happen. No, times had changed.

Supporters years ago stood shoulder to shoulder and cheered their team on. Or you could if you wished go to the end your team was attacking in the first half and at half-time you could walk a to the other end, passing the opposition's supporters who were doing the same without many problems. After the game you could all walk to the bus or train together and have a bit of friendly banter.

Over the years, Fulham have been pretty lucky in that we haven't have many problems regarding supporters getting out of control. We did have a hiccup though a few years back when in 2006, we finally beat our next-door neighbours Chelsea 1–0 at the Cottage, and a few Fulham idiots ran on to the pitch, baiting the Chelsea supporters, and even though they should not have done it, it was more out of relief and excitement that we had finally beaten them after years of being in their shadow. Even though one win didn't change our standing, it felt so good at the time. Sadly, that feeling doesn't last long.

Some people get carried away and their actions are more out of joy than to start any type of violent disorder. I remember back in the 70s once when we had an evening match against Arsenal. After the game three or four mates and I were in the chippy on the Fulham Palace Road when a few of their supporters ran in, threw a few punches at us and ran out. No particular harm done, but one of my mates kept complaining about his back hurting where this idiot had punched him, only to find out when he got home that he had been stabbed. Luckily it was more like a small puncture wound, so he had a couple of stitches at the hospital and was fine a few days later. It was just a rare incident, and I have never experienced anything like it since (I just hope it stays that way in future).

Another time at an evening match against Arsenal, a friend of mine, who is a gooner, came along with me to watch the game. It was his first time at the Cottage, and he was absolutely gobsmacked when after the game, both sets of supporters walked back to Putney Bridge Station together, through Bishops Park, in the dark without any trouble, and I'm pleased to say that it's still the same today as it was then (most games).

It was from the late 60s on when the hooligans started to come out in force, and there were some grounds where you were better off arriving early to avoid any problems before the game. For safety reasons they'd keep the away supporters in after the game to allow the nutters to get back home and into their cages. There were grounds where you couldn't wear your team's colours; grounds where there was wire fencing separating the two sets of supporters and a load of poor little sods wearing those bright yellow steward jackets. Some of these poor kids were so small their jackets looked as if they still had the coat hangers in them, and some so young-looking it seemed they would be better off at the Saturday morning pictures, watching kids' cartoons, or at McDonald's eating a kid's Happy Meal, rather than working as a human shield just for a little extra cash.

We had the Teds, rockers and mods upsetting our everyday lives in one way, shape, or another. Unfortunately, in our football lives we had football hooligans. We got that with the emergence of the dreaded skinhead. This species had not been seen or heard of since the last caveman, and it was thought that they had, or hoped to have, become extinct. This group unfortunately took society and football to a new low. They were so thick and gormless-looking with their shaved heads, scars, tattoos and Dr.

Martens boots (and that was just the women). They mostly listened to a mixture of reggae, ska, and blue beat: bands like The Specials, Madness, Desmond Dekker, and Bad Manners, all fabulous bands and music.

Most of the bigger teams had what was known as a 'crew' or 'firm'. They were nasty little bastards, who thought it took some sort of courage or bravery to run around in gangs, kicking the shit out of other supporters who had dared to come to watch their team on a match day. Teams like Birmingham had The Zulus; West Ham, ICF (Inter City Firm); Chelsea, the Headhunters; and the most fearful of all, the Grimsby Town crew known as the Cleethorpes Beach Patrol (now there's a crew to steer clear of, especially when you're on the beach). They possibly got their fighting experience from watching the Punch and Judy shows: 'That's the way they did it.'

Matches were full of trouble, inside and outside the ground, with fights starting at most of the big city grounds. There were also lots of problems during many of the local derby games, with rivals who tended to think that their team was better than yours, and they were tougher than you. The police managed to quell a lot of the fighting and made lots of arrest. Some of these thugs were taken to court and handed out silly little fines, and community services, and in some cases given a stadium ban. None of this did anything to deter them.

Due to the internet, football thugs changed their tactics and made arrangements with the opposition of the day to meet up somewhere out of the way of the ground, and the police. There they could fight till their hearts content, or until last man standing. These were not just fisty cuffs, a quick slap and tickle. These gangs came armed to the hilt, ready to cause damage: knives, knuckle-dusters, bike chains and various types of wooden batons.

Lots of films were made, sadly glorifying this mentality, films like *Green Street*, *The Football Factory*, *Awaydays* and *The Firm* with Gary Oldman. Books such as *Skinhead*, *Boot Boys*, *Suedehead*, and *Skinhead Girls* by Richard Allen are a great read, even though they glorify the violence Joe Hawkins and his crew dished out.

I'm pleased to say that we don't have too many problems at matches nowadays, and it's a lot safer to take our wives and kids. And long may that remain.

There have been behind-the-scenes TV documentaries about footballers and football families, such as *Sunderland 'Til I Die*; *All or Nothing: Manchester City*; *Take Us Home: Leeds United*; *The Class of '92* featuring six young lads at Manchester United; and *Make Us Dream*, which reflects on the career of the Liverpool legend Steven Gerrard.

There have also been great light-hearted shows, for example: *Mike Bassett, England Manager*, starring Ricky Tomlinson; *Bend It Like Beckham*, with Parminder Nagra and Keira Knightley; *The Dammed United*, reflecting on Brian Clough's short reign at Leeds United, with Michael Sheen; and *The Mean Machine* in 2001, starring the ex-footballer Vinnie 'Ha, ha, ha, ha, stayin' alive' Jones, and Jason Statham.

Unfortunately, there are clubs and players that love to be the centre of attention, and no matter where you look, they're there, in your face, day in and day out, and it's the so-called Big Six again: Manchester City, Liverpool, Chelsea, Tottenham, Arsenal, and Manchester United. It doesn't matter where you look, they're there. Sky Sports, talkSPORT, BT Sport and every single newspaper in the world. It does your head in. And now it looks as if Newcastle is sooner or later going to make it the Big Seven. So it's basically fuck all the rest of the teams. Who cares what's going on in their lives?

It's the same with the players: if Ronaldo farts, it becomes a headline or breaking news (should be breaking wind); if Jack Grealish buys a new hair-band, it's news; if David Beckham wants to wear a skirt, so what? And who cares that John Terry's mother and mother-in-law shop at Tesco, and forgot to pay? Who cares if a football player's baby gets its first tooth (I made that one up)? It drives you potty. It's got nothing to do with football.

Lots of other clubs live in the shadows of these financial bullies. Everyday life has always been a struggle for most clubs over the years. It doesn't matter whether you're posh and eating at the top table (Premier League) or poor and eating off a park bench (the Isthmian League, no disrespect intended), there is always someone or something to row with. But nine times out of ten, any disagreements or arguments on or off the pitch are normally sorted out in one big bust-up, then it's kiss and make up at the end of the game. Then it's back to normal (even if only for a short while, until the next game comes around).

Most teams stick together no matter how they feel about each other when a problem arises. No matter what happens to you in the rest of your life, your team and loved ones will always be there for you, and you for them.

Chapter Nine

Neighbours
DERBIES

Good neighbours, bad neighbours:
GOOD SUPPORTERS, BAD SUPPORTERS

Most people trusted their neighbours in those dark days gone by. Front doors were left unlocked and the neighbours who were always on the ear to borrow something (a cup of sugar or the like), well they would just push the door open, shout out a 'yoo-hoo, it's only me' and basically just stroll in. There was no real need for security alarms or three or four locks on the doors, or bars on the windows. More or less, everybody shared what they had with each other. Most neighbours got on well with each other. Although that's not to say that everything in the neighbourhood was hunky-dory. People in these towns and cities weren't living like Mormons, so there was always someone having a bit of trouble with someone else somewhere. But if you were incapacitated in some way, or needed any kind of help with things like shopping, household chores, cutting the grass, or looking after the kids, then you could always rely on the neighbours to give a hand or to send their kids in. Now it might cost you a shilling or two, but they were always there to give a hand until you got back on your feet.

People also seemed more tolerant towards each other. Most people had been born in the house that they lived in, and because people tended not to move around that often, we all got used to each other's ways. We knew where we all stood regarding the likes and dislikes of each and everyone around us.

After all the fighting that the War had brought, people were more interested in getting their lives back together and helping each other than having rows. As I said, front doors were never locked (how times have changed). Nowadays you wouldn't dream of going out and leaving the doors open, or the front door key under the door mat or hanging on a piece of string behind the front door so the kids can let themselves in when they come home from school.

I think things started to change in the late 50s and early 60s when new towns like Corby, Bracknell, Runcorn, and Washington on the Tyne and Wear were built. Communities were broken up and people were moved from one part of a city to the outskirts of these different towns. Now all of a sudden you had strangers living next door to each other, and most of them had very little in common, all coming from different backgrounds and lots of different countries, whereas before, all the men had worked together shoulder to shoulder in local factories. They would all meet up at the local pub after work or at the weekend and get pie-eyed while the wives stayed at home looking after the kids and getting the old man's meal ready for when he came home from work or the pub.

The kids all attended the same local school. Life was hard, but simple. No lack of sugar was ever a problem, you'd just pop next door and borrow some. If anyone was short of anything there was always a neighbour there to lend a hand.

The only thing the people of the new towns did have in common was that the War had changed all their lives forever. The conclusion of the War meant there was plenty of work in all areas of the country. The damaged factories, shops and houses had to be demolished and rebuilt, and due to the loss of lives that meant people had to be brought in from outer areas. People were invited from abroad to come to England to work on the trains and buses. Many people came from Ireland to help build roads and houses, but even though they came with good intentions to work and make better lives for themselves, it didn't go down well with the white British worker. Rooms in guest houses and pubs put up signs stating NO BLACKS, NO IRISH, NO DOGS. The British didn't want all these so-called foreigners coming over here and taking our work on the cheap.

In 1965, the BBC gave us the comedy show *Til Death Us Do Part* with Warren Mitchell playing the role of the racist bigot

Alf Garnett, and Dandy Nichols as his sad and long-suffering wife, Else (or 'silly old moo'). And in 1972, the ITV aired another comedy show, *Love Thy Neighbour,* with Jack Smethurst as the racist Eddie Booth, and Rudolph Walker as Bill Reynolds, his black next-door neighbour who suffered no end of racist abuse and insults. Even though at the time both these programmes were seen as hilarious and were a TV hit, both epitomised the way lots of the British public thought and acted.

In 1958, we should have seen the early warning signs of what was to come when the Notting Hill race riots blew up between the white British and the West Indian black community. Enoch Powell made his famous 'Rivers of Blood' speech, which made the country even more anti-foreigner. In those days, we didn't recognise it as racism; people were just wary of anybody of a different colour, or anybody who spoke a different language. Just about every community had some kind of trouble with neighbours fighting over and over again, and gangs got bigger and stronger. Local neighbourhood gangs would meet and fight it out over the running of each territory.

The 60s through to the early 2,000s brought in even more migrant workers, this time from countries like Pakistan and India, to work as cheap labour. More and more people were up in arms because as the country was starting to get back to what was classed as normal, the immigrants were seen as getting more of the jobs and council housing, and getting better financial aid when they had only just arrived in the country a few days before. Different commissions were set up to help people from overseas to integrate into the British way of life, but they were still not welcome. When we joined the EU, the country was even more open to workers from overseas than ever before, and even though we accept that there is still racism in many workplaces and society in general, people are working harder to try to solve the problem.

The country is slowly becoming more and more aware of not only the problem of racism but also sexism, homophobia, and all different types of diversities. Unfortunately, that neighbourly spirit isn't as strong as it was. Front doors are no longer left open. There is no more keys on strings behind the door. If you run out of sugar, then it's no good knocking on the neighbour's door. Sadly, most people don't even know who their neighbours are.

We now had a four-tier society: the poor, the working class, the very well off, and then there was the mega-rich.

The poor struggled each and every day, living on hand-outs, trying to keep their heads above water, unable to work for one reason or another. They were doing their shopping at some of the red spot shops, like the pound stores, or Primark or the local charity shops for their clothing.

The working-class families soon got their lives sorted out; people found steady jobs and became good stable families in the community and they would go about their daily chores in their neighbourhoods. It is the unsung heroes who do the jobs that go unnoticed: the lollipop ladies and men outside schools and on zebra crossings, school dinner ladies (are there school dinner men?), and people who work in the charity shops. All are working for a pittance, who have very little, but never complain.

How many of these people win awards or were recognised by the Queen or the PM when OBEs or CBEs are being handed out? These are the bargain bucket brigade. You don't see them in the big posh stores like Selfridges, or Harrods buying £2–£300 food hampers. The nearest they get to a food hamper is a family bucket from KFC (and there's nothing wrong with a bit of the colonel's finest chicken as a treat after a good honest day's work). They had no fancy cars and designer suits or footwear, no eating at the top restaurants.

The very well off we all noticed. They were those people that we thought had a good few quid. But, sadly though, it was all show, all put on (two cars in the drive, fuck-all in the fridge; all hat and no drawers). They thought that they were better than they were. They thought they were better than all the others like them. They turned their noses up at their neighbours, which caused even more problems between families. They were like Hyacinth Bucket (or should I say Bouquet), played by the wonderful Patricia Routledge in *Keeping Up Appearances*. You can just hear her when the phone rings: 'The Bouquet residence, the lady of the house speaking.' Marvellous stuff. There was also Margo and Jerry Leadbetter looking down on poor old Tom and Barbara Good in *The Good Life*.

The very, very rich families wanted for nothing; they had big houses, big cars, and even bigger bank accounts. They were happy to employ the cheap and overseas workers as nannies, gardeners, housekeepers, and chauffeurs. They were a lot like Margo Leadbetter, who had now changed her name to Audrey Forbes-Hamilton in *To the Manor Born*. Well, she was rich until her husband died and left her in an enormous amount of debt.

They could afford to pay whatever was required to keep them close to the top of the local tree and be the envy of everybody in the neighbourhood. The mega-rich oligarchs were totally untouchable, even looking down on the rich families from afar. For these people the sky was the limit, they paid other people to do the job of keeping them on top. And sadly, to this day, we still have the four-tier class society.

The poor are even poorer. The working class are working even harder and even longer. And the very well off are getting even more weller-offerer (I made that one up).

The very, very rich are even richer, and are basically ruling all the lives and the ways of the people of the local neighbourhood. They sit down with the LOCAL COUNCILLORS, BANKERS, WEALTHY LOCAL SHOP OWNERS, and basically anyone with some kind of letters after their name. They are all making local decisions for their benefit and bugger the rest of us, all getting their snouts in the trough or eating out of each other's greedy little trotters.

DERBIES:
Neighbours

Football over the years has taken the same route. Most clubs were owned by a local businessman, and most people supported their local team. Very rarely was there a problem between the football families or their supporters. Looking back to when I was a young lad in the late 50s and early 60s, football supporters like our neighbours caused very few problems. Down at the Cottage on match days both home and away, all supporters would use the same turnstiles. They would stand together side by side on the terraces, waiting for the teams to appear, never any real trouble, laughing and joking with plenty of verbal banter.

Once the teams had tossed to see which end they were attacking, their supporters would move from one end of the ground to the other, to the goal their team was attacking. Half-time would come and while the teams were having their slice of orange, a cup of tea and no doubt a quick fag, both sets of supporters would change ends.

In all my time watching Fulham I hardly ever saw any problems as the supporters passed each other. There was lots of verbal, but very little trouble. I remember when I was about seven or eight going to White Hart Lane with my brother-in-law Les, who was a big Spurs fan. He had a grocer's shop near the ground, so when I used to stay there some weekends, he would take me to see some of the great players that Spurs had back in the late 50 and 60s: Danny Blanchflower, Dave Mackay, Cliff Jones, John White, the list was endless. What a team they were that in 1960–61 season that went on to do the then magical double.

I remember one particular day, Spurs were playing the mighty Liverpool, and the place was packed. I needed to have a piss (or, as a little kid, I needed a wee-wee). Les asked if I knew where the toilets were, which I did, so off I went. (It was deemed to be safe in those days.) Business done, I tried to get back to where

Les was standing, which was down the front, right behind the goal. I tried to push my way through, and being so little, I tried to get through between their legs. I tried nudging them, but not being that strong I was getting nowhere. Then one of the Scousers asked me what I was trying to do. I told him I needed to get back to my brother-in-law who was behind the goal. With that he picked me up, and with the help of the Liverpool and Spurs fans, together they proceeded to hand me across their heads and back to where Les was. This wasn't just a one-off. Many times before, during and after a match, wherever it might have been, I have helped other teams' supporters or have been helped in many ways by them.

Once after Fulham had played at St Andrew's, the home of Birmingham City, I was leaving the ground with my daughter, son, and a friend, when a few idiot Birmingham supporters who were out for a fight, came along shouting, 'Let's get the southern bastards.' A small group of older Brummies, seeing we could be the target, gathered around us for protection until these dick-heads passed by.

The only funny side to this incident was that the very kind people who were helping us said, 'Quick, come and stand in among us and try to look inconspicuous.' Unfortunately, Fulham in their infinite wisdom had that season given us a sort of bright fluorescent green away shirt, so to be inconspicuous was really out of the question.

Thankfully we got out of there without any more problems. But, sadly, that day their supporters smashed one of our supporters' buses so badly that they had to get another one to bring the supporters back to London. When one of the Birmingham bosses at that time, a certain Ms Karren Brady was asked about the incident, she replied something about us playing Stan Collymore, who was an ex-Aston Villa player, and who is not exactly the fans' favourite, and she said he was the reason for it.

PATHETIC!

During the Second World War (that sounded just like Uncle Albert from *OFAH*), football Divisions One and Two were split into teams from the North and the South. This was to keep travelling down to a minimum. The leagues got back to normal not long after the War. 1957–1958 saw the amalgamation of Division Three, North and South, and also Divisions Four, North and South. The football world was a community again. We now had a 4-division football league. Local teams would help each other out. Movement of players was rare, and if they did move, the chances were that it would be to another local team.

Division Four was just where you didn't want to be. Teams in this division had virtually nothing and generally played to a small group of very loyal supporters. They were having to get players from wherever they could, at times, just to make the numbers up.

Division Three had slightly better prospects and fed off any decent players that Division Four might have had, working harder and harder to keep their place in the football middle-class world.

Then there was Division Two. These were the teams that wanted to get up the league as quickly as possible. These were the teams that thought they had the right to be up there. Most had more money than the teams in the divisions below and could get the pick of whoever they wanted, from almost anywhere they wanted. They had the lower teams doing their work for them: finding and training the players, getting them to a greater standard, and then they would jump in and offer the player more money, a better standard of play, and then pay the team they were going to snatch him from very little in the way of a transfer fee or remuneration for the hard work they'd done.

Division One had the top boys. This was the place where everyone in the other three divisions aspired to be. These were the super-rich of their day. Money was no object; the bosses paid the top people to do their work and keep them top of the pile.

But things changed in 1992 with the start of the Premier League. The football community started to break up. Teams were less willing to help each other out, the reason being that they were all now fighting for the same goal. Money had taken over the game. The game now became a business.

Why help your competitor? More foreign managers and owners took over. You now knew nothing about the people in your community. Managers like Alex Ferguson and Arsène Wenger had touchline spats, as did Kevin Keegan and Sir Alex, José Mourinho and Wenger. Later, like most neighbours, they would kiss and make up. Manchester United apparently had a very noisy neighbour in Manchester City, and what a noise they have been making ever since.

Division One became the Premier League, Division Two became the Football League Championship, and Divisions Three and Four became Divisions One and Two. Like the different classes in our everyday life, we now had a four-tier league. Division Two were still the paupers, Division One the middle tier, representing the working class, then the slightly richer in the Championship, and the mega-rich in the Premier League.

The teams in the top two divisions started to bring in more and more players from abroad: they were cheaper to buy, were paid less, and tried harder to get their first team place. This didn't go down well with the local players and supporters as they were taking the place of some of their teammates, and the supporters' heroes. The influx of foreign players has now totally taken over the top two leagues to the extent that some people are calling for a cap on the number of overseas players that a team can field or buy.

Sadly, like in our everyday lives the mega-rich clubs do what they want and when they want to do it, as they have shown lately by pushing and getting five substitutions instead of three for 2022–23, which again really only benefits the bigger teams who can afford to have a better stronger bench. They will set their terms and bugger the rest of the football society. And our football Government (FIFA, UEFA, and our own FA) will bow down to them. By doing so, they will join anyone with some kind of letters after their name, and they will all take their seats at the top table of sporting events courtesy of the TV COMPANIES, SPONSORS, THE MONEY MEN and LARGE CONGLOMERATES, all getting their snouts in the trough or eating out of each other's greedy trotters.

Chapter Ten

School to work
ACADEMY TO PLAY

Wise men say 'only fools rush in':
COACHES SAY 'STAY ON YOUR FEET'

At home in the 1950s and 60s our parents taught us to be respectful of our elders. We had to help out around the house before we could go out to play. We had to do the cleaning, the washing-up, and chasing after our older brothers and sisters. We were brought up well, and worked long and hard. Our parents watched over us and defended us to the hilt, protecting us against the problems of the world.

Then it was off to school to learn the wise ways of the world, and to learn for our future. In the mid-50s I went to Granard Infant School when I was about five years old. Infant school was about learning to play and share with the other kids: working together on how to build the Empire State Building out of used toilet roll tubes, or designing the Cutty Sark out of egg boxes; making spaceships out of empty Corn Flakes packets; and painting horrendous pictures of what was supposed to be your parents or your teacher, which made them look like something out of *Hammer House of Horrors* or an *Alien* movie. When I think back, they were good times.

The teachers were kind and patient, and did the best for us with what they had to work with i.e., toilet rolls, egg boxes etc. It was then on to Granard Junior School in Putney when I was seven. Schools back then were very basic, and you didn't need to take anything with you in those days. Leaving infant school and going up to junior school wasn't as daunting as I expected it to be as most of those in class at my infant school went up with me and into the same class. We all moved on together.

Then at about the age of eleven, I went to Elliott Comprehensive, also in Putney. Now, when you went to the so-called bigger school you needed a satchel, pen and pencil set, geometry set (protractor, set squares etc.) and text books.

We each had our own old wooden desk whose lid you could lift up and push forward so you were out of the teacher's sight. Then you could have a sly chat with your mate who sat alongside you, or pull stupid or silly faces to make you mates laugh during class, and get them into trouble. If they were caught once, they would end up with after-school detention. But if they were caught too many times, they would end up getting the cane or slipper across their arse, or even suspension. Now the best thing about this wooden desk lid was that if you pissed the teacher off, then when they threw the blackboard rubber (or whiteboard wiper, as I believe it is now known as), or slung the metal wastepaper bin at you, it would act as a great defensive shield.

The table also had a little ink-well which held pens with a rubber tube in them that we all had. We'd undo the barrel of the pen, pull out the rubber tube, which had the nib of the pen attached, stick the nib into the ink-well, push a small metal bar in against the rubber tube, and then release it. This would draw the ink into the rubber tube. Then we would screw it back into the pen's tube. Now this sounds dead easy, which it was, but what a bloody mess it made! You ended up with ink all over your fingers that stayed there for days on end. It didn't help the fact that as young kids we didn't exactly take kindly to washing ourselves. If you got ink on your nice new school shirt, God, were you in trouble when you got home. Your mum would do her nut because she'd probably only just bought it from Woolworths or British Home Stores, or, perhaps even worse, she'd had a loan from the Provident man, so she still had to pay for it on the never-never (weekly). With the interest charge on top, it was even more expensive than if she had paid cash for it (which sadly lots of families couldn't afford to do). Thank heavens for the invention of the Biro. (Mind you, even *they* leaked, but not as much.)

School was now a completely new challenge. After doing your eleven-plus exam you were graded on your exam results. So you were now placed into new classes with all different kids that you didn't know from Adam (or Eve), different social backgrounds, each kid trying to make their mark on their new colleagues, which didn't always work out as you can imagine. The loud and extrovert ones took to the fore, trying to undermine those who were quiet and less assuming. Those with the ability but had no ambition, made fun and disrupted the class for those with a lesser ability but who wanted to improve themselves.

It was a tough learning curve in life and it became dog eat dog (or God ate God, for those who had trouble reading). Aah, they were the best years of our lives, we were told, or so it was meant to be, and when I look back like most of us tend to do in later years, it was. But looking back, did we ever listen to our parents, elders, or our teachers then? Those people around us that knew what was right and what was wrong. Not really. They were old fogies. What did they know about our generation!! They were all out of touch. We never, ever got it into our heads that our parents did the same things when they were our age. So they probably did know the true consequences of our actions, but we still thought we knew best.

We couldn't be told, or if we could, we didn't listen. Basically, we couldn't be bothered. It was all too boring, boring, boring, or as Dame Lauren Alesha Masheka Tanesha Felicia Jane Cooper, aka Catherine Tate, would say, 'Am I bovvered?' We had got this far by learning day by day, so we thought we could carry on as we were. We didn't see the point of looking into the future. It was enough worrying about what was going on in our day-to-day environment. All we wanted to do was have fun with our mates, play sport, chase the girls, listen to music, and watch the television. We didn't want to worry about tomorrow because tomorrow would take care of itself when it came. Most of us weren't interested in what or where we would be in ten or so years. The past was a bore. Who cared about what went on in the past as in that great line in the Monty Python film *The Life of Brian*

178

that went, 'What have the Romans ever done for us?' Most of us didn't care what the Romans had done, we weren't interested in learning another language, we were English, most of the world spoke English, and if they didn't, then they should. Most of us were conceited and lazy and thought the world should go along with us. Today was today as far as we were concerned, and that was that.

Even some of those who had a gift never fulfilled their potential. I'm sure we all know old schoolmates who should have gone on to better things but ended up wasting their talent. They got to a certain standard, thought that was it, they were there, and they stopped listening to those who could take them on to a higher level, make them even better than they were. They let their egos take over. The you-can't-tell-me syndrome came into their lives, and alas they failed to reach the stardom that was theirs for the taking.

It was only the clever ones who took notice of what there was to learn, and most went on to be something or somebody. Everything should have been so simple. Some who had the brains to succeed chose not to. They wasted their lives away on drugs or drink. It seemed the older we got, the worst we got. Schools nowadays are so different with all the different types of technology that are available to the students. It's easier to keep up with what's going on in the world.

All schools back in the day were basically British and white. There were a few foreigners that stayed here after the War or came to seek asylum, but it wasn't until the late 50s and the early 60s when we started to get more people from overseas coming to Britain to live and work. Firstly, they came from Ireland and then the West Indies, and the Caribbean to work for London Transport. Then along came Sikhs from the Punjab, followed eventually by more and more immigrants all looking for work. The Government rubbed their hands together as did the large businesses, because this would amount to cheap labour. Schools now became multicultural and we started to take note of how other people from all around the world lived. Then, for some reason, over the years our mentality changed. Night schools became more prevalent; we began to study more and more as we came to realise that if we learnt more, then we have a better chance of success in life.

Lots of our parents seeing this started to take over the household chores. There was no more cleaning, scrubbing, and chasing around after everyone for us. Our family was more interested in our future. We still helped out at home, but the pressure of learning made it more important to study. Those that didn't quite make the grade started to become disillusioned and rebellious and started to upset the rest of the class. These were quickly moved on or were warned, and most after seeing the evil of their ways, buckled down and worked harder, having been given another chance. Some grabbed it with both hands, others just couldn't be 'bovvered'.

Private schools were the envy of a lot of the lower classes, and were only for anyone that was good enough or had the potential to be good enough to go onto bigger or better things, and of course those that could afford to go to them. But sometimes even money cannot produce a winner, especially if you don't have a certain amount of knowledge, skill, or the right attitude. Those who were really bothered about their own future worked hard and then went on to bigger and better educational institutes. Universities such as Oxford and Cambridge and colleges like Eton were their aim, but only a few back then made it, or could afford it. It was a massive achievement to get to this standard, but unfortunately most fell by the wayside under the pressure and the expectations.

About 40 or so years ago I lived in Eton Wick, which is just a short walk from Eton College. I used to see these college boys walking about the town in their robes, and I used to think about what a life those boys had. It seemed they were all born with that silver spoon in their mouths, with the rich parents, the big family homes, cars, boats, and holidays in exotic places. What more could you ask for? Then one afternoon I was having a beer and playing pool with a couple of mates at a pub in the Wick called the Three Horseshoes when three lads walked in. Straight away you could see they were from the college, just by the way they walked, their haircuts and the clothes that they were wearing, which possibly cost more than I got in wages in a month.

The landlord at the time should have asked them for their ID, but he already knew they were under age, it was quiet, and there was nobody around, so what the hell. They were just a few lads who used to come into the village for a sly drink away from the college masters. These three lads joined in with us playing pool. After a few games, we sat with them for a short while and I commented on what a great life they must have (and no doubt would have in the future). Then one of them said:

'Please don't take this the wrong way, but some of us would rather have a life like you have: the freedom of choice to go and do what you want, when you want. You don't have the problems and the pressure we have from our parents. We don't have a choice. If you failed at school, your parents would most probably be unhappy, but we don't have that privilege. We have to succeed, we cannot fail; it's not acceptable.'

You could hear in this lad's voice the pressure he was under. It made me realise money is not everything.

Top schools always have the top teachers; you wouldn't find 'old privet hedges' John Alderton out of *Please Sir!* teaching at Oxford or Eton, or Sydney Poitier out of *To Sir with Love* at Cambridge. No, all the top teachers tended to be dons or masters from the top institutes around the country. Very few, if any, kids from my school days went on to top schools or universities. Lots of them stayed on into the sixth form, and for some this was to better themselves. For others, it was a great excuse not to leave and it was a way out of having to find a job.

Many of them went on to college (not Eton, I hasten to say) and hopefully made names for themselves. Those that couldn't be bothered left school and got everyday jobs in factories, shops, warehouses, and the like. In the earlier years it was pretty easy to walk out of one job and straight into another; there were always local job vacancies at the local labour exchange. This was a government building where you could go if you were looking for employment. You could wander down there and there would be information cards pinned to boards, showing local companies looking for staff. You'd take the card to a receptionist who would fill out a form and then ring the company and make an appointment for you to have an interview with the said company.

As the years moved on, due to more people from overseas coming to work in England, jobs became harder to get, so if you left school without some sort of qualification jobs with decent pay were harder to find. Factories, shops, and warehouses were all now taking on more overseas workers on a lot less pay and in poorer conditions. The workers unions fought hard for the right of the British workers, trying to get the Government of the day to halt or put a limit on how many immigrants were coming into Britain to take our jobs. If, like nowadays, you left school and were out of work, you were entitled to unemployment benefit. To get it you had to go to the Labour Exchange once a fortnight to sign on. Due to the lack of permanent jobs, people would sign on and get their allowance and then go and do a day's work cash in hand, helping a local tradesman or friend who was also looking for cheap labour. This pissed the Government off no end, because no one declared it. It meant that some people got two lots of dosh *and* evaded paying any tax on the cash-in-hand job.

The Labour Exchange over the years became the Job Centre, which I'm proud to say I only had to use once for a short spell, and it was a complete waste of time. It has now been computerised, and there are hardly any jobs, or hardly anybody there to help you find a job. It all has to be done online. Nowadays, you don't have to sign on every two weeks, but you do have to have an appointment, to go along and show your face, and explain what you've been doing to try to find a job. And if you don't, they threaten to stop your monthly benefits. Lots of people ended up giving up the ghost after applying for endless vacancies without success, whereas years ago, if you went for a job and were declined, companies would write to tell you.

Nowadays, lots of companies have so many applicants that they no longer let you know either way. So, after application after application, lots of people give up trying, and sadly, quite a few end up with mental health problems and depression, all due to the inability of finding a job.

Many people had worked for years at the same company when out of the blue they were laid off for one reason or another. They struggled to come to terms with unemployment and the financial problems that it brings. So it was to your benefit that you listened and learnt in order to get a good education all those years ago.

There is very little loyalty now in life. When your expiry date arrives, you are no longer needed.

It becomes a little matter of:
'CLOSE THE DOOR ON YOUR WAY OUT
THERE'S A GOOD CHAP.'

ACADEMY TO PLAY:
School to work

Football, like our daily life over the years, has taken the same route. Years ago, young kids of maybe seven or eight would be scouted when playing in the local parks for their local team. If they caught the eye, then they would be invited along to have a trial with the local professional or semi-professional club. If they were seen to be good enough or had the potential to be good enough, then they were invited back to train, and to eventually join the Academy. Here you joined in with lots of other boys (girls at this time were not fully involved in football professionally) to start to learn, and nurture your football skills. Every boy was hoping to be the next Tom Finney, Jimmy Armfield or Bobby Moore.

In the early years as a young trainee, your job, first and foremost, was to wash and clean everything in sight, from the toilets to the changing rooms. The terraces had to be swept, the senior players' boots had to be cleaned and polished. And all this had to be done before your day could even start. Everything was very military. The coaches put you through a strict regime that you had to adhere to, and they were there to teach you the rules and regulations on how to become a successful footballer. Once all your morning chores were done, then off you went to your Academy to learn about fitness, teamwork, and your future skills.

Academies were fun if you were prepared to keep your head down and work as hard as you could, and do as you were told. Lots of young players worked hard, but, either through lack of skill or attitude, never quite fulfilled their potential. Lots thought they had arrived and the rest was going to be so easy. No need to keep pushing themselves. Nothing more to be learnt, the big time was here, and it was going to be a Glen Hoddle (doddle). These were the lucky few out of thousands of kids who had trials, and sadly, lots were turned away in tears. These were the ones all kids aspired to be, they all had the talent we all longed for, and when we saw their talent going to waste, we were all pig sick. David Bentley, Jermaine Pennant and Saido Berahino, just to mention a few of many players, were those who everyone thought would go onto greater things, but unfortunately their talent fell short. Whether it was the pressure of the big time, the expectancy of what was to come, they just seemed to take their eye off the ball.

Even though they ended up having a good career, they didn't quite reach the heights they should have given the talent they had. Most players dream of playing at the highest level: Real Madrid, Barcelona, Liverpool, Bayern Munich and Manchester United, but sadly for most it will never happen. Players like, and I've mentioned him before, Robbie (the robber) Savage (he'd nick the ball off you if you held onto it too long), who I thought was never the most talented player, has had a long and great career through working hard, along with dedication and listening to the people around him when he was young.

Other players in my mind who weren't as talented but who worked as hard are Jamie O'Hara, Paul Konchesky and Fulham's own Sean Davis, who wasn't the most talented, but boy did he work hard, and we loved him for giving that extra effort to the team. All these had great careers. Lots of young players who were turned away at an early age by one Academy or another pushed themselves on and went for more trials with other clubs. Great players like Roy Keane, Harry Kane and one of the all-time greats, the real Ronaldo (aka Bugs Bunny) were all turned away from Academies, but all went on to greater things and with greater teams.

Years ago, it was slightly easier to go from one team to another if you had a decent reputation. If you didn't make it in one division but you were seen as a half-decent player and seen to have the right attitude, then you could always drop down into a lower league.

Over the years the influx of foreign players has grown steadily. In the 60s there were very few overseas players. One person who stayed in England after the War ended was a German ex-prisoner of war by the name of Bert Trautmann. Trautmann was a wonderful goalkeeper, who in the 1956 Cup Final, while playing for Manchester City, had a terrible collision with the Birmingham player Peter Murphy. Trautmann played on for the last 17–18 minutes which City went on to win 3–1 only to find out a few days later his neck was broken, and not just cricked as first thought (and players today scream like billy-o if they get their toes stood on).

But it wasn't until the late 70s when the Ipswich manager Bobby Robson brought in players like the Dutch pair Arnold Mühren and Frans Thijssen. Spurs signed the Argentinian pair of Ossie Ardiles and Ricky Villa. Liverpool then brought in Avi Cohen, and as the years went by, more and more players arrived from abroad: Jan Molby, Jasper Olsen. The list started to grow longer and longer.

The English Academies and leagues today are now full of overseas players, some good, some not so good. Some people say it's a good thing to bring some of the top players in from abroad because it makes the leagues more exciting. Others say it doesn't help the young English players, many of whom are unable to get a shot at first team football, and more importantly, don't get the playing time to help their international careers. Clubs are happy to buy from abroad because overseas players are cheaper to buy than their English counterparts. Notably in 2015, Arsenal, under Arsène Wenger were the first Premier League team to field a team consisting only of foreign players. There are now so many players from abroad that the FA have been trying to put a limit on how many can be permitted to play in a team or be picked in their squads.

Lots of English players now have to go out on loan or leave their clubs. Ironically lots of British players now seek to go abroad, like Jadon Sancho did (and Jude Bellingham is doing just that at this moment in time). They do this to get regular first team football, and also to earn a wage and bonus money. Some sadly have to rely on the PFA to help them out financially if they can't get a regular club. Lots of older players have sold their medals, cups, and trophies to help pay their way. So, it is so important when you're young to listen and learn.

With the aid of the internet, lots of players that are now unattached from their last club for whatever reason and are struggling to find a new one due to the number of players coming in from all parts of the world, are now putting their names on various websites, aimed at league teams looking for experienced players to mix in with their younger up-and-coming players.

Sadly, lots of players with good talent are lost to the game each year due to depression and other mental issues, caused by the frustration of not being able to find a new team and regular football. Some that had given years to their clubs, but due to age or medical issues unfortunately meant they were moved on. Like life, there is very little loyalty in football. When your sell-by date has passed, you are no longer of value.

It becomes a little matter of
'CLOSE THE CHANGING ROOM DOOR ON YOUR WAY OUT
THERE'S A GOOD CHAP.'

Chapter Eleven

Pocket Money
WAGES

Money is the root of all evil:
MONEY IS THE ROOT OF ALL TRANSFERS

As youngsters in the dark days of the 50 and 60s, there was no way you could do anything with your pocket money your parents gave you each week (if you were lucky enough to get any at all). Lots of families were literally on the breadline, living hand to mouth. So, we kids had to work to get that little bit extra, unless you were one of the posh lot from up the road, who always had enough money for all the things that we yearned for. In 1958, at the age of about seven, I used to get about sixpence (2½ new pence) a week to spend on sweets. And if Mum or Dad were maybe a bit flush that week, I might also (if I was really lucky) get a comic, for example, *The Beano* with Dennis the Menace, Roger the Dodger, the Bash Street Kids, and Minnie the Minx; or *The Dandy* with Korky the Cat and Desperate Dan eating a massive cow pie. I can remember the horns popping out of the pastry, and being amazed that he could eat all that pie (a kid's imagination). As I got a bit older, it was the *Eagle*, with Dan Dare and the *Lion* with lots of spacemen.

Back then you could get quite a lot of sweets for six pence. Sweets like Black Jacks, Fruit Salads, sherbet flying saucers, and sherbet in a tube with a liquorice stick that you sucked, got it all wet, then dipped it in the sherbet. Most of the time before you'd even finished the sherbet, the paper tube was soaking wet and falling to pieces. Soggy sherbet was everywhere, and sticky black fingers stayed black forever and a day. I think you can still get many of these sweets even today.

Most of the little sweet shops had rows and rows of these great big glass jars, all full of different types of sweets, all different colours. It was just like going into Alice's Wonderland for us kids. It took what seemed like forever and a day just to decide what to have. Your mum and dad were forever telling you to hurry up. But you can't rush decisions on important things like this. Then after picking the ones, you wanted, and telling the shopkeeper how *many* you wanted, they would weigh them on these big scales, one ounce or two ounces, or as many as you liked (or could get with the little amount of cash you had). Then they'd put them in a paper bag, or some put them in cones made out of newspaper (that was even more fancy), then it was all-out eat yourself stupid time. The pocket money went up when I was 10 or 11. By then I used to get about half a crown (2 shillings and 6 pence, 12½p). It wasn't bad, but still not enough to do all things that our young lives required.

Now, who can remember going to Saturday morning pictures with their mates? I remember the cinema in Putney where I used to go. Once we all bundled in, we fought over the best seats. It would start with a bloke with a great big organ that used to rise up (no, not that type of organ, behave yourself), like the ones they have in a church. First of all, came this creepy haunting music, then it slowly rose from the pit. It always used to remind me of a horror film. This monstrosity of a machine would start to come into view. The horrific sounds always came from it. The sound made most of us kids look away, that chilling sound just before some grisly murder was about to happen. I kept expecting for the organ player to be wearing a black cloak and a top hat, and when he turned around ... it was Christopher Lee, with that deep echoing laughter that went right through you, his fangs dripping with blood and protruding out of his mouth ... but it wasn't. And the way he played it showed he certainly wasn't a young Elton John just starting out. All the kids down in the front few rows threw paper cups or anything they had at hand at him. Great fun. (Well, it was for us.) I don't think he was too pleased though. He used to play the same tune every week. I think it was called something like 'We are the Minors of the ABC' and there were words we'd sing along to it. I think it was called 'We are the minors of the ABC' (there's a coincidence). It went something like this:

We are the boys and girls well known as
Minors of the ABC (shouts out *ABC* very loud)
And every Saturday all line up
To see the films we like, and shout aloud with glee
We like to laugh and have a singsong
Such a happy crowd are we
We're all pals together
We're minors of the A-B-C (shouted loudly again).

I don't think it was written by Rogers and Hammerstein, more like a bloke named Roger from Hammersmith.

When I think back now to the early 60s, there were some pretty awful films showing at the Saturday morning pictures. For kids, films like *Flash Gordon*, *Buck Rogers*, *Roy Rogers*, the *Three Stooges,* and the brilliant Johnny Weissmuller as Tarzan, which were nearly all showing in black and white, were great at the time, but looking back on them now, did they really entertain me ...? Yes, of course they did. It was the best we had back then.

As we got older, if we wanted real money to buy clothes and records, or to take your girlfriend to the pictures, you would have to get some kind of after-school job, but a lot of the time you had to lie about your age as you weren't supposed to work until you were fourteen. Even then you were supposed to get permission from your headmaster at school, and permission was only granted if your school work was better than OK. If you were behind, you were not allowed to do anything other than your homework in the evenings or at the weekends.

Well, that was what was supposed to happen, but I, like most of my mates, sort of bypassed this slight problem, and the people who we went to work for couldn't give a sod about the headmaster's agreement (or about our education). That was our problem; they were only interested in us doing the job they needed doing.

I started off doing a paper round seven days a week when I was about twelve, walking around the streets, delivering, and selling the *Evening Standard* and the *Evening News*. Sunday mornings were the worst because not only did you get more thicker news-papers like *The Sunday Times*, *The Telegraph* and *The Observer*, because some started to put some kind of supplements in them too, making the bag weigh a bleeding ton.

On Saturday evenings after all the football matches had fin-ished (all matches finished about 4.50 p.m. in those days (Fergie hadn't yet taken over at Manchester United), *The Standard* and the *Evening News* brought out all the classified football results. It was great having all the results and write-ups a couple of hours after the games. There were no live games as such on the televi-sion. A cup match or England international was about the best we could hope for. So, to get all this information was good for all the supporters who couldn't get to the games.

People would check their Littlewoods or Vernons football pools coupons, hoping to hit the jackpot and solve all their fi-nancial problems. Lots queued at newspaper stands waiting for the vans from Fleet Street to deliver the bundles of newspapers. Sometimes you'd hardly had time to cut the strings to open them up before everyone was pulling and pushing to get a copy. For this seven-day stint I received about £1.50.

I then went on to work at the weekends, helping the local milkman, whose name believe it or not was Ernie (honestly, cross my heart and hope to die. Well, I don't really hope to die, but ...) All day Saturday, six in the morning until six in the evening, and Sunday mornings six in the morning until one in the afternoon. Then when it got too cold, it was time for a change. For helping old Ernie, my reward was £2.00 plus any tips I managed to get when collecting the milk money on Saturdays. As if by coinci-dence, some ten or so years later, after being made redundant from a job, I went and got a job at the local dairy and guess who it was that taught me the ropes ...? Good old Ernie ('the fastest milkman in the West').

I then started working two evenings a week, and every Saturday in a greengrocers. By this time, at the grand old age of fifteen, I was getting a princely sum of between £3 and £4 pounds for do-ing about 20 or so hours a week. It was hard work for very little, but, when in need, it's no good moaning, it had to be done. I remember my first full-time job at the age of sixteen. I was getting £7 a week and that was quite good, but that was only because I worked for my dad in the stables.

In the late 70s, when *Dallas's* J. R. Ewing (Larry Hagman) was showing us mere mortals how to be a nasty rich bastard, most of us had a little bit more in the way of savings and pocket cash to throw around. People were better off than they had been for many years, but as the saying goes, 'The more you earn, the more you spend' and 'the more you want.'

The rich kids, unlike us, didn't have these worries about earning pocket money or having to do work to earn a crust; they were eating the whole bloody loaf, *and* it had butter on it (not margarine like ours did).

Sadly, you hardly ever see a milkman or paper boy doing deliveries nowadays.

In fact, you hardly ever see a milkman because it's easier and cheaper to buy dairy products at the supermarket, and the newspapers can be got online. Having to work for your money should make you appreciate what you have in life. As I got older and into full-time employment, the wages went up, and so did the bills. Being able to buy a car was one thing, but being able to run it was another. As I already stated earlier in the book, companies bringing in people from abroad meant lower wages, which meant getting a position with a liveable income was harder to find. So, we had to work extra hours to earn that extra pay.

Obviously being at the age I am now, I don't mix with many kids, but from what I see and hear, kids nowadays seem to do quite well by their parents. I know mine do. It doesn't seem much of a problem for parents to buy designer this and designer that, top-of-the-range clothes, shoes, and electronic equipment. Unfortunately, it can get to a stage in life where kids are given too much too young, and then they start to get greedy. And then they take everything for granted, expecting to receive, rather than hoping to receive. Even my own three grandchildren are spoilt rotten, always getting what they want and when they want it. Yes! I'm as bad. I do spoil them rather than making them do some chores in the house to earn it.

I know, I know, I can hear all you youngsters saying, I'm an old fossil, living in the past, but sometimes I think that kids are given what they want just to keep them quiet and keep them happy. I wonder how many kids today get the same thrill out of spending their weekly pocket money as we did in the day. Every Saturday was like Christmas Day for as we went out to spend our well earnt pennies, or pocket money, in Alice's Wonderland of sweet and sugary delights. We'd worked so hard for our treats. But then again, I wonder how many kids still get pocket money as we knew it. I don't think many kids today have to work very hard to be rewarded as we did many years ago. They just get what they want.

Now as the years go by, the Government is worried that people haven't saved enough for their retirement and this is going to be a strain on the economy. I think the Government should realise that the cost of living has gone through the roof and wages have hardly increased at the same rate, meaning people don't have the funds to live and save for that rainy day. Allowing so many people to come and live and work (cheap labour) is fine in practice, but only if they work and pay their way. Otherwise, they become a massive strain on all our resources. Schools, hospitals, the local services have all had to cut back because the country is running out of money. And look at the housing market; if you're looking to get on the property ladder as a first-time buyer, well good luck to you. Most youngsters today can't even afford to buy the ladder.

Too many people and not enough properties mean it's a seller's market, and if you're looking to rent, well, the Government has given private landlords carte blanche regarding what they charge. My son has a wife and two young children, and they are having to pay £1,700 a month, plus Council Tax, for a small three-bedroom house that you could hardly swing a cat in. Hopefully one day the bubble will burst, but until then, those who have money are getting richer while the rest of us struggle on. And that is what is happening today. Foreign workers are sending money back home to help their families, which you can understand, but they're not spending it here to help build our economy and keep our costs down. All that money is leaving these shores sadly never to return.

WAGES:
Pocket money

Lots of youngster today who are trying to work their way up in the footballing world tend to take many things for granted. They don't realise that they don't have to do all the shitty jobs and the hard work that the up-and-coming pros did many years ago.

Kids in the 50s and 60s who were lucky to have that special footballing gift were reliant on their parents for their pocket money so that they could join a local team and pay to play. These lads and lassies played for fun, not money. In fact, for almost every one of them, most of their pocket money went on paying for a weekly club subscription, which all went to help the club pay for the pitch, the footballs, the kits, or other small things the club had to pay for.

Many parents were unable to support their children financially. So for those kids, an after-school job was essential to help pay for football boots and shin pads, as well as the cost of having a bit of fun with your mates after the game. Lots of the lucky kids were spotted by football scouts who were sent out by local professional football teams to the local parks in the area to find that special kid playing on a Saturday or Sunday in the Under-12, Under-14, and Under-16 leagues. These kids were then invited along for a trial with their local team. If they were good enough and passed all requirements, they would then be taken on and trained on a regular basis. Then, at some later date for the few that did pass, they would be offered some sort of contract or agreement, which would then tie them down to the club. And, that's when their work started, and so did the money.

No more having to pay to play, no more subs to pay. Most still had to buy their own boots and shin pads (no pampering or pussyfooting around). They were conditioned, trained, and paid very little. Their day, back then, started very early in the morning, and consisted of cleaning the showers and toilets, cleaning the pros' boots, and sweeping the terraces. It was all very military, and that was before they'd get anywhere near kicking a football in training. Wages for the youth team players was still piss poor, so even now on the brink of stardom, a second job was a must for most.

Once they got full-time contracts their wages got better. Their weekly wage was still low, but now they were on different types of bonuses. They could now earn a few extra pounds for winning games, scoring goals, and keeping a clean sheet. But even the great players through the years like Tom Finney, who was a plumber by trade as well as a brilliant footballer, still carried on plumbing when he wasn't playing or training. Geoff Horsfield was a bricklayer and a hod carrier, and Stuart Pearce was an electrician. These players, like many others, had to have two jobs just to keep them going financially until they made the grade.

Players supplied their own boots, and they were also expected to take home their kits after the match and wash them ready for the next game. They made their own way to the games, travelling on the bus or train, or maybe even walking to the ground with the supporters of both sides. There was no fancy cars or luxury coaches, no minders or bodyguards, no silly-looking headphones to alienate them from the crowd, they were just everyday blokes with a special talent that we all craved. They were footballers, not celebrities or wannabes. There was no fancy or famous Wags clinging to their arms and making a show for the media, all up themselves. Someone once asked Peter Crouch what he would have been if he hadn't become a footballer? His answer: 'a virgin'. And that just about sums up footballers. And what does that say about Mr Crouch's relationship with Abbey

Clancy ... is he saying that he understands that she's maybe only with him because he's a footballer, and that had he been a dustman, she wouldn't have been interested in him? Surely not!

Football in the early years was about the game and not the money. Players earned very little in comparison to today's salaries, but it didn't matter, they played for the love of the game. Don't get me wrong, they were still paid a better wage than most of the rest of us, and they got the little extras in life because of who they were. Becoming the local hero often got them free beers, bought for them by supporters, and restaurants often gave them a free meal or a bottle of wine, or a decent discount off the bill.

Life started to become financially a bit easier when the £20 maximum wage for footballers was abolished in the early 60s. Players could start to earn what then was seen as a decent liveable wage. Fulham's own legend Johnny Haynes was to become the first £100-a-week player (and worth every penny). But they still had to work hard. More and more, footballers started to be perceived as stars, and they were being chased by companies to advertise and endorse their products. Again, Fulham and England captain Johnny Haynes endorsed Kellogg's Wholegrain Wheats and Brylcreem in the 50s, along with cricketer and Arsenal winger Denis Compton. Of course, they were paid extra for these endorsements. Over the coming years, just as our pocket money increased, so did players' wages. Slowly at first each year ... until 1991.

It was then that football as we knew it changed from being a working man's sport, to a rich man's business, or for some, a rich man's plaything. For when, after trying and failing to purchase Manchester United, Rupert Murdoch's BSkyB set up Sky Sports, as we know it today.

Then in 1992 the Premier League was founded and the money started to flood in. Now even today, some clubs and players in these lower leagues can't complete with the clubs and players in the higher leagues in the footballing sense, so the change didn't make a big difference to them financially. The players still had to help out their clubs with the general running and up-keep, and pick up whatever wages at the end of the week if they were lucky enough and the club was in a position to pay them.

Most of the players still have to buy their own boots or wash their own kits. This is known as grass roots football. And this is financially insignificant yet one of the most essential parts of the footballing family, which, unfortunately, the faceless football bosses at the FA (and the teams in higher leagues) have all forgotten about. They treat the teams in the lower leagues like a music box. As soon as one starts to make a noise, they shut the lid down and put it to one side. Out of sight out of mind.

The clubs in this new Premier League were now awash with so much cash that they started to search the country for anyone that showed any kind of talent. When they were spotted, they were snatched off the local parks or out of the lower leagues and thrown into Academies as quickly as you could say 'Inverness Caledonian Thistle'. Some of the parents of these young talents were offered slightly smaller brown paper bags, or even houses, as incentives, just to get their kids to sign for the clubs involved.

Young up-and-coming players with that special talent now didn't have to do that hard slog to earn a wage. No more cleaning of boots, toilets, or showers. No more terrace sweeping. Now it was all about fitness and training. Their everyday lives were taken away and put into someone else's hand. They were pampered left, right and centre: no more supplying their own boots because Nike, Adidas, Puma, and many more were falling over themselves to supply whatever footwear or clothes they required. And they paid them for the privilege of wearing them. They were given free top-of-the-range cars; they were offered silly financial contracts even before they'd proven themselves.

Sadly, it's been the ruin of many a great prospect. They've been spoilt too soon, and at too early an age. Too much money and too much pampering, and in a lot of cases it's not been earned. In lots of cases, it's just to keep them happy and out of the hands of other opposing clubs' greedy little mits. Players like the ones already mentioned in previous chapters: Jack Rodwell,

Scott Sinclair, and John Bostock were players who were all too naïve as footballers, who never saw the bigger picture. Learn your trade properly and the glitz, the glamour, and the money will come. If too much is offered too young, it's not their fault. Their agents and their parents should have possibly given them better advice.

Here's a question to ponder: has Sky Sports been good for football? Or has it just been good for footballers?

It's definitely been good for the businessmen.

Unfortunately, what the football clubs and the FA, just like our Government, have failed to realise is that the cost of living for us mere mortals has gone up faster than a vicar's zip when compromised. And, if there's one thing that really gets under the skin of the supporters, then it's the price of today's season tickets and match day tickets. To purchase a season ticket at some clubs is now well into hundreds of pounds, and in some cases £1,500 (and more) for just a slightly better seat. When you weigh up all the cost of going to the game: travel, food, drink, programme, and the ticket, it comes out at a tidy old sum, and it's especially expensive if you've got a couple of kids.

Now should you be a shift worker, then you have another problem. By the time Sky Sports have fucked about changing the days and times of numerous matches just to suit the stay-at-home ('I'll watch on the box') fan, the sponsors, and most of Asia, the Middle East and America, you've got to decide whether to try and change shifts with someone, take a day's holiday, or pull a sicky. What's also worse is if you subscribe to Sky Sports, you're paying a fortune each month for the sports channel *and* an absolute fortune for a season ticket, and here you are, a shift worker, who for whatever reason, can't get to the game, *and* you're also unable to watch it if it's live on the box. It's not the same recording it and watching it later. You need to know what's happening while it's being played live.

Hopefully one day the bubble will burst, but until then those who have money are getting richer while the rest of us struggle on, and that is what is happening today. Clubs are now paying a fortune to agents to seal deals for players. They're also sending millions of pounds overseas to buy foreign players. All that money is going to help other countries' football economies when in fairness it should be spent here to help keep our football economy and costs down. All that money is leaving these shores sadly never to return.

Chapter Twelve

Love Letters
PROGRAMMES

Postman Pat:
PROGRAMME PETE

When you were at school years ago, love notes were about the only way to let someone know that you fancied them, without actually going up and telling them face to face. It also saved you from a mouthful of piss-taking and total embarrassment if your mates saw you trying to chat someone up.

At first it was just a single piece of paper with a small message to test the water. Some sent them anonymously at first, leaving it on their intended's school desk for them to find, and then watching their faces to see their reaction. Half the time you were kidding yourself that they didn't have any idea who'd sent it. Deep down you wanted them to know, maybe even by putting a little hint in it so perhaps when they'd read it, and were looking around to see who it might have come from, you might just let them see you looking back, before the pair of you stood looking like a pair of Royal Mail letterboxes, both bright red with mouths wide open in embarrassment.

You either had to be good-looking, a bit special or the class hard nut to receive a love note, or you (and whoever was sending you this message) were totally out there on your own academically, the classroom geeks. But, should you not be any of the aforementioned, then WOW, you were the lucky one, or someone was winding you up for a laugh. Most probably your mates were having a laugh at your expense. As the years went on, the short love notes got longer and soon became love letters.

Getting a love letter was so exciting. During the dark days of the War, those letters kept thousands of the troops who were fighting all around the world going, and gave them the will to survive. They gave the troops information about what was happening back home, and how that person back home felt, and more importantly, what they wanted to do to them when, hopefully, they got back home. Up-to-date pictures from home of their beloved and their family gave them hope. Love letters were an important part of life back then.

As I said at the beginning of the book, when you're very, very young, girls are play things, you simply don't notice there is a difference in gender. They were only there to bully, pull their hair and throw things at them, like worms or spiders, and to call them names to make them cry. They were not to be taken seriously. It's not until girls get into their early teens that they start taking shape, and you start taking notice. Unfortunately, this tends to be the time when they get their own back for all the crap you've given them. If there's one thing I've learnt over the years it is that women have long and unforgiving memories.

So, here you are: a young kid of about fourteen or fifteen, and all of a sudden that little girl from a few doors or desks away has changed shape overnight. Two small lumps appear on her chest, and all of a sudden, you've got a small lump in your pants. She's got you all hot and bothered. I remember back then, when I was about sixteen or seventeen, a lot of my mates and I would all go out with the same girls. After, we would give them marks out of ten (sad, but they most probably did the same. We was all young and stupid back then).

If you're old enough, you'll remember the days of SWALK (sealed with a loving kiss) or BURMA (be undressed and ready, my angel). Well, when you received a letter with these magic letters written on the back, you knew you were in. A love letter from an admirer told you everything you needed to know about what was or might be in store for you in the future.

In the early days it was just a short note like 'I really fancy you' or 'I think I'm in love with you.' And once they found out it was you who had sent the messages, if they were interested in you, as time went on the notes would go into more and more details. Pages of writing got more and more to the point with messages like 'Meet me behind the bike sheds after school' or 'Will your mum and dad be out on Saturday morning?' When you got a yes reply to these small messages, your heart would pump like mad, and so would your old chap down below in anticipation of what was, or might, follow. And the feeling you got when you saw them turn up was one of pure excitement. You couldn't wait to get started. The notes got meatier and juicier: 'I want to kiss you all over', 'I want to make love to you until you shout for me to stop.' And some were even more to the point, such as: 'How big's yer ...?' or 'Are your ... for real?' I'll leave it to your imagination about what else was said from then on.

Those letters were an important part of our lives back then. Lots of people who were the really romantic type kept these letters in boxes, hidden away from prying eyes and they were only brought out on the odd occasion to reminisce on the past. Handled with love and care so as not to crease or damage the pages, they were read with loving eyes and then stored away again for forever and a day. The one letter you didn't want to receive was a 'Dear John' letter that told you to take a hike on your bike, that it was all over, and you were now on your Jack Jones (own). Sadly, like most of us out there, I've had a couple of those myself.

Over the next 30 or 40 years, technology changed just about everything. Nowadays, I would think that just the true romantics out there are the only ones who might still be sending love letters in the traditional manner: all flowery and sprayed with perfume.

No, the days of the SWALK and BURMA letters have almost totally disappeared. They have been replaced by mobile text messages, such as LOL (lots of love), SHMILY (see how much I love you), or more personal ones, like GYPO (get your pants off), or IMEZYRU (I'm easy, are you?); and downright dirty, like SD (sucks dicks), J/O (jack off) and GNOC (get naked on cam).

Nowadays, email and social media companies like Facetime, WhatsApp, X (formerly Twitter) and Skype, keeps us up to date with what's been going in the daily lives of our nearest and dearest. If for some reason you don't have a mobile phone or any of these other different ways to contact the love of your life, then there's always the old dog and bone (telephone). That's if you can find a telephone box that is still in use, or hasn't been vandalised.

That old-fashioned personal touch between you and your special one which these letters brought you has slowly diminished. Now it's possible for everyone and their dog to keep up to date with what everyone else they know is doing. No more anticipation of what's arriving when your mobile dings that special ding when the message arrives. Now most of the time we can see who sent the message even before we open it. We can see the first few words straight away. We don't have to gently open this electronic envelope like we did all those years ago to see if the sender had put anything saucy in it.

There is no more waiting a week or two with bated breath for Postman Pat to slide that long-awaited letter through your letterbox for you to see what the situation is with a loved one. With the internet, information is now instant, just at the touch of a button.

PROGRAMMES:
Love letters

Match day programmes in the and 50s and 60s were very much like our first love notes. For most supporters and fans alike, they were a message from the team we were growing to love. Most of us young boys considered football in the same way that we considered girls. They were there to watch and play with, but that was it. Like with girls, football didn't really take shape for me until I was about thirteen or fourteen. That's when feelings for the club started to manifest. After going to a couple of matches at Fulham, I realised they were the ones for me. I bought my first programme (and to be honest, I don't remember what game it was) for the sum of about 6d (2½p), and even though, like our love notes, it was only a couple of pages printed on what looked like A4 paper, which told us very little, but it felt so special. It told me how the team was lining up, each player's name and number from number 1 through to number 11, and who was playing in which position.

The excitement we had as young kids seeing our heroes named in the starting line-up was just enough to keep our interest and our juices flowing. It was pretty basic to say the least. There would be the odd black and white photo of one or two of our players, and a list of the games that were being played elsewhere so you could check on the half-time results. It also had some advertisements from a few local shops and companies.

Over the years, programmes changed from being like our two-page love notes to being more like our full-blown love letters. They got juicier and juicier. There were more pages and more information on the players we cherished and loved. There was a lot more pictures, and they were now all in colour. These were much sexier than those dull old black and white ones. There was pictures of players in motion and information about their private lives, where they were from, if they were married, had a family, and lots of past history too.

The more pages there were to read, the more we got involved with the team, the players, and the club. These programmes told us what our beloved clubs intended to do to us, and where we were going to meet for our next date. Was it going to be Portsmouth? Charlton? Or maybe somewhere more out in the country, like Nottingham Forest. It was 'Oh so sexy'. Those programmes that started out costing us 3d (about 1p) in the 50s was now costing £3 or £4 at most grounds. We were drooling over just about everything the club was telling us. Most supporters and fans read these programmes over and over again to digest every little detail they had to offer.

Lots of die-hard supporters kept them in folders or boxes, which were only brought out on the odd occasion to reminisce on past games. They were handled with love and care so as not to crease or damage the pages, and they were read with loving eyes. Then they were stored away again for forever and a day. For most supporters the programme was a must-have. I used to buy them every time I went to a match. I remember one game when, owing to the traffic, I was late, and they had sold out of programmes. I was totally distraught, and coming away after the match, I felt empty. I know it sounds a bit pathetic, a grown man feeling this way, but there you are. I'd been buying them for so long it was part of the football day ritual, and going home not carrying that programme felt so strange. First thing on the Monday morning I was on the phone to Fulham and got a copy sent to me. (It just didn't feel the same though.)

The one programme you didn't want to get was an away day one (the 'Dear John'). This told us very little, or nothing, about our team; it showed no love for us at all. And we certainly didn't want to know about their team. But like most supporters over many years, I got loads of them.

Over the last 30 to 40 years, technology has changed just about everything. Nowadays, it's possibly only the true supporter who still keeps every programme in a file or box. With the internet, we can get all our loving details online. No more waiting two weeks for a home game to catch up with what is new at your club with social media companies such as Facetime, WhatsApp, X (formerly Twitter), and Skype keeping us up to date with what's been going in the daily footballing lives of our nearest and dearest. Many supporters have given up buying programmes due to the internet, apps on iPhones, iPads and all the other types of social media that are available, and sales of programmes are starting to diminish. Now it's only those who don't have access to the net or social media, or those who are true football romantics who still buy them.

Everyone can learn about your loved one on the internet. Information is now instant at the touch of a button. During Covid-19, many clubs packed up printing match day programmes due to the drop in attendance, instead putting everything about the game on their websites. If, for whatever the reason, you don't have the internet, you can always turn to Sky Sports, BBC, or BT sport, talkSPORT or Radio 5 live on the radio. Like those days of the love letter, that programme was a personal thing, it was like … like it was just sent to you, and only you, no one else got that message. Sadly those days and feelings are slowly disappearing.

Chapter Thirteen

Our Tunes
OUR CHANTS

Substitute The Who:
WHO'S THE SUBSTITUTE?

It was not only the love letters or programmes that sent us a message of love, but music did the same. Just as some might do today (not many, I don't suppose?), years ago, people used to serenade the ones they loved, like in *Romeo and Juliet*. There he was underneath his loved one's balcony, in the moonlight, singing his love songs. So romantic. But it was a bit of a bummer if her balcony was on the ground floor, especially if you were about 6 ft 6 in, and she was 5 ft 4 in. It didn't have quite that same romantic feel about it. I think people serenading must have stopped when high-rise flats started to get built. Let's face it, it's a bit difficult to serenade your girlfriend if she lives on the sixteenth floor, unless you have a voice like that bloke off the GoCompare ad.

If you were to ask most couples today, 'Do you have your own love song?' Almost certainly they would say yes. It was most probably the first one they heard when they first met, or the first one they danced to. A song that pulls on their heart strings. Nearly all of us have that special song. It might not be a love song, but a song that brings back memories of loved ones we may have had in the past but, for whatever reason, are no longer with us. Many of the singers and bands over the years can be identified by their songs, such as Elvis, *Jail House Rock*; Bill Haley, *Rock Around the Clock;* Rod Stewart, *Maggie May*; 10cc, *I'm Not in Love*; and *Hi Ho Silver Lining*, Jeff Beck. As soon as you mention any one of these great songs, then that singer or band will automatically come to mind.

Love songs back in the 50s used to be of the soft and genteel kind; music by the likes of Ol' Blue Eyes himself, Frank

Sinatra, who 'did it his way' and sang songs like 'I've Got You Under My Skin' and 'Strangers in the Night; and the 'Little Ole Wine Drinker Me'. Dean Martin, who sang 'Everybody Loves Somebody' and 'That's Amore', and Andy Williams who sang the one we've always sung at the Cottage, which is: 'Can't Take My Eyes Off You' (with the slight change of 'I love you, Fulham' not 'baby'). These were among many singers wooing the ladies in the 50s and 60s.

We had Shirley Bassey singing 'Kiss Me, Honey Honey, Kiss Me' and '(Hey) Big Spender'; Roberta Flack with 'The First Time Ever I Saw Your Face' and Dionne Warwick's 'I Say a Little Prayer'.

We had jazz from clarinet player Mr Aka Bilk, with his bowler hat and his jazz band, with 'Stranger on the Shore'. (I wonder, if we had had the betting companies back then that are so popular nowadays, would they have had an Aka Bilksie, instead of today's AccaBoost Akabusi? (Just a thought.)

There were also Cleo Laine and Johnny Dankworth, playing at the famous Ronnie Scott's jazz club in London. There were many different blues artists, such as John Lee Hooker, Muddy Waters, and B. B. King. Then along came The Fab Four known as The Beatles, who, it's said, changed the face of pop music. Well, they were 'twisting and shouting' quite a lot, and sending everyone into a wild dance floor frenzy. There was rock bands too like Mick (the lips) Jagger and The Rolling Stones, The Who, with Roger Daltry, Rod Stewart and the Faces, and there was Status Quo 'rocking all over the world (And I like it, I like it, I like it, I like it …').

Country music was, and always will be, popular. There were the likes of Kenny Rogers, Dolly Parton, and Tammy Wynette 'standing by her man'. We had great songs from bands like The Mamas & the Papas with 'Creeque Alley', 'I Saw Her Again', and 'California Dreamin' in the flower power era.

Then along came the Motown sound with the fabulous Diana Ross and The Supremes, Marvin Gaye, and Smokey Robinson; the list of Motown greats is as long as your arm. So many great hits from so many great artists. The Jacksons, with a young

Michael, The Osmonds, with a young Donny and Marie, and that little liar, Jimmy. Why? Because he reckoned he was a long-haired lover, and that he came from Liverpool? WHAT? A lover at the age of nine? Dirty little sod! And he didn't come from Liverpool.

We had some of the best music over the years, and we were blessed with some of the greatest songs, singers, writers, groups, and bands. But back then we also had rather crass comedy songs like 'My boomerang won't come back' by Charlie Drake; 'My Old Man's a Dustman' by Lonnie Donegan; 'Funky Gibbon' by The Goodies; and possibly one of the best loved, and truly funny in my mind was the great Benny Hill hit 'Ernie (The Fastest Milkman in the West'). BUT THEN!! Oh dear! Along came the Spice Girls, who totally changed pop music again (sadly).

Punk had evolved (if you could say that) with Malcolm McLaren, and the Sex Pistols, Johnny Rotten, Sid Vicious and the late Nancy Spungen (I think their names give you a clue as to what they were about), performing songs like 'Anarchy in the U.K.' and 'God Save the Queen' in what was thought to be a revolution in the music world.

All of a sudden, the genre of music had changed. Up until now, most songs of the past were basically about love, romance and being starstruck by the opposite sex. The punk scene was about swearing, spitting, and taking the piss out of society in general. Lots of the songs were rude and crude, nothing about love or romance, no more being starstruck (although you might get struck by somebody spitting a gobful of phlegm in your face). It was more about sex and drugs than the rock and roll.

It came as a shock to the average man and woman on the street because up until that point there had hardly ever been a mention of sex, drugs or violence in music (well, unless you include the very sensuous song 'More, More, More' by Andrea True, or 'You Sexy Thing' by Hot Chocolate, or the Beatles' song about Lucy being out of her head in 'Lucy in the Sky With Diamonds'. And on the point of violence, there was Tom Jones stabbing

Delilah to death, or Cher 'bang banging and shooting somebody down'. (She most probably had her ex Sonny in mind). The Bee Gees were about to get themselves executed, still trying to 'get a message to you. (Hold on, hold on!!'). And even the songs I've listed above were mainly love songs.

Unfortunately, some punk bands took things to a different level. On saying that, there were some great punk bands, such as Ian Dury with his band, Kilburn and the High Roads (and later with The Blockheads); The Clash with 'London Calling'; Siouxsie and the Banshees; and Sham 69.

Then along came garage and crap (oops, sorry, rap. No, I think I was right the first time): music that didn't have any meaning to the words. Just mixed-up rubbish, I'm sorry to say. Well, that's my opinion; yours no doubt may be different. The world of music had totally changed. It seemed that it was now acceptable to swear, insult, and mention drugs and some kind of violent act in most of the tunes. And they weren't about any kind of love.

In later years we had our comedy songs like 'Ullo John! Gotta New Motor?' by Alexei Sayle; 'Shaddap You Face' by Joe Dolce; 'D-I-V-O-R-C-E', a piss-take of Tammy Wynette's hit by the fabulous Big Yin himself, Billy Connolly; and also Chas & Dave giving us some fun songs like 'Rabbit', 'Gertcha', 'Margate', and many more.

Now we have the likes of Ed Sheeran, Lewis Capaldi, Sam Smith, Taylor Swift, and Ariana Grande bringing us our love tunes. Many of the great songs from the past are, and will still be, copied and re-released by many future artists. Lots of songs, like our love letters, gave us and our loved ones that special bond. Every person, as I say, will have a love song from many of the artistes that I have mentioned, and many others too. These are songs that will remain in their hearts forever.

OUR CHANTS:
Our tunes

If it was the match day programmes which sent a message of love to us the supporters, then it was the terrace chants we sang that showed our feelings of love for our team. These were songs that gave us all that bond of love. And how the terrace chants of love have changed over the last 50 or so years is quite amazing. But we continue to serenade our loved ones on the pitch with songs from the terraces.

Most of us and our beloved football clubs have our own songs. The most famous one of all I suppose is, 'You'll Never Walk Alone', which most football fans would recognise as the Liverpool and Celtic anthem. There is other tunes, such as 'Blue Moon' for Manchester City fans; 'When the Saints Go Marching In' for Southampton; 'I'm Forever Blowing Bubbles' in West Ham: 'Glad all Over' for Crystal Palace; 'Mull of Kintyre' for Nottingham Forest; and Everton take to the pitch accompanied by the tune of the old TV series called *Z-Cars*. These are just some of the songs and tunes that have taken their place with pride at these football clubs and they remain in our hearts.

Football terrace chants, like our music, have also changed over the years. Maybe because I was very young and a bit naïve (or maybe cos I'm old now), but I can't really recall any bad and abusive chants back in the day when I first went to Fulham. As I've already said, the chants were about the love we had for our team.

I remember we had the basic chants like: 'We love you Fulham, we do. We love you Fulham, we do. We love you Fulham, we do. Oh Fulham, we love you'; and 'Oh, when the Whites, go marching in, Oh when the Whites go marching in, I want to be in that number, Oh when the Whites go marching in.'

As the years have rolled on, so have different chants been rolled out, but still, I can't think of any bad chants (or perhaps we are all very polite down at our little Cottage). Later on in

1975, we sang 'Viva El Fulham' as we went to a Wembley Cup Final. (We lost.) In the 80s we sang 'Six-foot two, eyes of blue, Roger Brown is after you.' In the noughties, it was, 'We're going to score in a moto, Score in a moto, we're going to score in a moto' as we had just signed the Japanese international Junichi Inamoto on loan from Arsenal. I suppose the nearest thing to swearing we did was to chant, 'There's only one F in Fulham, one F in Fulham, there's only one F in Fulham' (effin').

Sadly, nowadays the chants that come from the so-called fans leave nothing to the imagination. Like most of the punk and rap crap, they are just vile abuse. I did a list of some of these so-called chants, and other than vile abuse they bring nothing to a football match. They are not about trying to cheer their team on to victory. All they do is let the name of their club down. It doesn't matter whether the song is racist, homophobic, or sectarian, they have absolutely nothing to do with football. But sadly, it seems to be a problem that not only football clubs need to eradicate, as society is having difficulty trying to stamp it out as well. Hopefully, like the music of days gone by, people will come to their senses and it will die out (although the odd bit of bad language can sometimes be quite funny if used in the right way).

We get our comedy songs from different moments in the game. For example, when we're three or four goals down, our supporters start singing: 'We're shit and we know we are, we're shit and we know we are'

Or if one of their players slings a long ball across the field to his teammate and it goes miles from where it was supposed to, the opposition start singing: 'What the fuck? What the fuck? What the fucking hell was that? What the fucking hell was that?'

There are so many, and I'm sure you have your own favourites.

Some football players in the past have made records, such as 'Fog on the Tyne' by Gazza alongside the band Lindisfarne. Glen Hoddle and Chris Waddle sang 'Diamond Whites'. And who could forget John Barnes rapping to 'World in Motion'? (One of the slightly better rapping songs?)

Many of the great chants from the terraces are, and will always be, copied and sung in many other grounds. Lots of chants, like our love letters, gave us and our loved ones that special bond. This got me thinking about some of the people in football today. If they were to record songs of yesteryear, I wonder who would record what. Here's my thinking:

'Stand By Your Man' (Tammy Wynette) by Roman Abramovich.

'My Best Friend's Girl' (The Cars) by John Terry.

Or maybe 'My Best Brother's Wife' by Ryan Giggs.

'Stuck in the Middle With You' (Stealers Wheel) by the Crystal Palace board on their Premier position each year.

'I can See Clearly Now' (Johnny Nash) by Arsène Wenger.

'You're SO VAIN' (Carly Simon) by The José Mourinho and Zlatan Ibrahimović Band, along with Ronaldo, Neymar, Cantona, Berbatov and special guest ('Why Always Me?') Mario Balotelli, singing a re-make: 'We're So Vain' for Football Aid.

'Give Me Just a Little More Time' (Chairmen of the Board) by most of the ex-Chelsea managers.

'We Gotta Get Out of This Place' (The Animals) by the Southampton manager after the 9–0 thrashing by Leicester at the St Mary's Stadium.

'The Long and Winding Road' (The Beatles) by, sadly, Bury FC, hoping to get back to where they were. (And let's all hope they do).

'Should I Stay or Should I Go' (The Clash) by Mike Ashley.

'If I Could Turn Back Time' (Cher) by most of the losing managers after their team's just let Fergie's Manchester United score a sixth-minute winner in the so-called fourth minute of extra time.

'I Don't Want to Miss a Thing' (Aerosmith) by Mo Salah.

'Everybody Get Up' (Five) by the council of the FA now they have agreed safe standing.

'Things Can Only Get Better' (D:ream) by the Fulham team trying to avoid relegation for a third consecutive year.

'Cruise Control' (Headless Chickens) by the Manchester City team whenever they play.

'Free Falling' (Tom Petty) by the Derby County team.

'Simply the Best' (Tina Turner) by Pep Guardiola and Jürgen Klopp.

'I Spy (For the FBI)' (Jamo Thomas) by Marcelo Bielsa (Spygate).

'Born to Run' (Bruce Springsteen) or 'Keep On Running' (The Spencer Davis Group) by Jamie Vardy.

'Umbrella' (Rihanna) by Steve McClaren.

'Strangers in the Night' (Frank Sinatra) by the Manchester United back line.

'Don't You Want Me Baby' (Human League) by Jesse Lingard to Ole Gunner Solskjær.

'Say a Little Prayer' (Aretha Franklin) by all the teams fighting relegation.

'War' (Edwin Starr) by Villa–Birmingham. Rangers–Celtic. Southampton–Portsmouth.

'I'm Still Standing' (Elton John) Jack Grealish just before kick-off.

'I Hear You Knocking, But You Can't Come In' (Dave Edmunds) by Peter Odemwingie banging on the doors at Loftus Rd back in 2013.

'Another One Bites the Dust' (Queen) by another manager sacked at Watford.

'Freed From Desire' (Gala Rizzatto) 'Mitro's on Fire'

And the last kick of the lot, as it was on that day:

'Go-o-o-o-ld' (Spandau Ballet) A-g-ü-e-r-o.

Finally, there's our national anthem, 'God Save the Queen' (unknown), and 'Three Lions (Football's Coming Home)' by Baddiel, Skinner and The Lightning Seeds.

Sadly,' God save the Queen' will no longer be sung, having now been replaced by 'God Save the King'.

Equally sad, 'Three Lions (Football's Coming Home' has now for some reason been changed to 'Sweet Caroline' (Oi, oi, oi). Unfortunately, Oi don't have a clue why, because it has sod-all to do with football.

Our love songs will carry on showing our feelings, and so will our chants.

Chapter Fourteen

Fashion Past and Present
KITS PAST AND PRESENT

From drainpipes to flares:
FROM LONG SHORTS TO SHORT SHORTS

There have been so many different trends in the world of fashion over the last 60 years or more, from the 50s Teddy boys with their long jackets and velvet collars, crêpe-soled shoes, and long thin bootlace ties to today's fashion of fake tan, spray-on jeans and over-sized egos, i.e., *TOWIE, Made in Chelsea, Geordie Shore* etc.

Due to this fact, I'm only going to highlight the ones that had any real effect on a lot of our everyday lives, the weird and outrageous styles that most of us followed at one time or another. Lots of these more weird and wonderful fashions that we wore came about via singers or bands and the music scene. When I think back to all those different styles that I wore in my younger days, I think 'DID I REALLY?'

In the 50s, the fashion was either the Teddy boy look, dressed as I've already stated in long jackets with velvet collars, crêpe-soled shoes and long thin bootlace ties. Or you could have the casual shirt, lightweight pair of slacks or drainpipe trousers, a pair of loafers, desert boots or 'Blue Suede Shoes' look, as worn by and bands like Tommy Steele and The Steelmen: Marty Wilde and the Wildcats: and Joe Brown and The Bruvvers.

Country music with Johnny Cash, Hank Williams, Jim Reeves, and the singing cowboy, Gene Autry, had everyone wearing cowboy hats and boots, check shirts, bootlace ties and jeans. Then they had everyone slapping their legs while trying to dance in a straight line, screaming and shouting 'yee-ha' and eventually throwing their hats in the air.

Things changed again when the 'SWINGING SIXTIES' arrived. It wasn't called the swinging sixties for nothing. People were doing more swinging than Tarzan and Jane, and if you didn't indulge, you were 'SQUARE MAN, SQUARE'. 'MAKE LOVE NOT WAR' was the saying of the day, and, my God, everybody did. People slept with anyone and everyone, no questions asked. Carnaby Street in the London's West End and the Kings Road, Chelsea, became not only world famous for the fashion scene, but also for the places to be seen. It was 'cool' for anyone who was anyone to be photographed in these areas.

With the emergence of flower power, the clothes and the colours went from being very straightforward in the fifties to mind-blowingly psychedelic. People started wearing long flowery bright-coloured outfits with flowery hair-bands in their long flowery hair (and that was just the men). Men wore kaftans, colourful beaded necklaces and rings on just about every finger, and flared trousers with CND and Make Love Not War badges sewn on them. They grew long beards and sideburns and went around in a daze saying 'Y-e-a-h, m-a-n' owing to the unprescribed medication that seemed a very popular thing to do in the day (as it still is today).

The Beatles in their early days gave us jackets without collars to wear, and mop hairstyles, and thousands of screaming girls, knicker-less as they left one of their gigs. In their later years, the Beatles took us on a *Magical Mystery Tour*, wearing way-out brightly coloured military-style outfits.

The fabulous Bob Marley and the Wailers brought us the reggae sound, dreadlocks and that red, gold and green chilled-out feeling, and rather large sweet-smelling roll-ups.

The 70s gave us the sound of ska and blue beat along with bands like The Who and The Faces. It also gave us the brilliant film *Quadrophenia*. The mods were wearing their button-down shirts, two-tone tonic strides, Harrington jackets, or parkas, driving around on Vespas or Lambretta scooters. The rockers were still dressed in leather jackets and denim jeans, as they had been in the 50s, and driving Triumph motorbikes, listening to old Elvis, Gene Vincent, and Bill Haley songs.

It also brought us the Bay City Rollers. All of a sudden, everyone was wearing all-tartan outfits (well, mainly the young females), long multicoloured socks that came up over the knees, and tartan scarves hanging from the wrist.

The film *Saturday Night Fever* starring John Travolta had us all wearing suits, shirts open to the navel, flared trousers and three or four inch platform shoes. These shoes were fine unless you suffered from vertigo. I would think more ankles were twisted, sprained, or broken due to people falling off them in this period than any other piece of footwear since. *Saturday Night Fever* also gave us the disco sounds of the Bee Gees, Gloria Gaynor, and Chic.

Adam and the Ants came on the scene, and everyone started to go out with a plaster stuck across their nose, and wore Dick Turpin outfits. The price of plasters went through the roof, I'll tell you. It was highway robbery. (Boom-boom!) David Bowie was at 'ground control' having terrible trouble trying to get in touch with 'Major Tom'. Perhaps he should have asked Michael Jackson to keep a lookout while he was doing his moonwalk, or the 'Rocket Man', Elton John. All these added colour and glitter to the fashion and music scene. I'm not sure if it was Elton John or Dame Edna Everage, the brilliant Barry Humphries ('Hello, possums') who started the quirky way-out glasses look.

Punk bands like the Sex Pistols, The Clash and Sham 69 became popular, and everyone then started to wear black bin bags, spiky hair, fishnet stockings and paper clips and chains.

Heavy metal bands like AC/DC, Black Sabbath, and Led Zeppelin gave us the early caveman look, open multicoloured tops showing a bare chest, long shaggy hair and beards, jeans and leather shoes or boots. There were glam rock bands like Queen, Slade, Sweet, and Marc Bolan, all wearing different types of outrageous multicoloured hairstyles, costumes, and face paint. Then there were Gothic rock bands: Siouxsie and the Banshees, The Cure, and Sisters of Mercy, mainly dressed in all black, looking like they were on their way to a funeral, or holding a wake for Uncle Fester of the Addams family.

The 80s heralded in very few bands or singers who brought us a new style. Most of the new bands and singers were influenced by bands from the past. I can't really think of any new bands that brought any major new styles as bands of the past had done. Lots of these bands are still as popular today as they were back in time. And it's thanks to the tribute artists and bands who keep the music and the memories of our youth alive.

The 90s and 2000s R&B singers and bands like Tupac Shakur, Eminem, 50 Cent, and The Notorious B.I.G. (Biggie), was about the only music to hit the scene that gave youngsters a new style of clothing to wear. This was bandanas, snapback trucker-style hats, big baggy jeans hanging around their arses, big baggy tops, hoodies, and long chains hanging around their necks with a medallion about the size of planet earth.

As I have already stated, there have been many other bands and singers in all different types of music genres, such as Motown, New Wave, garage, and grunge. And there have been lots of different boy bands all sounding very similar, from Take That to One Direction. The lists goes on and on of those that have had a small influence on us in our daily lives, but none like the ones I've mentioned. Sadly, for me today, music and fashion are just fun-less. (Is that a word? No? Well, it is now.) Lots of the music today is just continuous BOOM-BOOM-BOOM!

There have been many other changes in the way we have dressed over the years. From our heads to our toes. From the top hats, bowler hats and trilby hats of the 50s and 60s through to the bandanas, woolly hats, baseball caps and football caps, to the old-fashioned flat cap as in *Peaky Blinders*. Hairstyles have gone from the 50s short back and sides, the DA (duck's arse) and quiffs through to the shaggy perm, the Mohican, and today's top knot.

The 50s socks have gone from having loads of holes in them (well, mine did), through to long multicoloured worn-over-the-knee type, to bright fluorescent colours, to 'no socks baby, no socks'. Shoes have basically gone full circle many times over. Winkle-pickers, Chelsea boots, DMs (Dr. Martens), loafers, basketball boots and sneakers. They all have just been tweaked year on year to fit into the marketplace.

Oh, and I nearly forgot there was the Spice Girls.

One old thing from the 50s that has been recycled and dragged out at Christmas more times than Santa, is ... Sir Cliff Richard (bless him).

Fashion isn't just about clothing. Tattooing, piercing, hair transplants have been around for many years, but over the last few years they have all got more and more popular. Names, too, change over time and certain trends become fashionable.

Many years ago, the only people who had double-barrelled names were the lords and ladies, politicians, people with titles like The Right Horrible Sir Winston Brocklehurst-Fart (a fictitious name I hope). But nowadays it seems very fashionable to have a double-barrelled name. Lots of this is due to couples having kids before tying the knot, so they take both the parents' surnames. Others just want to be fucking flash.

Today's fashion seems to be about having a shit load of tattoos, a fake tan, a fake personality and giving your kids a shitty name. With names in mind, how fashionable it seems now to give your newborn baby, that beautiful little bundle of joy which you craved for over eight or nine months a bloody stupid name when it's finally born (just like some film stars and pop artists have done). I could be wrong, but I think the Geldofs started all this with Peaches (not too bad), Pixie (poor), and Fifi Trixibelle (sorry, but both are more suitable for a dog, not your daughter). And I don't know who it was that thought Heavenly Hiraani Tiger Lily Hutchence Geldof was a suitable or sensible name to give to a child. If I was one of those kids, I'd definitely have to change my name (I'd hate to be called Geldof).

Can you imagine registering these kids somewhere.

The registrar asks of the first one, 'What's your name, my dear?'

'Peaches Geldof.'

'OH, that's pretty, and what's *your* name?'

'Pixie Geldof.'

'OH, how lovely. And you?'

'Fifi Trixibelle Geldof.'

'OH, that's so beautiful, my dear. And what about you?'

'Heavenly Hiraani Tiger Lily Hutchence Geldof.'

'OH, my golly gosh, wonderful! And you must be Mr Geldof? And what wonderful exotic out-of-this-world name did your parents give to you, then?'

'BOB.'

'My God, why would they name you that? What is *wrong* with some parents? Do they never think about the poor child growing up with a name like ... BOB!'

But it *is* now fashionable today to give your kids an absolutely ridiculous name (and I don't mean 'BOB').

We used to take the piss out of Elton John's name, saying it sounded like a motorway junction on the M1, but it's nowhere near as bad as some of the names these poor kids are going to have to live with. Still, different fashions and trends will still come and go for years to come. We just wait with bated breath for the next one.

KITS PAST AND PRESENT:
Fashion past and present

Football and fashion years ago were never really mentioned in the same breath as they are today. But just as the film stars and musicians gave us our everyday fashions over the years, so football clubs and players do the same for us supporters today. When David Beckham had the Mohican hairstyle, so did thousands of supporters. That wouldn't have happened in the 50s and 60s. After all, would you really want to go into a barber's and ask for 'a Bobby Charlton or Ralph Coates comb-over please'.

When you look at old pictures of the fans at football matches in the 50s, most of the men are dressed in what looks like their suit, a white shirt, a tie, and a flat cap. They looked more like they were going to let out their pigeons, or going to a Labour Party meeting rather than a football match. And, because the coloured camera wasn't yet popular, most pictures were in black and white.

Back in the 50s, it was more about football passion than football fashion. The only fashionable things to have in football were a bobble hat, a scarf, a rosette and a wooden rattle, all in the club's colours. Football shirts in the early 50s were all very basic: big, heavy, long sleeve tops, and long shorts (if you can have such a thing as long *shorts*?) that came down over the knees. Teams chopped and changed their shirts, going from crew necks to collars to V-necks, and long sleeves to short sleeves and back again many, many times over.

Despite all the style changes, lots of clubs have kept the original colours they started with. But some have made changes. For example, Liverpool back in 1964 went from red and white to an all-red strip. Crystal Palace changed theirs from blue and claret to blue and red. I suppose the latest, and the one that caused the biggest controversy, was in 2012 when Malaysian businessman Vincent Tan, the then owner of Cardiff City, decided to not only change the team colour of blue to red, but also the team's nickname of The Bluebirds to the Cardiff Dragons. After lots of protesting from the supporters, Vincent Tan (feeling rather blue and red in the face, who might have wished his name was Vincent van Gogh after all the ear-bashing he got) changed it back again in 2015.

Lots of clubs have made other changes. Regarding their club badges, Fulham did just that when Al-Fayed took over. Some simply added another colour to the edges of their kit. The only thing I remember not changing colour was the goalkeeper's jersey (green, if I remember rightly). I think it was the colour worn by most keepers at this time (which, unfortunately, wasn't the same colour as the pitch for most of the year). Material for the shirts started to change about the mid-50s, moving from the heavy thick woollen material to a lighter more synthetic material.

For most of us older supporters, football fashion didn't really take off until the 60s. Football clubs since the 50s have always had three kits: one for home matches, one for away matches, and one extra away kit in case of any colour clashes with the opponents' colours.

Replica shirts have been around since the late 50s, but they were mainly produced for kids. However, sales took off more in the late 80s, and even more so in the 90s, and shirts have been a big part of our football lives ever since.

In our daily lives, over the years, we have had clothing brands like Ben Sherman, Calvin Klein, Gucci, Levi etc. In our football lives, we have Adidas, Hummer, Le Coq Sportif, Reebok etc.

The style of football kits over the years has basically stayed the same throughout apart from the chopping and changing of shirts: from round necks to V-necks to collars, and long shorts to short shorts, and socks by sports manufacturers such as Puma, Nike, Umbro, and Adidas. And I'm sure this will go on forever and a day.

Although back in 2002, the Cameroon team wore sleeveless tops, which FIFA said were illegal as they were vests, not shirts. So, they were banned. So to stick the ball back into FIFA's net, as they say, they then went to the 2004 CAFCO wearing an all-in-one strip (a onesie) and pissed FIFA off even more. It led to them getting a fine and 6 points deducted from their 2006 World Cup campaign.

In 1963 along came a young man by the name of Georgie Best who was to change style and fashion in the British footballing world. George, I suppose you could say, was the first real football super celebrity. Until now only a few footballers were seen as stars. Most footballers in Britain weren't really seen as anything other than sportsmen and women. Georgie Best did for football what the Beatles did for music. In fact, due to the way he had his hair and his style of dressing, he could have been the fifth Beatle. He was possibly one of the greatest British footballers I have ever seen. He had flair, balance, and unbelievable ball control while running at speed through the muddy ripped-up pitches, with defenders' tackles flying in from all directions. And he still had the ability to find the back of the net at the end of it all. Sadly, as well documented, George was not only on the back pages of all the tabloids owing to his sporting prowess, but he was also on the front as headline news owing to his way of life. Young fans wanted to play like him; older fans and supporters not only dreamed of playing like him but also wanted to dress and look like him. Fashion in football had started to take off.

Another Beatles lookalike Peter Marinello came to Arsenal in 1970. There was other players too such as the tall, good-looking, long-haired Frank Worthington at Leicester City; Malcolm Allison, wearing his fedora in 1975; Kevin Keegan and Craig Johnson with their shaggy perms; and Chris Waddle, Gerry Frances, and Barry Venison, all with the mullet hairstyle in the 70s and 80s.

Sadly, in 1990, comedians Baddiel and Skinner ('Three Lions' song) went a bit too far when they took the piss out of the hairstyle of one of the then Nottingham Forest players called Jason Lee, singing that he looked like he had a pineapple on his head owing to the fact that he had a ... I suppose you could say 'a high ponytail' on the top of his head. The song soon hit the terraces of opposing teams, and he was then subjected to abuse wherever and whenever he played. Unfortunately, this not only affected his game but also his life.

Since then, we have had David (pony-tailed) Seaman, David (the mop) Luiz, *'Peaky* Jack' Grealish, and lots more. Many supporters of all the aforementioned players have had their hair cut the same as their idols (well, sadly, perhaps not Jason Lee).

I must admit to being a big fan of Kevin Keegan back in the day, and in the 70s I did indeed have a shaggy perm (although nowadays, I tend to have more of a Jonjo Shelvey look about me).

Throughout my sixty or so years of following Fulham and football in general, I've seen all the different changes that clubs and players have made to supporters' lives. Supporters' fashion is all about the shirts we wear. When I think back to all those different shirts that I wore, I think 'DID I REALLY?'

Clubs bring out new shirts almost every year for us to wear, whether at matches, or just to wear casually. And that's fine. Now even though the styles have all basically stayed the same, the patterns and colours on the shirts have changed year upon year, and my God, haven't we had some bad ones! It always seems to be the away shirts that are the really bad ones, and they have been for many years.

But it isn't only Fulham who's had some fashion failures. In 1970, it looked as if Birmingham had simply decided to stitch together three pieces of someone's discarded yellow, red, and black curtains to make *their* shirt. In 1972, Cardiff went for a sickly yellow and mauve combo. The 1995 Liverpool goalkeeper's shirt looked as if the designer had been on a trip with Lucy 'in the sky with diamonds' (if you get my meaning). In 1993, Aston Villa brought out an away shirt that would have been better served for prisoners in jail. They certainly MULLER ... ED that shirt. (You need to see it to understand it).

The 1992 Norwich home shirt and the 1993 Peterborough away shirt looked as if they had had a paintballing contest and both teams sadly lost. These two teams should have been entered into the Johnson Paint Explosion Trophy. (You need to see it to understand it.) In 1994, Chelsea's away shirt of orange and grey was supposed to live up to its sponsor at the time, but unfortunately it wasn't Cool-s at all. (You need to see it to understand it.)

Then in 1996, the Manchester United players apparently couldn't see each other in their away grey strip as they got stuffed 6–3 by Southampton, even with the help of their sponsor Sharp Viewcam. (They should have gone to Specsavers?)

Let's face it, today's football for the owners is all about the money, and selling football attire, especially football shirts, and that is where we supporters come into the equation. Supporters nowadays are walking, talking billboards. Years ago, you would see some poor sod walking up and down the high street, sandwiched in between two blackboards, with a sign saying something like '20% off at Saucy Sally's Sex Shop', or '2FOR1 at Big Bad Brian's Tattoo Parlour'. The worst one was a bloke who looked like an undertaker, with a sign that said 'The end of the world is nigh'. He'd shout out, 'Jesus saves.' And the kids used to shout back, 'And Greavsie (Jimmy) scores on the rebound.'

I think football clubs should give us free shirts for advertising their sponsors, or at least give us some freebies of the products we're advertising for them. Since the 80s when Fulham had their first ever sponsorship deal with William Younger's beer company, I have advertised the GMB, casinos, internet companies, betting firms and Visit Florida. And out of all these companies for whom I, personally, have made millions of pounds, all I've ever got was a discounted pizza when we sponsored Pizza Hut.

We supporters don't care about who we have as a sponsor on the shirt, and we don't care if it's made by Adidas, Puma, or Reebok; we only care about our club badge being on that shirt close to our hearts, and for most, we like to have our favourite player's name on the back.

In the 50s, the shorts were that long that they met up with the big thick heavy socks that possibly weighed more than a full football kit would weigh today. Shin pads were as thick as a telephone directory. The ball was also made of leather and weighed a ton, and when it rained, it got clogged up with mud, which made it even heavier. It was a nightmare to head, feeling more like a medicine ball. It has been linked to the death of the ex-West Brom legend Jeff Astle in 2002, and sadly too the dementia of many other players.

By the mid-60s, just about every team had changed to the new lightweight kit with nylon socks. Football boots in the 50s were more like big old army boots that came up to the ankle, and apparently, they weren't originally made for kicking or running. They weren't even made to aid the player. They were designed and worn just to protect the feet. They were made of tough leather, and were heavy enough when they were dry. But they weren't waterproof, so when they got wet, they were like deep-sea divers' boots. If you look back at some of the pitches that have been played on over the years you could have understood if they had played in wellington boots. It was mainly in the 70s and 80 that the pitches were that bad, and some stayed that way even up until the early 2000s. Check out the Chelsea pitch. In a 2002–2003 season match versus Charlton, the pitch had more sand on it than most seaside resorts.

For the energetic football-playing supporters (a title to which I no longer subscribe), the new fashionable footwear is a must for most. Since the 50s when Adidas designed a boot that had the screw in studs made of plastic or rubber, boots have been made lighter and more flexible. The 70s was the start of the change from the original black boots only policy to today's multicoloured boots when the brilliant Alan Ball (1966 World Cup winner) wore a pair of white Hummel boots in a charity match for Everton versus Chelsea at Stamford Bridge. In the 80s we had Puma Kings, in the 90s the Craig Johnson (ex-Liverpool player) Adidas Predator boot. There has also been Nike Mercurial and so many more.

Boots today are more like slippers: lace-less, flimsy, multicoloured, personalised with the player's signature on them. And they also had GPS tracking to see how far the players have run. What I'd like to know from these multimillion-pound sports companies is this … how come they can pay players millions of pounds to wear their sports clothes and pay me fuck-all when I wear them?

Still, different football fashions and trends will still come and go for years to come. We just wait with bated breath for the next one.

Chapter Fifteen

Being Stood Up
BAD GAMES

I'll wait for her till the very end:
I'LL WAIT UNTIL THE FINAL WHISTLE BLOWS

OK, so now you're in your in your teens, and you've met someone who you're really keen on. You've met them a couple of times locally with your friends around, but now you want to move the relationship up a notch. So, you ask them out on a date. (When I was young, it was normally to the pictures, or the local dance hall.) You arrange to meet this new love you've found outside wherever, at an agreed time. Sadly, sometimes things don't always go to plan. I'm sure that over the years most of us have suffered the humiliation of being stood up for a date or two (come on now, own up, you're among friends).

Now you've been standing around for hours and she doesn't show up. What a bummer. You've rushed your arse off running around all morning, getting all spruced up, and gone to the bother of having a bath outside of your normal monthly sequence.

You've splashed on a bit of cheap aftershave that your sister bought you as a joke thinking it was funny to buy you a bottle that was endorsed by some overpaid footballer who you couldn't stand. (And my God, doesn't that stuff bloody well sting! Especially if you happen to splash some of it on the lower parts of your anatomy. Oh yes! It only happened to me once and I soon realised I'd make sure I had my pants on in future. A drop of that stuff on your old chap could make it go limper than Dale Winton's wrist.)

You've spent a fortune on a new shirt, a new pair of strides (why is it that when you buy a pair of trousers you only get one item and not two?), a new pair of shoes (you get two of them. It's just as well they don't use the same logic for shoes as they do for trousers or we'd all be hopping about the place), and you've had a dodgy haircut at the local barbers. (They were barbers in my day!) A short back and sides for two shillings was about the best they could do, and in many cases, it was about the only cut they could do. It looked like you'd had a bowl put on your head, and he'd cut around it. Then to finish it off ... he'd put a large lump of what looked like cooking lard on your head, but in fact it was called Brylcreem. He'd plaster this on to stop the remains of the hair from sticking up. (God, you thought you were so macho.) There was none of this poncy salon stuff we get today: anything from £25 up to £50 for a cut, wash, and a blow job, plus a tiny bit of hair gel gently rubbed in to make it look all spiky. This is so unlike years ago when the barber could do that quite easily without any hair gel. Your hair now makes it look more like you've just sat on a pair of your girlfriend's hot curling tongs.

Anyway, you're all pumped up and ready to go. You look at the clock. It says four o'clock, and you realise you got ready far too early. But that doesn't matter because years ago you would always meet at about six on a weekend or seven if it was mid-week. Nightclubs, pubs, and cinemas nearly all closed by about half past ten. There was no late-night drinking in those days, unless you were friendly with the landlord of the pub. Three or four hours together was about all you got before you had to get her home at a respectful hour. A quick snog and a grope if you were lucky, before her dad called her in.

Years ago, everything was supposed to be done in a prim and proper fashion. Respect was the name of the game. Well, that's what you hoped her parents thought you had in mind. But how times have changed (for better or for worse? I'll let you decide for yourself). Nowadays, with late-night pictures and some films lasting longer than the time you two spent together all those years ago, 24-hour drinking means that pubs and clubs can stay open all night and go on through to the next morning (although I don't think there are many pubs that do stay open all night outside of the big cities).

Also gone is the quick snog and grope when getting her home at a decent hour. A decent hour now is before the postman or milkman arrives. Now it's a full-blown 'wham, bam, thank you ma'am' sex session (and that's just before you go out). Oh yes, times have certainly changed.

OK, so being ready early is not a problem as you need plenty of time to get a couple of drinks inside you to help steady your nerves for when you meet (if only you knew). You phone a taxi as you don't want to rely on the buses or trains, which are normally late because the wrong type of snow, or a leaf, has fallen on the line. (Not a bloody great tree, a leaf, for God's sake!)

Also have you ever noticed that when you're going somewhere important, it seems some company has decided to dig a bloody great hole in the road, and there are always about six blokes just standing there looking in it. (Why? It's a hole that's been dug, presumably because there's a problem down there. So guys, hello, don't just look in it, get in it, and fix it, then fill it. It's not rocket science.)

There are always some kind of road works going on to hold you up, and they always seem do it at the busiest time of the day. If it's not road repairs, then the traffic lights are not working, and everything is at a standstill. And it's not the lights being out that's the problem, it's because a policeman is directing the traffic. When the drivers are left alone to sort themselves out, there are very few problems, but as soon as a bobby gets involved, it's mayhem.

Now you're in a rush to meet her, and it seems the whole world is against you, and you don't want her waiting around for you. That would never do. So you get a taxi, and this adds to the cost. So far you've already spent a fortune that you can't really afford, and you've not even met up yet. You keep checking your watch for the time. But, even after all these problems you've faced, you have still managed to get there a bit earlier than you had planned (about one hour). The arranged time to meet has now passed, but still you wait in anticipation for her to show up. In your head you start going through all the reasons as to why she hasn't arrived yet (well, she is only 15 minutes late). Maybe she missed the bus (it's walking distance). She finished work late? (It's Sunday, she doesn't work on Sundays.) Her cat got run over (that was the reason last time). You wait even though you know deep down inside she isn't coming.

You try to blend in with the scenery, making out that nothing's wrong, but you feel everyone's looking at you. Some are feeling sorry for you because you're standing there like a spare prick at a wedding or like Lily Savage at a bikers convention. Some of the guys are laughing under their breath as their dates arrive, and they all know yours hasn't (she's only one hour late). Still you look for that reason why she's a bit late. She's been abducted by aliens. A tidal wave has swept her away. There's been a military uprising in Putney. Or, Edward (Teddy) Kennedy (JFK the ex-American president's younger brother) has given her a lift. Back then you'd think perhaps George Michael had given her a lift and stopped at a set of traffic lights for a kip. She's now three hours late and you start to think that perhaps she's not coming.

The pubs, nightclubs, and the cinema are all closed. The rain's pissing down, which, thanks to the amount of greasy Brylcreem on your head, is just running down your back like Niagara Falls. Your ego feels like it's been kicked into touch by Johnny Wilkinson, and you finally realise ... she's not going to turn up. No matter how long you wait. You stand there, feeling the world is coming to an end. The rain is hiding your tears, you're just a sad and lonely lost soul.

Eventually you concede defeat and make that miserable lonely journey back home alone, absolutely gutted that the love of your life could do this to you again. The last couple of times you accepted her excuses, but not this time. This time she's gone too far, and you won't be doing all this again (well, that's what you tell yourself). You've now got to go home and face your family and friends, all of whom are going to want to know what's happened, and what went wrong. Your family will be sympathetic towards you, telling you 'she's not worth it' and advising you to tell her 'To sling her hook.' They will add, 'there are plenty more fish in the sea.'

While you can take all that from your family (after all, they mean well), and they don't understand what true loves about. But you are going to get some serious shit from all your so-called mates. They are going to give you such a verbal kicking while you're down, and it doesn't matter how much you try and make excuses, they are going to take the piss out of you big time, and ram it right up your... er ... where the sun doesn't shine.

You're going to hear things like, 'She was most probably out shagging another bloke and forgot the time' or 'Perhaps her pimp wouldn't give her the night off' or 'Maybe Cinderella said she had to stay in with her other sister and do the housework.' (These women don't realise what pain and suffering you go through when they don't turn up.) Still, tomorrow's another day, and after enduring all the flak from your mates (and don't kid yourself that you wouldn't do the same to them if the shoe was on the other foot), life goes on. The fact that she's gone too far this time in your eyes doesn't make you feel any different towards her. You will be told what went wrong, and why she wasn't there to meet you. And it doesn't matter what her excuse is, you will accept it because you are totally besotted with her. You will forgive and forget, and await your next date. Love is blind.

BAD GAMES:
Being stood up

Going to watch your team play has that same nervous expectation as arranging to meet your date, especially when it's away from home. You've been running around all morning trying to find your football shirt, your lucky socks or lucky underwear because you must have these as no others will do. Mum's gone out, and you don't have a clue where to look.

After ransacking the house from top to bottom, you finally find your whole kit at the bottom of the laundry basket where they've been for the last week. Unmoved by this slight setback, and after calling your mother all the names under the sun, you try to freshen up your clothes. You try and get the rancid smell of stale sweaty armpits out of the shirt, and the stinky smell of feet out of the socks by splashing them with some old aftershave you happen to have that has been endorsed by some ex-footballer who used to play for a certain football club in Manchester, and who now has his own football club in the USA. And now, as far as you are concerned, it's about all the aftershave is fit for. Although now it doesn't seem to make a big difference. You are now unable to tell which smells worse, the clothes or the aftershave.

You've only got the aftershave because your sister thought it a great joke when she gave it to you for your birthday. The silly cow, like some of the others around you just doesn't understand football and the passion that goes with it. The silly cow doesn't even understand the offside rule. (Come to think about it, I don't know anybody who does nowadays.)

What with the price of the coach fare, the cost of the taxi getting to the coach, and your ticket to get in (and you're not even there yet), so far, it's cost you a fortune. You look at the clock and you're early, but that doesn't matter. Years ago, nearly all League and FA Cup matches started at three o'clock on a Saturday so you knew exactly where you were and what was what. Some cup games, such as the League, the Milk, the Worthington (and whatever else it has been known as), along with the European matches, would nearly all be midweek and start around seven thirty. But how things have changed what with Sky and now BT TV throwing money at the game left, right and centre. Nowadays, nobody can be sure when the matches will be played: quarter to one this day, eight o'clock that day, a Sunday, or a Monday, or perhaps a Friday. It's difficult to make any long-term arrangements to go and see your team play.

A couple of beers are needed to steady your nerves. You get to the coach in plenty of time (an hour before its departure). You didn't want miss it. You want to be there when your team takes to the pitch so that you can cheer them on.

After a long and tedious journey, which according to Google maps should only have taken about three hours, it has in fact taken nearly five because you've had to endure more hold-ups than Dick Turpin ever did in his lifetime. If it's not accidents, or warnings of pedestrians or animals on the motorway (and this concerns me a bit as I can understand animals straying onto a motorway because they don't know anything about the highway code, but be fair, you have got to have a bucket of manure for brains to wander onto a motorway, and be even thicker to drive down the motorway on the wrong side of the road), then it has got to be the dreaded motorway maintenance brigade these people have made more jams than Hartley's). Armed with their dreaded orange and white cones, they can cause more trouble than you can imagine. Here you are in the coach, going along the motorway quite happily when all of a sudden it starts to slow right down. From cruising along at a nice steady 70 miles an hour, within a matter of a couple of hundred yards, you're doing 5 miles an hour, and then the cones come into sight, and you know in your heart of hearts the nightmare is about to start. Three lanes become two and two become one. You try to see as far ahead as you can, but the queue is miles long. You hope to see the orange flashing lights and not the blue ones (at least with the orange lights you should keep moving, even if it's only at 2 miles an hour). The blue ones can mean a bigger problem ahead.

You crawl along for what seems an eternity. Two miles of cones on the road soon becomes four miles then five, and you're at the point of giving up living altogether. Then suddenly hope comes into sight, and you breathe a sigh of relief as the orange flashing lights appear in distance. You *will* make the kick-off after all.

You crawl closer to these hypnotic flashing lights, and see the reason for the hold-up as it comes into view. You have just been delayed for almost two hours by about eight motorway maintenance lorries, which are scattered about the road, and a dozen men in yellow high-vis jackets, ten of whom are watching the other two replacing a piece of metal barrier. And they felt they had to shut down two lanes for about five miles for safety reasons! I can understand closing about one mile of road, causing a small delay, but five miles is a bit much. And if the other ten workers gave a hand it would have taken even less time. Then, when the work is finally finished, they have to drive backwards up the motorway collecting the miles upon miles of bloody cones that have been put out unnecessarily.

You finally get through all the obstacles the journey has brought, and you arrive at your final destination. You find a place to stand or sit on the terrace while you're waiting for you team to appear on the pitch and play out of their skins, to show the opposition who's who.

But after a couple of minutes, you go one–nil down, then two–nil, three-nil, four-nil. It's just like your date: it's like your team hasn't turned up. What's going on, you ask yourself. You try to think of the reason. You've got the wrong socks on (no, they're the right ones, just dirty). You've got the wrong pants on (no, they're the right ones, just dirty). Your own supporters near you start to look at you and they slowly begin to move away. You start to think it's your fault the team are losing, and that the other supporters know something about you that you haven't realised yourself. And now a very large space has developed between you and them, and you start to panic. You're wondering why they are treating you like some kind of leper. Why? Why? It's not something you are doing wrong. It's not your fault the team is losing. They're not blaming you, it's the poxy smell of that shitty aftershave you're wearing (or could it be your kit? I know which one I would blame).

On match days everything must be just right, from the time you get up in the morning to what you eat or drink, and especially what you wear. And every movement must follow the same sequence as the last match day. The fact you also lost your last game was not down to what you did or didn't do on the day. You did everything in your power to help, but again today it's all gone miserably wrong. They've let you down again. They've gone too far this time. You stand there, feeling the world is coming to an end. The rain is pissing down and hiding your tears. You're just a sad and lonely soul.

The home supporters are laughing at you knowingly. At 6–0, you finally concede defeat. There's no way back, they're not going to show up. So now it's time for that long, long, lonely journey home, and guess what? On that long, long journey back home to face your family and friends, those bastard motorway maintenance guys have put out some more of those poxy cones on the other side of the motorway: the same eight lorries, the same ten blokes watching the same two silly arses doing all the work.

After another lengthy delay you finally get home to face all the questions. Your family will try to be a little sympathetic towards you, saying things like 'Perhaps they will do better next time' and 'Oh, don't worry, there are plenty more games left.' They mean well, but they don't understand what football is all about. Your mates who all support bigger clubs are going to give it to you large: 'Six–nil. Close then, was it?' or 'Only six against your lot. Why? Did their team have some players sent off then?' or some just tell you straight, 'What did you expect? You're shit.'

When your team doesn't put up some sort of a show, they just don't understand how it hurts. Tomorrow's another day and you will hear all the reasons why your team didn't perform the way they should have, why they let down their supporters in front of the opposition, and humiliated you so badly. And no matter what the manager's excuse is, you will accept it.

Whether it's your girlfriend or your team who lets you down, it feels the same. You take the stick and put on a brave face, because you know that sooner or later, you'll get your own back. Your girl might not be the best looker or your team top of the league, but your love for them both is never in doubt. The stick you tend to get is mostly from your so-called mates, who get the girls that everybody drools over, and it seems that their team always appear to win.

Still, no matter what they say or how your girl or team treats you, the love for them will always be there no matter what, and so will you. Because you are totally besotted with your team. You will forgive and forget and await your next away day. Love is blind.

Chapter Sixteen

Home Cooking
MATCH DAY MEALS

No more feasting on fish 'n' chips:
NOW WE WATCH WHAT GOES BETWEEN OUR LIPS

It seemed that the word diet hadn't been invented back in the late 50s and early 60s. Most of us didn't need to worry too much about our weight though due to the fact that there wasn't a great deal dished up to us at the table. And even though a lot of it was fried, most of us didn't put on an ounce. Obviously, different parts of the country had their own delicacies. For most of us lower-class citizens living in the south, our food was very basic. Plenty of vegetables, not a lot of meat. Spam, corned beef, liver and bacon were the staples. Sadly, for some it was bread and jam, or bread and dripping with a large amount of salt. (Dripping was the fat which came from the Sunday joint if you were lucky enough to have one). Bubble and squeak was usually dished up on Mondays. This consisted of any left-over vegetables and potatoes, from your rare Sunday roast dinner, all mashed together and fried up in a pan. You might even be lucky enough to get a slice or two of any meat left over (that was as rare as the meat). But normally your dad got that and you had a fried egg instead. Lots of people also have bubble and squeak along with a traditional full English breakfast.

Puddings (or afters, as we called them due to the fact that you got them after your dinner) were things like spotted dick or jam roly-poly with custard, all thick and fattening.

When you think about it the timetable for eating food is quite confusing …

Breakfast is breakfast in any language (unless you live somewhere where it's not called breakfast, like Mexico for instance where it's called *desayuno*, or in Denmark where it's called *morgenmad*.)

So, thinking about it, breakfast isn't *actually* called breakfast in any language. Still, moving on ... lunch is eaten at lunchtime, unless you are at school, then school dinners are eaten at lunchtime, unless you can't afford school dinners, then you take a packed lunch for dinner (or lunch?). Many office workers take a packed lunch to work to have at lunchtime (or dinner time). Then is it teatime in the evening, or it that dinner time? Because when you come home from school or work, lots of people ask, 'What's for tea?' You can't ask 'what's for dinner?' because you had that at lunchtime (or was that dinner time?). Perhaps it's better to forget the what time *what* is and just ask, 'What have we got to eat?'

It's quite strange that as kids we would eat as much as we liked and no one could care less about weight or whether the food was good or bad for us. Nobody ever explained what too much fat and sugar could do to us. Schools at this time gave us miniature bottles of milk; they said milk was good for you. Apparently it *was* good for us back then, but not so good now (too much fat, unless you have skimmed or semi-skimmed).

Given the chance, we kids would just have eaten chocolate morning, noon, and night. We ate what our parents' pockets could afford for us to eat. Most of the kids going to school couldn't afford school meals, and lots of the working class, such as office workers, ate sandwiches at lunchtimes (or should that be ...? No, sod that, I'm not going through all that lot again).

Lots of manual workers, like builders and lorry drivers, went to the cafe (the greasy spoon) for a fry-up. But as we all got older, sadly, lots of us got wider, and not wiser, and still most of us didn't learn. I had always done a job (the doorstep milkman) which kept me quite fit, and I was not one to put on too much timber, so I never took real notice of what I was eating, whether it was good or bad.

But then I started to take more care in the mid-80s after having a stomach operation. I had started to become very bloated due to the fact that I could now eat more solid foods such as steak or chicken (I don't think drinking six to eight pints of beer each day helped either). But I did do plenty of exercise in the form of running. Unfortunately, the booze outran the running regarding the fitness. I think that it's only been over the last 30 or so years that people have realised that we are what we eat, as they say.

Nowadays fitness gyms and health centres are booming. I put this all down to one man and one man only, a hero who goes by the name of Mr Derrick Evans, aka Mr Motivator. He, in the early 1990s when appearing on breakfast TV, single-handedly got people out of their armchairs and in front of their TVs, bobbing up and down, marching on the step, to the left, to the right, backwards and forwards, step after step, every day for hours on end. (Mind you, I was like that most Friday and Saturday evenings after coming out of the pub!) What a man he was! Not only did he help us with our fitness levels, he also helped the keep fit industry start to grow. Not only that, he also helped keep the carpet industry going, because people had worn bloody great big holes in their carpets. Well done Mr M!

But seriously, we were now living in a different cultural world. With the influx of overseas workers and tourists coming to England, all different types of food became more and more available in shops and stores. Cooking programmes on TV were a-plenty: Fanny Cradock was one of the first I really remember with her pisshead husband Johnnie, who would say things like, 'May all your doughnuts turn out like Fanny's', which in the day was a bit raunchy. Then we had Graham Kerr, 'The Galloping Gourmet', which was the nickname given to him after he went to different restaurants around the world in 35 days, showing his viewers all different types of dishes from various countries.

Since those earlier years we've had a range of chefs on our TVs: Keith Floyd, Delia 'Let's be 'aving you' Smith, Ainsley Harriot, Nigella Lawson, and Jamie Oliver, all now showing us the right things to eat and the best way to cook them. Our diets for the most part have changed massively. Whether you're choosing to eat at home, at a local restaurant or in a pub, people nowadays have more knowledge and understanding of their bodies, and what food and diets mean.

Wraps and flat bread have for some taken the place of sandwiches; pasta has taken the place of potatoes. Salads, fish, and rice is more popular than pie, mash and liquor. It's olive oil instead of lard or dripping for cooking. Baked instead of fried. There are more vegetarian and vegan options on menus. Wine, spirits, and energy drinks have taken over, in some cases, from beer, lager and Guinness. And because of what we now know, it's helping us all to hopefully live longer and healthier.

Unfortunately, there are some people who have different kinds of health problems and trying to keep their weight down will always be a struggle. Sadly, there are also some people who are just not concerned about their health and fitness, so a Big Mac, KFC, or a steaming hot curry is for them ideal after 10 or 12 pints at one o'clock in the morning before going to their pit. Also, there are lots of people who are addicted to food, who just cannot seem to help themselves, who, for some reason or another, just have to eat. There are lots of different types of eating disorders that not only affect people's waistlines but also their mental health. Binge eating and drinking not only damages your body but also your mind. It's easy to fall into the addiction, but a lot harder to get out of it.

The richer classes (and I'm only presuming as I've never been invited to the home of anyone who is that rich) had the money to buy the best meat from the top butchers. Steak not Spam, sliced ham not corned beef, croissants and jam, not a slice of bread and butter, and any meat left over from their Sunday banquet was most probably given to the servants or the pets. They would have vintage wine or a glass of bubbly and they most probably had their posh nosh cooked by a Cordon Bleu chef and dished up on a silver platter. Ours was cooked by my dear old mum, and dished up on a 10p chipped plate from the local charity shop.

(OH my God, I'm so bitter.)
GOOD FOOD SHOULD MEAN GOOD HEALTH!

MATCH DAY MEALS:
Home cooking

Football teams all over the country years ago seemed to have had very little concern over what their players consumed be it food or drink. They were eating the same food as just about everyone else in the country. Players like the great Jimmy Greaves apparently on match days ate a roast beef and Yorkshire pudding dinner with all the trimmings, and followed that up with some kind of fruit pie or crumble and custard before kick-off. Lots of other players would have pie and mash, or steak, chips and peas, or a breakfast fry-up. Some would even prefer a few beers before kick-off. Some even took a hip flask into the changing room and had a calm-yourself-down drink. Some have even been known to turn up on match day totally rat-arsed!

After the match, it was normally time for a good old-fashioned piss-up. These could go on until the early hours of the morning, finishing off at some nightclub or another. Midweek after training, it would be down to the bookies, then on to the snooker halls for a few racks of snooker and a few beers, or maybe a few hands of cards, then on to their local watering holes for a few more beers.

Health and fitness were, at the very best, pretty poor. Players were just about match fit, but that was that it. Training was more about running around, passing and crossing, attack versus defence. Unfortunately, the years of alcohol abuse started to catch up with some of the great players, such as George Best, Tony Adams, Paul Merson, and the magical Paul Gascoigne. For many it also led to mental health issues. It's great to see that most of them are now dealing with whatever their problems may have been. And I hope it carries on being that way for these players who have brought us (whether you support the teams they played for or not) some great football memories over the years.

Paul Merson's books, *How Not to Be a Professional Footballer* and *Hooked: Addiction and the Long Road to Recovery*, both highlight how easy it is to fall under the influence of drink, drugs, and gambling. It examines all the problems addiction later brings, and also how difficult it is to break the addiction.

I think that it's only been over the last 30 or so years that players have realised we are what we eat, and now players and their football clubs are at another level. I put this all down to one man, and one man only, a hero who goes by the name of Mr Arsène Wenger, aka *Le Professeur*. In the mid-1990s when in charge at Arsenal FC, he single-handedly tried to put the makers of tomato sauce out of business, because he banned it at the club's training ground. No more egg and chips and ketchup. He replaced it with healthier options, such as fresh boiled vegetables, pasta, and rice, which, according to rumours, pissed off Ian 'Wright Wright Wright'. Lots of reports state that *Le Professeur* led the way in transforming other clubs to follow suit.

We were now in a culturally different playing field. With the influx of foreign players coming into our leagues, clubs had no real options but change. When Claudio Ranieri took over at Leicester, he banned chicken burgers, preferring to have pizza. Antonio Conte at Chelsea banned both types of sauce: brown and tomato. David Moyes at Manchester United banned chips.

The chairman and owner of Forest Green Rovers, Vince Dale, banned just about everything, because in 2015, FGR became the world's first vegan football club. Presumably it had some effect, because two years later they were promoted in the football league, and have now climbed up to Division One. (I'm not sure what their football movement is like on the pitch, but I'm sure their bowel movement off it must be working fine.)

Clubs and players now saw the benefits of heathier eating and drinking. English players were now having to change their diets after seeing their overseas teammates' eating and drinking habits. Pasta, salads, rice, chicken, and fish replaced all the pies, the roasts, and the steaks. A glass of wine or a couple of beers and plenty of energy drinks took over from the piss-ups. Early nights took over from the early mornings. A round of golf took over, for most, from the snooker halls.

Due to this new regime, players were fitter and heathier; football became faster and more intense and, in most cases, better to watch. The richer clubs always had more of a chance to change those bad old days into the new good days due to their financial clout, better training grounds and equipment, more trainers and health gurus. Unfortunately, for some players it didn't matter what they ate or how much they dieted, they'd struggle to keep their weight down, which can cause different types of mental health problems as well as fitness problems.

At most football grounds in earlier days supporters could only purchase perhaps a couple of types of pies: steak and kidney, or chicken: maybe packets of crisps or a few sweets: and Bovril, tea and coffee. You could generally also buy a carton of squash that was so diluted down it was difficult to tell what flavour it was. Nowadays, you can more or less have a full-blown meal: veggie burgers, soya hot dogs with peppers and onions, and curried pies. Beers, wine, lager, Guinness, tea or coffee, hot chocolate, and all different kinds of soft drinks are also on offer, and all at extortionate prices. With most clubs now, you can also get its corporate entertainment package: drinks and a three-course meal before the game, a drink and picky bits at half-time, and after the game, it's more drinks and meet a player from the past.

GOOD FOOD SHOULD MEAN GOOD HEALTH!!

Chapter Seventeen

Conscription
ENGLAND CALL-UP

Medals on your chest:
THREE LIONS ON YOUR SHIRT

When the First and Second World Wars were declared, to help bolster our troops and to help give us a fighting chance against the enemy, there was a large recruitment drive. You've seen the old posters: 'YOUR COUNTRY NEEDS YOU. Join up now!!' And there was Lord Kitchener pointing a finger at you, hoping you would sign up for a few years. Apparently the story has it that the poster actually came into being after the War had started and it didn't help recruitment as much as we were led to believe.

As the War escalated across Europe, the British Government brought in conscription, or as it has also been known in the past, National Service or Military Service. Conscription meant that anyone who was fit enough to go to war, between certain ages: 18–51 for men, and 20–30 for women, was called up to join one of the military forces. Later, as the War went on, more and more women of all ages were called upon. If you had a valid reason as to why you couldn't or shouldn't go and fight for your country, such as a medical, mental, or physical problem, but you couldn't prove it, then like it or not you were conscripted into the military.

Lots of youngsters who had such problems, or were under the requirement age, tried their best to hoodwink the authorities because they wanted to go and fight. A few managed to get through the interviews at the recruitment centres, but most were found out and turned away. So, once you did manage to get signed up, off you went to a military training camp where you were would meet up with lots of other recruits. You were all drafted into squads, all of whom were deemed ready to fight the dreaded foe. There was lots of exercise, training, and instructions from the military leaders there on how they wanted you to work as a team so that you would bond and watch each other's back. Lots of the recruits already had a small amount of military training and experience having been in other youth groups, such as the Boy Scouts, The Boys Brigade, Sea Scouts, or Air Training Corps. For them, moving up with the big boys wasn't so difficult.

Some of the top military brasses were there, making sure everything was in place, and that you were ready for when you were called upon whenever the fighting started.

Men and women who were over the age of conscription stayed at home and helped to make ammunition, bombs and aircrafts, and build ships. And of course, there were the famous land girls, or the land army. These were women who took the place of the men who had gone off to fight in the war. These were among some of the hundreds of other important jobs that all needed doing.

Many ex-World War One soldiers formed the Home Guard ('They don't like it up em' and 'Don't panic, don't panic, the Germans are coming.' Classic *Dad's Army*.) They were there to protect the country, especially the coastline in case German troops tried to invade. ('Who do you think you are kidding, Mr Hitler?')

Many young children were sent out of the cities and down to the countryside to be looked after by families who were living in safer areas where they were less likely to be in danger of the bombings. Sadly, some kids never, ever saw their true families again, as lots of families perished under the constant bombing raid on the cities.

When conscription was abolished in 1960 (I was only nine at the time), I am led to believe you could hear a sigh of relief from the young men and women over the age of 18, who at least for now could live without fear of the dreaded call-up. This meant that they could decide for themselves if and when they went to fight if it all went and kicked off again, and not leave it to somebody in high authority to decide whether to throw them in at the deep end.

There were the conscientious objectors. These were people who refused to go to war because of their beliefs, whether religious or just that they didn't believe in what the country was fighting for (or perhaps they simply weren't prepared to die at that age). I suppose one the most famous objectors at the time was Muhammad Ali, formally Cassius Clay, possibly the greatest heavyweight boxer to ever get into the ring. Due to his religious belief, he refused to go and fight for America in the Vietnam War. He was then arrested and stripped of his titles. It is quite strange to think that he could fight in the ring and hurt people but was not willing to fight for his country. I suppose his thoughts were that it's one thing fighting as a sport to earn a living, but it's another thing killing someone you don't know, or maybe, for something you don't believe in. Lots of objectors were willing to help the cause but in other ways. They did this by working in the factories, in hospitals, or doing other important types of work, but not physically going to the front.

Even after the tragic memories of the First World War, people were still prepared (in some cases, falling over themselves) to fight in World War Two and die for their country. Proud men and women's bravery and courage were honoured with medals such as the VC, the George Cross, and other such awards. There was heroes, such as Douglas Bader, who flew many missions despite losing both legs in a previous crash. Oskar and Emilie Schindler are credited for saving the lives of many thousands of Jews, even though Oskar, apparently, was a member of the Nazi party as portrayed in the film *Schindler's List* starring Liam Neeson. The British spy Odette Sansom, who was French-born but living in England, was awarded an MBE, George Cross, *and* the French Legion of Honour for helping the British Government and the French Resistance by going back to France and spying for the British and the French.

One famous name who gave everything for the French cause was the very funny René Artois from the wonderful TV show *'Allo 'Allo!'* This starred Gordon Kaye as René, the very sexy Vicki Michelle as Yvette, Kim Hartman as Helga, and Guy Siner as the gay Lieutenant Gruber; the list goes on (a programme not to be missed). There were many more unknown warriors all of whom were willing to risk life and limb to defend ours and other people's freedom and democracy and to defend the right to stand up and say what we think without any recrimination, to be heard, and hopefully make a difference to not only their own lives, but to the lives of other people living in this great country.

If in 1946 you could have asked many of the survivors whether it was all worth the fight and the loss of lives, I think most would say yes, because sad as it was for those who had died or were severely injured, and all the families that were affected, it was just to keep our identity and our freedom. But most important of all, it was to keep Britain British!!

After the War ended, lots were demobbed from the military and went back to civilian life. Many also chose to become reservists (reserves), meaning they were available should they be needed if there was another military threat, to be called upon in case of an emergency.

Sixty years on, I wonder what response you would get now if you were to ask those same people, who are now pensioners, that same question: was it all worth it? I'm pretty sure the answer would be very different. The tear of relief and the joyous victory of 1946 would be a different tear today. I think that today's tear would be that of sadness, dismay and disgust, and the question might possibly be answered with a few fucks, bollocks and arseholes, all aimed at the people who since the war, have given away just about everything we had.

All the brave men and women who fought for all those things years ago, are now fighting daily against a bigger enemy (their own Government) just to survive. Their voices, softened by the weapons used against them, are no longer heard. Their freedom is limited, and their democracy is all but down the toilet.

Their belief in a fight for a better future all those years ago has diminished year by year as shown by their war-torn faces, and their sad baggy eyes. It's a big question 'was it worth the fight?' It probably was then. But now? It's quite strange that many of the people in power who make decisions about war (who we fight, when we fight, which troops, and where we send them) have never, ever been to the front line, or stood in the bloodshed fields of battle.

NO WAR HAS EVER BEEN WORTH IT

Whether we like it or not, our governments over the years, the ones we elected to do the right thing by us, have sold us down the Swanee. Thousands of our people fought and died to keep our country out of the hands of the Germans, to retain our freedom only to sell us off to Europe years later and lose the very freedom we fought for. Thankfully, we have now managed to get out of the claws of Europe, where it seemed we were no longer going to be English or British, but where we were now all to be European. This also meant that we were unable to think or do for ourselves. Each year these faceless European MPs brought in new rules and directives from (no! not Westminster) but yes, Brussels, Brussels where the only thing they've ever had that was any good, is the sprout and pâté.

Mighty Brussels where they were now making world-changing decisions about how to make our lives much more enriched, decisions such as how long your cucumber must be, or how bent your banana was (no these are not euphemisms). You couldn't even bury your cat or your dog in the garden anymore, oh, unless you owned the property, which was great news for mums and dads, but a bit of bummer for the kids, who were now traumatised after just finding poor old Tiddles was brown bread (dead). Now instead of having a nice send-off, you tell your offspring, as you place their dead pet in a 20p Tesco plastic bag before putting it in the wheelie bin, that he's going to heaven to sit and purr alongside God (all because these bureaucrats had nothing better to do) This brings another problem; do you put him in the black bin (household rubbish) or the green bin (recycled). If it's the green bin, then you can't put him in a plastic bag to send him on his way. Then you try and tell the kids that the bin men are moonlighting for the Co-op Funeral Service. No, the European MPs did nothing for the betterment of this country.

Older people in Britain feel let down, and many youngsters are no longer rushing to join one of the world's best fighting forces: the Army, the Royal Navy, and the Royal Air Force. The country has opened its doors to anyone and everyone. We are now a multicultural society, which can only be good for our future, but sadly, we have had to give up most of our proud heritage. Once rulers of the world, now we bow down to those we once led. It's not only the Germans we've had our rucks with, the Falklands conflict brought us up against the Argies (which, again, we won). Years ago, we were a force to be reckoned with, but today we are now seen as just barnacles on the arse of Europe. We are no longer seen as 'GREAT BRITAIN'. Years ago, it seemed that whenever England went to war, the bloody Germans and the Argentinians were involved.

But, as I already stated at the time of writing this, we as a country have voted and decided to leave the European Union. At this point in time I'm not actually too sure who's running what and where, or where Brexit is going to take us regarding immigration and overseas workers coming into Britain. One advantage is that at least I can now decide for myself what size or shape my cucumber or banana can be, and I can now also decide what to do when my wife's pussy has passed it (behave!!). Can I bury it in the garden now, or what?

ENGLAND CALL-UP:
Conscription

Our football world has changed over the years as well. Like conscription back in the 50s, players were called on to play for their country. It was every player's dream to put on the white shirt with the three lions on the badge, and to win a cap representing not only your country but also your family. Very few players were lucky enough to get a call-up.

Once selected, off you go to the England training camps (now it's St George's Park) where you'd meet up with others called into the squad, all of whom were deemed ready to fight the dreaded foe. There you were trained hard by the FA coaches and given instructions on how to bond as a team, and watch each other's back. Most of the top FA brass was there making sure everything was ready and put into place.

Lots of the players there had already had a bit of international experience, most having played for the Under-15s and through to the Under-21s. Sadly, lots of top young players who couldn't get into their club's first team missed out on England call-ups. So, to help them get more on-field time, they would be sent out on loan to other clubs. Lots stayed after their loan period was up, and they never saw their parent clubs again.

International games were few and far between, so when you were called, you came running. Do you think that players in the 50s like Jimmy Armfield, Ronnie Allen, and Joe Baker, Jeff Astle in the 60s, all the World Cup squad, and later players, such as Tony Adams, Gazza, Darren Anderton, or Alan Shearer would say no to a call-up? They would have had to have been on their deathbeds not to turn up. (Although Darren 'Sicknote' Anderton might have been the exception, and that believe it or not would have sadly been through injury).

There have been a few who felt for one reason or another that they didn't want to play for their country. David Bentley refused to play for the Under-21s once, claiming he was tired (bless him). Jamie Carragher at Liverpool and Jamie Vardy at Leicester, and many more great players, have retired from the international scene, which was seen by many to have been far too early in their careers, but the only reason that they left was to prolong their careers with their clubs. Lots of them left the door open regarding a return (reservists) should 'THEIR COUNTRY NEED THEM'. (I can see the poster now with Gareth Southgate pointing his finger at them.) Many ex-international players still play seniors matches for their different charities, and it's a great job they do (football's *Dad's Army*).

Our stature as a footballing nation was never quite as strong as was our stature as world rulers or leaders, but even though this was the case years ago, we were still the team to fear, we were the country that every other country wanted to beat. We've won many battles on the football field over the last 60 years but never quite won the wars.

But that all changed in 1966 when our football equivalent to Sir Winston Churchill, Sir Alf Ramsey, sent our brave men into battle against countries that had dared come to invade England, to Wembley, to fight us on our own soil. These were countries such as Uruguay, with whom we drew 0–0 in the first battle, then we went on to fight the Mexicans who were blown away 2–0 (Charlton, Hunt). The lasts to fall were the French, because once again we were far too strong and celebrated another fine 2–0 (both Hunt goals) win. Victory took us on then to the quarter-finals, to battle with one of our biggest enemies… the Argies, who after the 'Animal' defender known as Rattin was sent off and left the battlefield, we went on to win 1–0 (Hurst). So then on to the semi-final against the legend that was the fabulous striker Eusébio, nicknamed the 'Black Panther' and the gifted left-winger António Simões Costa known as Simões. But again, we had too much up on the front line, and after a hard-fought battle we were victorious 2–1 (2 Charlton, 1 Eusebio, in penalty time).

We were now on the verge of our most famous football victory of all time. We were about to send in our bravest men into their finest hour (or just over as it turned out). Big players such as Gordon Banks, were holding our defence together, with our general on the pitch, Bobby Moore, big Jack Charlton, Ray Wilson, and because of my Fulham link, the bravest of them all, the great 'George Cohen' and Nobby Stiles, along with Martin Peters, Bobby Charlton and the late Alan Ball helping out both our defence and front line attack of Roger Hunt and Geoff Hurst.

There were many other unsung heroes waiting on the sideline ready to be called on to the battlefield should they be needed. Players such as the great Jimmy Greaves, Ron Springett, Norman (bites yer legs) Hunter were ready to fight it out against the might of the German FA. The battle seemed to go on forever and a day. They took the first strike (Haller 0–1) after only six minutes before the might of the English attack pushed them back and regained the ground which we had lost (1–1 Hurst). The fight went back and forth until we dealt them another mighty blow (2–1 Peters). With the battle almost won, and victory within our grasp, they pushed all their troops forward for a last-chance attack, and our defence was breached (2–2 Weber).

So it was into extra time when all hell was let loose: was the ball over the line or not? the Germans said no, the English said yes. It was now up to the UN peacekeepers (the ref and lino) to decide if England had played fair or overstepped the mark. After a long consultation it was decided that England had crossed the borderline fairly (3–2 Hurst) and we were now moving swiftly on, with the Germans on the verge of total disarray. England then dealt the final fatal blow as Geoff Hurst sneaked past the whole of the German rear guard and sent a rocket flying into enemy HQ. Another hammer blow (get it …? Hammer blow: Moore, Hurst and Peters, West Ham) and that blasted them out of the game. Finally the mighty Germans surrendered.

Those immortal words 'YOUR COUNTRY NEEDS YOU' are now replaced with 'THEY THINK IT'S ALL OVER. IT IS NOW!'

It's fortunate to say that we have had reasonable successes against Germany, such as in 1966 or 1–5 (and in their homeland), of which we hope there are more to come (on the football field, not the battlefield).

Due to Brexit, we will now have to wait and see whether, or how, the football transfer market will be affected regarding players' movements to and from Britain. Unfortunately, our beloved game will still be run by nondescript suits: UEFA and FIFA, and some of those people who not only pick the balls out of the bag, but also the cash.

Whereas it would be wrong to compare the two World Wars with the battles we've fought on the football pitches, I only do so to show the comparison for the sake of this book. Hopefully I haven't offended anyone by doing so.

Chapter Eighteen

Holidays Abroad
THE CHAMPIONS LEAGUE AND THE UEFA CUP

Margate or Brighton:
MONACO OR BARCELONA

In the 1950s and early 60s most families had more chance of flying off to the moon with Old Blue Eyes himself, Frank Sinatra, or
rocketing off with Neil Armstrong and Buzz Aldrin than they ever
did of going abroad to warmer climates for their holidays. We'd
heard and seen wonderful, exotic and mouth-watering pictures
of places like Costa del Sol, Rimini, and the French Riviera, but
to have a holiday abroad in these beautiful places for most working-class families was as I say a dream (and about as far away as the
moon). So unless you were lucky to be born with that proverbial
silver spoon in your mouth, you were probably like me (born with
a wooden one) and it wasn't going to happen. Overseas holidays
were considered a luxury that only the elite or rich could afford.

If you were really lucky, your parents might have been able to
afford to take you on a day trip to the seaside. Or, a day trip to
the Garden of England, as Kent is known. Here you could have
some great but absolutely back-breaking fun by going fruit picking. This meant filling your face while filling your basket: getting paid to work by the farmer who owned the land. But it also
helped to fill your pocket. You got paid in line with how much
fruit you had in your basket. It's a wonder that they didn't weigh
the picker before they went in, because I'm pretty sure that each
one weighed a lot more when they came out due to the amount
they ate on the way round. The farmer knew you'd been scoff-
ing the fruit by the colour of your lips. Light red (strawberries),
darker red (raspberries), blue (blackberries).

For the average working-class family, many factories and in-
dustrial workplaces would normally close down for an annual

two-week holiday. You didn't get to pick and choose the dates that suited you in those days, you just thought yourself lucky if you got two weeks' paid leave. Back in the bad old days, lots of companies couldn't (or said they couldn't) afford to pay holiday pay, so you had to put away a few shillings each week to help pay for any holidays you might get. If your family was fortunate enough to be able to afford to get away, then you most probably spent your holidays sitting on a beach that had less sand than the bottom of a budgie's cage (it probably had about the same amount of shit on it too). Lots of South Londoners went to seaside towns such as Margate, Herne Bay, Bognor, Whitstable, or Leysdown-on-Sea, on the Isle of Sheppey.

I unfortunately spent about the first 14 years of my life going to Leysdown-on-Sea for family holidays. We had our own caravan there called Bingo, on a site which I think was called something like Harts Caravan Park or Harts Holiday Camp. I must admit it was great fun in those days (only cos we didn't know any better) just to enjoy the freedom away from the big city and the brick and concrete jungle that London had become.

Sadly, due to the lack of sand on most of the beaches, we kids were unable to build sandcastles, but the good news was ... we were able to build Stonehenge. Blackpool, Scarborough, Margate, Brighton, Cleethorpes, and Southend were just some of the 50s and 60s holiday hotspots (most times without the 'hot'). The sun seemed to hardly ever shine, the sea was cold, dirty, and full of oil. There was rubbish left lying all over the place from the previous year's beach bums. Popular donkey rides along the beach left donkey shit all over the place.

If by chance you went somewhere where there was sand, then you'd have a plastic bucket and spade to dig a great big hole where you could bury your siblings. Then you would sit back with a big grin and listen to them screaming for someone to come and dig them out. You would try to make a sandcastle, or something resembling such a thing. Most kids built these so close to the sea that unfortunately the tide would come in quicker than you could build it, and it would get washed away before it was finished. Unperturbed, they would move their building site back 10 feet and start again. The sea would continue to advance up the beach by another 10 feet and they would have to start all over again. Strange thing was you never realised the advantage you had back then to do away with your annoying sibling by burying them closer to the incoming tide. In Leysdown you didn't bury your siblings, you stoned them. Also there was no chance of my Stonehenge ever getting washed away. Still, as much as I have put down our coastline, those were happy days.

One thing I could never understand were those people who brought those great big multicoloured beach balls with them. They were so light that most of the day was spent chasing it miles along the beach when the wind blew too hard. Half the time you were chasing a lost cause. Everything on the beach was against you trying to catch up with the bloody thing when it took off. You were either tripping over, or knocking over, some poor kid's perfectly built sandcastle (they probably grew up to be a top architect or construction worker due to the number of times they had to rebuild the bloody thing), or tripping over his siblings head that was popping out of the sand (they'd break their toes on my Stonehenge).

Also, I could never understand how other beach users could watch as this missile the size of a planet, that was bouncing towards them with some poor little sod chasing after it screaming like fuck, 'STOOOOOP IIITT'. They would just smile at them and give an apologetic nod as if to say sorry, 'if I'd seen it, I would have stopped it'. There you were hurdling over old people sitting in deckchairs with their grubby string vests, knotted hankies on their heads, short trousers and long socks that came halfway up their calves (all looking like the Gumbys out of one of the great Monty Python sketches), all the while doing your best to avoid treading on sunbathers and donkey shit, trying to catch it before it got too far along the coast and reached the next resort.

Everyone had a soppy kiss-me-quick hat on. For years I thought there was some sort of secret society, cult, or strange religious order of pink-bearded men and women whose job it was to walk up and down the seafront every day until I discovered they were people eating candy floss, which was sold along the prom or on the pier.

The top delicacies to tickle your taste buds were cockles, winkles, jellied eels, pie mash and liquor, or fish and chips, which would all be washed down with a nice glass of brown ale, a Mackeson stout, a pint of local bitter or a pint of Watney's Red Barrel. Your lodgings were either a tent, a chalet, or a caravan, or in our case, because there were so many of us, we not only had our own caravan, but one year we hired one that turned out to be an old converted horse box (by fuck, did it smell like it). I had to sleep in it with my brother-in-law Les, who had to sleep with his legs out of the window because the bed wasn't long enough.

Because lots of Britain's factories were closed for the two-week holiday period known as factory fortnight, during the day you would spend your time on a beach. This was so cramped with thousands of families with crying kids, waiting for someone to dig them out of a hole. Everyone was fighting with everyone else to get a good patch of beach where you had room to lay out your towel. After a day of lying on a stony beach in Leysdown, you had indentations all over your back and your arse looked like a golf ball, so you looked like an alien from a *Star Trek* film. You very rarely went home with an all-over suntan as the beach was so crowded. The worst thing was that when you went home, people would say, 'My God, hasn't the sun brought out your freckles.' (Freckles my arse! That was my suntan.)

The early evening entertainment was prize Bingo down at one of the many arcades. If you won, you would get a token or a voucher which you could exchange for many wonderful items. One or two tokens would get you something like a fluffy toy, or a plastic bucket and spade set, or a lightweight multicoloured bloody useless plastic beach ball. So, unless you had twenty or thirty tokens, it was a complete waste of time and money. It cost you about £5 (a lot of money back then) and it would have been cheaper to buy the things straight from the local shop. Then it was back to the campsite for the night-time entertainment of more prize Bingo, followed by the camp entertainer. (*Hi-de-Hi!*) There was a talent show that was amusing to say the least. Usually there was some old pisshead trying to sing 'Roll out the barrel'. (The daft old bastard looked and sounded as if he'd just drunk one!) Or it was 'We'll meet again, don't know where, don't know when' and to be quite honest, I really couldn't toss if we did, or we didn't. If you remember the song 'Cwying' sung brilliantly by Philip R J Pope, or perhaps better known as Tony Angelino in *Only Fools and Horses*, well, some of these singers made him sound like that big fat bloke Wynne Evans on the GoCompare ad. What a fabulous voice that guy has! Although my old mum didn't do too badly. She had quite a good voice and she won quite a few talent shows. Unfortunately, the first prize for the women always seemed to be a ladies' brush and comb set. Cheap as chips (only five tokens down at the Bingo arcade).

If you tended to be more in the middle-class bracket, you might really splash out and stay at some old biddy's guest house. Here you were really spoilt with clean bed sheets, a hearty breakfast and a homemade evening meal. The downside staying at a guest house was making sure that if you went out in the evening, you were back by eleven o'clock, which is when the old cow who owned the place locked the front doors. A typical day for the slightly classier, more managerial, or middle-class type of worker, would be a nice stroll along the promenade. There they would pay to hire a deckchair to sit on and watch all of us poor people fighting for a few grains of sand to lie on. They would sit there like Roman emperors watching gladiators fighting to the death. Then it was back to the guest house for a wash and brush-up before perhaps going to a local music hall and having a glass of sherry at a local bar before retiring for the night.

The very rich had already been sampling these far-away places we only saw on posters for many years plus, places such as The Caribbean Islands, Monte Carlo, Monaco, places we didn't even know existed. They would fly in on their own private jets or sail there on their luxury boats and yachts. They would eat exotic food while staying in the top hotels all around the world. And they would be pampered by the hotel staff.

I remember a while back I was listening to a radio station which had Noel Gallagher on as a guest. One of the presenters, seeing that he had a lovely tan, asked him if he had been sunbathing. Noel jokingly said, 'No, I pay somebody else to do that for me.'

As the years moved on into the late 60s and 70s, we started to expand our tastes in travel as the cost of flying and general travel became more affordable. More and more travel agencies opened up to help with our overseas travel plans, which made life easier regarding when and where to go. People sold whatever they could, and sacrificed just about everything they could, to save up for the chance of a trip to a far-off land. Far-away places didn't now seem so far, or so much of a dream.

Schools, for those parents who could afford it, started to take groups of students away on school trips to the likes of France, Germany, and Italy to explore the different cultures and languages.

Freddie Laker had started up Laker Airways with cut-price cheap flights. Slowly, places like Spain with its Costa Blanca and Costa del Sol; Italy with the Riviera; and Greece with Corfu and Rhodes became more popular with the younger population and they were easier to get to.

Holidaymakers were lying on the beaches of countries where we had previously been fighting only a couple of decades ago. These were now clean golden sandy beaches to lay down your beach towels, no stones and donkey shit to worry about, and your multicoloured beach ball floated on the warm light sea breeze, like floating lanterns or hot-air balloons. On lots of the beaches, young ladies were allowed to go topless, which for a lot of the young English ladies at first was a big fat no-no. But after a few days and gentle persuasion by their boyfriends (who had their own agenda for getting their birds to get their thrupenny bits out), they seemed only too pleased.

There was no more having to watch people in string vests and knotted hankies. Spaghetti, pasta, ravioli, and salad with olive oil and a glass of wine became our holiday diet. Places like France and Germany were more for the sightseeing than the beaches, where they ate frogs' legs and escargot, sauerkraut and frankfurters, and all different types of cheese, some which smelt like a frightened skunk.

Hotels were being built more quickly than my Stonehenge. It was up in the morning, or for those that stayed out all night, it was up in the afternoon, although it didn't really matter what time it was, the sun seemed to be shining from dawn till dusk. So, it was up, a continental breakfast, and then down to the swimming pool or the beach for the rest of the day to swim in the deep-blue sea. And there was plenty of sand for everyone, and sun loungers or beds too. Then when the sun had had enough of you, it was back to the hotel for a shower, a kip, or a leg-over, depending on how fruity you and your partner felt, especially after you'd been watching the birds with the big tits, and your girlfriend had been drooling over the bronzed Adonis (David Hasselhoff from *Baywatch* lookalike) lifeguard. For some reason or another, your girlfriend has been admiring his bulging swimming trunks, thinking to herself 'my God, look at the size of his snorkel!'

From the 1980s on, the world became as big and as colourful as that poxy beach ball we chased forever and a day. People started to go to places like France, Germany, Holland, and Belgium for the day. They would take their cars and vans over on the ferry, spend the day there and fill their cars up with all different types of alcohol and cigarettes and tobacco (the booze cruise). Sadly, lots of British holiday makers went slightly overboard with the sun, and especially the booze. We started to get ourselves a bad name in lots of countries, especially Spain. There was bar and nightclub fights in places like Benidorm and Ibiza, which had become places to go for the young holidaymakers, and those on stag night and hen nights. Lots of drink, meant lots of clink. Stag and hen nights are now banned in some of these popular overseas resorts. Even in Britain and Ireland stag and hen nights are banned in many places, which is all due to the loutish behaviour of some of our young. But for many of us menials, the holidays that we dreamt about were now no longer a dream. We were going to places that we couldn't pronounce let alone spell.

After the dissolution of the Soviet Union, now known as Russia, in the 90s, breakaway countries like Moldova, Estonia, Belarus, Ukraine, and Georgia all became popular places to visit. In addition, with the dissolution of Yugoslavia, places like Serbia, Croatia and Bosnia were also on many people's lists of places to go to for their holidays, as they still are today. Many people chose to visit Africa, Asia, and South America, backpacking around all the different continents. Lots of people who have since visited these different countries have loved them so much that they have decided to uproot and move there to work and learn about the difference in cultures.

Nowadays, I don't think there's a place or country on this planet that you can't get to. And with technology the way it's going, sooner or later you will be able to holiday on that moon, or perhaps have a life on Mars. If you can't afford the price to travel to all these wonderful places, then buy a poxy multicoloured beach ball, hang on for dear life, and wait for the wind to blow and see where you land up. (Knowing my luck, it'd most probably land up back in fucking Leysdown-on-Sea!)

THE CHAMPIONS LEAGUE AND the UEFA CUP:
Holidays abroad

Football clubs and their supporters had the same dreams all those years ago as we did with regard to our holidays in the sun. But for the supporters, their dream was to go abroad to watch their beloved team play. However, this was usually only for the elite at the big rich successful clubs.

We'd heard with envy about some of the top European clubs, teams like Real Madrid, Barcelona, Benfica, and A C Milan. These teams were far, far away and totally out of our league. We would be watching our teams playing in Blackpool, Preston North End, Bolton, Wolves, and Huddersfield Town, which were all some of the top teams in England at this time.

Holidays for us football supporters were only on the domestic front, very few teams were in a position to play abroad. Lots of firms in the 1950s used to close down a bit earlier on Fridays for the weekend, which was great. But some firms had you in to work on a Saturday match day morning, which was a real pain in the butt because there was no real time to prepare for the game. The blast of a factory horn went, or a whistle was blown by the shop steward to signify the end of the morning shift, and there would be a loud shout of 'everybody out' (much like the shop steward Paddy Fleming, better known as Miriam Karlin, in the 1960s TV series *The Rag Trade,* which also starred Reg Varney, later better known as Stan ('I hate you Butler') in the TV series *On the Buses*. Once that whistle was blown, then all workers would drop their tools quicker than Monica dropped Bill's when Hillary walked into the Oval Office. Saturday was the weekend break, the mini holiday.

Supporters would get to the ground where it would be packed with a lot of their workmates. It wasn't until the late 50s that floodlights were introduced into grounds so all matches were played on a Saturday afternoon, only one game a week or once a fortnight at home. So it was quite an occasion on match day, fighting with the crowd to get a good view. And crowds in the 50s and 60s were generally quite large.

It was off to the away match with a sandwich and a flask for refreshment, notwithstanding the typical British weather. When you see the old black and white pictures of all the supporters on the terraces, it seemed as if there were about 80 per cent men, 10 per cent women and 10 per cent kids. Most of the men were dressed in a white shirt and tie, a jacket, a pair of dark-coloured trousers and a flat cap, or a trilby hat, looking like they should be on the set of *Last of the Summer Wine*. The way they dressed looked more like they were going out for the evening, not going to a football match.

Those that were lucky enough to be able to afford to go and watch an away match most probably went on the many coaches that the clubs supplied, or by the trains that were put on by British Rail (known as the Football Specials). These trains were put on for supporters only on a match day. They took us to places like Blackpool, Portsmouth, Southampton and so many more. In the 1960s, British Rail threatened on numerous occasions to cancel the running of this service due to vandalism, staff intimidation and violence. British Rail did eventually keep the service running by putting British Rail police on the trains as a type of deterrent (sadly to very little effect). Some clubs put on their own Football Specials, but after the privatisation of the railways came into effect in the 1990s, these trains no longer ran. Fortunately, this put an end to many of the thugs and football hooligans who didn't bother to travel as they couldn't do the same damage to the coaches as they could to the trains.

Lots of things started to change in the late 50s when a few supporters started to follow their teams abroad. 1958, for many Manchester United supporters, it was meant to be the breakthrough year. Now it was time to venture abroad for their holidays with their loved ones. Sadly, disaster struck at Munich-Riem Airport, when the plane that was taking the Manchester United squad to Belgrade to play a Champions League semi-final game against Red Star Belgrade, crashed during take-off. This resulted in the death of eight of the players known as the Busby Babes. In total, twenty-three players and passengers out of the forty-four on board perished.

It wasn't until the 1960s when supporters' overseas holidays with their beloved teams changed. Up until that point, Europe felt as if it was miles away, full of foreigners, who only a few years earlier we had been fighting on the pitches in the World Cup. International matches were the height of our footballing year. The World Cup was as near as we got to going to overseas matches. It was Celtic in 1966–67 who then became the first British team to win the European Cup, and they were given the nickname the Lisbon Lions.

British teams and supporters now started to take part and win in Europe, which changed our footballing lives. Up until then we'd never really thought about going abroad with our teams.

In 1968, ten years after the tragedy of the Busby Babes, Manchester United became the first English team to win the European Cup by beating Benfica at Wembley. Having a taste of success overseas was the start of a long and loving relationship for United supporters, not only in Europe, but they became worldwide travellers, backpacking and playing in all the different continents. They played and won in all the different competitions, going to places like Germany, Portugal, and Turkey. And in 2000, they played and won the Intercontinental Cup in Tokyo, beating the Brazilian side, Palmeiras.

Liverpool in the 70s and the 80s was doing the same thing in the European Cup, travelling to Italy, Belgium and Spain, year in year out. Tottenham Hotspur and Chelsea were holidaying abroad with their supporters, with slightly less success on a regular basis. West Ham, Aston Villa, Nottingham Forest, and Leeds popped overseas for a few visits here and there. Some had a reasonable time, some suffered having to travel the long distances. European matches in those days were one-legged affairs, unlike today when we have two-legged games. So if your team was going to play in France, Germany, Holland, or Belgium, then lots of supporters would treat it like the booze cruise. With Laker Airways starting cheap flights abroad in 1966, it also made travelling abroad quicker and cheaper.

Lots of companies and travel agents started to organise football supporters' trips for away matches abroad, to help with travel, accommodation, and match tickets. A lot of fans begged, stole, and borrowed to make the trips. Some, it's said, even sold some of their household goods, like the TV or the fridge, when the wife was out, and apparently, they didn't even tell her they were going to the game. Some booked for a one-night stay, and after a night sleeping rough on the beautiful warm sandy beaches or on a lounger under the stars, missed their flights back and thought to themselves 'what the fuck' so came home one month later. But sadly, some never got to see the match due to getting pissed and causing trouble before the game, which led to getting themselves locked up and deported the very next day.

Unfortunately, in the 80s British football fans started to get a bad name right across Europe for the trouble they caused wherever they went. It was already bad enough in Britain. But just like on the holiday stag nights and hen nights, wherever they went, football fans got drunk and started fights, which eventually ended up as full-blown riots. Police with riot gear and water cannons were sent out to try and quell the wanton violence caused by these drunken thugs.

In the 1985 European Cup final between Liverpool and Juventus in the Heysel Stadium in Belgium, disaster struck when a dividing wall collapsed after fighting broke out between the two sets of fans. Sadly, 39 people died and almost 600 were injured. UEFA pointed the finger at the Liverpool supporters, and due to the way that English supporters had been causing so much trouble in Europe, all English clubs were banned from European competitions for the next five years, ending in 1991.

With the break-up of the Intertoto Cup, the Europa League, better known as the Losers League (for teams that are knocked out of the Champions League in the first rounds) was created. Teams get to have another go by winning the Europa League, which most tended to do, for example when Fulham lost the Europa Cup Final to Atlético Madrid, Madrid had lost in the Champions League first round so automatically they dropped into the Europa League.

We now also have the ridiculous Europa Conference League (better known as the Dog and Duck Pub League). Now teams from all over Eastern Europe were becoming involved on our travels. Moldova, Estonia, Belarus, Ukraine, Georgia, Serbia, Croatia, and Bosnia were all places we were now visiting. Supporters of all these, and other lucky British teams now flooded not only Europe as we know it, but we were now travelling worldwide.

Teams were now starting to play tournaments in countries like Dubai and Saudi Arabia, and all over Asia, America, and

Australia. Lots of players that played in these different countries enjoyed it so much that they eventually decided to go and play there before feeling homesick and returning to these shores. Players such as like Gary Lineker (Barcelona, Grampus Eight), Kevin Keegan (Hamburger SV), Emile Heskey (Newcastle Jets), Paul Ince (Inter Milan), Ashley Cole (Roma, LA Galaxy), and David Beckham (Real Madrid, LA Galaxy, AC Milan, and Paris Saint-Germain) were among these. One of the first players to venture abroad was the great John Charles who in 1957 went over and played for the mighty Juventus for five years. After that, he played for one year in Rome with Roma. According to the rumours, lots of the Celtic supporters that travelled to Lisbon to watch Celtic back in 1966–67, have never been seen again.

Nowadays, I don't think there's a ground or country on this planet you can't get to, and with technology the way it's going, sooner or later you will be able to have a footballing holiday on that moon, or perhaps have a match on Mars.

Chapter Nineteen

A Marriage Licence
A SEASON TICKET

The wedding bells ring to start our future:
THE REFEREE'S WHISTLE BLOWS TO START OUR GAME

Wedding bells:
FOOTBALL CLAPPERS

The registry office
    'Do you (groom) take (bride) to be your lawfully wedded wife.
    To have and to hold from this day forward,
    For better, for worse, for richer, for poorer,
    In sickness and in health, until death do you part?'
    'I do.'
    'I now pronounce you man and wife. You may now kiss the
    bride.'

> You can change your wife or partner,
> but you can't change your team

Getting married is possibly one of the most important decisions most of us have to make during our lifetime. Most of us at some time or another will go through that marital lottery, perhaps not just once, but sometimes more, trying to hit the jackpot in finding that perfect partner.

So, after doing the rounds, as they say, going on a few dates here and there, with all sorts of different people from different walks of life, maybe a young professional high-flyer, a nurse or doctor, or maybe a road sweeper or bin collector, it doesn't matter what class bracket they are in, you finally meet the love of your life, the girl (or man) of your dreams.

After taking stock of all the pros and cons, you decide to dedicate yourself to that one special person who has given you so much in a courtship that has lasted as long as it took for you to decide that they were the real deal for you, the one and only. Some courtships can go on for years while others are whirlwind, in-the-blink-of-an-eye romances, love at first sight, you could say.

Years ago, when you found who you thought was the right one for you (remember this is from a male point of view) you would then not only ask the young lady for her hand in matrimony, but you also had to ask her father for permission. That in itself was a daunting enough experience. If you didn't have good breeding, good prospects, or a good few quid in the bank, then there was a good chance he'd say, 'You're having a laugh. On yer bike.' Now if he said that, then that was it more or less, you were history, no room for negotiations.

Back in the dark ages the father found the daughter a husband to be. She had absolutely no say in the matter, and if Dad was convinced that he was the one, then that was it, there was no arguing. It didn't matter if the future husband looked like Quasimodo (does that name ring a bell?) or the Elephant Man, you married him. Full stop. You didn't dare go against your father's wishes; that would be seen as sacrilege. The fact that the chosen one was the highest bidder for your hand, and about to pay your dad a few quid, OH no, that had nothing to do with your dad's decision. He was only doing what he thought was best for you. And his pocket.

Nowadays, things are totally different, you can marry who you want, when you want, and where you want, and it may not always be with your parents' blessing. There will most likely be a good few arguments over your choice of partner, being totally opposite to the one your parents thought was right, the one they might have hoped you'd go for. But too bad, it's good enough for you so tough shit if it's not good enough for them. It's your life and you'll spend it with whoever you want. After all, you're the one who's going to spend the rest of your life with them (or so you hope).

You've decided that you've been in love for long enough, and you know what you and your partner both have to offer each other. Hopefully now there's something wonderful to build upon. Hopefully there will be a prosperous and successful family in the future. After ticking all the good points and crossing off the very few bad points, you feel you know enough about each other, and what you both want from each other in life. Honesty, loyalty, support, and affection. No more fooling around with the ex-girlfriends for you, no more gallivanting about, no more playing away from home. You've finally decided to take the plunge.

Now after taking those sacred vows, 'Do you take etc.' and you've responded in the affirmative, that's when your life is about to change. Committing yourself to the marriage licence means you've signed your life away. Now you can't just come and go as you please, doing what you want and when you want. You're in a partnership and you've committed yourself to being there full-time. You don't choose the when, the where and the how anymore. Now your partner has a big say in what you do and when you do it. No more fanny and fart-arsing about for you. You've gone in with both feet (red card?) and eyes wide open, turning your casual relationship into that total commitment. You've tied the proverbial knot. You've thrown your hat into the ring, and all the other clichés that go with it.

Now it's the exciting fun time, building a future together, making a home together, and going out to work to help pay the bills. Hopefully you'll end up being parents, teach your kids the rights and wrongs in life, and watch them grow up to have happy and successful lives, and children of their own. This in turn will bring you more joy and happiness, and you can help the family move on up in the world.

Now that you've set up your home, you'll have your own front door and front door key, your own chair to sit in, as your father did. You'll have your next-door neighbours, with whom hopefully you'll become friends, so you can have a good old chat about the rights and wrongs, the good and bad things you see going on, not only in your family, but in other families around you. You'll have disagreements about how the families are doing, you'll have different views on how your family should be run, and where you expect your family to be in a year or two. But no matter what your family does, or gets up to, you're there for them, supporting and fighting for them all the way.

Sadly though, not all marriages last. It's one thing courting, seeing each other every so often, but it's another thing giving yourself full time, body and soul. When there's someone else who has a say in your life, after a while you start to realise that maybe there are other things you need from the relationship that you begin to feel your partner isn't providing. You're not playing the same game. This is when things start to fall apart, and relationships turn sour. The vision they promised for you both never came to fruition. Their personality has changed as the years have moved on, and all of a sudden life isn't what you wanted it to be. You're both struggling day in day out and you feel that your relationship is going downhill fast. There is money problems, and the kids are not doing what they're told. You eventually get to a stage in life where you feel that you don't want to go home anymore, so it's going to the pub, rather than going home. You may even get to a stage in life where you feel the need to try and meet another more exciting partner, one that will re-ignite that love you once had, bring back that excitement that you have lost with your partner. It may well lead to you having an affair. You stay with your partner but see someone else on the sly now and again (while the cats away, the mice will play).

Eventually you decide enough is enough, and although you part company with your ex, your feelings for them will never diminish. You keep an eye on them from afar, through friends, the old neighbours and on social media, wishing them well for the future. You may never, ever again find that true love you had. You may meet someone else, but will the love be as strong? Will that love ever feel the same again?

For some people commitment is out of the window. They will do the rounds, partner after partner, never feeling able enough to give their love to just one person. Lots are happy to sit on the sidelines and watch their friends take the plunge. Many nowadays have overseas relationships, partners who live abroad, so they have to travel to places like France, Germany, Spain as well as other parts of Europe to see them. These people prefer the foreign types of lovers and their lifestyles. They also find it cheaper than it is in England when committing themselves fully to their foreign beauties. Lots of couples now go abroad to get married as it can work out a lot cheaper than in England. Marriage isn't seen to be as sacred today as it was all those years gone by.

THE REFEREE'S WHISTLE BLOWS TO START OUR GAME:
The wedding bells ring to start our future

FOOTBALL CLAPPERS:
Wedding bells

The ticket office
'Do you (supporter) take (team) to be your only football team. To follow and to support from this season on.
For better, for worse, for richer, for poorer.
In winning, drawing or losing until death do you part?'
'I do.'
'I now pronounce you a season ticket holder. You may now kiss the badge.'

SEASON TICKET:
Marriage Licence

Now the season ticket is the supporter's equivalent of the marriage licence. It doesn't matter how long you've supported your club, some like me it's many years, but I never actually committed myself to a season ticket, even though I was there week in and week out.

I never gave myself totally in the relationship until I did finally take the plunge 24 years ago. But that was after a courtship of almost 40 years. (It was love at first sight with Fulham, but not exactly a whirlwind romance.) For most supporters, after doing the rounds, as they say, and going to watch a few teams like Southampton, West Ham United, Leicester City or slightly lower league teams like Cardiff, Bristol City, Harrogate Town, or Windsor FC, it didn't matter what division they were in, you would eventually find the one for you. The team of your dreams. Other people would go to just two or three games and they're all ticketed up. It was love at first sight, a whirlwind, in-the-blink-of-an-eye romance.

Years ago, it was the done thing to fall in love with the team your father supported. To even think about choosing another team wasn't an option. If you asked him if you could support another club, there's a good chance he'd say, 'You're having a laugh. On yer bike.' And that was the end of that story, no room for negotiations. It didn't matter how bad your dad's team was, how poorly they played or how ugly the football was, that was it, you supported them. Full stop. You didn't dare go against your father's wishes; that would be seen as sacrilege.

Nowadays, things are totally different. Kids can support who they want, when they want and where they want, and it may not always be with your parents' blessing. It will most probably cause a good few arguments over your choice of team, regarding what your parents thought was a good choice and what they might have hoped for. But too bad. It's good enough for you, so, tough shit if it's not good enough for them. It's your life and you'll spend it with who you want. After alL you're the one who's going to watch them for the rest of your life (or so you hope).

You've decided that you've been in love for long enough, and you know what you and your team both have to offer each other. There's something to build upon, hopefully a prosperous and successful team in the future. After ticking all the good points and crossing the very few bad points, you feel you know what you both want from each other in life: honesty, loyalty, support, and affection.

So now you've finally decided to take the plunge. Now after taking those sacred vows, the words, 'Do you take etc.' and you've responded in the affirmative, that's when your life is about to change. Committing yourself to a season ticket means you've signed your life away. Now you can't just come and go as you please, doing what you want and when you want. You're in a partnership. You don't choose the when, the where and the how anymore. Now your team has a big say in what you do and when you do it. No more fanny and fart-arsing about for you. You've gone in with both feet (red card?), eyes wide open, and turned your casual relationship into that total commitment.

No more fooling around for you with other teams you've watched before, no more gallivanting about, no more going away from home (well, only with your team). You've tied the proverbial knot. You've thrown your hat into the ring, and all the other clichés that go with it. You and your club are now both kicking in the same direction, and you realise that you both agree that what you want are the same things for the future.

The ground is now your home. You'll have the same gate (turnstile) to enter each game, a key to enter the gate (a plastic season ticket, a swipe card or whatever they give you to gain access), your own chair, which is for only you to sit in. You've now got a lot of other new supporters sitting around you (neighbours), who you meet up with to discuss what's going on with your football family, the rights and wrongs of what's happening with the team. And you're bound to argue and disagree over what's going on, not only with your club, but other clubs as well.

When I first started going to Fulham, I saw players who were obviously a lot older than me, and they were like older family members (uncles or older cousins). Then when I was in the period from my late teens through to middle age, it was as if they had become cousins, mates or friends because we were almost the same age. But now that I'm in my seventies, I see them as my kids: players like Tom Carney, Harry Wilson, Marek Rodak, Tim Ream and the brilliant Joao Palhinha. And watching them grow up, I know I have some wonderful grandchildren to come: , Luca Ashby-Hammond, Jay Stansfield, and Tyrese Francios to name just a few of some of the young talent we have at Fulham.

Sadly, not all football marriages last, and it can be the same with your team. It's one thing courting, going to games every so often, but it's another thing giving yourself full time, body and soul when there's someone else who has a say in your football life. After a while, you start to realise there are other things you need from the relationship, which all of a sudden your team isn't providing. That's when things start to fall apart, and relationships turn sour. Sadly, the vision they had promised for you never came to fruition.

The playing style (personality) changed as the years moved on, and all of a sudden, your football life isn't what you wanted it to be. You're struggling day in and day out, you feel that your team is going down the divisions fast. This is due to money problems and the players not doing what they're told on the pitch. It doesn't take long before you decide you don't want to go to matches anymore. You'd rather go to the pub than the stadium. Some supporters decide to start following other teams, looking for a club that brings back the enjoyment and excitement that their club has failed to give them. They still go to most of their team's games but also watch other teams on the sly when their team is playing away (it's like having an affair). At this point I must admit to two-timing Fulham with Windsor FC. I take my grandson to watch them whenever we can't get to see Fulham (there, I've owned up and feel a great weight off my shoulders).

Eventually you decide enough is enough, and although you stop going to matches, your feelings for the team will never diminish. You keep an eye on them from afar: on social media and TV, through friends, the old football neighbours who you used to sit next to, and who still go. You wish them well for the future. You may never, ever find that true love you had again. You may go to watch other teams somewhere else, but will the love be as strong? Will that love ever feel the same again?

For some football fans commitment is out of the window. They will do the rounds going to as many grounds as they can in a season. They will have their favourite teams and favourite grounds but will never commit to just one, happy to let their mates take the plunge while they swan around the country. Lots of fans nowadays have overseas relationships with teams in France, Germany, and Spain as well as other parts of Europe. For them, they prefer the foreign teams and their style of play and the players. They also find it a lot cheaper than it is in England to follow a team abroad with the price of the season tickets. Football loyalty isn't seen today as it was all those years gone by.

Chapter Twenty

Marriage Guidance Council
LEAGUE MANAGERS ASSOCIATION

Red roses will keep us together:
RED CARDS WILL KEEP US APART

The relationship between men and woman nowadays doesn't seem to be as strong as it was many years ago. Years ago, most husbands and wives stayed together no matter what problems they might be facing. They stood together, hand in hand, and worked out what their problems were and how to sort them out. Whether it was a family problem or a financial one it didn't matter. Lots of the time it was driven by the lack of money due to excessive drinking or gambling (usually on the part of the husband). The wife was given whatever money that might be left to run the household after the old man had finished up down at the pub or at the bookies, which put heavy pressure on their daily lives. As we know, all relationships hit the rails now and again, and usually after a few days of silence, a few broken cups and saucers, then everything is normally sorted out and everyone lives happily ever after (some of the time).

In the earlier years in a male-dominated Britain, things didn't always end up in an amicable way. The husband usually had the last say in any domestic dispute, and the wife rightly or wrongly did as she was told, or else!! 'Or else' back then was commonly known as a back-hander. For many families this was a common occurrence. Sadly though some were more volatile, more intense, and could never be sorted out. Men and a smaller minority of women preferred to use their fists rather than words to sort out their problems to get their own way. Women who were battered did their best to hide their bruises from their family and friends, even though everyone knew what was going on. The women not only took the beatings but they also blamed themselves by saying things like, 'It was my fault, I shouldn't have kept going on at him.'

Unfortunately, many of the men were not only hen-pecked like Richard in *Keeping Up Appearances*:

'Oh Richard, do mind those pedestrians over there, and do slow down, we're going much too fast. I don't know what the neighbours will think if you go racing around streets like Lewis Hamilton.'

'But we're only doing 20 miles an hour, dear.'

'Don't argue with me, Richard.'

'No dear.'

But lots of men were also beaten by their wives. They were now in a catch-22 situation and they had very little choice as to what their options were. To speak up would show their family and friends that they were weak, pathetic, a coward or a wimp for being bullied by a woman. If they left home, they would have been accused of being a bastard for deserting the family. You were supposed to be in charge, you were supposed to be the 'king of the castle'.

People couldn't understand or comprehend that some men were timid and soft by nature. Their mates who could see what was happening kept telling them, 'You want to give her a fucking good hiding. Put her on her arse, for fuck's sake!'

Sadly, for some, that's easy, for others it's not.

For the abused women there was no way out. Many had nowhere to go. Most just stayed for the sake of the kids. Where could they to go with two, three or maybe four kids? Family members were sympathetic but in many cases didn't want to get too involved. In many cases the husband or wife would alienate their partner from their families so that they had no backup at all: divide and conquer. Many stayed and put up with the violence rather than be seen to have been some kind of failure: a bad wife. They tried to hide it from their kids.

There was marriage guidance counsellors and places to go to seek help, to try to help the relationship get back on course, but for most men, the male ego would not even allow the thought of such a thing. No, it was a matter for most of the abused to shut up or ship out. Unfortunately, for a lot of them the latter was not an option. It wasn't only physical abuse, there was also mental, verbal, and sexual abuse. So many of them thought they were on their own and suffered in silence.

Things changed slightly in the 60s. Women seemed to become a bit more independent. Don't get me wrong, the abuse still carried on as it sadly does to this day, but the abuse came more into the public eye. Men and women started to fight back (not with violence) as they were pushed by family members and friends to report their spouses. Hospitals got even more involved by reporting any incidents to the police. Eventually due to the media bringing it to the fore, this then prompted a public outcry, and lots of men and women managed to get their partners to seek help and advice with the marriage guidance counsellors.

The 60s not only brought us 'make love not war' but also 'the swinging 60s' and that's what a lot of married men and women did: not only with their other halves but everybody else's other halves as well. For lots of men and women, one partner was not enough. Many married two, and in some cases three partners even though bigamy was illegal.

Quite a few famous people seemed simply to enjoy wedding cake. Liz Taylor, for example, was married eight times, Zaza Gabor nine times, actor Richard Pryor seven times, and Tony Curti six times. God only knows why! I bet their houses must have been full of toasters, dinner sets, kettles, cruet sets, etc. Just what they all really needed.

Marriages were stating to fall apart under everyday pressures of life. More and more people were seeking an answer to their situations. More and more councillors saw more and more people to give sound advice on how to end their domestic disputes. From this day on, disputes between partners will always be on going.

Nowadays divorce is on the up. Couples no longer have to put up with the situations they had to endure in years gone by. Marriage guidance was a great help for lots of couples, but it didn't always have the right outcome for many others. Sadly, many ended up in the divorce courts.

Some marriages only lasted a short spell due to couples taking the plunge too soon, not really knowing each other for long enough before tying the knot. Britney Spears and Jason Alexander's marriage lasted a mammoth 55 hours (well, at least the champagne was still chilled). Nicolas Cage and Erika Koike's was four days; Cher and Gregg Allman's nine days; and Eddie Murphy and Tracey Edmonds' fourteen days; and the list goes on and on. Lots of men and women are now seeking partners from abroad, partners who were in many cases living and working in perhaps a poorer environment and only too glad to come to England and into a relationship, no matter what the conditions were. However, a lot of them come here with the promise of a better life only to find that it isn't quite as easy to adapt as they thought it would be. Many relationships break up. Many soon return home back to a familiar and less stressful environment. (Normally also a lot richer).

The marriage council has helped many many families solve all types of problems with great success, but some sadly only for a short while.

LEAGUE MANAGERS ASSOCIATION:
Marriage Guidance Council

Over the 60 or more years that I have been watching football, the relationship, or should I say 'the marriage', between owners and managers nowadays doesn't seem to be as strong as it was many years ago. Years ago, loyalty between managers and chairmen was the thing, and no matter what the problems were, they tended to stick together. It didn't seem to matter how badly the owner treated the manager, the manager put up with it. The owner always had the last say, he was the boss, he ran the club, even though he may not have known much about the footballing side of things. The manager had to do what he was told. It was a matter of shut up or ship out. Unfortunately for most, the latter was not an option.

Managers didn't move around as much in those days as they do now. Managerial positions were few and far between. Managers took the blame and abuse from the chairman when things were going badly but very rarely got the praise when things were going well. Lots of the arguments back in the day, as it still is now, was about money, or should I say lack of it. The manager was basically given very little funding to strengthen the team, so each game, week in and week out, was a struggle to get the results the owner and chairman wanted.

Back in 1919, a union was started to aid football league managers and secretaries in troubled times, but due to the lack of members, it didn't really pull a lot of weight. In the next couple of decades, managers started to fight more for their rights and working conditions. Managers employed agents to speak on their behalf, helping to ensure better contracts, pay, and one could even say 'marital rights'. In 1992, the League Managers Association was formed and started to take on the fight for certain rights for all their members, trying to act as a go-between in all kinds of disputes between managers and clubs. If the two parties could not come to an amicable agreement, then it would end up going into the hands of the LMA. Just like the Marriage Guidance Council had tried and failed to help in some of our family domestic issues, many football relationships also ended up in the divorce courts, with the manager moving on.

Unfortunately, the turnover of managers and the words loyalty and love have been replaced by results and money. Manchester United and Arsenal are perhaps the exceptions to the rule. The way both clubs stuck with Sir Alex Ferguson and Arsène Wenger shows how loyalty pays off. Perhaps some of the other league clubs should take a leaf out of their book.

Whereas it suited some managers to feel safe and happy at one club, like Sir Alex and Arsène Wenger did, it wasn't that way for lots of managers. For some managers one club was not enough. Managers like Big Sam Allardyce, Steve Bruce, Roy Hodgson and Harry Redknapp have all managed what seems to be about 100 clubs between them. It seems that it has now become a lot easier nowadays for managers to split from their football marriages.

There have been lots of managers that have tied the knot with different clubs but after a short spell both parties have realised it wasn't going to work out. To give some examples, Leroy Rosenior (2007) lasted a mammoth 10 minutes at Torquay United; Dave Bassett (1984) lasted 4 days at Crystal Palace; Micky Adams (1997–80) lasted 13 days at Swansea; and possibly one of the most famous of all the short managerial spells of a manager in charge is Brian Clough's (1974). He lasted 44 days at Leeds United. The book and film *The Dammed United*, released in 2009, tells of the 44 days that Brian Clough (portrayed brilliantly by Michael Sheen) was in the managerial hotseat after taking over from one of his biggest rivals, a Leeds legend, and the longest serving and most successful Leeds manager Don Revie.

Managers nowadays have a lot more security with the backing of the LMA, working on their behalf.

Lots of owners now go abroad to find their managers, thinking that because they have done OK in lesser leagues abroad, they can cut the mustard over here. Managers who were, in many cases, managing in perhaps a lesser league were only too glad to come to England and enter into a relationship no matter what the conditions were. However, a lot of them come here with promise of a better life only to find that it isn't quite as easy to adapt to the leagues and the style of play as they thought it would be. Many football relationships break up. Many managers soon return home back to a familiar and less stressful environment. (Normally also a lot richer).

NSPCC

The National Society for the Prevention of Cruelty to Children does an amazing job protecting and assisting children from all different types of dangers. There are no real words to say how vital and this organisation is and what a wonderful job they do under great pressure. Long may they carry on helping young children to move away from all the bad things and people there are in life.

PFA

The PFA do a similar job to the LMA in fighting for the rights of the players (our children). Instead of ending in a football divorce court, this can end up in football adoption. It's also there to protect and aid in any form of football abuse.

There is absolutely no comparison between the amazing and truly wonderful work that all people connected to the NSPCC do and the good work the people at the PFA do. So I will leave it at that.

Again, I hope I have not offended anyone by linking these two organisations. I do so for the sake of the book.

Chapter Twenty-One

WARNING … WARNING
THIS NEXT CHAPTER CONTAINS DISGUSTING
LANGUAGE AND SEXUALLY EXPLICIT DESCRIPTIONS
AND SHOULD NOT BE READ BY ANYONE OF A
NERVOUS DISPOSITION OR AN IMMATURE AGE

Sex
SCORING GOALS

The erogenous zone:
THE PENALTY BOX

One of the most important things that helps to keep a relation-ship or marriage together, along with love, loyalty and money is SEX. Getting on the job or getting your first ever leg-over was always so exciting, even if losing your virginity wasn't the re-sult that you'd hoped it would be.

Sex over the years hasn't really changed much since the days of Adam and Eve, or Mary and Joseph. Perhaps a few different positions might have got more popular than the old missionary one. Being taken from behind is one way. Standing up (the old knee-trembler) is another. Talking of knee trembles, I remember a great line in an episode of *George and Mildred*, played brilliant-ly by the fabulous pair of Brian Murphy and Yootha Joyce, in which Mildred was asked what her married name was. 'Mildred Roper' she replied. She was then asked what her maiden name was, and with a totally innocent face, she replied: 'Tremble, Nee Tremble' (knee tremble, get it?) absolutely brilliant!

Now before you start to even think about getting it going with your partner, both of you need to get yourself warmed up with a bit of foreplay. A bit of kissing and canoodling to start off, then a bit of groping and fondling, then on to the old French kiss-ing, or maybe a bit of Australian kissing (it's the same as French kissing, only down under, if you know what I mean). And a good old 69 (dinner for two, as it's also known). Then there can be a bit of tossing off, just to finish the warm-up phase. Then it's a matter of getting down to it. And sexual games can be played out in all different ways. Some start by going down on one knee and working their way up the body gently and respectfully before they really get going.

Once you start, some people don't want to be just fucked, they want to be made love to, slowly, sensually, and erotically. But for others, they just want a good old rumble on the bed, a good old wham, bam, thank you, ma'am is all they really require for their sexual pleasure. Lots of people can last the distance and get to come, ejaculate, or shoot many times during the course of the action. For some, sadly, all they can manage is a five-minute cameo appearance, only perhaps getting to shoot just once before they're done for. But if they can succeed and bring sexual satisfaction to their partner in that short time, then there's no problem.

Some don't like to keep putting it straight down their partner's throat, they want to try for other openings. Some like to dominate, take full control of play, be the one on top. Others less experienced like to let their other halves show the way and just lie back and think of England. Some partners like to fight while playing the game. They want their partner to fight for the right, to break them down and split their defences wide open before physically slamming it in.

Lots fantasise, thinking they're having it away with somebody else. For the men (and in some cases women), it might Halle Berry or Emma Watson. For the women (and perhaps again the men?), it could be Tom Cruise or Daniel Craig. Some might have a slightly different taste and may prefer someone like Onslow (as played by Geoffrey Hughes in *Keeping Up Appearances*), or Wayne, played brilliantly by Harry Enfield in *The Slobs*, or maybe Onslow and Wayne's other halves as in Daisey, played by Judy Cornwall in *Keeping Up Appearances*, or Waynetta played by Kathy Burke in *The Slobs*. It could even their best mate's partner as in the case of John Terry. Well, there are some strange people out there. Still, whatever rocks your boat.

Some of those who are not too sure about what sexual positions there are often revert to the *Kama Sutra* for guidance, looking at the different pages and different positions, feeling one way was not working for them, and so needing to try a different way to play.

Nowadays, a bit more equipment has been added to the fun of it all. Whips, vibrators, handcuffs, chains, and masks all help get the best out of their sex lives. A lot more people are using cameras to film their sex games, and then they watch them back many times over, just to see how they can get a better result. Some download them onto DVDs and sell them to make a few pounds for someone else's sexual gratification. Whatever your sexual preference, maybe there's only one spot that sends everyone into a frenzy when found, and that's the erogenous zone. Sadly, for a lot of people, they struggle to find it, but when they do, it's all there ready. It's the spot, it's the opening they have been looking for over the last 90 minutes. The opportunity is there now for you to dive in with your head, or do what Maradona did and use your hand.

Without a good sex life, life itself can become dull and boring. If your partner is not sweating buckets or moaning and groaning for more and giving it all, then not matter how hard you try, without much enthusiasm coming from them, this can cause a big problem in reaching your goal. Just to hear them screaming and shouting encourages you on, pushing both of you to reach that peak, that climax, pushing you on to shoot.

If you're not hitting the right spot or the right zone, firing blanks or not shooting when it's the right time, all can be lost. Now if you're not getting the right result, then your partner might start looking for a substitute or three (a *ménage à trois*, or even five in the case of an orgy) to come and join in the fun; someone whose different way of playing with them might just be what they need to find that right zone.

They want you to be nice and hard when your tackle's going in; it's no good you being all soft. Sliding in when it's nice and wet is fine, but make sure you're in control of your tackle because you don't want to be coming in there too soon. If you're not pulling your weight when playing around, they might find it better to bypass you and play on their own. For some people, masturbation (or pulling yourself off, as it's also known) is the only answer if you're not getting the right results with your partner. And if you're playing away from home sexually, then it's so important that you play in a neat and tidy way so that you don't get caught out by dirty sheets. You want to keep the sheets as clean as possible.

The name of the game is to shoot, and the more times you shoot, the more chances you'll have of getting a baby.

SCORING GOALS:
Sex

One of the most important things to keep a team together with its supporters is winning games: being successful by scoring goals. Getting on the pitch for your first game has always been exciting, even if losing your football virginity wasn't what you dreamed it would be.

The playing of football hasn't changed much since the Romans were kicking shit out of the Christians. Although a few different ways of setting out the team have perhaps become more popular than the old 4–4–2. Lots of clubs nowadays often prefer to play 3–5–2 (taking it from the back), or 4–1–2–1–2 (the diamond formation), or 4–3–2–1 (the Christmas tree formation), or 4–4–1–1.

But before you start to even think about getting the match started, you need to get yourself warmed up with a bit of a kickabout, or 'foreplay'. Then it's time for the toss-up. This is the moment in time when the excitement starts to creep in. And just before it all kicks off; some take the knee to show equality and respect. Football can be played in so many ways. Some teams like to play with the ball on the ground, they don't want to just kick the ball long and hope, they want to play slow sexy football to tease the opposition. Others like the ball in the air so they can put their head on it. And others just want a good old rumble on the pitch, to kick it up field and try to win that way: a quick wham, bam, thank you ma'am is their way of trying to get a result by having the ball in the net as soon as possible.

Some players can go the full distance in a match and have several shots on target during the course of the action. For some, sadly, all they can manage is a five-minute cameo appearance, able only perhaps to shoot just once before they're done for. But if that can succeed and a goal is scored in that short time, then there's no problem. Some just don't like kicking the ball long because they simply end up putting it straight down the keeper's throat. They want to look for other openings.

But the way you play is also utterly important to the supporters (they're the partners) who want to see their team perform, to dominate. They want to see sexy football, they want to see their team give a good account of themselves, put on a good show. If the team is performing well, the noise that emulates from the supporters spurs the team on. You can feel the temperature rising with each tackle, attack or goalmouth incident, and when there's a goal, the whole place erupts with pleasure. Watching the ball hit the back of the net is the best feeling ever. The excitement is in the build-up to the goal, the passing and movement, slowly, slowly at first, teasing, tormenting, getting your playmaker on the ball. Then when you get the opposition into a position just where you want them, and when the time is just right, you ram it home.

Now, as we supporters know, it doesn't always go well for some players, so they end up getting pulled off, and then as I've said previously someone will come on as their substitute for a five-minute cameo. Hopefully that is all they need to shoot once and get the right result required.

Some teams like to dominate, take full control of play, be the one on top. Others less experienced like to let the other team have the ball and control the way the game plays out, preferring just to sit back and defend and dream about one day playing for England.

Some teams like to fight while playing the game. They want the opposition to fight for the right to try and break them down and split their defences wide open before even getting a chance of slamming it in.

Lots of players fantasise about being Ronaldo, Messi, Pogba or Mbappé, and try silly manoeuvres and shots from impossible angles. Some might have a different type of player in mind such as Massimo Taibi, goalkeeper at Manchester United (1999–2000); Igors Stepanovs, a forward at Arsenal (2000–04); Eric Djemba-Djemba, mid-fielder at Manchester United, Villa, Burnley, and St Mirren. He was pretty bad with all of them during the noughties. (Well, there are some strange people out there. Still, whatever rocks your boat.)

If a team is in trouble and not getting anywhere during play, they tend to switch things around and get out their book of different football positions (the football equivalent of the *Kama Sutra*), hoping to find a way to break down the other team's defence.

Nowadays, a bit more equipment has been added to the game to help it move on: yellow and red cards, VAR (if you think that helps), goal-line technology, and the referee's foam to mark the place where a foul has taken place. Lots more cameras are being used to film the play and are used to rewatch games. Or they are sold on DVDs for other people's football gratification.

Now there's only one spot on the pitch that sends all of its supporters into a frenzy when it's hit and that's the penalty spot (the erogenous zone). Sadly, for a lot of teams it's hard to get the ball exactly where it's needed, but when they do, it's all there ready, it's the spot, it's the opening they have been looking for during the last 90 minutes. The opportunity is there now for them to dive in with their head or do what Maradona did and use their hand.

Watching a team play badly can become dull and boring. If the supporters are not screaming, moaning, or groaning for more, then not matter how hard you're trying, without that enthusiasm coming from them, this can cause a big problem in reaching your goal. Just to hear them screaming and shouting encourages you on, pushing your team to reach that peak, that climax, just pushing you on to shoot.

We want to see our players beathing heavily and sweating, giving it all. If you keep playing a ball that is not hitting the right spot or the right zone, if you're firing blanks or not shooting when at the right time, the game can be lost. Now if you're not getting the right result, your supporters will start looking for a substitute or five to come on and take your place. You might find it better asking to be pulled off for the sake of the team. Someone else whose way of playing with them might be just what they need to find that right zone, to put the ball in the box where the supporters require it.

They want to see you nice and hard when your tackles are going in; it's no good you being all soft or losing control. Sliding in when it's nice and wet is fine, but make sure you're in control of your tackle, because you don't want to be coming in there too soon.

If you're not pulling your weight when playing, they might find it better to bypass you and try to do it all on their own (playing one up front). And, it doesn't matter if you're playing at home or away, the most important thing you need to do is to keep your defence neat and tidy so that you can keep a nice clean sheet.

The name of the game is to shoot, and the more times you shoot, the more chances you'll have of getting a trophy.

Chapter Twenty-Two

Babies
TROPHIES

Men and women try for babies:
OWNERS AND MANAGERS TRY FOR TROPHIES

Now ever since Adam met Eve, the main aim in life for most couples is to be successful and have a happy and fulfilling life. And they do say that children bring couples closer together and make a marriage. Well, I don't know who actually said it, but it was most probably some unmarried hippy yoghurt-knitting social worker who has never had children. I can tell you that because I've got two kids, and many, many times they have driven my wife and me to almost come to blows. I'm sure those of you with children have also experienced the same thing. And as they get older, they seem to get worse. Some kids have caused so many problems at home that it has ended up with big family arguments, and have eventually caused the break-up of some marriages. But where would we be without them? (Well, that's what the wife asks me. A lot richer, I say).

To some couples, pregnancy comes easy (if you'll excuse the pun). A couple of attempts with a few shots on target and you've scored. Unfortunately, for some, things don't quite work out that way. You've been trying and trying for ages but to no avail. You've tried all different angles and positions, you've tried most of the *Kama Sutra* positions, but it seems that you're never going to hit the jackpot, and then all of a sudden ... you're merrily shooting away and you've BANGED one in, as they say. And finally, you've got the result you've been trying for.

Now in the early years, once it was confirmed you were pregnant, you could pop down to the local hospital for a scan, just to make sure everything was alright. There they could see that the baby was fine and kicking about (into football already) and there it was waving away at you. But, one thing they could not tell you was what sex it was, or how healthy it was. Nowadays, with advanced technology they can scan you and confirm if it's going to be male or female without doubt. And if you're rich enough to pay, your scan can show you your growing foetus in 3-D or 4-D, giving you its height, weight and anything else you want to know.

Now most pregnancies last around nine months, but some babies don't go the full term and arrive early. Some women don't even show signs of being pregnant, then all of a sudden out of the blue and to everyone's amazement out pops a baby. But hopefully at the end of whatever the amount of time that it is, you end up with a pretty and healthy bouncing baby, one to be proud of and to cherish. One you want to be able to show off to the world, to be admired by everyone and envied by all those around you. Although it will upset some of those around you who have been trying for years without success, some will sadly find fault with the end result: the baby's ugly, or its head's too big for its body. It's got funny ears. They will find any fault just out of envy or jealousy.

Now prior to the joys of giving birth (sadly for some not so joyous) the mother has to decide how she's going to play it out. She has to choose which will be the best and easiest way to get the right result without too much pain and pressure, when the final day arrives. Whether it should be a home birth, a hospital birth or in the bath, is a crucial decision. After consulting with the family and reading up on reports about how others suggest the best way is to play it, they have to decide which is the best way to get a comfortable result for them. And then, when everything is finally over for you, it's a dream come true. Something you have been trying for, for so long has now come to fruition. To lift that baby up in your arms is such a special moment, the feeling is overwhelming. With tears of joy, a lump in your throat as large as a football, you just want to celebrate with everyone around you.

All those family and friends who have been there to support you through it all. It's a slap on the back all round. It all ends with a massive piss-up, champagne and cigars all round. Although when my wife gave birth to our two kids, they both arrived after closing time (typical, she's not changed after all these years, my dinner's still never on the table on time), so I had to wait until the next day for a pint or three.

Some mothers are lucky and go through a pregnancy without much pain or discomfort, a wonderful exciting experience, fully enjoying the anticipation of the forth-coming event. But unfortunately, others don't have the same luck; they suffer sickness, nausea, pain and intolerable agony. Even though they are suffering, they carry on with life regardless until the end. My wife was quite lucky with our two; a bit of morning sickness and backache, but all in all a reasonable time. And even though I moan about them, we were lucky that both were born healthy and without too many problems.

Through all the troubled times that a pregnancy can cause: the morning sickness, the times when you are so tired you wished it would all come to an end, everyone around you at the time getting on your nerves, everybody having to put up with your mood swings, tears one day, fun and laughter the next, it should be said that without everyone's help, things could have been a lot harder. Relatives on hand to help with the general everyday duties when you were at your lowest point made such a difference. And now it has all come to the end, you want to milk every last second that this magical moment has brought to you and your family and friends.

You're tired and worn out after a long and enduring pregnancy. But now you feel it was worth every minute. Everyone around wants to share this special moment with you. They all want to take pictures or videos to remind them of the day, this special event, to keep for years to come, a record of joyous memories to look back on when they're older. And it helps you to reflect on how you were then and how you've grown up and where you are today.

*Unfortunately, some pregnancies don't always have a happy ending. Sadly, for some families, the pregnancies have to be aborted along the way for one reason or another. For lots of men and women, having kids is the be-all and end-all in their relationship, and if for whatever reason, one or the other of them is unable to make this work it can end up with the pair splitting up, such is one or the other's desire for a baby.

Money is always useful and can help in many ways; it can get you better hospital treatment or medical care. If you're not happy with one doctor, then you can afford to go private and see a top specialist. And with a few shillings at your disposal, if you're unable to conceive for whatever reason, you can pay to have fertility treatment to help. If you're not financially flush, then you have to put up with whatever comes your way regarding any pain or suffering.

Over the years, having a baby hasn't changed much, but who can actually afford to have children has. The cost of having a baby and the associated upkeep has spiralled. Some families already have so much financial commitment that they have to wait quite a few years before they can even consider trying. Sometimes they can wait a bit too long and then age catches up.

Years ago, when a child was due to be born everybody in the family would give a hand to make it as easy as possible. The neighbours were there to give help in any way, shape, or form, for example by running errands. And when the baby finally arrived, they were genuinely over the moon for you and shared in this joyous occasion. Family, friends and neighbours would all come from miles around to join in on your special day. And as soon as you could possibly get out of the house, out came the pram, pushchair or buggy, and you're parading the baby around the streets so that all those local friends and neighbours could rush out to see your newborn treasure.

Some women have difficulty getting pregnant, or have sadly arrived at a certain age where getting pregnant is a problem (or maybe they want more children but don't have the time, or they don't want to go through the whole pregnancy thing), so they look at adoption to help solve their dilemma. There have been lots of people who found it hard to adopt in this country, so they have had to look at adopting from abroad. Sadly, this doesn't always get the result they're hoping for. There have been lots of famous people who have already had their own children and then gone abroad and adopted kids from all over the world without any problems, which is perhaps a problem some of the lower-class applicants come up against. These are celebrities, such as Elizabeth Taylor, Julie Andrews, Angelina Jolie and the singer Madonna, just to name a few. The bigger the name, and the bigger the bank balance, the better the chance of success when adopting as many kids as they require. Having enough finance makes trying for a baby so much easier to get the result that you have worked so hard for.

All the above information regarding pregnancy and child birth was given to me by my wife as obviously I have very little knowledge of how giving birth feels. Although I do still have the scars on my hand because I held hers while she was pushing away not too merrily. And I don't think the names she called me she really meant (well, not all of them because she met both my parents, so that one goes right out of the window).

TROPHIES:
Babies

Bringing home a trophy is a must in helping to bring the owner and manager closer together. If the trophy is not one of the bigger ones, then this can cause a right old ding-dong between the two of them (and it isn't the Avon lady calling). Then it's likely to be a managerial change and the dole queue (well, for about ten minutes).

The football season is very much the same as a pregnancy in that it also lasts about nine months (mid-August to mid-May) and at the end of this time, some teams are lucky enough to be handed a beautiful trophy to keep and cherish, to be admired by everyone and envied by all. Like the pregnancy that no one saw coming, some teams never, ever thought they would get a sniff at winning a trophy, then out of the blue and to everyone's amazement, they do.

In 1988, Wimbledon beat the mighty Liverpool in the FA Cup final. In 2013, it was Hull's turn to beat the odds, winning against Manchester City, also in the FA Cup final. And I suppose the greatest shock of all in the history of the Premier League so far was when in 2015–16, Leicester City shocked the other football families by winning the Premier League. No one saw that coming (well, apparently one man did, winning £20,000 in the process).

Some teams are lucky enough to win a cup after only a few months or a few matches. Years ago, some teams won and lost important games over bad decisions, chalking off goals, saying the ball didn't cross the line, but nowadays, with goal-line technology, there's no doubt. And if you can afford it, there's also the wonderful VAR (cough) so that you can see it in 3-D or 4-D.

The manager has to get his players shooting and scoring in every game they play; it's the only way to get to where they want to be. If they don't shoot, they don't score, then they'll have no chance of getting the trophy that they so longed for. The thought of lifting that trophy up, to hear all the supporters of the club go wild, is what everyone at the club will strive for over the next few months. And then hopefully it will all end up with slaps on the backs, and a massive piss-up with champagne and cigars all around.

However, some other clubs' supporters will find fault with what you've achieved. They'll say you were lucky in one game or another, you should have had a player sent off in another, and if Joe Bloggs hadn't missed a sitter in that game against whatever team it might have been, then you would have gone out in an earlier round. This is criticism through pure jealousy and bitterness by those around you whose clubs have been trying for years to win a cup or a trophy without success.

For some teams, cup matches are a bit like some pregnancies. They only last a few months and some end up winning and some fall by the wayside. Most clubs crave success and trophies mean success. Some clubs are happy just to play along and hope something comes their way. But for most managers and owners, winning a cup or trophy is a must. Now if one of them cannot produce the requirements, then after a while it will no doubt result in their relationship breaking up, such is one or the other's desire for cup or trophy success. Some managers go through similar problems as some women do when trying to get their bundles of joy. Some get the luck of the draw and end up with a couple of bad days but basically go through the competition without too much pain or agony. But most suffer the turmoil of ending up with a phantom pregnancy, and then have to forget it for now and try again the next year.

The manager during the season also has to decide the best way to play so as to get to the final. Should it be a 4–4–2, a 3–5–2, or a 4–5–1? It's a crucial decision, but after consulting with their assistants and reading reports on the other team, they have to make the right decision to end up with a comfortable winning result. Winning a league title in any division is everybody's dream, but along the way, just like the pregnancy that some mothers experience, some managers also experience the same terrible feeling of pain and sickness and those continual headaches. And most don't have the comfort of a financial cushion to help.

The bigger, richer clubs can use their financial clout to help get their baby. The managers at clubs like Chelsea, Manchester City, Manchester United and Liverpool have the money to succeed in winning trophies. And if need be, they can afford to get their own type of fertility treatment by way of bringing in a new player or two to help them reach their goal. Then after the nine months, you can bet your life they will end up with a trophy or two. To win the league and a cup is like having twins. Manchester United in 1998–99 won the Premier League, the FA Cup and the Champions League, so for them it was triplets (Ahhhh, bless them).

Some of the slightly better off managers sometimes try to help some of the less fortunate managers to help them win important matches by giving them information about other teams they're about to play. They might even loan them a player if it would help them succeed.

Before a woman falls pregnant, she may suffer with the dreaded PMT (pre-menstrual tension. If you're young and don't understand what this is, ask your mother), then she falls pregnant and it goes, until after the baby is born. Managers suffer a similar experience with PST (pre-season tension). This occurs during the close season, but once the season gets going so does the feeling. Unfortunately, then it turns into PMT (pre-match tension).

Supporters of all different clubs would try to get tickets on Cup Final Day, going to give support to one of the teams or just going to enjoy the special day, though always wishing it was their team out on that waiting area (the pitch). And, as soon as they can, the winning team gets out the open- top bus and parade that well-earned trophy around the street for the rest of their fans to admire.

Some teams have found as much success in winning trophies abroad as they have in England. Teams like Nottingham Forest, Derby County and Ipswich Town are such teams which have had success in this country then gone abroad and had perhaps bigger results. Unfortunately, lots of clubs, like my own team Fulham, and Middlesbrough, have gone abroad and sadly have struggled to bring back the trophy they required. The so-called bigger, more famous clubs go abroad and manage to bring home whatever trophy they try for without too many problems. The bigger the name and the bigger the bank balance, the better the chance of success. Sadly, I have been at the games where my beloved team have tried to bring home that precious trophy without much joy, and I still bear the scars.

*I would like to make it quite clear that losing a football match of any kind and losing a child during pregnancy are not in any way comparable, and I can only apologise if this should cause offence or distress. But for the sake of the book, I use it as a comparison.

Chapter Twenty-Three

Retirement
THE FINAL WHISTLE

It started with a kiss:
IT ENDED WITH A HANDSHAKE

I've come to realise, now I'm at the age of seventy-two, that there comes a time in everyone's life where the body and mind says 'enough is enough' and starts to slow down. The enthusiasm and energy are not what they were. What used to be seen as a big 'WOW' or a 'OH MY GOSH, THAT'S AMAZING' becomes more like 'THAT'S NICE' or 'OH, WELL DONE.' Our expectations for the future become less and less, and they are not the same as they were when we were younger. At Christmas and birthdays (we see this now as being more for the kids), we don't tear the paper off the presents in anticipation of what we were hoping to get. Now we try to take the paper off gently so perhaps we can use it again the next year. Going out in the evenings is fine, but a lot of the time we're only too glad to get back home for a nice cup of tea and an early night. We are now at a stage in life where we look back on our memories rather more than wondering what the future is about to bring. When meeting up with family and friends, we tend to chat and reminisce about the past more than talking about our future.

As I sit here now, I don't know what the future has in store for me, or how long I'll be around, but whatever it is, I'm happy with the good memories I've already had over the years (and no doubt you will all have your own), like being at the birth of my daughter and son; seeing their faces when they first saw Mickey and Minnie in Disney, Florida; the births of my three grandchildren; watching them grow up; our short spell living in Tunisia. I think fondly about going on a mini world trip to visit my sister in Perth, visiting countries like Singapore, Australia, Tasmania, New Zealand and America, and meeting so many good people on our way. I've enjoyed meeting many TV and film stars when I was working in the family's riding stables, such as Peter Wyngarde (aka *Jason King* and *Department S*), Peter Bowles (*To the Manor Born*) The West family, Timothy and Prunella, and so many, many more. I've been lucky enough to go to the fortieth *Only Fools and Horses* Appreciation Society where I met a lot of the cast, and there was a very special moment when I met the great Sir David Jason. To top it all was meeting the superstar that is Whoopi Goldberg in Florida and a having a picture taken with her.

Unfortunately, there are a few memories that are not so good. Not getting to the hospital before both my parents passed away. Losing my sister Pat and nephew Simon suddenly. The loss of good friends like Dougie, and Roger. Letting friends and family down too many times over the years. The worst was when we found out that my grandson Oscar was suffering from a condition called panhypopituitarism, which is a life-threatening condition, and for which there is no cure. It's controlled by daily medication. But he is doing well now at the age of twelve, and may it continue like that for the future.

THE LAST KICK:
Retirement

I'm finding going to football matches nowadays at the age I am has changed totally from when I was much younger. The enthusiasm and excitement are not pumping through the heart like they were a few years ago. Not long ago I was chomping at the bit to get ready and out of the door as quickly as I could. I'd be shouting at the kids: 'COME ON QUICKLY, HURRY UP' and 'COME ON OR WE'LL MISS THE KICK-OFF.' Now it's more likely they're shouting at me: 'AREN'T YOU READY YET, OLD MAN?' or 'IF YOU DON'T PULL YOUR FINGER OUT, WE'LL BE LATE.'

And my reply, 'OH, DON'T RUSH ME.'

Don't get me wrong I still love going to the game and watching my team, and I'm as happy as a pig in poop when I get there, but regarding the build-up to the game, because I've been there so many times, you get to the stage where the excitement of what is going to happen in the game isn't there anymore. I don't expect anything now. If it happens, then I'm over the moon. When we score, I stand and give the kids a high five and I clap, but the days of jumping in the air and screaming have long passed. For me, now, it's about the memories of the years gone by. When we sit with fellow supporters, we talk and reminisce about yesteryear. I have lots of great memories of watching Fulham over the years. Seeing Fulham in the Cup Final at Wembley, and winning the Play-Off Final also at Wembley. Going to Hamburg for the Europa Cup Final. The Clint Dempsey goal against Juventus when time seemed to stand still as the ball went over the keeper's head and into the back of the net. Growing up watching the likes of Johnny Haynes, George Cohen, Allan Clarke, Les Barrett, Jimmy Conway, Rodney Marsh, Sean Davis, and so many more Fulham greats. Another great memory was being at the birth of Louis Saha at Tiverton Town FC, where he played in a pre-season friendly, one of my all-time favourites, along with Luís Boa Morte. And to top it all, Barry Hayles, Sean Davis, Elvis Hammond, and some of their friends made it a special day when they came along and entered a 5-a-side tournament that we organised to raise money for the Pituitary Foundation.

Unfortunately, some memories weren't always as we would have wanted, such as all the relegations we went through. Losing cup matches to teams in the leagues lower than us. I also regret that Fulham had to sell top players over the last twenty or so years like Steve Finnan, Louis Saha, Edwin van der Sar, Sean Davis, Steed Malbranque, and, of late, Fabio Carvalho, all great players sadly let go for one reason or another. (MONEY?)

Bill Shankly once said:

'Some people think football is a matter of life and death. I don't like that attitude. I can assure them it is much more serious than that.'

Well, that may be not quite be true for some. But, sadly, through our lifetime we will all suffer the pain and heartache of losing someone very special whom we dearly love. For the die-hard football supporter, a Cup Final loss or relegation can come very close to that feeling. We see people of all ages on the terraces, grown men and women crying on each other's shoulders, trying to console one another. Small children sobbing their hearts out after Cup Final defeats, and especially after relegation.

For the owners of a football club, football is no longer just a game. Sadly, it's a business.

For the lifelong football supporter, football is no longer just a game. It's a way of life.

WELL, THAT'S IT,
THE FINAL WHISTLE HAS BEEN BLOWN.

I hope you have enjoyed the light-hearted look at what I think makes a real-life football supporter. I apologise if reading any part of this book has upset or hurt anyone's feelings (except the so-called southern supporters of the big northern clubs that never go there).

NOW, IF IN YOUR OPINION, AS A WRITER I'VE COME OUT LOSING 10–0 WITH THE RESULT OF THIS BOOK BUT YOU'VE STILL MANAGED TO STAY UNTIL THE END (UNLIKE SOME FANS DO), YOU HAVE DONE REALLY WELL (OR YOU'VE HAD SOD-ALL ELSE TO DO). BUT, THANK YOU ALL FOR DOING SO.

BUT HOLD ON, IT'S NOT QUITE OVER YET, THERE'S EXTRA TIME BEING PLAYED IN THE AFRICAN NATIONS CUP, SO LET'S GO STRAIGHT OVER TO TUNISIA AND OUR REPORTER THERE (THAT'S STILL ME, BY THE WAY) AND FIND OUT WHAT HAS ACTUALLY BEEN HAPPENING THERE.

COMING SOON...

FOOTBALL, THANK GOD FOR MOHAMED: EXTRA TIME
A True Account of Our Life and Football in Tunisia
and the 2004 Africa Cup of Nations

EXTRA TIME is a true account of our short life in Tunisia and of a three-week football bonanza at the 2004 Africa Cup of Nations which was held there. My family and I owe a great deal to our good Tunisian friend Mr Mohamed Amroussi, without whose help, his clapped-out car, his local knowledge, connections, and Del Trotter dealings, we would never have experienced the other side of a totally different way of life and footballing culture at this tournament in Tunisia.

This is where we exchange prawn sandwiches for a shawarma (similar to a type of kebab) and caviar for couscous, a £200 thousand plus (per week) player for a 12,000-dinar (per week) player (that is approximately £5,000), and the type of supporters Roy Keane would have loved at Old Trafford: passionate to a fault 8 games in twenty days took us on an experience of a lifetime, seeing a different type of passion in a part of the world where football and poverty are as natural to these people as getting up in the morning.

We saw the friendship and the hatred, the fun and the fear, which each of the 7 games brought, feelings we very rarely get with British football (and perhaps in some cases we might not want). If you think we have a passion for the beautiful game in England, then you should try to get to see a match in what is still very much considered a Third World country where supporters are herded like cattle into the stadium, pushed, pulled, and punched. Where to moan or complain is not such a good idea for fear of being physically removed. Where it seems that 30,000 tickets are sold at a ground that only holds 20,000 people, and if you don't get to the ground two, three, four or maybe even five hours before the game, you may not get in at all (these hours are for the big games). That is their equivalent to our Champions League, Europa League or a local derby.

Acknowledgements

Firstly, the biggest thank you has to go to Sasha Smith, Elizabeth Prcha, Viola Milacek and the team at novum Publishers, who have been so much of a help to a now semi-retired lorry driver who had no idea what he was doing. Thank you all. To my wife Carol, who put up with all my rants and raves when things weren't going right during the writing of this. To my daughter, Gemma; son, Lee, and his wife, Lyn; my three wonderful grandchildren: the beautiful Ella, 'Orrible Oscar and Terrible Tommy. All of them I love so very much. Thank you all for making my life what it is today. I'd like to also give a big thank you to my sister, Joan, and her partner, Tommy, who over the last couple of years have helped my wife and I so, so much. A big kiss and a thank you to you both.

A very special mention goes to Dougie's wife, Marie, their son, David, and daughter, Michelle, who over the many years of our friendship, have always been there. And even though Dougie is sadly no longer with us, they will always be part of my life.

I'd also like to thank Paul (aka, ICKY, the two-timing bastard) Whitmore, who sat tirelessly in Wetherspoons, The Alpha Arms, The Herschel Arms, The Wheatsheaf, and any other establishment in Slough (against his wishes), but he said they were the only places he could find peace and quiet while reading the first draft, and giving me his honest opinion and thoughts. I did ask him why he didn't try the library. His reply was, 'What's a library?'

I'd like to thank Nick (West Ham) Davies for no other reason than being a top, top man, and a great friend to my family and me for many years. Also, Chris and Pauline Baker, the QPR (Ha ha ha ha ha) at the Alpha Arms in Slough, to whom I give so much stick. My neighbour in Bracknell, June Smith, and her grandson Alfie, who are Fulham through and through.

I'd like to give a big thank you to Jonathan Leighfield, sports journalist, who has since left the *Swindon Advertiser* and is now writing for *Golf Monthly*, who again kindly gave his time to meet up with me to offer his advice, thoughts and football knowledge. (Good luck on your new position, fella, and to Swindon Town FC!)

I'd like to thank Ian Powell, without whose knowledge of IT I would most probably still be trying to find out how to switch on the laptop, or I'd still be on page one.

I'd like to thank Mark Rayner, a patron of The Boot P.H in Bracknell, who through his constant piss-taking regarding my attempts to ever get this manuscript finished, made me even more determined to get it done. Also at The Boot are Mick and Pat Gissing. I'd like to give thanks to them for their help in keeping me mobile when my car broke down. And thanks too to the crazy but lovable Gemma Baker behind the bar.

One very special person whom I have to acknowledge is Roger Lewis Baldery, who is sadly no longer with us. I first met Roger in March 2018, in Wexham Park Hospital where we were both having treatment for cancer. Through our love of football (Roger was an Arsenal supporter) and our health conditions, we became good friends, and we kept in touch after we were discharged. My cancer was removed, and thankfully I've now passed the five-year surveillance period, but sadly there was nothing they could do for Roger. He is sadly missed by Jane, his wife, and all his family and friends. RIP, boss.

Sadly, also no longer with us is one of the Mohameds: that is Mohamed Al-Fayed, who had not only been a big part of my football life, but also in the lives of thousands of other Fulham supporters.

And finally, to all the players I've watched over the last 60 plus years who have given me so much pleasure, and to all the members of my Fulham football family, such as my nephews Mark Lewis, Luke and Craig Fontana, also Mark (Mouse) Teefey, Bill Dineen, and Mike Jewsbury. Also the four lads who sit behind me at the Cottage. They are Chris Lai (who can see a penalty from 80 yards away), Andy Hodson, Darren Holmes and Alan Johnson, who between them will make sure I never, ever have to wear an hearing aid.

'COME ON YOU WHITES!'

EIN HERZ FÜR AUTOREN A HEART FOR AUTHORS À L'ÉCOUTE DES AUTEURS MIA ΚΑΡΔΙΑ ΓΙΑ ΣΥΓΓΡΑ
HJÄRTA FÖR FÖRFATTARE UN CORAZÓN POR LOS AUTORES YAZARLARIMIZA GÖNÜL VERELIM SZÍVÜ
CUORE PER AUTORI ET HJERTE FOR FORFATTERE EEN HART VOOR SCHRIJVERS TEMOS OS AUTOR
HERZ ÕINKÉRT SERCE DLA AUTORÓW EIN HERZ FÜR AUTOREN A HEART FOR AUTHORS À L'ÉCOUTI
CORAÇÃO ВСЕЙ ДУШОЙ К АВТОРАМ ETT HJÄRTA FÖR FÖRFATTARE Á LA ESCUCHA DE LOS AUTORI
AUTEURS MIA ΚΑΡΔΙΑ ΓΙΑ ΣΥΓΓΡΑΦΕΙΣ UN CUORE PER AUTORI ET HJERTE FOR FORFATTERE EEN HA
YAZARLARIMIZA GÖ ÕINKÉRT SERCE DLA AUTORÓW EIN HERZ FÜR A
VOOR SCHRIJVERS TEMOS OS AÇÃO ВСЕЙ ДУШОЙ К АВТОРАМ ETT HJÄRTA FÖR

The author

Born in 1951, Tom has lived and worked in London all his life. He is married to Carol with whom he has two children. He also has three grandchildren. He has had a wide range of jobs, such as being a milkman, teaching people to ride in the family stables business, and driving a Class 1 HGV. He's also been a debt collector and a shop manager. He has travelled to numerous countries, including Australia, New Zealand, America, Spain, Tunisia and more. This is his first book, which he initially began writing in 2005, but long hours in his lorry meant it was completed at the end of 2023. Over the last seven years he has had cancer, a silent heart attack and a mini stroke. These incidents have served to make him more determined than ever to pen his footballing memoirs. Tom has already planned his next book, Football, Thank God for Mohamed: Extra Time, which tells of a three-week football bonanza he enjoyed at the Africa Cup of Nations in 2004.

*He who stops
getting better
stops being good.*

This is the motto of novum publishing, and our focus
is on finding new manuscripts, publishing them and
offering long-term support to the authors.
Our publishing house was founded in 1997, and since
then it has become THE expert for new authors and
has won numerous awards.

**Our editorial team will peruse each manuscript
within a few weeks free of charge and without
obligation.**

You will find more information about
novum publishing and our books on the internet:

w w w . n o v u m - p u b l i s h i n g . c o . u k